FATE'S FABLES

BOOK 1 OF
HER DARK DESTINY

T. RAE MITCHELL

ORIGINAL MIX MEDIA

PRAISE FOR FATE'S FABLES

"FATE'S FABLES IS ONE OF THE BEST AND MOST UNIQUE FANTASY STORIES I HAVE READ IN A LONG TIME."

"I couldn't get enough of this book and with every page I felt myself overcome with a wide range of emotions. The action scenes in this tale will have you on the edge of your seat with your heart pounding, while the romance will leave you longing for someone to hold. Fans of Gail Carson Levine and Cassandra Clare will want to add T. Rae Mitchell to their reading list."

~ Readers' Favorite Editorial Review ★★★★★

'THIS BOOK WAS EVERYTHING I'VE BEEN MISSING IN THE YOUNG ADULT SCENE."

"It has the imagery and the storyline of a great fantasy novel. I have not read anything this imaginative since Lord of the Rings or even Harry Potter. The book is so beautifully and creatively written that I was lost in the story the minute I started."

~ The Passionate Bookworm ★★★★★

"NOT YOUR TYPICAL YA NOVEL"

"T. Rae Mitchell has taken our love for fairy tales and put a spin on the idea by intertwining her main characters into the fate of each fable. As a lover of fairy tales, I was intrigued throughout the whole book."

~ Top Knot Librarian ★★★★★

"GREAT DEBUT"

"One of the things that impressed me more about this book is the countless types of characters Fate encounters: Goblins, Trolls, Sorcerers, Fae... the list is long. And if like me, you cannot live without romance, you will not be disappointed. His name is Finn and he has a Scottish accent. Prepare to be swooned."

~ Book Cupid ★★★★

"AMAZING START TO A NEW FANTASY SERIES!"

"Combining some wonderfully creative fables, a romance born from strange circumstances, and some incredibly delightful, colorful characters resulted in a stunning first book."

~ Parajunkee ★★★★★

"FRESH AND ORIGINAL FANTASY!"

"Fate's Fables is unlike any other fantasy novel I have read. Ms. Mitchell has a unique writing style with a quality almost like great fantasy novels of the past such as Lord of the Rings."

~ A Walk On Words ★★★★★

"THIS BOOK WAS MAGICAL, FUN AND REALLY ENTERTAINING."

"I love the idea of the fables and the 'Words of Making'. Instead of just living in one story, I got to move through several and it was great to have both a dark and light element playing throughout the book."

~ Pieces of Whimsy ★★★★

"I RECOMMEND THIS BOOK TO EVERY FANTASY LOVER"

"The richness that every fable had and the different elements each of them brought into light made me sink deeper and deeper into the magical places the author created."

~ Secrets From Books ★★★★★

"FATE'S FABLES IS A FANTASTICAL PAGE TURNER"

"I seriously couldn't put it down. Poisoned oaks, druids, faeries, and trolls… Fantasy buffs will be all over this first novel in the series."

~ A Book And A Latte ★★★★★

"WHAT A PAGE TURNER!"

"Once you start you can't put this book down. If you love faeries, trolls and such you will want this novel in your library collection."

~ Books, Reviews, Etc. ★★★★★

"I CAN'T WAIT TO READ THE NEXT BOOK."

"If you loved The Lord of the Rings or Game of Thrones, I'm sure you'll enjoy Fate's Fables."

~ Lite,Rate,Ture ★★★★

An Author's Circle Novel of Excellence Winner

Original Mix Media Inc.
1685 H Street #1046
Blaine, WA 98230
www.originalmixmedia.com

Ordering Information:
Quantity sales. Special discounts are available on quantity purchases by corporations, associations, and others. For details, contact the publisher at the address above.
Orders by U.S. trade bookstores and wholesalers. Please contact Big Distribution:
Tel: (604) 725-4284 or visit www.originalmixmedia.com.

Printed in the United States of America

Library of Congress Cataloging-in-Publication data
Mitchell, T. Rae.
Fate's Fables / T. Rae Mitchell.
p. cm.—(bk. 1)

Summary: Seventeen year old Fate Floyd is mysteriously trapped within a deadly fairy tale world bound by the Book of Fables. Her only way home is to travel through the book's 8 unfortunate fairy tales and change them into happily-ever-afters.

ISBN 978-1-9990241-9-2 (hardcover)
ISBN 978-1-9990241-1-6 (paperback)
ISBN 978-0-9917987-1-1 (eBook)

[1. Supernatural—Fiction. 2. Fables—Fiction. 3. Secret Portal—Fiction. 4. Magic—Fiction. 5. Fairies—Fiction. 6. Druids—Fiction. 7. Fairy Tales—Fiction. 8. Sorcery—Fiction. 9. Romance—Fiction.] I. Title.

Special Edition

10 9 8 7 6 5 4 3 2 1

For Tony

OLDWILDE
Icewall Cliffs
Twisted Bone Forest
Sunder Run
River Torle
Mount Helgunth
Brynmoor Highlands
Duenthorn
Well of Eyes
Mount Alderath
BELDERETH
Springs of Almsdeep
Dragon's Bite Ridge
Loch Windmere
NORTH ENDLUND
Kildaer Peak
Mystwitch Woods
River Torle
Raven's Run
Peldoril Forest
Glormer Mountains
Peldoril Forest
Glyndaer
Swamplands
Shadowless Moors
River Torle
Mornavar Valley
Great Oak
Lake Lathrea
SOUTH ENDLUND
Shytuckle
SERPEN EMPIRE
Mount Fargrum
Innith Tine
Dreaded Oak Wilds
Bloodthirsty Oak
Eldunough Islands
ASGAR
N
W
E
S

CHAPTER 1

FATE STILL COULDN'T BELIEVE all these people were here to see her. No matter how many book signings she'd done, she never got used to the rising level of excitement or the increasing numbers showing up at each location on her tour. And this last book signing in her hometown of Seattle was by far the biggest yet, leaving the beleaguered library staff struggling to control the unexpected mob.

"Um...hi." Four shy girls made up like pixies from her book, *Magic Brew,* stood on the other side of the table. They were trembling with so much anticipation their dark wings quivered on their backs. Lately more people had been showing up dressed like her book's characters, which Fate loved. It was like her own personal Halloween.

"Hi there." Fate sat straight and smiled. Caught daydreaming, again. "Awesome costumes! Where'd you find those wings?"

"Oh thanks. We made them!" One of the girls tilted her shoulder forward to give Fate a better look.

Another pixie hugged her book after Fate finished signing it. "I'm taking Kung Fu now, all because of the kickass girls in your book. It's changed my whole life!"

Was her book really that good? Fate doubted it. More than likely her surprising success was just another big fluke in a long list of others.

Cursed with a name like Fate, her luck had never been average or ordinary. It was either spectacularly terrific, or horrifically bad, and the two were often intertwined. Like the time she found a diamond tennis bracelet in the hidden pocket of a purse she bought at a thrift store, only to lose it four weeks later on a rollercoaster ride she hadn't even wanted to go on. Or the early edition Green Lantern comic she got at a garage sale for a buck and sold for $10,000, which she thought had been an amazing deal. A week later she learned the comic was actually worth a quarter of a million.

That was pretty much how life went for Fate. Though if she were being completely honest with herself, she'd have to say her luck leaned more towards the bad. A meteor, of all things, destroyed the car her dad had given her on her sixteenth birthday. Out of everyone at a high school football game, a bat chose her hair to get tangled up in, which turned her into a freaked out, screaming hot mess in front of her whole school. She'd been stuck with the horrible nickname, Batty, ever since.

And of course, there was the incident with the worms back in grade school. No! She wasn't going there. Fate shivered and took a deep breath as she forced the scarring experience from her mind, choosing instead to focus on this nice piece of luck with her book.

This was a dream come true. She'd been making up stories since she first learned to write and had always toyed with the idea of being an author someday. She had simply never expected her career to begin, let alone take off, at the age of seventeen. Either way, she was determined to enjoy her moment in the sun before her name jinxed it into a rainstorm.

Maybe this time would be different. She discreetly knocked on the wooden table.

A guy dressed as a shadow elf pushed past the pixies. When Fate saw his eyes sweep over her, she blushed, rethinking the wool tartan mini and snug blouse she'd chosen to wear. When he saw he'd been caught staring, he sheepishly dropped his gaze to the floor, but inevitably followed the line of her bare legs from her Doc Martens to the hem of her skirt.

A girl dressed as a Goth witch in vintage black and lace-up boots stepped forward, elbowing him hard in the ribs. She didn't look happy about his ogling.

Fate tugged at her hem and smiled ruefully.

"Ow! Er…hi, Fate," the elf said, his waxed anime-style spikes wobbling on top of his head. He held out his book, holding firm when she grasped it. "We represent the very first and best unofficial dedicated *Magic Brew* fan club website on the 'net…"

Fate waited for more but he trailed off, staring at her with a stupefied grin.

The witch let out an annoyed huff and pushed him aside. "Hi, I'm Darcy, and we're proud to announce we're holding the first official *Magic Brew* Convention at the Paramount tonight. I sent you a message on your website, but I guess you didn't get it. We're really hoping you'll attend—as the guest of honor, of course."

"Wow. Really?" Fate was stunned. Now she had her own personal Comic-Con. "Uh, yeah!"

It was Darcy's turn to look surprised. "Uh…oh good." The rigidity in her posture relaxed. "Okay, we'll send the limo for you at nine. It'll be stocked with all your favorite foods." She smiled proudly. "We have them listed on our website."

Fate thought about it while she signed their books. The list couldn't be that extensive: Mounds of Parmesan with anything Italian underneath, and chocolate-covered everything, except maraschino cherries and fruit cream.

"May I cut in?" a smooth voice interrupted.

Thanking her, Darcy and her elf boyfriend stepped aside as a tall slender guy in his early twenties came forward. He was dressed as a warlock from her book, looking regal and sexy with long sable hair blending into an ebony overcoat. He doffed his top hat and gave her a graceful bow. Poised there, he leaned in closer, his mirrored sunglasses catching a twin reflection of her.

Spotting her wild mane of auburn curls filling the frames, Fate smoothed her hair in a lame attempt at taming the volume. She should've worn a ponytail. She had to admit, the flip side of all this attention was the magnification of every irksome flaw she'd neglected to attend to. But hey, these were her peeps, right? Nobody here was calling her Batty.

He removed his sunglasses, revealing sky-blue eyes rimmed with eyeliner applied way more expertly than hers. He pulled a black silk rose from his lapel. "Allow me to introduce myself." He handed her the flower.

Smiling, she twirled the rose. "I already know. Rade Silverhand. You look so much like I imagined him. Better, actually."

He seemed to grow a few inches taller.

She picked up the pen, ready to sign his book. "And your real name?"

"Unimportant." He sighed with a wave of his gloved hand.

She understood. He was in character. And who could blame him for casting aside his normal persona? Who wasn't either bored or troubled with their own story and only too happy to leap into someone else's? It further confirmed her motto: Reality sucks. Make-believe rocks.

All of a sudden, three boisterous green goblins wearing hooded purple boxing robes clambered around the table. "Hey, you're holding up the line," one of them said, his row of plastic vampire fangs making it hard to speak with any dignity. "How bout letting ush in for our turn?"

Fate stifled a chuckle behind her hand. They were more comical than scary-looking, with warty gray rubber noses sticking out like sore thumbs on the green makeup covering their faces. She was about to respond when the warlock lifted his walking cane, smacking it across their chests. "Back, inferior scum! Retreat to your squalid sewers before I'm forced to vanquish you with my shadow fire!"

The goblin with the loose fangs rolled his eyes. "Oh, come on, Shteve. You know that doeshn't work on demon goblinsh. We'll jusht abshorb your dark power and turn it back on you."

"The name's Rade, half-breed."

Fate laughed out loud, amazed by how much they were throwing themselves into their roles. But when all three of them pounced on Steve, she jumped to her feet so fast her chair tipped over. The warlock dodged them with surprising skill, but his stately carriage crumbled the moment his top hat was knocked off and crushed under a goblin's boot. As Steve came at them with cane swinging and a litany of curses, the goblins grabbed hold of the other end of his cane and a clumsy tug-of-war ensued. Fake noses, ears and fangs flew in all directions.

"Hey guys, *stop*," Fate said, raising her voice. Distressed by this unforeseen turn of events, she looked for Eustace, her steadfast father. Always neatly dressed in slacks, with shirt and tie under a sweater and blazer, he stood by the side door. He was her tall pillar of strength, protective, kind and eternally patient. Part of a dying breed, Eustace was a true gentleman in every sense of the word. Giving her a reassuring wink, he gestured to let her know that security was already on the way. Then he returned his attention to Lana, her publicist, who hadn't stopped jabbering at him for one second.

Fate narrowed her eyes on Lana. She didn't care for the way the woman had been looking at Eustace throughout the month-long book tour. Like she even had a chance with the confirmed widower. Eustace was just being nice. He listened to everyone in that caring, attentive way with his head tilted and thick, silver-dusted hair falling down over a quizzical expression. Then again, that was pure catnip to cougars like Lana.

Laughing at something Eustace said, Lana turned and trotted over, her speed hindered by high heels and small steps enforced by a narrow skirt. Her smooth coif bounced neatly around her polished face and red lipstick. She bent to speak in Fate's ear, her perfume enveloping her client in a cloud of floral fruitiness. "This is *fantastic*! We couldn't ask for better publicity. I'll send out the press release." Without waiting for Fate's response, she snapped a photo and started speed texting.

"How can this be good?" Fate muttered. Did this happen to other writers? Or were her readers going nuts because the book was all about a gangland war between supernatural species? Had she ruined everything by unintentionally glamorizing violence? It wouldn't be the first time something delish had spoiled earlier than the best-before date.

The skirmish continued with a tangle of purple robes and black silk rolling about the floor with the occasional grunting face rising up for air. They were so jumbled together, it seemed as though they might stay that way until security arrived to break them up. But much to everyone's surprise, they got back on their feet.

Two of the goblins had Steve by the arms, while the third prodded him in the ribs with his own cane. The goblin doing the poking shoved his fangs back in his mouth and glared at the disheveled warlock, whose dark eye makeup had streaked down each side of his flushed face. "Admit you've losht the battle, and we'll take mershy on you, warlock."

Steve lifted his chin. "*Never.*" He kicked the goblin between the legs, which took the confrontation to a whole new level.

As the security guards pushed their way past the crowds circling the scuffle, an abrupt rumbling distracted Fate. The floor heaved beneath her feet. The walls leaned at threatening angles. Frightened, she grabbed the table, realizing quickly that no one else was reacting to what she thought was happening. Everyone carried on, distracted only by the immediate mayhem. She appeared to be the only one experiencing the distressing upheaval of her surroundings.

The hairs on her arms rose.

Was this another one of those internal quakings? The last one she'd had was when her grandmother had died. It had been the shiver of an inner knowing, a whisper of sorrowful change in the air. But this one was a shout, a warning that her entire world was tilting on its axis, shaking the earth out from under her. Then just as swiftly, the walls returned to their normal positions and the ground stilled.

Fate let go of the table. She felt different all of a sudden. Or maybe everything else had changed. Her surroundings had become flat, colorless and plain, like she was looking through a clouded lens. The air seemed thick, the ceiling too low, the swarm of people stifling. She didn't understand why she felt detached to everything taking place around her. It was as if she'd fallen into a hypnotic trance.

As she stared past the milling heads, a pinprick of light penetrated her filmy gaze, opening her inner eye to a sheltered valley where rainbows curve over green, blossoming fields. As the deep gold of tulips and dewy leaves flashed bright in her mind, a spectral hook sank deep in her heart. The ghostly line began reeling her in, beckoning her gently to that meadowy wonderland she'd abandoned years ago.

She needed to go there. She knew where it was. Sort of.

Grabbing her purse, Fate stepped backward, edging along the wall until she reached the side door where her father stood.

Eustace bent his head, concern showing behind his scholarly glasses. "Don't let this bother you, Doodles."

She gave him a frown. "*Eustace*, no baby names in public."

"Sorry." He smiled, not looking sorry at all.

"I'm going to scram while the scramming's good," she told him.

A stickler for keeping commitments, he checked his watch. "Oh, this should've ended a half hour ago." He looked at her, raising a brow in surprise, scrutinizing her in that thoughtful way. "Didn't you say you could do this twenty-four-seven?"

"I'm pretty sure I said that at the beginning of the tour."

"I'll get the car."

"No, that's okay. I think I'll take a walk, maybe grab the bus over to Jessie's later." Her stomach knotted with guilt. Why was she lying to him? She'd always been honest with her father. He wasn't strict in the usual sense. If anything, he was constantly coaxing her to get out into the world. He couldn't seem to accept that she was perfectly content with creating her own interesting and much more entertaining worlds from the comfort of home with her favorite playlist inserted in her ears and her cat, Oz, batting at her pencil while she wrote and doodled. As far as she was concerned, the world could keep its harsh reality to itself.

Eustace smiled with approval. "Good idea. I'm sure your BFE missed you."

Hearing her egghead dad trying to speak her lingo was about as mismatched as a hammer decorated with pink ribbons and rhinestones. "BFF. At least try to get it right," she said, rising on her toes to give him a peck on the cheek.

"LYF. That's one I never get wrong," he said as she slipped out of the auditorium.

Darn, he had to go and make the guilt worse. She stopped and glanced over her shoulder. "LYF too…" She trailed off when she saw that Lana had recaptured her father's attention. Annoyed, Fate turned on her heel.

The escalator was in sight when a forbidding form blocked her way. "Going somewhere?" a hushed voice asked.

"Foiled," Fate muttered. It was the dreaded dark angel from her book, an androgynous character she'd always found unsettling. The angel towered over her with a crown of thorns resting on limp raven hair. Blood dripped down a painted white face with eyes darkened into disturbing hollows. Enormous wings framed the tall willowy frame and the long cemetery-gray gown effectively disguised the angel's gender.

"Bathroom break," Fate said, trying her best to appear nonchalant.

The dark angel stood very still, watching her with a stony, unreadable expression. "You're leaving aren't you?"

Was it that obvious?

The angel gave her a solemn nod. "I understand. You've seen through the illusion of this world now that you're ready to move onto the next life. Not to worry, I will raze the landscape with a ruinous blaze and turn the world into a massive funeral pyre, just for you. But…"

"Yes, Anguish?" she said, going along with the role-playing now that she knew how far some people were taking it.

"Can you sign my book first?"

"Oh. Sure." Relieved, she scribbled a nice message inside. The dark angel stepped aside and she hurried onto the escalator. She made it to the top and continued through the vast atrium toward the main entrance, hoping no one else would catch her sneaking out.

As she neared the entrance, the sounds of the busy street outside urged her on. Fate pushed through the doors, breathing in the smell of car fumes and rain on fresh asphalt like it was ocean air. Falling into a run, she hailed a cab.

After showing proof of payment because she couldn't tell her driver where to go exactly, he became surprisingly tolerant with her vague request to head north on Interstate 5.

They were less than an hour from the Canadian border when the tugging in her chest yanked hard to the left. Fate grabbed the back of the driver's seat, pointing into the dark. "Borys. There. Take this exit." Almost two hours of driving had given them plenty of time to chat and get on a first-name basis. She knew all about his wife and their eight children.

As he swerved off the highway and followed the overpass, she felt the unrelenting pull grow stronger than ever. There was no question anymore that her destination was near. She was on autopilot now.

When Fate directed him to turn onto an obscure road leading to what seemed like the very outskirts of civilization, he slowed the car. "Are you certain?" he asked in his thick Polish accent. "Looks like it goes nowhere."

She didn't answer. Her gaze was fixed on the lit edges of the road. As the headlights grazed over a broken-down tractor, she watched for the weather-beaten paddles of the windmill farther up. Her heart thudded with a joyful ache when she saw it. "Once you pass over the covered bridge, go right," she said, her voice but a whisper.

Borys turned his head as if to speak but remained silent. The cab bounced over the rickety bridge's warped planks. As they passed through the wooden tunnel Fate held her breath, her muscles tight with anticipation. She felt like she was entering a time portal into her past.

On the other side thick brambles and tall grass crowded the dirt road, blocking her view of the outlying tulip fields. They would be in bloom about now, a golden blanket woven together by bands of April Moons, Apollos, Goldstars and Yellow Giants.

Her grandparents had given her mother the field as a birthday present, allowing the eight-year-old to pick all the bulbs. She'd chosen only yellow, selecting them by interesting names alone. Fate had grown up making the trip to Gran's with

Eustace every April 3rd to celebrate the birthday and memory of the mother she had never known. But Gran, widowed by then, had filled that hole, telling stories about her mother's childhood—always starting with how her precocious daughter had described the annual bloom as the time of year when sunbeams fell in the back yard just for her. The best birthday present ever.

As the car turned right, Fate sat straight, watching the high beams illuminate a large brick building a half-mile down the lane. She could hardly believe her eyes. Fables Bookstore. She was amazed she'd found it. The last time she'd been there was when she was ten and totally clueless about directions.

"I should take you home now?" Borys asked.

His voice brought her back to the moment. "No, that's okay. I'll get out here."

He shifted in his seat, turning to look at her with some effort since he was a heavy man. She avoided his troubled expression, ducking her head to search for her credit card. He handed her the terminal so she could pay. She passed it back with a hundred-dollar tip folded on top.

"Oh, too much!" he protested.

"You deserve it. You have the patience of a saint." She climbed out.

He gave her another look of concern.

She feigned a carefree smile. "It's perfectly safe. I own the building." She wasn't lying. She'd inherited the bookstore when her grandmother had died seven years earlier, though she hadn't returned since. The pain that had always kept her away was already flooding in. She shut the car door and waved goodbye.

As Fate stood in the pitch-black watching the lights of the cab disappear, she felt anything but safe. Not because of the inky darkness wrapped around the secluded vale or absence of close neighbors. But because the inexplicable compulsion that had propelled her there was terrifying.

She had lost her mind. Why else had she talked Borys into leaving without her?

Yet here she was, standing in front of the century-old bookstore, where she'd spent all her childhood summers burrowed deep within its vault of stories—tumbling down a rabbit hole with Alice, skipping along the yellow brick road with Dorothy's gang and flying to Neverland with Peter. Indeed, Fables Bookstore was where she'd first started writing her own adventures.

All the sweet memories rushed in, making her yearn for a time long gone.

The clouds shredded thin, allowing enough moonlight to give her a better look at the building. It looked more like the granary it had originally been with its stark façade and entrance and windows boarded over. The sign, which had been made to look like a giant book with *Fables* written on it, was gone. Had someone stolen it? This worried her. She could easily imagine someone taking it as a unique piece of art for display in some metropolitan apartment. She stared at the worn letters painted over the brick, which spelled out *Bookstore* in all caps. The quaint, old-fashioned flourishes that once surrounded the sign now looked bizarre without the book to complete the design.

It made her angry and sad to see the place looking so forsaken. Fables had been loved by generations of loyal customers throughout the county. Not to mention all the tourists who came to visit the historic bookstore on their way to the quaint countryside getaways peppered throughout the valley.

Her stomach knotted with guilt. Why had she promised her grandmother she'd run the bookstore someday? Maybe because she'd thought Gran would always be there, creating the perfect haven for fellow bookworms. But Fate didn't know how to do that. Especially since the heart and soul of Fables Bookstore had died with Gran.

A brisk wind swept past her, rustling the brush and trees with a mournful moan. She shivered, feeling small, wanting more than anything for her grandmother to run out, wrap her in a blanket and take her inside where a cup of hot chocolate and a good book was waiting.

The desire to go inside the bookstore was overpowering. But she remained rooted to the spot. She may have been lured there by a sudden burst of nostalgia, but now she felt like a fish caught on a line, struggling to swim in the opposite direction while the hook dug deeper. How could she go inside without Gran being there? She couldn't. Just thinking about it was too painful.

A fat raindrop smacked the top of her head. The moment she looked up, the sky dumped a torrent of rain in her face. She shrank under the deluge. Within seconds her hair was plastered to her head and her clothes were drenched.

Glancing up, she blinked into the pelting rain. "Really?"

Knowing she had no other choice but to surrender to this untimely force of nature, she ran around the corner looking for the delivery door. Thankful it wasn't boarded over like the front entrance, she fished in her purse for her keys.

Fate froze as she moved to put the key in the lock. Strange that she hadn't taken the key off the ring after all these years. Then again, having it there had helped her pretend Gran was waiting for her at the bookstore. She was a pro at pretending, always had been. But there was no room for that now. Shoving the key in, she turned the lock and pushed the door open. It was time to grow a spine and face why she'd come back to roost like some absentminded homing pigeon.

CHAPTER 2

THE MUSTY ODOR OF DAMP PAPER filled the dark interior. The moment she stepped inside, the temperature seemed to drop a few degrees. Clicking on the tiny flashlight attached to her key ring, Fate directed its modest beam at a cluttered storeroom. Without stopping to scrutinize anything in particular, she navigated her way through a maze of boxes, bypassed a door labeled Janitor, and slipped past a panel of green velvet curtains.

As soon as she entered the main floor, another wave of nostalgia hit her. She'd expected the place to be empty, but it was just as she remembered. The cozy reading nooks still contained the comfy wing-backed chairs, though there was nothing inviting about them now. Under the cold, meager beam of her flashlight they looked as gray and forbidding as tombstones.

She pointed the light at the rounded cashier's counter, her chest tightening, her eyes stinging with tears. She could almost see Gran standing behind the counter, sorting through piles of books or looking up over her reading glasses with that lopsided smile and eyes twinkling with childlike wonder.

Sniffing, Fate blinked to hold back a flood of tears, but they escaped, rolling down her face unchecked. She looked away, unable to bear the overwhelming sadness and turned her attention to the rows of towering bookcases filling the large, open interior of the bookstore. They were still brimming with books. Wiping her eyes, she walked over to a bookcase filled with classics. She ran her fingers over the spines before pulling out a random book. It was Oscar Wilde's The Picture of Dorian Gray. A shower of paper dust fell from its warped hardbound cover, drifting to the worn cedar floor.

Perplexed, she stared at the husk before checking several other volumes. They were all crumbling. What could've caused this? Books, no matter how dusty and neglected, simply didn't disintegrate as if they'd undergone some sort of weird time warp. She suddenly had the heebie-jeebies.

Shivering from a mixture of nerves and wet clothes, she glanced around, disliking the shadowy corners keeping the dead spaces hidden from view. As she stared into the dark, her skin prickled with a sense of being watched.

Fate pointed her flashlight into the blackest regions of the store. The light bounced off a framed poster, which she recognized as the Moonlight Rider, then grazed over a whole series of old fairy tale posters she knew well. When the round beam moved across a bookcase off to her right, she held still as something darted from the light.

It looked like a gray cat jumping from one shelf to another, except its movements seemed more halted than lithe. She knew it couldn't be the former bookstore cat. Oz lived with her now.

"Here, kitty, kitty…" She started to follow, but an appalling stench stopped her and she was quick to make an about face. No doubt this was where the stray was leaving its unsavory victims to rot. And if the cat was feral, she was best to leave it alone.

A metallic clanking sound came from the front of the bookstore. She swung around, grabbing at her chest, adrenaline shooting to her heart. She wasn't alone. Pointing her flashlight in the direction of the noise, she froze in place, unsure if she should run away or investigate. Running felt best, but she could hear the rain beating against the roof. It was really coming down out there.

Fate turned off the flashlight and tiptoed forward. Peering around a bookcase, she spied a faint light casting flickering shadows against a wall lined with windows. She smelled smoke, thick like smoldering paper. She frowned. Who had started a fire in her bookstore?

Roused by sudden indignation, she moved to the next bookcase and peeked around the corner. The contents of a metal wastebasket burned high with crackling flames, its light revealing the vandal. He stood in front of the Fables sign, where it leaned against a stairwell leading to the second floor. Relieved to see the sign had been moved inside, she fixed her eyes on the intruder.

He was a tall dark outline against the fire, his back to her and a huge iron key in his hands. She puzzled over the key, certain she'd never seen it before.

She shrank into the shadows, nervous about what to do next. A confrontation might be dangerous. He could be a creep. But she couldn't just let him do whatever he liked in her building. What if he burned the place down? She dug inside her purse, feeling for the phone. When she found it, she made her way to the back of the store, dialing 911.

"Damn, no signal," she whispered. Now she was really stuck.

Knots of panic and frustration formed in her stomach. Why was this happening? She wanted out of there. She wanted to be home. "Start dealing," she told herself. Taking a deep breath, she dropped the phone and flashlight in her purse, searching for the small can of pepper spray Eustace had given her. She pulled out a vial of perfume instead. Great, the mace was in her other purse.

"Fake it," she murmured as she snuck to the front of the store. Relying on the element of surprise, she stepped into the light, the pink cylinder aimed, finger on the trigger. "*Hey!* What're you doing here?"

He dropped the key, whirling around in alarm.

"Don't move unless you want a face full of hurt!" she said in her toughest tone. She tried to keep her arm steady, but she was wet and cold, and couldn't stop shivering.

He stood motionless, his face cast in darkness. She couldn't tell what he might do, and the longer he remained silent the tenser she became.

"You gave me a fair fright," he said at long last. "I didn't expect I'd be discovered."

The lilt of his Scottish accent threw her off. "Yeah?" she stalled, unsure what to say next. "Well, I wasn't expecting to find my place broken into."

Keeping the perfume pointed, she eyed the inviting flames, her frozen limbs craving the warmth. Raising his hands in surrender, he stepped aside so she could move close to the fire. Giving him a wide berth, she kept her eyes trained on him as she sidled over to the metal wastebasket. She glanced at its contents, quickly returning her gaze with a disapproving frown. "There's something deeply wrong with people who build fires in a place that's basically a tinder box. You do realize it's a bookstore and full of paper, don't you?"

The dying embers in the can collapsed, nearly extinguishing the flames. She couldn't see his face, especially since he continued to retreat into the dark. "You'd be right if these books were filled with pages, but they're no more than empty husks," he said. "I'm sorry for trespassing, though I assure you I was being extremely careful." He waited a moment. "If it's all the same to you, I'll be on my way."

Deciding he wasn't a hoodlum, Fate dropped her arm. "Hey, before you leave, can you get this fire going again? I haven't got a lighter."

"Uh...sure," she heard him say in confusion just as the last flame winked out.

The sudden black made her anxious. What if he was pulling a Norman Bates on her? Still clutching the perfume in one hand, she hoped it would at least sting his eyes enough for her to get a well-targeted kick in. She groped inside her purse for the flashlight, her fingers fumbling through endless junk in the way.

She went rigid as something brushed her arm. He was right next to her, rustling around, *breathing*. Just as she pointed the bottle, light sparked on, revealing him kneeling over the garbage can. He was holding a lighter under a wadded piece of paper he'd retrieved from the recycling box. A few seconds later, flames blazed high.

Fate whipped her hand behind her back before he could see how close he'd come to getting sprayed in the face with the flirty fragrance of candy and cupcakes. "Thanks." She leaned into the heat.

"Happy to help." When he stood, the warm glow illuminated the dark gold of his hair and stunning features.

Her heart lurched, a reaction that floored her. She dropped her gaze for a split second, but couldn't resist revisiting the strong line of his jaw and the friendly curve of his mouth. Her pulse shifted into high gear as she followed the rising arc of his ruddy cheekbones to eyes that had the same luster and greenness of rain-washed leaves.

Wow, talk about bite-the-back-of-your-hand beautiful. And eerily familiar. So much so, she simply gawked as she tried to place him.

His expression closed and he swallowed hard as he diverted his gaze.

Oh no. She'd embarrassed him. Heat rose into her cheeks as she cringed inwardly. Despite feeling like a total loser in that moment, she couldn't help peeking through the curtain of her wet curls for a quick sweep over his braided leather necklace with its Celtic pentacle, long-sleeved shirt and olive army pants. His clothing hung loose over his tall frame, but there was no concealing the lean, muscular build underneath.

He turned away. "I should be off."

She found herself grasping for a reason to stall him. "So where'd you find that big key? I've never seen it before."

Without stopping, he nodded over his shoulder. "It was lying next to that big book."

When he disappeared from the light, her heart lunged forward in her chest as if to chase after him. A bewildering sadness filled her as she stared at the fire, dumbfounded. She didn't know him, yet she desperately wanted him to stay. And as crazy as it sounded, she suspected she was missing him the way she missed someone she was close to. A tear trickled down her cheek. She dabbed it with a finger, looking at the teardrop in surprise.

"Uh, I left my coat behind."

She swiped at her watery eyes—mortified she'd been caught swooning—then promptly worried if she'd smudged her makeup.

He scooped the jacket off the floor, brushing at some brown powder that wouldn't come off. As he shrugged on his coat, he asked, "Which way is out?"

"The same way you came in?" she said, her tone more edgy than intended.

"Right. It's mighty dark back there."

"Wait." She couldn't bear to see him go again. "It's terrible outside. You should stay 'til the storm passes."

He flashed a smile that made her heart flip-flop. She bit her lip, baffled by the involuntary, knee-jerk reactions she was having to him.

"I'd be grateful of that," he said, stepping back into the ring of light.

Needing something else to focus on other than his overwhelming good looks, she glanced at the oversized key on the floor. "So what do you make of this key?"

He walked over and picked it up. "I'm certain it fits in the lock keeping this book closed."

"It's not actually a book," she said, looking at the ten-foot tall Fables sign. She was well acquainted with how it was made to *look* like a book, with an elaborate oak tree carved in relief on its wooden cover. But being up close to it for the first time, she was surprised by the line of smaller words above the large gold-leaf letters spelling *Fables*, disclosing its true title: *Book of Fables*. Inlaid at the center of the trunk where the branches curved with an abundance of oak leaves and acorns spreading out to the edges, was a round starburst of tarnished bronze, patterned with leafy scrollwork surrounding a large keyhole.

Astonished, Fate stepped close and ran her hands over the dips and curves of the carven wood to the cold metal of the lock. "I always imagined this was a real book lost by a giant. Not the club-carrying kind with a face full of carbuncles, but the ones my grandmother used to call the chroniclers of old magic and history." She moved to the side, looking at the pages pressed tight between the covers, touching them with eager fingers. They were thick, but definitely made of paper.

Fate turned to him. "Hey, it's a real book!"

He nodded, obviously not surprised.

"What're you waiting for? Let's see if the key fits."

"As you wish." He hefted the key up to the lock. It slid in perfectly. He turned it, activating a series of gears and slide bars, all turning and sliding in clockwork fashion beneath the wrought ornamentation. Within seconds, the tumblers clicked and the cover sprang ajar. A cloud of dust wafted out from between the book's covers as the stiff pages ruffled loose.

"I can't believe it!" She waved away the dust and pulled at the heavy cover. As she pried it back, the book's spine creaked like it hadn't been opened for a very long time.

Fate could barely contain her excitement. She stared in awe at the first fable penned in old-world calligraphy upon yellowed pages spotted with age. She brushed her palm over the broad expanse of rough paper, feeling where the ink had raised the fibers.

The fire was dying down again. She shivered with the anticipation of reading the story, as well as a deepening chill.

"Here, put this on before you catch your death." He held his coat open. "Sorry about the muck on it. Smells like some kind of herb. Anyway, it's all around the book, almost like someone spread it about."

Fate could care less about a little grime as she wriggled into the sleeves. The arms ended well below her hands, but the coat was still warm from the heat of his body. "Thanks." She pulled the collar close to her face, soaking up the warmth and the scent of soap and spice lingering within. "You know, I generally make it a rule not to wear strangers' jackets without knowing their names."

His lips curled into a smile. "Finn."

Her mouth fell open. "What? Did you say *Finn?*"

He nodded. "Aye, I did. And what would your name be? Because you know, I generally make it a rule not to hand my jacket to every stray lass who shivers in my presence."

"F-Fate," she said, barely able to speak. His name kept ringing in her head. How was it possible that a complete stranger could look that amazing, have a Scottish accent and that name? The odds were infinitesimal at best.

Finn raised a brow in amusement. "Are you sure? You seem confused—"A noise from within the shadows had him staring into the dark recesses of the bookstore. "Did you hear that? It sounded like a voice." He tensed with his arm held out in front of her in a protective manner.

"It's probably just a cat I saw earlier."

"I'll have to differ with you on that." He grabbed her hand.

The warmth of his touch caught her unaware, sending a surprising thrill through her. "Uh, y-you don't want to go that way," she stammered, thrown off balance. "There's a rodent graveyard back there and it reeks like Bigfoot."

When he didn't say anything, she rattled on to keep from focusing on her hand in his. "Not that I know what Bigfoot smells like, mind you. But from all the first-hand accounts I've read, it's supposed to be seriously unpleasant."

He remained intent on pulling her along behind him. Other than her aversion to the stench they were headed towards, she felt safe with him and wasn't concerned with what might or might not be in the bookstore.

But just as they rounded a bookcase, something gripped hold, stopping them in their tracks. Fate couldn't move. An unseen yet tangible force pressed in on her, locking her in place. Terror coursed through her veins as prickling sparks flared over her skin, thickening into a caustic fume that stung her unblinking eyes. Afraid to breathe it in, she fought to move her body, but her tightening muscles wouldn't respond. She knew Finn was beside her. She could feel his hand, but he was also paralyzed. When she couldn't hold her breath any longer, she inhaled. The taste of copper and heat filled her mouth, electrified air entered her lungs, scorching like an explosion of hot cinders. The fiery vapor spread, permeating her entire being with excruciating pain. Her scream came in the form of a strangled gurgle when it hit her locked vocal chords.

She was shocked by her utter helplessness.

The muscles in her legs convulsed, suddenly moving of their own accord, each limb thrusting stiffly like a toy soldier. She could see Finn doing the same out of the corner of her eye. They were turning around, marching robotically back to the *Book of Fables*. All the while, a spreading numbness replaced the agonizing pain. The relief was tremendous. But the numbing was becoming more like a horrible deadening, traveling up from her legs, into her belly to her chest. The moment it silenced her pounding heart, Fate realized a new terror.

She was dying.

CHAPTER 3

FATE WAITED FOR THE MOMENT OF DEATH, but it never came. Her heart continued to beat, despite the awful numbness throughout her whole body.

A splash of light appeared on the floor. It took every ounce of will power to bend her head enough to glance down at the haze of liquid gold pooling around her feet. She stared in disbelief as the light coiled around her legs–hot and electric against her skin–snaking its way up her paralyzed body.

As soon as it reached her head, her vision filled with a blast of white, burning away all thoughts. This left an emptiness, which then filled with a torrent of emotions. Desperation and fear churned together with rigid determination and a primal need to survive. A presence, strong and frightening, invaded her being, bringing with it a craving, burning desire for one thing: a tiny golden rod engraved with symbols held by a wise-looking old man in a white robe.

The light waned and the invasive presence withdrew, leaving Fate to float in a fog of forgetfulness. She could feel herself slipping deeper into the nothingness, but she knew if she didn't fight it she'd be lost forever.

A stomping sound broke the quiet. "Useless bones," someone said in a raspy voice.

Fate clung to the voice like someone drowning. Fighting to keep from sinking into unconciousness, she forced herself to look over her shoulder.

"Turn around," the voice said.

Fate's body tried to obey as the cloud of forgetfulness pressed in, but she pushed against the command with everything she had. Holding her position, she focused on who was speaking.

Sitting a few feet away, a withered old woman stared angrily back at her. Who was she? Did she have anything to do with putting her and Finn in this paralytic state? If so, how? Finn had said some sort of herb was scattered around the *Book of Fables*. They must've inhaled some of it.

The old woman struggled from her seat and shuffled across the floor, dragging a bent leg behind her. With her head pitched to one side like her neck was broken, she drew within inches of Fate's face, squinting through eyes clouded with cateracts. A nauseating stench oozed from her. This wasn't a musty old person smell, she reeked of rotting meat. Fate choked on the foul air between them as bile rose into her locked throat. She wanted to run but her body refused to budge.

Fate recoiled inside herself when the mummified crone touched her cheek. As she scraped her dry, skeletal fingers along Fate's skin, her shriveled face twisted into a frightening, hateful expression. What could she have possibly done to make this stranger hate her so much?

The woman jerked her hand away. "I am Brune Inkwell," she croaked.

Fate repeated the name over and over in her head. She was determined to remember it.

"I'm sending you on a very important mission, for which failure is not an option," Brune continued. "You will die before you give up. Do you understand?"

Fate nodded her head as she listened in horror. Mission? Die? She tried to shake her head no, but her body wouldn't behave.

"It doesn't matter how long you take to accomplish this task. Time passes differently in the *Book of Fables* than it does here. I'll experience a few minutes from the time you leave to when you return, whereas you might experience months, or even years.

So there's no need to hurry and make unnecessary mistakes."

Fate's heart thudded with panic. The paralyzing herb must be hallucinogenic. She had to be tripping out or something. There's no way some stinky, hideous witch was trying to force her on some crazy mission inside the *Book of Fables*...it was ridiculous!

Brune's creepy clouded eyes narrowed on Fate. "Tell me what it is you're supposed to bring back."

"The Rod of Aeternitis," Fate replied, so fast it shocked her. What the–?

"And who has the Rod?"

"O'Deldar," Fate answered, the name coming out of nowhere. Who the hell is O'Deldar?

Satisfaction formed on Brune's face, but as she stared at Fate her expression softened to what could almost be sympathy. "What's your name?" she asked.

Fate gave her name before she could stop herself. Damn, the last thing she wanted to do was give her evil puppet master any personal information.

"You'll be needing this." Brune unpinned a Victorian piece of jewelry she was wearing and clasped it onto the waistband of Fate's skirt. "You'll know what it's for when you read the warning at the beginning of the book. Do that immediately after you enter the first fable."

The command buried itself deep in Fate's mind, even as she tried to write off everything that was happening as a side effect of the paralyzing herb. But that was hard to do as she watched a fly skitter over Brune's eyeball. Flies are drawn to dead things. What is she, a freakin' zombie? Fate dismissed the thought as absolutely insane.

Brune batted at the fly, almost losing her balance. She teetered on her one good leg and frowned at Fate. "Time to read those fables you're so curious about."

Fate tried to keep her gaze from moving to the open pages of the giant book. She screamed silently against the command, but curiosity weakened her resolve as soon as she laid eyes on the ancient text.

Brune studied Finn. "Don't know about this one, but hang onto him if he proves useful."

But Fate had no further thoughts regarding Finn, or anything else for that matter. The veil of forgetfulness had closed back in around her as she spoke the first fable's title, "*The Lonely Sorceress.*"

The Lonely Sorceress

In the morning of the world when the very air swelled with magic, an enchanted island floated against the currents of the ocean. Its captain was Elsina, a sorceress whose beauty was as cold and remote as a marble statue. She was capable of charming the winds and seas to her every whim, and there was no place she could not go by water. The island was not only her home, but the source of her power. Therefore, she could not leave her precious isle even once, or she would lose her powers of enchantment forever.

To protect her secret, she lived alone. Because of this, Elsina grew lonely and missed the companionship of others. She turned to the island's animals, rocks and trees to fulfill this need. Under her magical touch, the animals were formed with human-like qualities. She also gave them the gift of speech and clothed them like people. She delighted in how outlandish they looked, especially when it suited her to mix a bee with a lizard, or a fish with a bird. She brought boulders to life and shaped them into giant bulls, elephants and lions. The plants and trees were granted the ability to move so they could gather close to her, offering both beauty and protection. She even infused the water of her fountains and pools with song and music.

One day while the sorceress basked in the hot sun, Hatho, her closest and most trusted aide drifted down out of the sky and landed on the terrace. The soldier hawk told her the previous night's storm had caused a fishing boat to crash on the rocks of the cove. Now a young man lay unconscious on the beach.

Elsina had her winged granite ox fetch the storm's survivor. For three days and three nights he slept. While the sorceress watched over him, she could not help admiring the gentle curve of his lips and the coppery sheen of his wavy locks. When at last he opened his eyes and smiled at her, Elsina's closed heart opened like a flower opens to the sun.

Torrin was his name and from one full moon to the next, he shared in the wonders of her island. Elsina grew to believe that he loved her. In truth, Torrin was grateful to her for giving him food, shelter and good company. But his first love was the sea, and as time passed, his gaze turned away from Elsina, back to the ocean. By and by, the time came when Torrin spent his days walking the beach and staring at the swirling tides as a prisoner might gaze past the iron bars of his window.

One evening he did not return to the palace. Fearing for his safety, Elsina sent her owl to search for him. The long wait seemed like days to her before the silent winged creature glided into her bedchamber. Torrin was quite well, the owl told her. He was in the cove, but not alone. A golden haired sea nymph with eyes as stormy as the sea had him wrapped in love's embrace.

The sudden piercing in Elsina's heart was so painful she thought she might die. Her anguished scream resounded throughout the island. Every creature, tree and plant trembled. Before she could take her next breath, Hatho was by her side, holding her in his strong arms. Yet Torrin never heard the heartbroken cry that shook the island. He had fallen under the siren's spell.

Elsina was determined to reveal the sea nymph's monstrous nature to Torrin. So she entered the tower where she stored her darkest magics. For seven days and seven nights, she gathered the vilest ingredients of the sea and added them to a boiling, hissing broth of hatred and vengeance. On the seventh day, the sorceress poured her bitter concoction into an urn carved from the branch of a cursed oak tree, the most menacing instrument used in the spell.

Carried on the back of her winged lion, Elsina landed in the cove before sunrise. Robed in black like a specter of death, she crept under the cover of darkness to where the sleeping lovers lay entwined. She stole to the water's edge, waiting for the twilight hour. When the moment hit and the air pulsed with magic, she poured the thick ooze into the water. Once the potion spread through the cove, she left.

Soon afterwards, the sun rose, warming the two lovers. The sea nymph, who was ready to relinquish all gifts of the sea to live as a mortal with Torrin, was anxious to reunite with the ocean one last time. She dove into the waves while he waited on the beach. But the waters started to churn. Something huge thrashed in the roiling froth. A spiked fin sliced the briny foam, followed by gnashing fangs and a giant tentacle snaking skyward. Torrin raced to the shoreline. Unarmed as he was, he was ready to battle with the beast that he believed had devoured his true love. He did not know Elsina's potion had turned his beautiful sea nymph into a mindless monster. The creature's bulging eye fixed on Torrin, lunged with staggering suddenness and dragged him into the deepest hollow of his beloved ocean.

When Hatho reported the tragic news, Elsina's heart burned as hot as a thousand candles. Her sorrowful wail penetrated the island. The cliffs crumbled, the stone palace cracked and all her creatures fled, leaving the sorceress alone and bereft. Try as he might, Hatho could not console his mistress. Her guilt and sadness ran too deep. All the same, he stayed by her side.

Days stretched into years, and years became decades. The loyal soldier hawk kept his silent vigil, always perched somewhere nearby, until the time when he grew so old and feeble, Elsina took pity and turned him to stone. And so it was that the sorceress found herself lonelier than ever before. All because she could not see whom her most loving companions truly were.

CHAPTER 4

FROM THE SECOND FATE SPOKE the fable aloud, the inked words lifted off the book's ancient pages and a flurry of letters swirled around her. Then, like tiny pixels, the letters combined into a scene formed by her imagination, bursting into life all at once in a symphony of sights and sounds. The fable flowed through her. She became its voice without knowing the words, each sentence generating more and more of the living, breathing story. She was part of it, yet each time she reached out to touch the rich reality encircling her, the images rippled like a drop of water disturbing the reflective surface of a still pond. When at last the tale came to an end, the fantastical characters and enchanting scenery splintered into a storm of letters, the release so abrupt she thought she was falling from a frightening height.

Her knees hit something soft, moist and gritty. Dizzy and nauseated, she kept her eyes shut, the sound of the ocean still lingering in her mind. Though now she smelled the brine blowing off the waves.

There was something so wrong about that.

Finn touched her arm, his fingers squeezing lightly. "Are you all right?"

She focused on the warmth of his hand, her mind trying desperately to reject what felt like sand beneath her. "Please tell me we're still in the bookstore," she said, before turning her head in the direction of his voice, opening one eye and then the other.

"Uh, sorry. I'd venture to say, we're far from it," he said, his tone uncomfortable.

He looked pale. Was he as frightened as she was? She kept her eyes glued to his face, refusing to look elsewhere, willing the setting behind him to change back into the dim interior of the bookstore. The backdrop remained stubbornly bright and sunny as he stood and tilted his head to the sky.

"I'm guessing this is Elsina's drifting island," he said. "At least I think so. Those gulls look normal enough. Course they could've hitched a ride from some other port, but I'm surprised we're not being greeted by her circus animals."

Curiosity got the best of Fate. She glanced up at the seagulls circling overhead. When she saw they were ordinary, she wasn't sure if she was relieved or disappointed they hadn't been feathery freaks. But now she'd gone and looked. Giving up, she dropped her gaze to where the *Book of Fables* leaned against wet shale stretching high into towering black cliffs. She broke out in a rash of anxiety as she turned, her knees digging an arc in the sand as she stared open-mouthed at a breathtaking beach of white sand set within a sheltered cove. Beyond the breaking shoreline, the ocean stretched away from them into an endless, empty horizon.

She wasn't in Kansas anymore.

"How's this possible?" she muttered, her breath coming in shallow bursts. "This just doesn't happen in real life. It has to be a dream."

"Then we're sharing the same one."

"No, you're in *my* dream," she said, frowning at him.

His lips curved with mischief. "Or you're in mine."

Her heart reacted to his smile with a surprising thud despite the added jolt of fear his remark had caused her. The very idea of being only a figment in *his* dream, or anyone else's, scared her. No wonder Alice had cried when Tweedledum told her if the Red King woke from dreaming about her, she'd go out like a candle. What a terrifying thought! Out of all the baffling reasons for why she was there, that one was the least desirable.

She closed her eyes, reaffirming in her mind: *I am real, damn it! I exist!*

"Fate? What is it?" Finn asked. "Are you in pain?"

She felt embarrassed. Here she was totally losing it while he remained calm. He certainly wasn't questioning if he was real or not. What was wrong with her? She had a whole life back home filled with solid evidence proving her existence. Even if she didn't know how she'd ended up in a freaking fable, she could count on one reliable fact: She was a real flesh and blood person.

Phhh…silly!

Smoothing the panic from her face, she peeked at Finn through cracked lids. A look of genuine concern had replaced his smile. She opened her eyes fully, scrambling for something to tell him, other than confessing her insane thoughts. "Uh…for a couple of hairy seconds during the ride here, when my stomach turned inside out and dropped to my feet before sloshing up into my head…I…uh…I thought I was dying."

He nodded in agreement. "I recall feeling something along that line."

Annoyed that he didn't appear traumatized by *his* near death-like experience, she frowned, groping for more. "Right…but you know what I was thinking?"

"What?"

"I…kept wishing I was at home having a staring contest with my cat. Now that's upsetting. What kind of person thinks about something like that when they're about to die?"

"Someone who'd rather be at home having a staring contest with her cat, instead of dying?"

"Yeah, I guess that makes sense. Thanks for restoring my self-respect." She attempted a smile, but it felt more like a grimace. "Speaking of out-of-place felines, the last thing I remember was telling you about the overachieving mouser in the bookstore."

"Aye, I remember saying it wasn't a cat."

"Oh yeah," she agreed, but try as she might, her memory blanked beyond that. Except of course, the vivid reading experience of the fable. But why couldn't she recall the circumstances just before? She was missing time just like alien abductees.

Or maybe she didn't want to remember. Uh-oh. Was she to blame somehow? After all, she was the one who'd read the fable. Had her insatiable curiosity caused them to slip through the Looking Glass?

She had the sudden need to hide her guilt behind some fresh lipstick. A glossy mouth might distract him from seeing the guilt in her eyes. Of course she probably needed more help than color on her lips. Her clothes were still damp and she didn't even want to think about what her hair was doing. She shoved the sudden image of Troll dolls from her mind.

Twisting in all directions, she looked for her purse. "Do you see my handbag anywhere? It's red plaid with black piping."

"No."

Doubt pricked at her mind, stinging it with renewed paranoia. That purse contained proof of her life. Her wallet was in there, the sparkly notebook she jotted ideas in, her phone. Oh no, Eustace. She was close to tears now. "Finn, I *really* have to find it. I need to call Eustace! Tell him I'm…okay?"

"Who's Eustace?"

"My dad." She was on all fours, glancing around, scouring the white stretch of sand for a spot of red.

Kneeling, Finn pulled gently on her arm, putting an end to her frenzied activity. She looked at him. His color had returned…nicely. "You're scared," he said. "That's only natural. But you won't fare well if you keep panicking. Understand?"

She gulped, nodding like a bobble head. He was right. She really needed to get a grip.

He gave her an encouraging smile as he rose, offering his

hand to help her up. "Let's take a look inside the big book. It's the only other thing that's come with us."

He pulled her up so quickly she collided against his chest. They created an instant gap, her jumping back, him sidestepping, nearly tripping. Regaining his balance, he cleared his throat and pulled the book's cover back. She gave one of those laughs, the kind that sounds so stilted she wished she'd been born mute. Hiding her red face, she made a big show of brushing away the sand sticking to her legs.

Her composure regained, she joined him in front of the book. But the moment she looked at the pages, her vision blurred and everything around her tilted. Or so she thought. Finn caught her before she fell flat on her back. "Thanks," she mumbled, going blank for a second as a piece of information slotted itself into her brain. She acted upon it by turning the title page to a passage written on the other side.

"I don't remember seeing this." He looked at her, his eyes clouding with uncertainty. "How'd you know it was there?"

Hearing the edge in his tone, she took a step back. "I don't know, I just did."

She could see him wondering about her, but he kept his thoughts to himself and turned his attention to reading the passage instead. She peered around him, eager to know what it said.

~ Reader Beware ~

If these Words of Making are spoken into the air,
these ∞ fables shall become your world forever.
Your fate may very well be pressed between these pages
like last summer's rose, unless you can unmake each fable
into its mirror opposite with new Words of Making.

Finn pointed at the peculiar mark within the text. "Do you think that's intended to be an infinity symbol?"

"If it is, I'm really not liking the spooky emphasis on forever."

"No, me either. But at least this warning explains why we were pulled into the story. It happened when you read the title of the first fable out loud."

So it was true. She was responsible for this. Guilt erupted, flushing her face with a telling heat. "I'm sorry. I honestly didn't know that would happen. In fact, I don't even remember reading the fable. I mean, I *remember* reading it, but I don't know *why* I read it."

"There's no blame, lass. It's obvious there are hidden forces at work here."

She dropped her gaze, staring at her shaking hands, fighting back the tears. The sun glinted on something shiny clasped on the waistband of her skirt. She grabbed at it, an antique clip linked by a chain to a fancy locket dimmed by the patina of age. Most of the silver plating had worn away from the original brass underneath the raised parts of the design.

"How'd this get here?" She unhooked it, seeing paper pressed between the metal coverings. It appeared to be some sort of vintage notepad.

"It's not yours?" he asked, looking puzzled.

"No. I've never seen it before."

"Oh, I noticed it." He shrugged. "Just thought it was some sort of fashion bauble."

"Uh, not exactly my style. Someone clipped this on me. Hey, maybe there's a message inside."

"In that case, open it," he said, stepping close.

She pulled a little red pencil from the slot holding the notepad closed. The lid sprang open, revealing a thin stack of tiny pale-green pages about half the size of a business card. The top sheet was blank. Fate thumbed through them, ripping loose several pages in her hurry to find something, *anything* that would explain what she was doing there, and why.

Finn cupped his hands over hers. "Whoa, lass. Careful there."

She watched the squares of paper fluttering on the wind through rising tears of anger and frustration. "The stupid thing's *useless*." Pulling her hands free, she slammed the notepad against the ground so hard it stood upright in the sand. She stormed off down the beach, but not before grinding it into the ground with her boot.

She stopped at the water's edge, staring at the ocean without seeing it. Why was this happening? Surely there was some reason. Or was it ridiculous to expect an explanation? No one ever spelled it out for Alice or any other fairy tale or comic book character that had ever tumbled, slipped or phased into some other world. They just accepted their lot and did what needed to be done, sometimes even having fun with it. So why wasn't she welcoming this like an adventure in Wonderland? Why was she reacting as if she'd been dumped in Dante's Inferno?

Before she could answer the question, Finn walked up to her. She kept her gaze fixed on the seagulls diving into the water and coming up with silvery rewards.

"Sorry for the big baby tantrum," she murmured.

"No harm done."

She turned to him, the warm wind whipping her unruly locks across her face. He reached out, slowly brushing her hair back. The sparkling ocean reflected in his eyes as his mouth parted with something unspoken. She waited, but he held her gaze without saying a word.

Hot spots burned into her cheekbones. "I'm ready to behave now," she blurted, when she caught herself leaning in toward his lips. "No need to worry about diving for cover every time we get bad news."

He smiled. "Best not to make promises you can't keep. I've

never known a fiery temper to go on holiday."

She stared at him open-mouthed.

Laughing, he ducked away from her fist flying at his arm. By the time she'd chased him back over to the *Book of Fables*, she was laughing too. She rested her hands on her knees, catching her breath. When she straightened, he was holding the ornate notepad out to her.

"Aw look at you, rescuer of the downtrodden," she said, taking it from him. "And you saved it so I can apologize in person?"

"I thought you might give it another look to see if it jogs your memory."

"Sure," she said, shrugging, "I guess it can't hurt to try." She rubbed her thumb over the embossed surface, surprised it had remained intact after being stomped on. The design was actually quite magical looking. Her gaze fixed on the face, a fairy she decided, since it had those butterfly wings behind the head and an elfin smile.

An old woman's mummified face flashed in its place.

"Yikes," she said, jumping back and dropping the notepad.

"Ah, you remember something," Finn said, scooping it up and handing it back.

"Uh huh...Brune Inkwell. *She's* the one who gave me this." The memory of being trapped in a noxious cloud of revolting smells came rushing back. "Ew, her breath was so gamey it made my eyes water. It stunk like meat smothered in Limburger cheese left out in the desert sun to rot and then eaten by coyotes. But it killed the coyotes and then *they* rotted in the sun—"

"I get the picture. That's one overactive imagination you have."

"Yeah, I'm paid quite well for it."

"So how do you know this manky woman?"

"I *don't* know her. She told me her name...and she was going on about some other stuff I...can't quite remember." Fate stared at the notepad, trying to retrieve Brune's exact words.

"I don't know…the memory keeps fuzzing in and out like a bad cable connection."

"This Brune Inkwell sounds dodgy to me," Finn said. "Good money says she's behind me waking up in the bookstore without knowing how I got there, and us ending up here."

"Do you think she knocked you out and kidnapped you?"

"Not likely. I was in Scotland at my grandfather's." He shook his head. "I'm sure he's wondering what's become of me, seeing as I vanished from my bed."

Fate frowned. Surely he was joking.

"Lucky for me, *and you*," he continued with a wry smile, "I woke fully clothed, since I was completely starkers when I slipped between the sheets." Chuckling, he looked away, not seeing how much she blushed from the mental picture forming in her mind.

She forced a laugh, deciding he had to be messing with her.

"I should've left that bloody bookstore. But no, I had to go poking my nose into a big bad book," he said as he walked over to the *Book of Fables*.

"And then I came along and got us trapped on this miserable, yet postcard-worthy beach," she chimed in.

She trailed after him to where he stood reading through the warning again, his hand cupping his chin, his brows knitted together in concentration. "Ah, I was afraid of that," he said, sounding troubled.

"What?"

He frowned at the page, gripping the edge of the book's cover white-knuckle tight. "We can't be free of the book without unmaking each fable into its mirror opposite."

She reread the warning several times, certain there must be another meaning. "No, there's no way we're supposed to take this literally."

He turned and looked at her. "Look at where we are. How

else can we take it?"

Panic prickled beneath her skin, threatening to erupt into a full-blown nervous breakdown. Taking a deep breath, she pushed the anxiety down. "Okay, so we have to change the endings. Big whoop. It shouldn't be too difficult," she said, an out-and-out lie. But somehow pretending she wasn't flipping out on the inside helped—a little. "How hard can it be to rescue a princess, slay a dragon or two, find the Holy Grail along the way and play cupid here and there?"

Finn looked both surprised and impressed. "Aye, how hard can it be?"

"So how many fables are we talking about?"

He parted each page just enough to see the text, counting silently as he went. At last he said, "Eight in total."

Eight? Fate gulped. She'd hoped for four at the very most. So much for putting on a brave face. Her thoughts returned to Alice and her trusting, playful attitude toward the wacky characters she'd encountered in Wonderland. That was the outlook she needed to adopt if she was going to get through this with her sanity intact. Fate found herself smiling as a spark of excitement ignited in her. She'd have fun with this, make it a game. Like a big chessboard in which she had to make it to the eighth square, first as a pawn before she was made a queen, the way Alice had been.

But then it hit her like a punch in the gut. What if that's exactly what she was...a pawn in a sick, twisted game of chess?

CHAPTER 5

THE TOWERING CLIFFS LOCKED IN THE COVE, leaving no way out except by sea. Finn persisted in looking for a way out long after Fate gave up. Her brief spark of enthusiasm had been snuffed out by a growing sense of dread. But she wasn't letting on. She had gone back to pretending she was dauntless, feigning excitement when he discovered some stairs cut into the rock hidden behind a thick stand of bushes.

Forcing a smile, she helped him gather driftwood, kelp and palm fronds to camouflage the book before making the steep climb. He bounded past her like she was standing still, proving just how out of shape she was. Halfway up, her lungs and legs were burning so badly she had to sit down and rest. At least the exhaustion provided a little distraction from worrying whether she was Brune's puppet.

When at last she reached the final step, Finn was lying on his back staring up at the sky and whistling a tune. "Oh, you made it. I was beginning to think I'd have to carry you—" he chuckled, "—or perform CPR."

"Your confidence…in me…is overwhelming," she gasped. She staggered up next to him, taking in the landscape. The peaks of Elsina's palace crested above some distant hills near the center of the small island. There was also a clear path leading into the woods, most likely the way to the sorceress.

Finn jumped to his feet, gesturing to the path with a princely sweep of his arm. "After you. Unless you need to rest a while longer."

"I can handle it." She was shocked by how shaky her legs were. She'd been ruthless with her characters, putting them through much worse than hoofing it up a mile of stairs. There was no longer any question she preferred writing about strenuous activities to actually doing them.

They had walked a fair distance and were strolling through a dense patch of forest when Finn slowed his step to listen intently.

"What's up?"

He put a finger to his lips. "It's the trees. They've begun to notice us."

Speechless, she stared at him. "What?"

"The trees," he whispered. "They're waking up to our presence."

He grabbed her hand and didn't seem to notice that she was staring at him like he'd just sprouted a hairy mole on his face. That was the second disconcerting thing he'd said. She'd let the last crazy remark go by as a joke, but he seemed so serious at the moment. Dry humor wasn't really her thing. But what if he wasn't actually playing around? Ew, she didn't want to think about what that might mean.

"We should keep moving before they let Elsina know we're here," he said, pulling her resistant weight behind him.

Maybe he was treating this insane situation like a game, the same as she was trying to do, or applying some sort of twisted logic to it because he didn't know what else to do. Fate picked up the pace. She could play the game just as well. "Maybe it's best the trees announce us," she said, fighting the urge to smirk. "It's pretty rude to show up without calling first."

He stopped to look at her. "She's a sorceress. From what I've been told, they're enormously territorial. She'll most likely turn us into frogs first and ask questions later."

He was really getting into this. "Uh…right," Fate agreed, matching his serious gaze.

Finn dragged her along at a fast jog. After the climb, she

tired quickly and was about to say game over when the narrow path ended abruptly. They had reached an impasse where a high ridge overlooked a gleaming palace of pale yellow stone extending high into the deepening sky.

Five slender towers curved around a turret-shaped castle. Terraces overflowing with blossoming gardens linked each tower together. Further down, two gigantic stone lions with grim human faces sat on either side of the main entrance.

Finn pulled a small spyglass from one of the pockets of his army pants and aimed it at the terraces.

"Where'd you get that?" Fate asked.

"Found it on the beach."

"Beats the rusty nail *I* found," she said. "Can I have a look?"

He handed her the spyglass. She stared at the oddly mixed creatures in awe, realizing with a cold chill that the fable had actually become a real place and she was standing right in the middle of it. Disbelief tried to assert itself again. But she could no longer deny the truth when she saw the tall, pale woman who strolled out onto the balcony toward a large table laden with food. Dressed in a shimmery crimson robe, she glided past an exotic array of flowers with an open hand, drawing their fragrance to her nose to breathe in their scent. Her serene features were unnaturally beautiful, like the carven image of a stone masterpiece. And her hair, black as midnight, hung in silky plaits to her ankles.

"Elsina…" Fate said under her breath.

"Oh, let's have a look." He took the spyglass back and whistled softly.

As he continued to stare, Fate grew impatient, her thoughts turning to the delicious banquet she'd seen. Her stomach growled. "Do you think there's any chance we can get our hands on some of that food? There's enough to feed an army."

He didn't answer.

She waited a few more seconds for him to look away, but the longer he gaped at the sorceress, the more agitated she became. "Hey. *Answer me!*"

When her voice echoed out against the stone palace, she clapped her hand over her mouth. Birds scattered from the surrounding trees, sounding calls of alarm from the sky. Grabbing her arm, Finn pulled her away from the path into the shadows of the trees. They ran long and far until she tripped and fell, scraping her knee.

Holding her bleeding leg, she bit her lip to keep from crying.

Finn shook his head and kneeled down next to her. "What got into you back there?"

Her knee throbbed. Actually, *everything* hurt. "Other than being stuck here with *you?*"

His eyes widened with surprise. "Did I do something wrong? Or is hunger bringing out the grizzly in you?"

Fate dropped her gaze, too overwhelmed to keep up with his overzealous game playing. She needed him grounded in reality, or she was going to lose her own mind, if she hadn't already.

He pulled out a small tin and dabbed some thick brown salve on her bleeding knee. "There. It's an old family remedy I like to have on hand. You'll be good as new in a few days."

The touch of his fingers sliding over her skin caught her off guard, a confusing distraction from the pain and anger.

He rested his elbow on his knee, studying her with amusement. "I think it's time you drummed up something for us to eat, missy. I fear I won't survive that blistering temper if we don't calm those nerves with some food in short order."

Irritation rushed back in. Clearly, he wasn't going to stop messing with her. "Oh sure, no problem." She feigned a perky grin. "I'll just run down to the corner berry bush. Then stop by the convenience stream and spear us a fish. And after we're done pigging out on too many berries and parasite-ridden sashimi, we can look forward to one of those super-fun gastronomical hangovers."

"We could do that, but I thought maybe you'd try writing up our dinner on that wee notepad. Maybe that's why it came with you." With a patient smile and a curious glint in his eyes, he pointed at it dangling from her waist.

Her jaw dropped. "You think if I write up some sort of description, it'll just appear out of thin air?"

"I suspect that's how it might work. But we won't know unless you try. Will we?"

"The verdict is in. You are completely certifiable."

"Why else would that smelly old woman have pinned it on you if you weren't supposed to write 'Words of Making' in it?" he said, making air quotes.

Fate's stampeding anger skidded to a halt when she realized he was referring to the warning in the *Book of Fables*. And then Brune's words came back to her: *You'll know what it's for when you read the warning at the beginning of the book.* She unhooked the notepad from the chain and pulled out the tiny pencil.

Finn sat down amongst the moss and fern beside her. "Now, what mouth-watering grub are you going to write up?"

"Pizza?"

"Aye, perfect. A lass after me own heart," he said, throwing the Scottish brogue on thick.

Fate couldn't resist smiling; that Scottish accent made her feel all warm and fuzzy. She scribbled out a hasty description. "Okay, here goes nothing. *From out of nowhere, I am ordering a freshly made, hot pepperoni pizza with Parmesan.*"

When nothing happened that very instant, she felt stupid for letting him make her think she could magically conjure food. But then the air distorted visibly, wavering like heat waves in front of them as the smell of freshly baked dough and spicy pepperoni met her nose. Seconds later, a pizza on a platter came spinning into view. Finn caught it with both hands.

She jumped to her feet, amazed. For the first time since she'd been thrown into this mess, she felt excited. Confident even. "Do you realize what this means? Getting out of here's going to be a snap! I can literally write all our problems—" she looked at Finn, "—away."

Still holding the pizza, he was frozen, his eyes filled with awe.

Grinning, she bounced up and down. "I know, pretty mind-blowing, huh?"

He set the pizza down with an air of reverence. "We have to be very careful with this, Fate."

"With the pizza? No way I plan to destroy it with much chewing." She grabbed a piece and took a bite. "Mmm. Have some. It's pure cheese heaven!"

"No, I mean the Words of Making," Finn said, his expression grave. "To be honest, I'm gob smacked they can be used this simply. I was sure we'd have to combine them with magic of some sort to get them working. But this…this is straight from the source. This is *true* power."

"Explains why the pizza's so good."

He shook his head. "Is any of this sticking in that head of yours?"

"Yes, I understand, Uncle Ben. With great power comes great responsibility."

"Aye. As well as great danger," he added, still giving her a serious stare.

"Would you relax?" She handed him a wedge dripping with cheese. "This is the best piece of news we've gotten since we first landed in this big steaming cow pie."

"Maybe," Finn said.

"Maybe? This makes me the dungeon master." She frowned when she saw he didn't understand. "That means *I* get to call the shots now."

"Don't confuse overconfidence with blind certainty."

"Killjoy."

He bit into the pizza, a blissful smile melting away the tension on his face. "You're right. This is *wicked good*." He paused, his expression turning thoughtful before tapping the brass-covered notepad. "We'll make it all work."

She settled down on the ground next to him, relieved and happy. They both ate hungrily, hardly talking until the pizza was gone. Then she ordered up a chocolate milkshake for herself and a root beer float for him, in as few words as possible. She'd counted forty-two sheets in the notepad, figuring she'd better save the majority for more vital matters.

They were both overly full and lying on the ground staring up at the gray swollen clouds when it started to rain. The promise of an impending storm came from a sudden flash of lightning and thunder rumbling in the distance.

"I'll write up a nice cozy cabin," Fate offered.

Finn jumped to his feet. "I like your line of thinking, but something much smaller would be better."

"Ew, you mean a tent?"

"A tent's perfect," he said, too busy filling his palm with pebbly white dust from a pouch the size of his fist to see how displeased she was. She watched him place the powder on the ground, followed by three more handfuls around where she stood. Using a lighter, he lit the piles on fire, muttering something under his breath.

She watched the peculiar ritual with increasing horror. "What did you just do?"

"I made this patch of ground around us invisible to unwanted eyes. Now nothing can see us or the tent as long these protective wards are in place." Flashing a satisfied smile, he wiped the dust from his palms. But his smile faltered when he saw her obvious dismay as she spoke her written description of the dreaded tent. "Sorry about the cabin," he said. "I've tried larger objects before, but anything over a couple of meters won't work."

"That's great. I feel safer already," she said, her tone flat as she watched the quivering air solidify into a camouflage-colored tent. Why was he still playing make-believe when they had the real deal? Where was the invisibility he was talking about? She could see him and the tent quite clearly, not to mention herself.

Frowning, she went back to writing down all the camping gear they'd need.

"The wards are tried and true," he said, trying to convince her of their worth. "I should know. I used them when the wolf wraiths were after me in Black Spout Woods. They ran right past me."

She jerked her head up. "What did you just say?"

"I said the wards worked on the wolf wraiths."

The rush of blood pounding in her ears muffled his voice. Her heart was in her throat, making it impossible to speak. She stared at him, helpless to look away as her vision magnified on every perfect detail of his face.

He'd gone quiet as well, his eyes locked with hers as a certain knowing passed between them.

Flustered, she tore her gaze away, pressing the pencil so hard against the paper, the lead tip broke. "*Damn.* I wasn't finished."

He kneeled down, pulled a Buck knife from his thigh pocket and sharpened the tiny pencil. She watched in silence, remembering all the peculiar things he'd taken from the multitude of pockets in his army pants. A rash of goose bumps ran down her arms as each item took on new meaning, the sum total adding up to a conclusion so far-fetched it made being tossed into a world of make-believe seem normal.

As the storm raged around them, the lantern's soft light filled the tent while they each sat wrapped in the warmth of their respective sleeping bags, staring at the blustering fabric walls in awkward silence.

Finn was the first to speak. "Since we'll be spending a lot of time together 'til we get out of here, I thought maybe we might get to know one another a bit better."

Fate wriggled inside her sleeping bag until she was lying down and tightened the drawstring along the top. "Sorry, my tank's empty," she said, hiding within her nylon cocoon. "Not only have I been bamboozled into a magic book by some stinky old crone I've never met, but my legs are pretty miffed about all that hiking. There's a strong possibility they'll go on strike."

"Oh." He sounded disappointed.

She sighed and peeked through the small opening of her sleeping bag. "What do you want to know? But only one question," she warned. "Something tells me we'll have plenty of time to hear each other's life story later."

He nodded. "I've been wondering what you were doing before you came to the bookstore. You already know I was sleeping in the buff before I got there."

She loosened the drawstring and pushed her face out. "Just so we're clear, there'll be no sleeping in the buff while I'm around. Not that I'm against buff, because I'm not. It's just that you need to keep your buffness to yourself."

He laughed. "Not to worry. The clothes are on."

She receded back into the folds of her sleeping bag.

"So?" he asked. "What were you doing?"

"Signing books in Seattle."

"Were you now? And what kind of books would these be?"

"That's *two* questions."

"Please?"

The playful glint in his eyes stopped her breath for a split second. She couldn't refuse and briefly described *Magick Brew*. When he said he hadn't heard of it because he didn't read those types of books, she was surprised. And confused. If he wasn't a fantasy geek like she'd initially thought, why all the make-believe nonsense?

A jittery sort of hopefulness bubbled to the surface. Could he really be who she'd begun to suspect he might be? She could ask a few key questions. But what would happen if she confirmed her suspicions? That could open up a whole new can of worms she really didn't have the energy to deal with at the moment. Her body was bent on sinking into a comatose sleep.

His mouth curled into a devastating grin. "So, you're a famous author."

She closed her eyes to the thrill his smile provoked in her. Upon opening them, she avoided his gaze. She didn't want the humiliation of getting caught staring again. "That's what they tell me. But don't go getting all impressed. I didn't write some literary masterpiece. I'm just a mediocre writer with an overactive imagination."

"You're being modest. How else did it happen, if not by talent alone?"

"It was a total fluke. It all started with an English assignment where we got to pick any book about gangs in the 1960's and put our own spin on a favorite chapter. Being the nerd I am, I turned mine into a big rumble between a bunch of supernatural gangs. But my teacher liked it so much she talked me into entering it in some contest. Then before I knew it, a big publisher was asking me to expand the idea into a book."

His eyes widened. "Do four-leafed clovers always grow under your feet like that?"

"Believe me, it's not always green clovers, pink hearts and yellow moons for me. Sometimes it's broken mirrors. And I think we both know we're probably in for at least seven years bad luck on this one."

"You're way too young to be so fatalistic."

She frowned. "You expect someone named Fate to be anything but?"

"Aye, I do. With a name like that, you should feel in control of your destiny."

"Have you ever looked up 'fate' in the dictionary?" She didn't wait for his answer. "'The development of events beyond a person's control, regarded as determined by a supernatural power.' If you need an example, just look around."

"I'll agree our predicament appears to look that way. But I'd also argue that what we're thinking and feeling day in and day out is the determining force behind our destinies, making us, as the poem goes, 'the masters of our fate, the captains of our souls.'"

"How can you say that? I know *I* wasn't wishing to get trapped here, wherever this is."

"Are you sure about that?"

Squeezing a fistful of the sleeping bag, she drew in a shaky breath. "Yes, because I'm so *not* thrilled about being here." Terrified was more like it. And she was homesick for Eustace, the comfort of her bed and Oz purring near her head.

"What is it you spend so much time writing about again?"

"Adventures about make-believe people and places," she muttered.

"And where are you?"

Frustration welled up, flushing her face with heat. "I did *not* make this happen! And what about you? What did you supposedly do to get here?"

Finn leaned away from her angry tone. "Well, I'm always getting into strange situations, usually on purpose. But when it seems like pure chance, I know I've got to take responsibility for it."

"What's any of that supposed to mean?"

"It's what I was taught since I was—"

"You know what? Never mind. I don't want to hear it."

"I didn't mean to upset—"

"Forget it," she said, jerking the bag over her head. "I'm too tired to talk anymore."

She waited for him to say something but heard nothing, save for the wind battering the tent and the sound of the lantern being turned down. As she lay in the noisy dark, curling into a tight ball, she puzzled over why she'd lost her temper so completely. But deep down, she knew the reason. There had been a stinging ring of truth in what he'd said. And if she was really being honest, she knew she'd always wished for real adventures over making them up.

Well, she finally had her wish. Only one problem, she wanted safe adventures, an oxymoron, if ever there was one.

The melodic chirping of birds woke Fate from a dead sleep. As she lay half awake she smiled, knowing Eustace was making breakfast. Hopefully, pancakes. Yawning, she opened her eyes, seeing an ugly camouflage pattern in place of the sparkly blue netting above her bed. She sat up, gulping for air, disappointment weighing heavy on her chest as she realized yesterday really wasn't a bad dream. Fighting back tears, she looked over at Finn. Her stomach dropped. His sleeping bag was empty.

Had he vanished back to Scotland? Had he ditched her? She shoved her head out through the tent flap. He was sitting on a log, whittling a stick. She ducked back inside, shaking with relief. Grabbing the notepad, she wrote up a change of clothes, opting for a pair of pink tartan jeans and a black argyle top.

When she whispered her description of being showered and groomed, her skin felt instantly cool and clean, and her hair actually smoothed into shiny waves. Now *that* was something she could get used to.

Feeling a little better, she stepped out of the tent. Finn looked up. When his gaze meandered down the length of her body, she blushed, unsure if he liked what he saw.

"I didn't see any luggage full of clothes," he said.

She tugged the notepad from the pocket of her jeans. "Abracadabra."

"And I see you fancy the tartan weave."

"A homage to my Scottish roots," she said, leaving out the fact that she'd been obsessed with everything Scottish her entire life.

"You're Scottish?"

She smirked. "Royalty even. I was born in Edinburgh Castle. Only because I arrived seven weeks too early while my intrepid parents were touring the place." Her smile faded. "But…there were complications. My mom died before the ambulance got us to the hospital." She shrugged. "I guess I almost went with her. That's why Eustace dubbed me Fate."

"I know how it feels to lose your mum. I lost mine when I was five," he said, adding another clue to the growing list.

She thought about pushing for more, but when she opened her mouth, something else came out. "Uh…sorry I dropped the grumpy bomb last night."

"All's well. I survived the fallout."

"Can I interest you in a change of clothes?"

Finn nodded. "Aye, that'd be excellent."

While he was changing in the tent, Fate glanced up at the powder blue sky, her thoughts spinning in circles. "It can't be him," she whispered to herself. "Stop thinking about it."

She breathed in the earthy scent of last night's rain hanging in the air. Smiling, she stepped forward, almost tripping when her foot sank in the soggy ground. "Oh great," she mumbled, bending to see how much mud was on her boots.

She screamed.

Finn bolted out of the tent with his new shirt half on. She scrambled onto his bare back, flinging one leg over his shoulder, digging the other knee into his spine and pulling back his head to hoist herself up onto his shoulders.

He pried her hands off his eyes so he could see. "For God's sake, Fate! What's going on?"

"Don't drop me!"

When he let go of her hands she grabbed hold of his hair.

"Ow, I promise I won't let you fall. Now what's got you so blinking scared?"

"Don't you see them?"

His body tensed as he turned his head side to side. "What? Where? I don't see anything!"

She tilted his head down. "No, *there*. On the ground!"

He stared at the surrounding flora.

Fate lost all patience. "How can you ***not*** see those squirming gelatinous tubes of pure gore? They're all over the place! Look at them with their slimy snouts poking the air."

"Do you mean the worms?" he asked, his tone incredulous.

"What *else* could I possibly mean?"

His muscles relaxed beneath the death grip she had on his head. "Oh I don't know. I was thinking something silly like an ambush."

Hatho circled high above the encampment, eyeing the two strangers' every move before flying back to the palace to report to Elsina.

The sorceress was pouring cream over her breakfast of wild

berries and curds when Hatho sailed down and landed on the terrace. Dismissing her butler parrot, she invited the soldier hawk to sit next to her.

He remained perched on the parapet, bowing his head before speaking. "I have important news, milady."

Elsina smiled at her loyal companion. "I hope it's interesting, Hatho. I will admit we're certainly due for some excitement. It's been much too long."

Hatho shifted his weight, gripping the balustrade with his talons. His mistress was kind, but unpredictable if the balance of the island became unsettled. And knowing what he knew, the scales would tip very soon indeed. "There's a shipwreck in the cove. And a young man lies unconscious on the beach."

The sorceress snapped her fingers. A large sparrow with sharp human features darted forward. "Send word to the ox to fetch this young man." Like a shot, the sparrow seemed to vanish from there to other parts of the palace.

"There is more, milady," Hatho continued. "A sorceress, or witch of some sort, and her apprentice have trespassed. She possesses a powerful tool. I witnessed her conjuring clothing into being with a tiny magic book, and she wrote her spell with a sliver of wood that needs no ink."

Elsina turned a brooding gaze out over the forest sprawling beyond her terrace. "Bring me this magic book. And send Sithias to watch for anything else they may possess."

"Consider it done, milady." Hatho climbed high into the cerulean sky, letting out a piercing cry that echoed over the island. Within seconds, ten soldier hawks gathered behind him.

CHAPTER 6

AS EMBARRASSED AS FATE WAS about freaking out and climbing Finn like a tree, she remained on his shoulders. She just couldn't get down on the ground with those worms. At least he seemed to be okay with waiting while she wrote in her notepad and spoke the words to clear their campsite.

As the tent vanished and breakfast appeared in her hand, she felt him laughing beneath her. "Well? Aren't you going to tell me how this fear of wee wrigglers began?"

She shoved a warm, gooey cinnamon bun into his hand. "No. Just get me out of here, please."

"Must've been painfully bad to make you so mental," Finn said, biting into his bun. He started to leave, but stopped to stare at one of his protective wards. The pile had been flattened into oblivion by the rain. "Uh-oh, we've been living on borrowed time. The rain washed away the—"

Suddenly the forest walls rattled with shrieks and a battery of beating wings. Startled, Fate fell backwards into a patch of ferns, her scream cut off as the air slammed from her lungs.

A strong hand grabbed her by the arm, jerking her upright. Gulping for air, she stared through the slit of a silver helmet into the glinting eyes of a white, overgrown hawk with muscular arms. As shocked as she was by the bizarre, totally unreal sight, she recognized him as Hatho from the fable.

"Surrender your magic book, witch." His voice was surprisingly deep for a bird.

Still winded, she twisted in his grip, straining to see where Finn went. He was nowhere in sight.

"Stay the witch's hand," Hatho ordered.

His soldiers pinned her arms down while he searched the pockets of her jeans and pulled out the notepad. He was stealing her only means of survival and she couldn't stop him. Hating how powerless she felt, she kicked at the hawk's head but missed, hitting his shoulder instead.

He grabbed her throat, choking off the air. "I'd kill you now, but milady has seen fit to let you live—for the moment." With that, Hatho and his soldiers launched skyward, vanishing from behind the treetops.

Coughing, she rubbed her sore neck just as Finn appeared out of nowhere. "Where were you?" she croaked.

He ran over to her. "I threw a circle of invisibility around us, but you fell off." He looked frustrated.

She glared up at him. "Thanks for leaving me alone with the hawks on steroids!"

He clenched his jaw, biting back a response.

"They took my notepad! We'll never get out of here without it!"

"We'll get it back."

"How? March into Elsina's palace and demand she fork it over?"

"I say we head back to the big book and read through the fable again. Maybe we'll find something in the story that'll help us hatch a plan."

Something cold squirmed under her palm. Lifting her hand, she squealed when she saw a worm stuck to it. She jumped up and clamped onto him, her feet on top of his. An awkward moment dragged out between them.

"We'll make better progress if you get on my back," he suggested. "It's the least I can do."

As much as she wanted to refuse, she didn't argue. After they reached the worm-free path, she climbed off, walking the remainder of the way back to the cove in uncomfortable silence.

Hatho placed the small brass notepad in Elsina's hand. She closed her eyes, feeling for the heat or tingle of magic within the curious piece. Frowning, she opened her eyes and rubbed her finger over the filigreed surface in an attempt to awaken the indwelling spell. When the metal remained cool and unresponsive, she pulled the thin red stick from its holder. The lid sprang open. She flinched, expecting the air to charge with hot sparks or bolts from whatever enchantment she was certain she'd just unleashed. But nothing happened. Not even the slightest shift in the wind.

More puzzled than ever, she stared at the pale-green paper covered in light scratchings. Squinting at the marks, she recognized they were letters, though sloppily written. No doubt it was a spell or incantation. She read the words aloud. "From out of nowhere, I am ordering a freshly made, hot pepperoni pizza with Parmesan."

There should have been the usual heat and coppery taste in her mouth. Even the weakest of spells left a slight aftertaste. She shot Hatho a black look. "There's no magic in this thing, or the incantation. And who is this Parmesan? Did you see a third trespasser?"

"No, it was only the witch when we attacked," Hatho explained. "I thought I saw her apprentice from the air, but he was gone when we landed."

"Did the witch use her magic against you?"

"No, we gave her no time." He paused. "She seemed weakened after we took the book."

"That makes no sense." She slammed the notebook on the table. "It's only a piece of tin." She fell quiet, her confusion and concern building. If the book wasn't the witch's source of magic that meant the magic was in some other object. *Or someone else.*

Most likely the so-called apprentice, or this missing Parmesan. "Find Sithias. He'll have found out more by now. I want to know exactly who I'm dealing with."

Finn suddenly rushed down the last stretch of steps leading to the cove.

"Hey, slow down!" Fate called out. "Jeez, I'm already in danger of breaking a sweat." Plus her legs were way too sore from yesterday's hike to even think about running after him.

"Don't you hear it?" he said, without stopping. "That singing—that voice, it's like nothing I've ever heard before."

"You mean that seal barking?" she yelled.

He left her standing there without answering.

Irritated at having been abandoned yet again, she took the steep steps at a more hurried, torturous pace. By the time she pushed through the bushes, he was halfway down the beach, walking into the ocean toward what looked like a girl who was skinny-dipping.

"For crying out loud." Fate ran down the beach as fast as she could. Waves smacked against her knees as she waded in and grabbed him by the arm. "What…do you think…you're doing?" she said, out of breath.

He shot the girl in the water a lovesick grin. "She's singing to me. She wants to take me somewhere."

She was a knockout, super model kind of knockout, unless you count the fish scales from the waist down. Fate dug her fingers into his skin. "She's a sea nymph. Probably *the* sea nymph from the fable."

He pulled away from her.

Planting her heels in the sand, she yanked on his bicep. "*Finn*, she's luring you in with her sireny ways."

"She wants to take me away with her."

"And where do you think that is? Down to her giant clam shell where she'll smother you in kisses and hand feed you soggy shrimp popcorn? Try rolling you in seaweed and serving you to her bottom-feeder friends."

He continued grinning like a fool. "She'd never hurt me."

Fate scowled at the sea nymph. "Don't come any closer. I know what you're up to."

The sea nymph bobbed in the frothy waves, her eyes wide and staring, but with a hint of something wild and dangerous in the stormy blue of her irises. She reminded Fate of the raccoon she'd thought she'd tamed by feeding it from her bedroom window. Cute and cuddly, until the night it skulked in through Oz's cat door and stuffed its furry burglar face with most of her Halloween candy. When she'd woken to Oz's growling and the crinkling of wrappers, the ungrateful bandit had spit and hissed at her.

The sea nymph ducked under the water, only to pop up twenty feet away. Fate managed to pull Finn back onto dry land, but his eyes were glued to the siren.

"Oh for Pete's sake, would you stop staring at her?" She pushed him down in the sand and blocked his view. "We're in trouble here, and I need you to focus—*on me*."

He leaned over to see around her. She blocked his view again, but he tilted in the opposite direction, craning his neck, a sappy look on his face.

She picked up a rock, threw it at the sea nymph and watched it miss by a good ten feet. Huffing, she looked for something else to throw, but stopped short when she saw the wreckage of a broken ship near the edge of the cove. "Finn, look. A ship crashed on the rocks last night."

He didn't respond.

She gripped his head between her hands, forcing him to look at the wreckage.

He resisted until his face squished up in her hands. "I can't see her," he complained.

"Snap out of it. That must be Torrin's ship, which means we're at the beginning of the story." She let go of him, panic unraveling her self-control. She wanted to slap him out of it.

Thinking better of it, she told Finn not to move and ran back to the *Book of Fables*. Sweeping aside the branches and driftwood, she opened it up to the first fable and read through a few lines. She glanced back at Finn. He was still sitting forlorn on the beach. When she saw the sea nymph had gone, she went back to reading.

"Well that was about as useless as Dumbo's magic feather," she muttered, when she found nothing helpful in the story. Maybe she should explore the wreckage. Fate turned, expecting to see Finn. He was gone.

She ran back, stopping where his footprints led into the ocean. "Finn!" she yelled, rushing into the water up to her chest. Pushing against the rolling waves, she screamed his name at the top of her lungs, but the rising swells splashed into her mouth, drowning her voice. She paddled back to shore, coughing up seawater, ashamed for being so easily beaten.

Dropping into the sand, she hung her head. Why had she turned her back on that predator? She grabbed a nearby stick and slashed it across the smooth sand. The deep line sparked an idea when she realized what she was looking at.

She wrote furiously in the sand, then read it aloud. *"When the sea nymph took Finn down into the deep ocean, he found that he could breathe, and the spell she had over him broke. Forced to free him, the sea nymph let go and Finn swam safely to shore."*

She searched the water, but the cresting waves tossed without disturbance. Her heart sank. So the magic was in the notepad just as she'd feared. Grief hit her like a fist in the gut as tears welled in her eyes. Stiffly, she rose and turned her back to the ocean, her feet dragging in the sand.

"Fate."

She stopped. Was her mind playing cruel tricks? She looked over her shoulder. Finn was staggering knee-deep in the water. He collapsed on the shoreline before she could get to him.

At the same time a gigantic wave rose behind him. The sea nymph rode within its foaming coil, her face twisted in rage. Fate pulled on his arm. "Get up! She's coming back!"

Dread splashed across his face, but before he could get to his feet, the siren gripped hold of his ankle.

A terrible tug of war ensued.

"What sorcery is this?" the sea nymph roared in an inhuman voice that made Fate's blood run cold. "If the sea cannot claim him this day, it will swallow this island whole to have him."

More outraged than scared, Fate held tight. She wasn't letting go now that she had him back. "Why *him?"*

"The souls of every doomed ship are the sea's due," the sea nymph raged.

"He wasn't on that ship!" Fate yelled. "The sorceress has the one you want."

She let go of Finn's leg and they both tumbled back. Pushing her tail into the sand, the sea nymph slithered forward, looming over them. "Bring me the doomed soul and I will spare this one from taking his place."

Fate scrambled backwards, but faced the creature nonetheless. Though Finn was running as far from shore as he could get, leaving her in jeopardy once again. "I don't need to bring the sailor here. He'll come to you on his own," Fate explained. "And I also know the sorceress plans to turn you into a brainless sea monster for taking him away from her."

The sea nymph grabbed Fate's leg with astonishing speed. *"You lie."*

She shrank from the rank odor of the sea on the siren's breath.

"No, it's true!" Finn called from where he stood by the cliffs. "You can read about it in this book."

The sea nymph narrowed her wild eyes. The second she let go of Fate, her fishtail fluidly transformed into legs. Her long golden locks were all that clothed her—barely. She made her way over to the book with zero modesty. Finn's gaze scarcely flicked over the unpredictable siren. It was obvious he wasn't going to burn his hand on that stove again, and jogged back to stand next to Fate.

When the sea nymph finished reading, she returned to the water and dove in. There was a moment of uncertainty before she surfaced. "I have heard of a book, which dictates the destinies of those who are written on its pages. Until now, I thought it was a myth." Her gaze locked on Finn. "I will allow you to live, and I will grant you a boon for giving me fair warning." She removed her pink pearl and coral necklace. "I gift you with my glamour. When it is worn, you may become anything you wish by changing your form. It is no mere illusion—it shifts flesh and bone and other matters into whatever you desire."

She threw the necklace on the beach. Her beautiful face lingered for the briefest moment before her eyes bulged and her mouth widened into a fishy grin. Her golden hair turned to green slime and her barnacled neck split open with gills. She arced out of the water, her spiked dorsal fin slicing the waves before she plunged into the deep.

Finn shuddered. "And to think I wanted to kiss *that.*"

"Yeah, you were all over it." Fate picked up the necklace and put it on. "Okay, let's test this baby out." Closing her eyes, she pictured a green and blue parrot about half her size like the one she'd seen at the palace, wearing a simple dress, apron and ruffled maid cap. She braced for a painful experience, but a strange, rather pleasant sensation flooded down from her head to her toes instead. Like warm oil oozing over her body, seeping in, softening her, molding her into a new shape.

Hearing Finn laugh, she opened her eyes.

"Quit messing about, Fate."

She raised her arm. It was short with stubby hands covered in fine down. Bending, she wiggled the toes of her talons. "Holy cow, it worked!" she said, startled by how the wings on her back fluttered in response to her excitement.

"And what exactly do you expect to accomplish in that getup?" he asked, clearly skeptical.

Frowning, she crossed her arms. "I'm going to make sure this story ends in our favor."

"Now hold on. Don't be hotheaded about this. We should plan this out."

"Right, because that's been working like a dream." Taking a run at it, she flapped her wings as hard as she could. She lifted off, wobbling and dipping like crazy, certain she would never clear the cliffs. But she wasn't about to give up. She'd rather hurl to the ground than suffer the humiliation of having to admit defeat.

Fate crash-landed on an empty terrace. Unfortunately, a cranky parrot in a butler's suit witnessed her clumsy arrival.

"What are you doing out *there?*" he squawked. "Get your feathered fanny in here. I need every piece of silver polished before we serve dinner."

She waddled inside. When she saw the stacks of tarnished serving platters, bowls, tea sets, goblets, urns and utensils covering the surface of a gigantic table her beak dropped. "Don't you have house-elves for this kind of thing?"

"If only such things existed," he said as she headed in the opposite direction. She didn't get far before she heard the quick scratching of his claws over the marble floor as he beetled behind her. "Where do you think *you're* going?"

"Sorry, there's been a mix-up."

The butler parrot slid past her, skidding to a stop, his wings flapping to catch his balance. "Why haven't I ever seen you before?"

"I don't know."

With his head cocked sideways, one yellow eye darted over her face and feather markings. "There's something not quite right about you…"

Glancing past him at the mountain of tarnished silver, she heaved a sigh of dread. "Where would you like me to start?"

Several hours of non-stop polishing along with a feather duster shoved in her face every time she made the slightest complaint, had given Fate enough time to cool off, at least about Finn. She felt downright sheepish for thinking he'd purposely deserted her during the ambush. And it wasn't like he'd willingly fallen under the siren's spell. She felt awful for losing her temper and ditching him. He'd been right. They should've made a plan.

The whap of sooty feathers over the head startled her. "It's time to serve dinner."

Glaring at him, Fate stood beak to beak with the butler parrot. "Listen, Jeeves. If you do that one more time, *you're* going to be the feather duster."

He reared back, looking indignant. "Insolent," he muttered. But he left it at that, gesturing for her to push a cart filled with a delicious array of food. She followed him down a long hallway full of activity. Lizard-headed bluebirds darted past her head, carrying flowers to a raccoon arranging bouquets. Winged squirrels flitted about dusting fixtures and furniture with their tails, while a bear with sad human eyes mopped the marble floors.

Fate slowed as she passed a chamber, where a pale, but really good-looking guy slept in a massive bed. A lioness bent over him with a cloth to his brow. Despite her predatory face, she looked almost angelic with the white veils she wore and outspread wings. Fate knew the patient had to be Torrin. Everything was in place now that the sea nymph was out of the picture. All she had to do was suss out the situation with Elsina, get back to Finn and figure out how they'd play cupid between the sorceress and her reluctant companion.

The butler hustled her out onto a large terrace glowing with colorful paper lanterns floating overhead and thousands of fireflies hovering in amongst the lush foliage. A fountain burbled with soft tinkling music, while a group of toads with dragonfly wings added melodic bass notes. Elsina sat dressed in a satin azure gown at the head of a very long table filled with a bizarre company of dinner guests—a bull, a giraffe, a wolf, a lynx, a gazelle, a horse, a ram, a lion and a swan—each animal endowed with human bodies from the neck down and as elegantly dressed as their hostess. A sight that was both confusing and disturbing.

Hatho arrived last, his helmet off and wearing a general's uniform. He sat next to the sorceress as Fate set the platters on the table. She spotted her notepad next to Elsina's jeweled hand. She started reaching for it when the butler pulled her back by the tail feathers, motioning with stern eyes to stand next to him.

Elsina cut into a plate of quail stuffed with herbs, nuts and raisins. "Where is Sithias?" she said to Hatho before taking a small bite. "These intruders confound me. I need to know more."

The hawk's golden eyes slid to the others at the table. They were being entertained by a troupe of winged rabbits performing acrobatics in time with the music. "There is no word yet," he said, turning back to her.

An ominous smile curved Elsina's ruby lips. "He must have discovered something of great interest for him to be gone so long. He is clever and sly, if nothing else."

"If you say so," Hatho said.

"You've seen his plays—full of mystery, deception and intrigue."

Just then something huge descended with a loud flapping noise, scattering the floating lanterns and disrupting the flying rabbits before landing on the balcony. Swaying upright —standing a good six feet tall when coiled—was an ivory-colored snake with a suede hunter's cap shadowing large amber eyes. The snake folded its brown-speckled feathery wings, while doffing its cap with a rather skilled tail.

"Finally, Sithias," Elsina said, eagerness disturbing her smooth brow. "What do you have to tell me?"

"Mistresss," Sithias hissed, "forgive me for not coming sssooner to warn you. The witch'sss apprentice held me *temporarily* under a minor ssspell with hisss magic flute."

"So it's just as I thought," she said. "The apprentice is the one with the power."

Fate listened with surprise.

"It would seem ssso, but we can't be sure. We mussst be careful. The witch isss here." He looked around, his eyes widening on Fate. "Oh dear, there she *isss*."

The sorceress turned her head, looking past Fate and the butler parrot to other servants bringing in more trays.

Fate froze, afraid to move.

"Where?" Elsina said. Ice crystals formed over the spheres of each eye and her breath turned to frost even as a terrible heat came off her, forcing nearby guests to back away.

"There mistresss…the parrot!"

A bolt of red flames poured from Elsina's hand, striking the butler parrot. He vaporized into a cloud of smoke and feathers. Fate screamed, jumping away. She removed the glamour, thrown further off balance by the dizzying sensation of stretching back to her normal size and shape. "*Please.* Don't shoot," she begged, holding her hands up.

Elsina kept her lethal hand aimed at Fate, her fingers feeling the air like a blind person. As the ice melted from her eyes, tears trickled down her pale skin. "So this is our *witch*." A wintry smile formed on her face as she dropped her arm. "You have no magic. Do you?"

The smell of burnt poultry in the air had rendered Fate momentarily speechless. All she could do was shake her head.

Elsina stood, closing the space between them. She dangled the notepad by the chain. "And this is nothing more than a trinket."

Fate nodded.

"Take it, little would-be witch."

The soldier hawk and snake exchanged a confused glance. "Milady, I strongly advise against it," Hatho warned, as Sithias shook his head with a worried look.

Fate reached for the notepad.

Elsina dropped it in her palm. "Now tell me about the wizard you traveled here with. I want to know what his source of power is."

"Uh..." Fate stalled, grasping at the first thing she could think of. "The snake's right. He gets his power from the flute."

"Do you know how he uses it?" Elsina asked, feigned puzzlement barely disguising her shrewdness.

"Sure. He...plays musical spells on it," Fate said as an idea blossomed. "If you'd like, I can write one of them down for you."

"Please do," the sorceress said, her smile carefully grateful.

Biting her lip to keep the nervous smile off her face, Fate pulled out the pencil and wrote: *I am on the beach with Finn*. Glancing up at Elsina, she muttered the words under her breath, astonished when the sorceress and her creatures blurred away.

Back on the beach—after Fate had flown away—Finn found a hideous, winged snake reading the *Book of Fables*. Afraid it may have seen Fate change into a parrot, he couldn't let the snake fly off and tell Elsina. To keep it grounded, he did the only thing he could think of. Mesmerize the serpent with his Druidic inscribed wooden flute. The music had worked like a charm, except he couldn't keep it going. The moment he ran out of breath after hours of playing, the snake made a swift escape.

He needed to warn Fate. And fast. The snake would arrive at the palace any moment and reveal her disguise.

Placing his palm on the sand, Finn pushed his senses into the earth. His first lesson as a youngster, taught to him by his grandfather, the Grand Druid of Scotland, was to connect with all living things through the earth. In this way, he'd learned to communicate with the trees and hear their voices.

Connecting with a human was new to him, but he had no doubt he could connect with Fate. They were inextricably linked somehow. From the second they'd met in the bookstore, he'd been drawn to her like no one he'd ever known. At the same time, she mixed him up. His skin felt on fire every time he looked at her, yet her presence was as comforting as going home—like when he'd first set foot on Scottish soil and knew he belonged there.

Sometimes he was so overwhelmed by his feelings he could barely meet her gaze for fear of blurting them out. The last thing he wanted to do was scare her off. So he waited in silent anguish for one small gesture or glance that she felt the same way. There were moments when he thought he glimpsed an inkling, but her moods changed like quicksilver, leaving him more confused than ever.

The link to Fate blazed up his arm, her core essence exploding in his chest. She was inside him, a blizzard of wildfire, cinnamon candy and crisp autumn air. She soaked into his blood, flowed through his veins straight to the heart of his soul, taking his breath away.

He wanted to stay there, dive deeper, drink her up. But he had to pull back, focus on her present condition. He sensed she was safe for the moment. There was still time to send the warning.

Then he suddenly felt a jolt of fear run through her. She was in trouble. He hadn't been quick enough. Powerless to protect her yet again, he pounded his fist into the sand. He stared at the indent he'd made. If Fate could write Words of Making, he should be able to as well. Scribbling a sentence in the sand, he read it aloud, *"I am now in Elsina's palace standing next to Fate."*

He waited for something, a sensation of traveling, anything that would indicate it had worked, but nothing happened. "Bollocks!"

He jumped to his feet and raced toward the cliff steps.

"Hey! Where are you going?"

Skidding to a stop, he turned to see Fate running up to him, her cheeks flushed, her eyes lit with excitement. She grabbed his hand, pulling him toward her with an urgency that made his heart skip a beat. He stepped close, expectant, reaching out with his other hand to pull her into his arms.

She twisted away, yanking on his hand, tugging him over to the *Book of Fables*. "*Come on*, we've got to move into the next fable. Now!"

Disappointment hollowed him out, slowing his movements.

A roar echoed out over the cove. Finn glanced up as a winged granite lion glided past the cliff walls, descending swiftly, shaking the ground upon landing. The sorceress slid off its broad back as Hatho touched down with a dozen other soldier hawks.

Rushing now, Finn pulled open the book. He looked back as Fate turned the pages. Elsina radiated deadly power. Her eyes turned white, the air around her body rippled with heat waves.

He sensed her drawing strength from the island, charging up. As she raised her arm, a fireball burst from her palm.

He grabbed Fate's hand. "Time to read that first word," he urged. But an inferno blasted toward them. There was nothing he could do but shield Fate with his body.

Squeezing his eyes shut, Finn braced for the flames to consume them both.

A Dark Faery's Love

Shrouded within the mists of time when the elusive realm of faery had few boundaries, one could easily trespass into a world of enchantment that sometimes offered rich reward but more often led to danger. Within these realms dwelt scores of magical creatures. The forms of faery were varied and numerous, with many names.

One such faery, that of a dark ilk, is the subject of this tale. This deadly faery took on the guise of an irresistibly beautiful human so as to spellbind its victim until the moment it revealed its hideous form.

So it was that a young maiden named Mae was picking berries in the forest one day. She knew the berries were most plentiful near the heart of the forest, even though she'd been warned never to go more than ten trees deep into the woods. It was said that an evil grove had grown from the acorn of a cursed oak. These sinister, pixie infested trees moved to confuse many a woodsman's path and steer him to certain danger. But Mae trusted that there was goodness in all things, even in the heart of the most evil of creatures. Therefore, she ignored the warnings and went in alone.

Yet she was not alone. Something hid in the shadows. A repulsive creature crept from behind and slithered up a tree to hang its loathsome head over her crouched figure. While Mae sang and filled her basket, she was unaware that the dark faery of those cursed woods was taking in the delicious odor of fresh human meat.

When she felt a tickle on top of her head, she lifted her hand and touched something unfamiliar. Curiosity, rather than fear, kept her hand exploring. The dark faery froze under her inquisitive touch while her fingers ran over its misshapen face, and when Mae felt its row of sharp fangs she did something quite unexpected.

She giggled with delight.

In that very moment, something miraculous took place within the dark faery's heart. Warmth never felt before began to spread where only ice had lived for centuries. When Mae lifted her gaze, the dark faery vanished before she could witness its true form. For the first time in its ancient existence, it felt searing shame for its evil intent.

Mae called out to it, saying not to be afraid, that she meant no harm. The irony was not lost on the dark faery and, try as it might, it could not find any malice in its heart to harm her, nor could it leave her welcoming presence. So it shed its monstrous skin, and out from the scaly heap stepped a handsome young man.

He appeared before Mae. His noble features were warmly colored, his eyes a gentle brown. He wore the garments of a hunter and carried a crossbow in his hand. Giving her a gracious bow, he introduced himself as Callum and reassured her he'd killed the horrible monster that had come all too close to devouring her. Mae was horrified by this and sobbed. Callum was both surprised and confused by her reaction. When he tried to console her, she would have none of it. She told him she could never forgive him for killing her new friend, and ran home.

Contrary to his malicious nature, the dark faery allowed her to leave, not by means of compassion, but because he loved her all the more for the grief she felt toward a vile monster's demise. Yet here was a true dilemma. If the dark faery could not have Mae's love, he did not want to live.

The next day, Mae's father discovered a crate containing twenty chickens outside the door of his humble cottage, a welcome gift for a poor family. Thereafter, the family received ten goats, then five cows, one bull, four fine steeds, six turkeys, a hundred bushels of wheat, bolts of fine fabric, rounds of cheese, barrels of apples, an array of spices, a new wagon, a sack of gold, and finally, a silk wedding gown trimmed in pearls.

Upon the arrival of the last gift, Mae's father opened the door and welcomed Callum with great enthusiasm. When he asked for permission to marry Mae, her father gave her hand gladly.

Mae was far less willing to marry the man who had murdered her friend, but she couldn't ignore Callum's generosity to those who had known only poverty. And she didn't doubt the love in his eyes when he looked at her. She agreed to marry him that very day, but only on one condition. She pledged that her heart would beat solely for him if he vowed never to kill another living thing again. The dark faery willingly whispered this promise to her.

Word spread, and many came to witness the marriage between the mysterious nobleman and the peasant girl. One of the guests, a wise man with the gift of Sight, was horrified to see a monstrous creature of fae standing next to Mae. With his staff pointed at Callum, he spoke an incantation for drawing false veils aside and revealed the truth to everyone.

The frightened guests drew back when they saw Callum's true form. Mae was the only one who stayed by his side. She put her hands on the gruesome face staring back at her and smiled in recognition.

Those carrying swords were quick to attack the revolting creature. The dark faery could have killed every one of them, but he would not break his vow to Mae and surrendered. His attackers did not care that he didn't fight back. They slashed the dark faery into bloody pieces.

After the chaos ended, Mae's father wailed with grief. His dear daughter lay lifeless on the floor without injury. Her death remained a mystery. No one could have known that her heart beat solely for Callum, whose promise to never kill another living thing had also unwittingly meant the death of his one true love.

CHAPTER 7

THE FABLE'S OVERWHELMING IMAGERY disintegrated into a torrent of letters that rained onto the yellowed pages, falling back into their original order.

Gripped by nausea, Fate staggered, waiting for the lightheaded feeling to stop. Slowly, the sounds of wind through trees and the scent of pine brought her around. It was hard pulling out of Mae and Callum's tragic story. She needed to shake it off, get her bearings. As the queasiness subsided, she remembered the flames shooting at them.

Finn.

Panicked, she straightened, blinking through watery eyes, turning in every direction. Still dizzy, she lost her balance and fell against him. "Oh thank God," she said, planting her forehead on his chest. "For a second there I thought you'd been Caspered."

"You're not the only one," he said, wrapping his arms around her.

He held her like it was as natural as breathing. He felt so good. Warm and safe. She started to melt against him, but realized something was wrong. "You're shaking."

"Just a side effect of being lightly killed." He pulled away, showing her the top of his left shoulder. There was a singed hole in his shirt, revealing an angry burn, weeping blood.

"Oh no!" she cried, sick to her stomach. "It's all my fault! This never would've happened if I hadn't taken off like that. I'm so horrible, completely thoughtless and selfish and—"

"Whoa. How about you trade your cane in for a cat o' nine tails? It's not a proper flogging without one."

Fate sighed. "From now on we'll plan everything out together."

"Your reasonableness will be much appreciated." Giving her a weary smile, he pulled out the tin of salve stashed in his pocket.

Fate took it from him and dabbed it on the wound, wincing as she did so. After she finished, she wrote up some bandages and carefully applied them. "There. I'm no Doc McCoy, but I think you'll live."

"Thanks, Bones," he said, walking over to the *Book of Fables*. "Shall we see what we left behind?"

"Do we have to?"

He was already turning the pages, his expression carefully blank as he read the ending to *The Lonely Sorceress*.

"What does it say?" she said, afraid to look.

"Well, it seems Torrin was so desperate to strike out to sea he cut down some trees to repair his ship. But that infuriated Elsina, so she imprisoned him for a month, as what she called, a slight punishment. When she let him out, he threw himself off the cliffs. She still ends up lonely."

"Oh that's just terrific. Now we've got to go back and keep Torrin from killing himself?" She kicked the dirt. "What if we screw up all the other fables too? We could be at this *forever*."

"Don't fret, lass. We'll get the hang of it. Starting with this new one. And the Words of Making will certainly help. Who knows? We might be able to write *all* the endings. It could be as simple as that, so long as we put careful thought into it first."

The conviction in his eyes sparked hope in her. "You think?"

He chucked her chin gently. "Never give up, missy."

"No, you *musssn't* give up," a sibilant voice hissed from somewhere behind them.

Fate jumped, grabbing Finn's arm as Elsina's winged snake rose up from behind a bush. "Sithiasss, at your ssservice." The snake bowed, tipping off his hat to them, a wide grin revealing long fangs.

He returned the hat to his gleaming head. After several strained moments of silence, Sithias said, "Allow me to begin the peace talksss. I hitched a ride with you mossstly becaussse I could no longer sssuffer the sheer boredom of my life. You two were the mossst exciting thing to come along in a very long time. But I alssso came for the chance to help you turn all thisss gloom into sssomething a little more…upbeat shall we sssay?"

Finn stepped between her and the serpent, his face flushed red with a look of revulsion. "And we're supposed to trust a *snake?*"

Sithias appeared offended. "As rumorsss would have it, we're not *all* bad."

Finn clenched his fists. "Hmmm, let's see…does the term snake in the grass mean anything to you? And you *are* Elsina's spy."

"Please, I'm not here to ssspy." The snake swayed on his coils. "If anything, I can be of great ssservice to your mission."

Swift anger cut through Fate's shock. "Oh, and by help you must mean blowing my cover and nearly getting me killed? Elsina vaporized one of her parrots because of you. He was a bossy pain in the butt, but he didn't deserve *that*. And I would've been next, except I managed to outwit her."

"There'sss no outwitting my mistresss. She clearly underessstimated you." He batted his eyes with a guilty smile. "But you're quite right, I did—how did you put it? Blow your cover. I wasss merely doing my job. You don't *not* do your job around Elsssina. The consequencesss of that are dire."

Finn took her by the arm, leading her several yards away. "We need to get rid of him."

She glanced over her shoulder, regarding the snake with equal suspicion. "I'd like nothing more, but he knows all about the *Book of Fables*. He could cause some major trouble if he wanted to. I say he stays so we can watch him."

"But he's a *snake*." His face twisted in disgust. "I *hate* snakes.

And I'm surprised you don't feel the same, especially since he's all but an oversized worm."

She shuddered. "Snakes aren't like those sticky tubes of ick. They're dry and smooth…and clean."

Sithias stuck his head between them. "That'sss quite right, I'm spotlesss—"

Finn punched the snake in the nose. "Not so *close*."

"That hurt!" he whimpered, rubbing his nose with the tip of his tail.

"If you sneak up on me again, I promise, I'll skin you for a pair of boots."

Fate cringed. "Kinda harsh, Finn."

"I agree, Finn," the snake added.

"That's, *sir*, to you!" He turned his heated gaze back to Fate. "If you knew how my mum died, you'd understand."

"Was she bitten by a rattlesnake on a hiking trip in the Rockies?"

The anger drained from his face.

She immediately regretted speaking before thinking.

"How could you know that?"

She stepped back. "I, uh—"

"I'm terribly sssorry to hear that," the snake interrupted, his amber eyes round with contrition. "Ressst assured, sssir, I am *not* poisonousss."

He threw the snake a scathing look. "Do you mind? We're talking here." He turned to her. "Tell me how you know that."

Fate's throat closed around her voice. She finally had confirmation. He was exactly what she'd suspected from the moment she'd laid eyes on him. She simply hadn't been willing to admit it. Even now she was having trouble believing it. But should she tell him? Part of her wanted to confess everything. But a bigger part resisted. He wouldn't welcome it. Who would?

Instead, she found herself saying the first stupid thing to pop in her head. "I-I'm a little psychic. I get these flashes, and then poof, they're gone. Just like that," she said, snapping her fingers. She gulped, quite certain he wouldn't buy her lame explanation.

Finn's shoulders drooped with disappointment. "So… you're psychic."

She forced a smile. "That's me, your very own psychic hotline, right here."

"*Ooh*, do me," Sithias said, excited. "Tell my fortune."

She turned to the snake, actually grateful for the diversion. "Sure, but you'll have to wait for a flash," she lied, knowing one would never come.

"I'll be *counting* the minutesss."

Finn grabbed her arm. "You're not going to tell his fortune, because he's not staying."

"I won't be any trouble, I promissse."

Finn lurched at Sithias, who dodged the attack by weaving out of the way. "*Listen*, we don't trust you. Besides being Elsina's spy, you could be one of those bloody squeezers that eats anything from goats to humans." He eyed him up and down. "You're big enough to do it."

Sithias gagged like a cat coughing up hairballs. "Goatsss? Humansss? How *utterly* revolting. I prefer ham. Mistressss alwaysss feedsss me sssweet honeyed ham."

Fate hid a smile behind her hand. "See? He's domesticated—nothing to worry about."

"I don't like it," Finn grumbled.

She took out her notepad. "Hey, I don't know about you, but I've got a yen for spaghetti."

"I'm not hungry," he said, still glowering at the snake.

She left him to his fuming and wrote up a big side of ham for Sithias and two bowls of spaghetti smothered in Parmesan. The snake thanked her profusely. Before he began swallowing his ham whole, which was gross to watch, he talked on and on about how excited he was about their upcoming adventures. By the time they finished the meal, the snake had charmed her.

Even Finn seemed a little less hostile, the black look gone as he busied himself with placing protective wards around the *Book of Fables*. She finally had a moment to sit back and really look at him, see his actions through the lense of knowing who he truly was. Now it made perfect sense why he placed the powder, which she knew to be crushed chicken bone and sulfur, in the four cardinal directions. And she recognized the invocation he muttered to empower the wards. But she also knew it was a bunch of mumbo-jumbo.

The giant book vanished from sight.

Astonished, Fate stood and walked over to it with her hand raised. When her fingers hit the book's hard surface, she gasped.

Finn stepped up next to her. "There, that should keep *him* from sticking his nose in the book." He fell quiet. "Something wrong?"

She snapped back to attention. "No…I was just thinking he also watched you put the wards in place. He knows where it is, same as we do."

He let out a frustrated sigh. "I know, but it eases my mind to have done so. And he's not the only one I'm worried about. We don't need the dark faery catching a glimpse of it. But we shouldn't leave the snake alone with the book—all he has to do is read a few words out loud and disappear with it."

Struggling with the urge to stare at Finn in amazement, she glanced at Sithias and the engorged ham-sized lump stretching his scales. "We don't need to worry about him right now. He's about as frisky as a beached whale."

"Maybe so," Finn agreed. "But we can't go trusting him when he's slinky again."

"So we'll keep an eye on him after he's out of the fat farm.

Until then, let's take a look around and find out what part of the story we're in."

He gave her a reluctant nod.

She had to work to keep the awestruck smile off her face and was glad he was distracted, or he might start asking questions again. She turned to Sithias. "We're going to scout around. Be back shortly."

"*Very* shortly, so no funny business," Finn warned.

Sithias belched. His drowsy eyes rounded with surprised embarrassment. "I'm too ssstuffed to do anything but sssleep." He flopped his head on his bulging belly.

Smiling at the snake, Fate whispered to Finn. "I should probably make his next helping smaller."

Giving her a frown, he turned to leave. "Stop looking at him like that."

"Like what?"

"Like you just brought home a stray pup."

"Oh, come on. How often do you meet a talking snake? I feel like Dr. Doolittle, or Harry."

"He has fangs the size of my fingers!"

She laughed, catching up to him. "Stop worrying. You know what they say about sleeping dogs…so let this one lie."

"That's exactly what I'm worried about."

CHAPTER 8

THEY WALKED THROUGH THE FOREST, looking for a road or nearby village. But it seemed as if they were heading deeper into the woods, the undergrowth dense with blackberry bushes. There was little room to walk without becoming tangled in brambles, which is exactly what happened to Fate. She waited for Finn's help, but he was just standing there staring straight ahead.

"Hey, I'm stuck," she said, wincing from the thorns wrapped around her legs.

As he carefully extracted her from the thicket, he kept looking over his shoulder.

"What's wrong with you? You look like you're expecting the sky to fall."

He gripped her hand, holding tight. "I'm not sure. I'm getting the feeling there's something hiding itself—watching us."

Other than the stinging scratches the thorns had given her, she wasn't sensing anything. But that didn't mean a thing. She knew Finn's abilities too well. If he said something was watching, then there was.

"Do you hear that?" she asked.

Nodding, he put a finger to his lips to keep quiet and motioned for her to follow. They edged up behind some bushes and peeked through the branches.

A young woman about Fate's age was carrying a basket of blackberries and singing. Her fingers were stained purple and she wore a homespun dress mended with patches of random cloth. A frayed rag held her copper hair back, but none of this marred the sparkle in her blue eyes and the rose in her cheeks.

"That must be Mae," Fate whispered. "The story's already in full swing. We need to warn her about the dark faery before—"

"Too late." Finn pointed at the bowed, swaying branches six feet above Mae. The leaves rustled as a gruesome face emerged, its mouth a gaping grin of curved fangs. There was no nose or eyes to speak of, only a snarl of yellowed flesh wrinkled into an evil scowl. A web of veins throbbed beneath skin stretched thin over a bulbous skull. Four long, sinewy arms pulled it further out onto the limb, revealing an emaciated torso. Its membranous hide clung to a deformed ribcage and spikes protruding along its back. From its waist extended a tangle of long, writhing tentacles, which lashed round the branches, enabling the monster to slowly lower itself down over its victim.

Fate trembled. Never had she seen anything so hideous. Her heart pounded with fright as the dark faery sniffed the top of Mae's head. She wanted to yell out to her, but she had to trust the story would play out as written. Holding still, she held her breath as Mae reached up without looking at the horror fest looming above her. As she ran her hands along each side of its repugnant features, her trusting expression turned to one of surprise, even amusement.

An unnatural hush had fallen over the forest. No breeze, no bird song, no droning of bugs. It was as if every living thing in the area—even the elements—held still as the creature's jaw unhinged, widening into a cavernous, steaming maw above Mae's head.

Then she giggled. Her laugh broke the silence, crisp and clear as a bell, ringing through the air with the purity of a child's delight. Birds joined in song and the wind broke free to whistle through the leaves. The dark faery held still, its jaw snapping shut. As Mae glanced up, the beast recoiled, vanishing within the foliage. Movement in the treetops marked its swift escape.

"Ew, now that's what Eustace would call uglier than a war wound," Fate said, a hand to her heart as she started breathing again.

"Agreed," Finn said, as they emerged from their hiding place and walked over to Mae.

She whirled round, an expectant smile lighting her face. When she saw them, she looked disappointed. "And who might you be?" she asked. "'Tis certain you're not my newly made friend of these mystical woods."

Finn eyed her with an appreciative smile. "No, but you can consider us new friends all the same. I'm Finn, and this is Fate."

Fate tried to ignore an uncomfortable pinching in her stomach and waved hello.

Mae curtsied. "Pleased, I'm sure. My name is Mae of the Glen."

"Good to meet you, Mae of the Glen." Finn's Scottish accent grew even more pronounced in the presence of Mae's Irish cadence. He stepped close to her. "Who was with you before we arrived?"

A smile lit her face. "That was my new friend. I must say, you no doubt scared him off before I could get a peek at him. He's a shy one, he is—"

"Sorry to rain on all this Irish freshness, but we got a good look at your 'friend'," Fate said. "And he wouldn't be described as appealing to anyone blessed with sight."

Finn flashed Mae an apologetic look, before whispering to Fate, "A little tact here, please."

"I could've said worse," she whispered back.

He turned back to Mae, whose smile had dimmed. "I think what Fate means is that your new friend would've frightened you if you'd seen what it looks like."

Mae shook her head. "I may not have laid eyes on him, but I felt his face with my hands. I could tell he's not bonnie to look at, which means he's in great need of a kind touch and a friendly heart."

The pinching in Fate's stomach worsened as Finn's eyes filled with admiration.

"I see your point," he said, his tone soft, patient. "But we need to warn you about something, and I don't want you to be frightened by what I have to tell—"

"Oh for crying out loud," Fate interjected. "Mae, that thing you made friends with is a dark faery, and it's going to appear to you as a man named Callum who wants to marry you. But if you do marry him, he won't be bringing the usual problems, like flirting with every pretty face he happens to run into, or leaving you to face danger all by yourself. He'll be bringing you death on your wedding day."

Mae drew away from them both, making a sign to ward off evil. "How do you know this? Are you witches come to curse me?"

Finn held out his hand, but she kept backing away. "We don't wish you any harm. We only want to help."

Mae studied each of them. "I do see truth and kindness in you, Finn. And though Fate is tetchy—" she paused to survey Fate's jeans, "—and in men's clothing, no less, I'm certain there's goodness deep down inside."

"I'm not tetchy. Irritable maybe, but not tetchy," Fate grumbled.

Finn threw her a sharp look, which stung, especially when he smiled warmly at Mae. "Don't mind her. She means well. She's just not good at delivering bad news."

Mae's blue eyes widened with trust. "I believe you have my welfare at heart. I'll return home with a mind to turn this Callum away if he should show his face."

"Good," he said, openly relieved.

She turned to go. "Safe journey, and may the good spirits smile upon you both."

He waved. "And to you."

After she left, Fate rolled her eyes. "Ugh, how sickeningly sweet. Like those chocolate eggs with the white goo and off-putting splotch of yellow in the center. Hated them so much, I wrote the Easter Bunny to tell him to stop putting them in my basket. Of course, I found out much later I should've been writing Cadbury, but you get the point."

"Why must you be that way?"

"What way?" She knew she was being a complete brat, but hadn't been able to stop the rant once she started. She felt all messy and confused inside.

"Sour about someone you've barely met. Mae's probably one of the most sincere people you'll ever run into."

His obvious disappointment in her riled her inner brat even more. "Sincere? You do realize you're defending someone who's not real. None of this is. It's all a work of fiction, albeit with incredibly good special effects. Hollywood would be all over this place if they knew about it."

His expression grew fierce as he took her by the arms, nearly lifting her off the ground with his intensity. "This is as real as it gets, lass. You'd best wrap your head around that, or you're in for a great deal of trouble down the road."

There was fear in his eyes, the same fear she'd seen in Eustace's eyes when she was little and got lost in the mall. She'd hated causing that pain in her father, and this felt just as bad. "I know it's real," she said, unable to keep her voice from shaking.

He let go of her.

"I don't know why I've been in denial. Hard to believe, since I've done nothing but write about stuff like this for years. But now that it's here—and you too—I can't help thinking I've either bumped my head, or I'm dreaming, or just stark raving mad."

He had begun to relax, but his brows shot up, puzzled. "What did you mean by me too? Is there something you want to tell me?"

"I…I'm just glad I'm not alone in all this. I know we've gotten off to a rough start, but I'm really grateful you're here."

"That's it?"

His eyes begged for more. She dropped her gaze and nodded.

"Fine. We should get back, figure out what we need to do next and make sure that snake is behaving," he said, his voice gruff as he stomped away.

Fate watched him go, a sick feeling starting in the pit of her stomach. She wanted to tell him. He deserved to know. But it would be rotten timing after her callous remark about Mae. She'd have to wait just a little longer.

They were traveling in circles.

The same hollowed-out tree stump appeared for the fourth time. On their way back, they had come upon the dreaded grove of twisted oaks and now there seemed to be no getting away from them.

Glancing up, Finn frowned at their dark branches lacing over the gray sky like stiff, gnarled tentacles. "Even though we've seen no sign of the trees moving, I can't help feeling we keep getting herded back here somehow."

Fate sighed with relief. Finally, he was talking to her again. She'd been so uptight and distracted by the tension between them she'd forgotten she could write them back to the *Book of Fables*. She started to tell him when something cracked beneath her boot. She lifted her foot off a thin white branch. It looked wrong somehow. As she bent to pick it up, her gaze followed the fragile line to a tiny skeletal hand. She broke into a sweat, gulped a deep breath as she staggered back.

Finn stepped around her, anxiety showing on his face. She followed stiffly as he pushed through the thickets into a small clearing. He turned abruptly, his hands up to stop her from going further. "Don't look," he said, his voice choked.

It was too late. She stared at the tangled pile of skeletons strewn amongst shredded, bloodied clothes and scattered belongings. Terror and sorrow crashed together. She stifled a sob behind her hand as Finn pulled her away, thorns tearing at them. She ran blindly, seeing only the delicate bones of the infant's hand, a woman's locket, a little girl's torn doll, a man's broken crossbow.

Finn slammed his back against the trunk of a thick oak, pulling her close to him. "Stay still and be very quiet," he whispered.

His tone frightened her. She huddled close, her arms round his neck, heart racing, thoughts muddled with fear. A piece of bark moved just above Finn's shoulder, like something was pushing from underneath. She pried it free, thinking it felt too thin and papery to be bark. As she placed the brown leafy thing in her palm, spidery legs unfurled and a gruesome little head with almost human features blinked at her.

Startled, she screamed and flung it.

At that moment, everything happened in a terrible blur. All of the bark dislodged from the trunks of the surrounding oak trees, becoming a disorienting swarm of shrieking pixies. She clung to Finn, but as the pixies smacked into them, she flailed and fell away from him.

The earth groaned with the sound of roots ripping free of solid ground as the oaks joined the fray. Clods of dirt flew everywhere, a multitude of branches lashed through the air. Fate dropped, scrambling on all fours to escape the writhing tree limbs. Pixies pelted her, from all angles, pulling her hair, tearing clumps from her scalp. Tiny claws clung to her face, prying her eyes, nostrils and mouth back, digging in her ears.

The pain and terror fractured into pure hysteria. Her scream blended into the cacophony as she twisted onto her back, kicking wildly, slapping at her face and arms to get them off. Then something snaked around her waist, squeezing so hard she thought her guts were squishing into her chest. As the branch snatched her off the ground, she saw Finn bound in the tree next to her, covered in pixies. His face was flushed and scratched.

She was stupefied. The fable hadn't exactly specified manhandling trees and *rabid* pixies.

She watched the trees burrow their roots back into the ground. The pixies had suddenly fallen silent, settling on the circle of oaks. She still had her share of pixies crawling over her, tugging at her hair, pinching and poking her skin but with much less intensity. She squirmed, trying to shrug them off. Another branch slithered over her, tightening around her ribcage so hard she could barely suck air into her lungs.

"Stop struggling…you'll make it…worse," Finn warned, suffering from the same shortage of breath.

Just then, the trees parted, allowing a young man to step within the tight circle of gnarled oaks. He stood out bright and beautiful amongst the wild, gray woods like a cultivated rose. The moment Fate looked at him, a pleasant heat rose beneath her skin, dispelling her fear and discomfort.

He wore a long coat of brushed suede over an olive vest, tan breeches and shiny black riding boots, but it was the glow of his sun-kissed skin that captivated her. Looking into his eyes was like being dunked in melted chocolate. He planted his polished walking stick into the ground and leaned on it. "Allow me to introduce myself. I am Callum, lord and master of these cursed woods."

The silvery timbre of his voice coaxed an involuntary moan from her throat.

Callum stared at them expectantly. "And you would be?"

A chill passed through her for a fraction of a second, like

someone had flapped the covers, waking her enough to realize who he was before the drowsy warmth returned. "Oh…he's the dark faery," she informed Finn. "And *damn* gorgeous."

"Thanks for sharing," Finn said, his jaw clenched. Then he glared at Callum. "I'm Finn McKeen."

Hearing his full name hit Fate like a freight train, driving the truth home like nothing else had before that very moment. Finn McKeen, the name she'd written over and over for the last five years. "It really is you," she said.

Finn's gaze flicked to her before returning to Callum. But in that instant, his eyes burned with a desperate need to know.

"And your name?" Callum said, netting her back into his entrancing gaze. His voice sent delicious shivers up her spine, pulling her thoughts away from Finn.

"Fate," she croaked.

Callum raised a brow. "Fate? What an apropos name for circumstances such as yours." He turned to the trees and their little parasites. "Don't you think so?"

The twisted oaks groaned, creaked and cracked while the pixies screeched with laughter.

Callum strolled up to her. His scent flowed over her like a balmy breeze, a full-bodied blend of woodsy musk and winter spices. "Yes, dear Fate, you will definitely be meeting your namesake very soon." He waved his cane at the trees. "Hold these meddlers as long as it takes my pets to pick their bones clean."

The dark faery chuckled as he turned to leave.

"Why don't you eat us yourself? Better yet, I challenge you to a good and proper brawl. Just you and me!" Finn called to Callum's departing back.

Callum stopped, then turned to face him. "Tempting, but I don't wish to stain my fine attire with your blood." He caressed the fox-trimmed lapel of his coat. "My children must eat, though it'll be a while before their appetites return. We just feasted on an entire family. I must say, the baby was a rare delicacy." He licked his perfect lips and bowed. "I must be off now. I have much to prepare for my wedding. Oh, and since you've warned Mae about me, I've decided to introduce myself as Ennis. Ennis and Mae. It has a nice ring to it, don't you agree?"

Finn struggled all the more, but the tree squeezed until he groaned in pain. Callum smiled with satisfaction. "And I think I'll marry her post haste. No need to allow the lovely Mae anymore time to dwell on those troublesome seeds of doubt you planted in her mind."

The dark faery whistled a cheerful tune as an oak ambled aside, allowing him to leave the circle. As the whistling faded, the pleasing fog in Fate's mind cleared. Fear slammed back in. Her skin crawled with hyperawareness. She felt every pixie tangling in her hair, worming down her shirt, scrabbling up her pant legs with needle-sharp claws pinching and scratching, even tickling.

She remembered the pile of skeletons. As soon as the pixies grew hungry, they'd eat them too. A sweating panic erupted. She thrashed against her bindings, desperate to escape. The branches constricted all the more, crushing her chest. "We're…going to die…like that…family!" she gasped.

"Fate, *stay calm*," Finn urged. "Try to hold still."

How could she relax when she couldn't get enough air? With each hyperventilated sob shuddering through her, she bruised her ribs against the rigid branches.

"Just let go," he said.

Frowning, she looked over at him, certain she'd heard him wrong. Did he really mean what she thought he was saying? Give up? Die? But she couldn't see him anymore. Sparks floated across her dimming eyesight. Maybe he knew it was best this way, more merciful to slip into oblivion.

Sorrow welled up inside her. There was still so much she wanted to do. But this was it. The end.

As her lungs and brain screamed for oxygen, a roaring wave of darkness engulfed her. She panicked as she felt herself sinking into the deep. Then two green eyes, a pink nose and orange-striped face appeared. It was her cat, Oz, his stare watchful and dignified. He started purring, a sound that ran through her like a powerful tranquilizer.

Stop that, Fate told him. *If I fall asleep, I'll never wake up again.*

Oz's face faded away. Only his eyes remained. *You should be so lucky*, he purred. *Unfortunately, you're destined to live. So sleep, and enjoy a little slice of peace.* With that his pupils expanded, eclipsing the light of his green irises and plunging her into an ocean of nothingness.

CHAPTER 9

FATE WOKE TO THE SENSATION OF FALLING. Her face hit moist earth. Bewildered, she sat up, rubbing dirt off her sore cheek. She glanced around just as Finn stepped out of the morning mist curling through the trees.

Before she could say a word, he clamped his hand over her mouth. "Be dead quiet," he whispered, scooping her up off the ground.

Gripping her hand, he led her through the still oaks. Slumbering pixies slipped off her and landed on the ground. Having lost their cozy sleeping place, a few woke, screeching in alarm when they saw their breakfast leaving.

She ran blindly, letting Finn lead her past a blur of trees. As they pushed through the brambles, she barely felt the thorns scratching her hands and face. Her attention was on the angry, shrieking swarm of pixies gathering force behind them. It seemed as if they would never outrun the raging sound, but instead of getting louder, the noise receded.

They came to a breathless halt as soon as they realized the swarm had given up the chase.

Fate staggered to a harmless birch tree, clinging to it for support. Gulping air, she stared at Finn in amazement. "How…did…we…get out of there?"

He wiped the sweat from his brow. "I waited 'til the trees fell asleep and joined them in their dreams. It took all night, but I was eventually able to convince them they had no prisoners, so they relaxed their limbs."

Even though she knew without a doubt who he was and

what he could do, she still stared at him, half in wonder half in disbelief. "I was unconscious all night?" she said, shaking herself out of it.

"No, most of that was sleep."

"There's no way I could've slept."

"You snore…like a kitten of course."

"What do you think is keeping those nasty pixies from coming after us?" she said, hurrying to change the subject.

He shrugged. "Can't be sure. They must be bound to the oaks."

"I'd love to get my hands on one of those little shi—"

"Looks like you'll have that chance." He reached out and plucked one of them from her curls. Pinching the pixie's leafy wings between his fingers, he dangled its limp body between them. It was either still sleeping, or weak from being so far from the oak grove.

She took it from him, frowning at the creature. "Hey there, unlovely little bug-thingy," she said, her voice momentarily singsong. "And I thought pixies were supposed to be cute and glowy—and *nice*."

Opening its beady eyes, the pixie bared its fangs and shrieked.

Startled, she dropped it to the ground, lifting her foot to squash it under her boot.

"Whoa, hold on there," Finn said, grabbing her arm and throwing her off balance.

"Are you serious? We were just on the menu for the all-you-can-eat breakfast buffet and your little friend here was at the front of the line."

"That's just its nature. It's nothing personal."

"It was to me," she argued as he shivered and folded his arms. "If I look anything like you, I'm the poster kid for chicken pox."

He turned and started walking.

Fate regarded his hunched shoulders and the drag in his step with concern. "Are you okay? You're looking a bit slumpy."

"Gee, thanks."

"No, really. Did something happen you're not telling me about?"

His jaw muscles contracted as he trudged through the thinning brambles. "It was those oaks and the things they were dreaming—it was bloody disturbing." He gave her a dismissive wave. "I'll be fine. Mae's the one in trouble right now."

She grabbed his hand to stop him and held up her notepad. "Let's take the transporter back and make sure the *Book of Fables* is where we left it. Then we can think about how we're going to help Mae. Okay?"

"Aye," he said with a weary sigh, "sounds like a plan, Scottie. Beam me up."

Sithias was coiled up in front of the book, reading its massive pages when they arrived.

The snake turned his head all the way around to look at them, a wide grin baring his fangs. "Ahh, you're finally back. What wasss ssso dire that you were out all night long?" His scolding tone softened when he saw how scratched and beaten they looked. "Whatever did you two get into?"

Finn charged over to the snake. "Bloody hell! What happened to my wards?"

Sithias drew back with a pained expression. "I grew concerned, ssso I disssturbed the little pilesss you made. First I tried to sssee if you'd changed the fable, but there wasss no mention of you. Ssso far it'sss the sssame terrible end." He started talking faster and with increasing excitement. "Then out of sheer boredom I read through the other fablesss—all but the lassst. I was getting ready to read it when you arrived. You should know there's a common thread throughout each one. I sssuspect a sssinsister force working behind—"

"What if the dark faery had found the book?" Finn interrupted, his eyes red-rimmed and crazed as he glared at the snake. "But I suppose you were thinking you'd be off with the big book long before that happened."

Sithias uncoiled with hat in tail, his head down. "It'sss true. I did read sssome of the wordsss aloud. Just to tessst it, mind you." His worried glance bounced between them.

Forming a fist, Finn punched his other hand. "I *knew* it."

"But I'm ssstill here," Sithias reminded him. "It would ssseem only one of you two can transport usss from one fable to the next."

Finn turned to Fate. "See? He can't be trusted."

Slithering closer, the snake stared at them with round watery eyes. "You *can* trussst me. I promissse. Even if I had been able to read my way out of here, I would've returned for you."

"Aye, I believe that like I believe in old Saint Nick."

Fate tried to ignore the snake's big crocodile tears. "Finn, at least we know we don't have to worry about him or anyone else taking off with the book. I say we give him one more shot."

Finn looked ready to argue, but exhaustion had taken over. He slumped against a tree, his eyes shut. "Fine, I'm too wrecked to bother with him anyway."

"Oh thank you, misss. You won't regret it."

"One chance," she warned. "If you do anything, so much as sneeze wrong, I'll use my magic notepad to write about you floating out in deep space."

He nodded with a timorous flutter of his wings. "I undersssstand, misss. You both have my undying allegiance."

Finn slid to the ground. "I need an hour to catch a wink."

She wrote up a large canvas tent with two soft beds inside, a bowl of hot water and some warm towels to clean his wounds. "Lie down," she said, leaving Sithias outside. She guided him to a bed. He collapsed into it. "While you're asleep, I'll go over to Mae's and warn her father about what's coming."

His brow furrowed with worry. "No, if the dark faery's there, you'll fall under his spell again. I need to be with you. It's not safe. The last time you flew off without me, you nearly got yourself killed."

She dabbed at his pixie-bitten chin with a moist cloth. "True, but I managed to escape."

He winced. "That stings."

"Who's the big baby now?"

A mischievous smile formed on his lips. "If I'm the baby, does that mean I get a kiss goodnight?" he murmured.

Fate's heart raced at the mention of a kiss. He looked so weak and vulnerable, and absolutely irresistible. She smiled. Finn McKeen…in the flesh. *Unbelievable.*

She leaned close enough to feel the warmth of his breath against her mouth. Closing her eyes, she waited for his kiss, *the* kiss she'd imagined a million times but knew could never happen.

Seconds ticked by.

She opened her eyes. He was fast asleep. She pulled away, feeling silly and more disappointed than she had a right to.

"Ladies and gentleman, I give you another cringeworthy moment in the life and times of Fate Floyd," she muttered. Rising to her feet, she stared at his angelic face, then leaned down. "Sweet dreams, Finn McKeen," she whispered in his ear. She hovered there, itching to nibble his earlobe.

His mouth curled into a faint smile as he turned over, hugging his pillow.

She drew back. If she stayed any longer, she could really misbehave. Using every ounce of willpower, she forced herself to step away and promptly marched herself out of the tent.

CHAPTER 10

SITHIAS WAS WAITING outside the tent. "I have an idea, misss. Sssince you've been told to ssstay put, I thought I might help you write a happy end to thisss fable. Being a ssstudent of the heart, I fancy myself a bit of a writer. I've dabbled in a little poetry, but mossstly playsss—"

"First off," she interrupted, "Finn's not the boss of me." Pulling the tent flap back, she stuck her head back inside to see if he was still sleeping. He was out cold, but a fretful almost feverish expression had replaced the peaceful look he'd had only a moment ago. "I guess I should stick around. I'm a bit worried about him." She regarded the snake with curiosity. "Okay, we'll give it a go. But first, I have some pixie crust to wash off."

She could've cleaned up in an instant, but decided to soak in a hot bath so she could unwind. Afterwards, she treated her scratches, bites and bruises, combed out her washed hair and dressed in fresh clothes. Then she wrote up a cup of hot chocolate, a pen, sheets of paper and a comfy winged back chair. Sithias settled onto the silk pillow she provided.

Once she was sitting comfortably, she held her pen poised to write. "Okay, where should we start? I vote for bringing in a prince to slay the dark faery and marry Mae."

Sithias tilted his head and tapped his chin with the tip of his tail. "Hmmm, I'm not ssso sssure that alignsss with the ssstory's purpossse."

She raised a brow in surprise. "Oh really? And what do you think is the purpose?"

"Well, if I were to hazard a guesss, it isss to unite thessse two unlikely characters and experience the joy of the dark faery's transformation made posssible by the love of sweet Mae."

Fate choked on her drink, quickly rearranging her expression from shocked to unimpressed. "That's all well and good if you're writing for writing's sake. But just so you know, that dark faery is a mean piece of work. I don't think there's enough sweetness in any one person to transform *that* monster into anything trustworthy."

"Exactly what happened out there?"

"The dark faery had his evil oak trees hold us prisoner while a swarm of pixies snacked and napped on us." A shudder ran through her as she put a hand to her sore ribs. "If Finn hadn't dreamed with those trees and tricked them into letting us go, we'd be a pile of bones like that poor family we found."

Sithias looked horrified. "Oh, how terribly atrociousss. No wonder you look like a beekeeper after a bad day at work. Well, the dark faery sssimply mussst die. Now then, let'sss discusss how we'll bring hisss villainy to a wonderfully disssastrous end."

They worked for several hours, laughing at the silly story lines they were inventing before settling on the one they felt most confident about.

Fate stared at what they'd written. "It sure feels good being the one who's making things happen for once."

"Yesss indeed."

She took a deep breath. "Okay, I'm ready if you are."

Sithias dipped his sinuous neck in a royal bow. "Begin your recitation of our eloquent prose. I assure you, the applaussse will be deafening."

Fate cleared her throat and began, *"Before the dark faery could reach Mae and present himself in human form, Fate intervened by calling on the God of the Woods, that wise and gentle spirit who is the sap within the roots and whose ancient face peers through every branch and leaf in the world. The Green Man rose from his bed of earth to restore the cursed oak grove to natural order and bless Mae with a bountiful harvest every season for as long as she lived."*

She looked up from the passage. "Well, it sounds like a happy ending to me—no more evil faery and free groceries for life. But how will we know when it's done? There's no way I'm going back to that grove to see if it worked."

"Maybe our happy ending hasss been freshly inked onto the pagesss of the *Book of Fablesss?*" Sithias asked.

Fate jumped up from the chair. "Brilliant, my dear Sithias. Let's have a look, shall we?"

A deep rumbling suddenly ripped through the earth.

She stumbled as roots tore from the ground like buried rope. Sithias whipped his tail round her waist before she fell.

The surrounding forest seemed to buckle and bend inward, with a horrible cracking and toppling of timber. Then the earth swelled several yards ahead of them, heaving into a mound of tangled bush and roots. A gnarled knot pushed its way through the thick greenery, forming a fierce, disturbing face and green eyes glittering with eerie luminescence.

Fate and Sithias froze in place as two massive hands of twisted roots broke through the ground, lifting a giant head and torso out of the ruptured earth. The smell of soil saturated the air as the giant rose ever upward—towering over them a good hundred feet—showering dirt and leaves on them.

And worms.

Fate muffled a frantic scream behind her hand. Sithias tightened his grip on her, his head snaking close as he hissed under his breath, "Be ssstill, misss. We don't want to draw undue attention. You can ssscream all you like once he leavesss to go after the dark faery."

She tried to stuff down the horror building inside her. Shaking, she held still, her eyes squeezed shut. Then something slipped from her hair and landed on her chest, cold, wet and squirming. Shrieking, she tore away from Sithias, slapping at herself to get the worm off her skin. It went flying, landing a few feet from her.

Relieved to be free of it, Fate looked up, only to see a mammoth hand filling her field of vision.

Finn woke with a start, soaked in sweat as Fate's blood-curdling scream ripped through the dark fabric of his nightmares. Feeling her terror like it was his own, he leaped out of bed and raced from the tent, heart pounding in his throat. He skidded to a halt when he saw a giant made of earth and vegetation take one enormous step and disappear from sight with Fate clenched in its gnarled hand.

He kneeled, gripping the loose soil strewn around the encampment. Every muscle within him pulled tight with fear as he pushed his senses into the earth. Within seconds he touched the giant. The sheer enormity of its presence and the vast, ancient wisdom dwelling within the entirety of its being was so overpowering he had to break the connection. It was an elemental, one of thc Olde One's his grandfather had told him about. At least he knew the Dark Speech, the secret language of Druids that spoke to nature's elements.

Finn looked up in grim surprise as Sithias emerged from his hiding place. "She summoned the Green Man?"

Still mute with shock, Sithias nodded.

"Why?"

"To dessstroy the dark faery and ressstore balance to the foressst."

Finn shook his head. "No, the Green Man sees *Fate* as the imbalance to the natural order of the forest."

"But how can that be?"

"Because there is no imbalance here. The dark faery is here

to protect a gateway between worlds. Any trespassers disturbing this place must suffer the consequences."

Sithias's eyes widened. "You know all thisss from feeling the dirt?"

"That, and my lingering connection to the oak grove," Finn said, curling his hands into fists as the monstrous visions he'd woken from came rushing back. He couldn't bear the thought of Fate becoming a part of those nightmares. "I have to get to her *now*."

"I can take you," Sithias offered. "Of coursssе, it will involve sssome touching."

Finn glared at the snake's ivory scales and the strong ripple of muscle moving underneath. His skin crawled with disgust. "If that's what it takes," he grumbled. Shutting his eyes, he tensed against the snake winding around his waist. As Sithias lifted off the ground, he squeezed hard, the upward motion so swift it knocked the air out of his lungs.

He watched the ground shrink beneath him. As they crested the forest canopy, he saw the Green Man towering over the barren oak grove, looking down at Callum.

"Set me down there."

"But sir, you'll be sssorely outnumbered."

"Just do it."

Sithias swooped down and dropped him.

He landed near Callum, startling him. "I don't know how you two escaped, but I'm pleased you've returned so we may finish what we began."

Finn crouched in place. "I've come to help you win Mae's heart in exchange for the life of my fair lass." He chanced a quick glance upward, his gut wrenching when he saw the wild look of desperation on Fate's face.

Callum laughed, as did his pixies and the sinister oak trees. "What a fool. Why would I need your help? I've already sent

Mae's dowry. Her father has given me her hand, and she has agreed to marry me this very evening."

Finn gave him a cold, knowing smile, a look that disrupted Callum's confident grin. "That may be, but someone there will see through your false veil and know you for the hideous monster you really are."

Callum's grin turned wooden.

"Your life is in danger," Finn continued, "as is Mae's."

Fury flashed over the dark faery's face. "Who would dare harm Mae?"

"No one but you," Finn said coolly.

Callum lashed out with his cane, rage twisting his face.

Ducking out of the way, Finn sprang to his feet.

"Take him," Callum roared, his voice an unearthly growl.

Before Finn could move, a branch snaked out and grabbed him.

He heard Fate's cry from above, but kept his gaze fixed on Callum and delivered his message. "Don't let Mae swear any promises to you—or you to her…besides that of marriage."

Callum's murderous expression paled, betraying recognition and fear. "What promises?"

The tree tightened its hold, crushing his chest. He could barely get enough air to speak. "That her heart…will beat only… for you as long as you…never kill another living thing."

The dark faery marched up to him. "And what do you think would happen if such promises were exchanged?"

"You'll both die."

Callum's lips twitched. "Those vows were spoken last night. How can you possibly know what we whispered to each other? Are you a sorcerer?"

Finn tipped his head back, looking up at Fate where she struggled within the Green Man's immovable grasp. "If you… let us both go," he gasped, his head falling limp, "I'll hand over…what you and Mae need…to live a long and happy life…together."

Callum hesitated.

Finn could see him wrestling with his thoughts. After his hellish connection with the trees, he knew too well what carnage the dark faery was capable of. He wasn't one to capitulate to demands of any kind.

The moment stretched into torturous doubt.

At last, Callum signaled the oak and the Green Man. "Release them."

The tree let go. Finn dropped to the ground, his already bruised ribs in excruciating pain as he sucked in lungfuls of air. He glanced up, expecting to see Fate being set down, but the Green Man hadn't budged. "You get nothing until Fate's released," he said, rising to his feet.

Callum turned to the giant, speaking in a language that charged the very air with crackling power. Finn recognized a similarity to the Dark Speech, suggesting the ancient tongue bore the same roots.

Staring down at the dark faery, the Green Man spoke. His rumbling voice embodied the terrible rending of trees and the deep roar of a rocky avalanche, a sound that thrummed in Finn's chest and communicated the Olde One's message like an arrow piercing his heart: *The human must die*.

Fear clouded Finn's thinking, buckling his knees. He hit the ground, tormented by his inability to save Fate. He couldn't imagine being without her. He suddenly knew she'd always been with him, part of his dreams until the moment she'd stepped out of them to stand before him in the flesh.

Love surged through him, sweeping away the fog of fear.

Looking up at the giant, he cried out in the Dark Speech, beseeching the ancient spirit to spare her.

The Green Man tilted his massive head, but did not respond.

Finn clutched at the earth, linking directly with the colossal being—a move that could get him crushed like a bug under his massive foot.

The Olde One peered back into Finn's mind, a piercing gaze that laid his soul bare with careless abandon. The violation was agonizing and, just when he thought he could take no more, the torture ended abruptly. Only a vague, portentous message hovered in the back of his brutalized mind, one that vanished the second he grasped for it, but left him with a lingering sense of doom.

With the connection severed, Finn knew he'd failed to save her. The fear pumping through his veins was deafening. His surroundings blurred behind hot blinding tears as grief shredded his heart. How would he endure the pain of Fate's death? Surely it would kill him.

Movement wavered behind his tears, a figure in blue plaid jeans and gray argyle sweater. Unable to believe what he was seeing, Finn rubbed his eyes dry as he struggled upright. Fate's face came into view as she ran to him, her body crashing into his. He grabbed hold of her, burying his face in the perfume of her soft curls. She wrapped her arms around his neck, squeezing like she'd never let go. The rapid thud of her heart against his chest flooded him with relief. He was home again.

"Now that you lovebirds are reunited, I'd like to attend to my problem," Callum said with impatience.

"I have your word you'll let us leave safely after I've given you what you need?" Finn directed the question at Callum, but he was looking around for the Green Man. The Olde One was gone, having left a massive mound of roots and shrubbery in his place.

"My solemn word," Callum said, with a slight bow of his head.

"How can we trust *him?*" Fate whispered.

Without taking his eyes off Callum, Finn pressed his lips

to her ear. "Give me the sea nymph's glamour and write down our escape."

She jerked her head back, questioning him with an are-you-crazy-look? but did as he said and pulled the glamour from her pocket. Finn tossed the pearl and coral necklace at Callum while Fate wrote in the tiny notepad.

"What's this?" Callum asked.

"A powerful glamour. No one will be able to see through to what you truly are, not even you," Finn explained.

Callum appeared disappointed. "*This* is our salvation?"

"It is, if you decide to use it."

"I'll have to try it first before I allow either of you—"

"Time to read, love," Finn said.

With a nod, Fate read the words and returned them to the *Book of Fables*.

Fate reeled from the dizzying sensation of the sudden shift of the grove melting back and the encampment materializing in its place. She was shaking, the adrenaline rush of absolute terror gone. She felt wobbly, like her bones were turning to mush. She held onto Finn for support, savoring the secure feel of his arm wrapped around her waist and the sweet collision of heat and nerves swirling between them.

Sithias flapped several feet off the ground in front of the *Book of Fables*, his wings dropping precious feathers. "Oh thank goodnesss!" he said when he saw them. He landed in a coil, looking fretful. "The ssstory's been changing on the pagesss every few minutesss! It's been a sssuspenseful, confusssing messs to follow. I was jussst about to read how you essscaped, but here you are."

Finn let go of her and stomped up to the snake. "You'd know first hand if you'd stayed—or even possibly *helped*."

Sithias gave him a pitiful look. "I've never been much of a

fighter—more of a lover if truth be known."

Fate wavered in place. The sharp pang of separation she felt when Finn removed his arm surprised her. "No time for arguing, you two," she sighed, suddenly exhausted as more tension drained away. "Just read the ending to us, Sithias."

The snake nodded eagerly, making a big show of clearing his throat and humming a few test notes like he was preparing to sing.

"*Read*," Finn said, crossing his arms.

"Oh, all right," Sithias said, his excitement dampened somewhat, but he still spoke with plenty of melodrama when he began reading. "To conceal hisss true form, Callum wore a powerful glamour made by Possseidon'sss daughter and married the lovely Mae. He helped her father create a prosperousss farm and built a grand manor for his new bride, her family and the ten children they would have. Callum usssed his magic to heal and help othersss. The king took notice and granted him a noble title with a generousss amount of property. Callum's magic and Mae's goodness ssspread throughout the land and the kingdom prossspered for fifty yearsss."

Sithias looked at them. "Thisss soundsss promisssing—"

"Keep reading," they both said.

"It came to passs that in the late winter of Mae'sss life, Callum, who only appeared to age, was forced to watch her wither and die. When he placed her body in the earth, his tearsss caused a downy coverlet of emerald-green mossss with white ssstar-ssshaped blossoms to ssspread over her grave. Heartbroken, Callum bade hisss grown children and grandchildren goodbye.

"He returned to the evil oak treesss, where he lissstened to the malignant murmurings of the oaksss and pixiesss. With a sssweep of his arm, he sssealed the gateway between worldsss and burned the grove and pixiesss with a white cleansssing fire. The cloud of asssh became a flurry of birdsss, butterfliesss and flower seedsss. Callum left the foressst, never to be ssseen again. However, it was sssaid that a dim figure could be ssseen ssstanding over Mae'sss grave during the hour of twilight, in that fleeting moment when light and dark are made one."

Sithias sniffed, dabbing at his tears. "Ah, a truly touching end."

"You were right, Sithias," Fate said. "True love really did transform the dark faer—"

"You two are bloody lucky the story turned out well," Finn said, startling them both with his sharp tone. "Summoning a force like the Green Man was bold and reckless."

His sudden anger shook her.

"Whose idea was it in the first place?"

"Mine, sssir," Sithias confessed, his eyes blinking with contrition.

"No, it was my idea," Fate said, not wanting to give Finn even more reason to hate the snake. "I did a lot of research on the Green Man when I was writing about…well you know, my stories."

Finn let out a weary, frustrated sigh. "I thought you understood how careful you have to be with the Words of Making."

"I know. My bad," she murmured. Shifting uncomfortably, she stared at the ground. "I should've waited 'til we all agreed on what to do."

He took her hand, forcing her to face him. "Do you have any idea how close you came to dying?" he said, pain clouding over the anger in his eyes.

Seeing how affected he was frightened her all over again. As terrified as she'd been only ten minutes before, she never really believed she'd die. The concept was too unreal, not to mention everything else that had happened from the moment she'd arrived in the book. But Finn seemed to know exactly how grave her situation had been. Fear iced through her as she thought back to it. The bruises and bites made by the oaks and pixies were nothing compared to the bone-crushing grip of the

Green Man's thorny, gnarled fingers. Her legs and waist still ached. She shuddered, realizing the not so Jolly Green Giant would've squished her if Finn hadn't stopped him.

"I just wanted to help us get home," she whispered.

"I know," Finn said, his expression softening. "And we're that much closer. We can move onto the next fable knowing this one is a job well done. Just promise me you won't do anything that rash again."

"I *swear* I won't," she assured him. Not once had it entered her mind the Words of Making could backfire on her like that. Using them for conjuring the bare necessities was one thing. Writing anything of real consequence was another entirely. She would never use them again so carelessly. The next time could get everyone killed.

Disappointment caved in on her. Here she was with the power to rewrite destinies, but as always, her cruel namesake was still the one running the show, proving she didn't have control of her life and never would.

The Goblin Queen

In a time when humans lived weakly within the folds of a wild and magical world, there was a girl named Glenna. For one so young, she carried the burden of feeding and caring for her ailing mother. A sickness of heart had taken the woman, making her eyes dull and her mind a fog. Glenna's greatest desire was that her mother be well again, for she wasted away with each passing day and Glenna feared the worst.

One morning while selling bundles of kindling at the market, Glenna spied a colorful caravan. Dark-skinned ladies with flashing eyes and gold bangles danced around it. They pointed at the caravan's gilt door and told Glenna her deepest wish would be granted if she but dared to enter.

By some means of magic, the caravan's interior was made larger than the outside. Standing amidst many riches was a veiled woman. She drew a knife, saying she needed to cut a lock of Glenna's hair in order to divine the wish she would grant her. The moment she held the flaxen strands in her hand, she knew Glenna's mother was sick. She spoke of a golden goblet that wept dewdrops of healing water. Anyone who drank from the cup was granted good health and long life. But swamp goblins had stolen the goblet from its makers and kept it hidden within their murky kingdom.

The swamp goblins were difficult to find, she told Glenna, for they moved their kingdom once every thirteen moons by riding the currents of underground rivers 'til they found a blooming hawthorn tree. There they lived deep beneath its roots, sapping the tree's life force until it withered. When spring came, the kingdom dislodged in search of another hawthorn. Upon finding a new tree, the earth cracked open to reveal their foul waters for one day, the perfect time to snatch the goblet.

The only way to find this place was to follow the elusive will o' the wisp to the goblin's location. The woman gave Glenna a crystal bottle in which to capture the will o' the wisp when she found the swamp. She explained that the goblins had a weakness for shiny things, and taught Glenna how to use the light catcher to entice them to the surface.

Eager to help her mother, Glenna turned to leave. But the veiled woman stopped her, saying there was a price for granting her wish. The girl offered all the money she'd made at the market. The woman refused. Her price was the goblet, so she could return the healing cup to its rightful owner. Glenna happily agreed, but mere words were not enough for the woman. She wrapped Glenna's hair around a small twig taken from a cursed oak and uttered a mysterious incantation to bind the agreement for all eternity.

Glenna returned home, whispering assurances to her ailing mother as she fed and bathed her. That night after sunset, she watched for the will o' the wisp. By some good fortune, she saw a glowing spark dancing low to the ground near the woodland's edge. She raced after the darting light as it threaded deep into the forest to a hill. At its peak stood a hawthorn tree in full bloom. Beneath the tree's gnarled roots, a mossy swamp festered within a deep crevasse.

Saying the magic words she'd been given, Glenna captured the will o'the wisp within the bottle and dangled the sparkling light over the surface of the swamp. The murky water rippled and frothed with a multitude of slimy heads. Horrid little faces with bulging eyes and leering smiles stared up at her, while spindly fingers grabbed for the bottled light. But she held it out of reach, saying she would only trade it for the golden goblet.

The swamp goblins writhed and whispered to one another before sinking back into the mire. Moments later, they returned with a gleaming goblet. Eager to hold it, Glenna reached out. But this time the goblins held back, telling her she could only possess it for one night and one day. Their price was the light catcher, in addition to something else.

Their pale, bulging eyes drank in her milky skin and delicate features. Too many moons had passed since they'd looked upon such unspoiled beauty. They were moved to make her their queen, for they had all been human once, and she had awakened those dim memories.

Glenna had no intention of becoming the queen of such undeserving thieves and wanted only to honor her agreement to the veiled woman. So she made a hollow promise to be their queen and ran home as fast as her feet could carry her. One drop from the goblet brought a spark to her mother's dull eyes. A few more drops had her jumping out of bed and, by the time the sun rose, she was sweeping the floors and delighting Glenna with her stories the way she used to.

Glenna told her mother how she found the goblet with the help of the veiled woman but said nothing of her false promise to the swamp goblins. Her mother removed a silver locket and latched it around her daughter's neck as a token of her love, then told her to deliver the goblet to the woman at dawn's first light and settle the debt.

The next morning when Glenna opened her door, a slimy swamp lay outside her step. A blue-green light glowed from its center and she fell entranced. Kneeling down, she allowed a host of slithery green hands to pull her into the swamp.

Even though water filled her lungs, she did not drown. The spellbinding light had changed her. They pulled her down into the deep to a shimmering palace of unusual beauty and sat her upon a throne of woven roots inlaid with pearls and shells. They then placed a crown of delicate fish bones on top of her head and draped an emerald robe of kelp over her shoulders. Strangely, Glenna welcomed its cold touch on her skin, relishing in the scent of rotting earth and fish.

She had become the new goblin queen. As she gazed out over her splendid kingdom, a shadow fell over the swamp. She glanced up, seeing a vaguely familiar face staring down at her. The goblin queen rose to the surface. Glenna's mother gasped in horror when she saw her daughter's locket on the neck of a hideous little goblin. Struck by a thin remnant of love, the queen reached out to her, but Glenna's mother beat her back with a broom. Hatred for humans flared in the queen's heart as she sank into the quagmire and sealed the earth shut. The kingdom dislodged and drifted away.

In that moment, whatever was left of Glenna faded for all time. As queen, she turned her attention to finding the thief who'd stolen the golden goblet forged by swamp goblins eons ago. Yet it would be an endless chase, for the veiled woman hid under the protection of the stolen locket of Glenna's hair bound to a piece of cursed oak.

As for Glenna's mother, she was doomed to live a long and healthy life, in which she would forever grieve the murder of her dear daughter by a vicious swamp goblin.

CHAPTER II

VISIONS OF HOMELY GOBLINS, a shimmering castle in the murk and a mother's grieving face shattered before Fate's eyes. The fragments became a swirling cloud of letters before sudden blackness swallowed the last glinting shards of an imagined world. A streak of white blurred across her line of vision and she blinked as Sithias came into focus.

He smiled at her. "Feeling woozy, misss?"

Finn pushed the snake's head aside and steadied her. "Yeah, a little dizzy," she agreed, "but I'll take that over the feeling of my organs being rearranged."

Finn nodded. "This jump did seem easier than the last for a change. Though your snake here, didn't feel so much as a twinge of discomfort."

They both looked at Sithias.

The snake made a sort of shrug with his wings. "What can I sssay? I'm resssilient."

"Lucky you," Fate groaned.

His wings drooped. "But what a sad story that wasss. The pain of a parent's losss is truly heartbreaking."

"As sad as a child losing a parent," she said, her gaze flicking first to the surrounding woodland sprawling with thin birch trees and then to Finn.

He was staring intently, his green eyes burning with questions. She knew he was ready to return to the moment she'd recognized him. Her stomach clenched into a tight ball of nerves. She looked away, glancing up at the bleak sky. The chill of winter lingered in the air, but a few trees were starting to blossom with leaves unfurling from the buds. Shivering, she hugged her arms.

Drawing up from behind, he wrapped his arms around her. He seemed to radiate heat just for her. With his chin resting on her shoulder, he whispered, "I know you have something to tell me."

She started leaning into him, but stopped short. Would he still feel the same about her after he heard what she had to say?

Finn raised his voice for Sithias. "But first we could use something warm to bundle in."

Sithias folded his trembling wings close to his tubular body. "I agree, it'sss quite chilly. I would love a wool blanket to sssnuggle under."

"Coming right up," she said, reluctantly pulling free of Finn's embrace.

Two coats and a blanket shimmered into view within seconds of reading the descriptions aloud. When she handed Finn his coat he thanked her with such open anticipation of her news, her heart almost broke.

"I suggest we go on a scouting mission before we plan this fable's end." He winked to let her know he planned to get her alone. "But first I need a good scrubbing." He plucked a squished worm off her sleeve. "And so could you."

She gagged when she saw the revolting carcass. "A bath can't happen soon enough," she said, quickly jotting down a few words in her notepad. *"Finn and I are showered and clean from head to toe, and dressed in a fresh change of clothes."*

As she felt the cool, breezy sensation of her skin being cleaned in an instant, she laughed at Finn who had the startled look of someone being touched inappropriately.

He ran his hand over his spotless clothes. "That's wicked! And a touch unsettling. You won't take advantage of that will you?"

She gave him a mischievous smile. "Only when it suits me."

Grinning, he took her hand, pulling her along behind him. "Come along, vixen. There's a stream over there. I say we follow it to see if anyone's living nearby. No doubt it'll be Glenna if my guess is right." He stopped and turned to Sithias. "Stay by the big book and keep it safe."

Already nestled beneath his blanket, the snake poked his head out in surprise. "And what will I do all by myssself? Twiddle my tail?"

"Whatever butters your biscuit," Finn called back.

As they followed the creek, he seemed content to walk in silence for a while. Fate would've enjoyed the quiet stroll, but she was too nervous to relax. She was certain he would press her to talk at any moment, but she was wrong. He spotted a dilapidated mud hut through the trees and picked up the pace.

The thatch on the cone-shaped roof was in desperate need of repair, and the rounded mud walls were crumbling in places that left holes for the biting cold to seep in. A harsh winter of heavy snow had broken branches off the surrounding trees and the spring thaw had caused the ground to turn to mud.

They strode up to the door and knocked. Scuffling sounds came from inside before the door cracked open to reveal a wary eye peering back at them. "What 'tis it ye want?" a young girl's quavering voice asked. "We have not a thing of value for the taking."

"We don't want anything," Finn assured her, "except to offer a trade of service for some food and a few nights' shelter from the cold."

Fate stared at him in surprise, unable to hide her objection to his impromptu plan.

"It's the first thing I thought of," he whispered out of the side of his mouth.

The door opened more. Glenna stood before them, pale and

delicately boned with large hazel eyes and flaxen hair worn in a long braid under a blue tartan scarf. She smoothed down her rumpled dress and shyly invited them inside.

A warm fire blazed in a deepened well at the center of the round hut with a large kettle hanging over the flames. Hugging the curved walls was a long earthen ledge covered in furs, blankets and a myriad of woven baskets, pots and utensils. Glenna's sick mother lay close to the fire on a bed of thatch. Her breathing was labored and her hollow eyes were closed to the world.

As they sat down by the fire, introductions were made while Glenna ladled hot water from the steaming pot into cups and sprinkled cinnamon bark into each one.

"I saw the new thatch sitting outside the door. I can do the mending on the roof for you, and there are cracks in the walls I could patch easily enough," Finn offered.

"Oh, bless ye. That would be most welcome," Glenna said in round-eyed amazement. Her timid gaze flicked to Fate.

"And Fate can darn your socks or do some sewing for you," he added.

Glenna looked overwhelmed. "Thank ye both many times over."

"It's our pleasure." Finn set his cup down and rose. "We'd best get back and gather our belongings. We'll return shortly."

Glenna smiled brightly. "And I'll have some bread and broth waiting on yer return."

"Oh don't go to any trouble. We could be a while actually. It's a long walk," Fate said, directing a pointed gaze at Finn.

After they left, she walked fast alongside the creek, stopping after they were a fair distance from the hut. "Listen, I can't sleep on those flea-infested furs. Call me crazy, but I'm just not into icky rashes."

Disappointment moved in Finn's eyes. "I never figured you

for a snob."

His criticism stung and she rose to defend herself. "I'm not. But if the option's there, I'll take Egyptian cotton and a goose-down comforter complete with a yummy chocolate mint on my crisp, clean pillow."

He stared at her blank-faced.

"Okay, that didn't sound nearly as justified as it was supposed to," she sighed. "Go ahead, crown me Queen of Snobdom."

"Very well, Your Majesty." He cracked a smile. "I know sleeping in Glenna's hut is unappealing, but it's only for one night. Just long enough for us to make sure she doesn't go to that caravan alone." He glanced back at the mud hut. "She's too young to be carrying the weight of the world on those small shoulders."

He looked tormented by the young girl's plight. Fate could tell he was thinking back to his own burdened childhood. A wave of guilt rose to the surface. She wanted to run from it, deny she was responsible for his pain. But she couldn't turn her back on the truth anymore. She had to confess what she knew before another minute passed. If she didn't do it now, she never would.

"Finn, I need to tell you something."

He shifted his gaze to her, a new look of concern in his eyes.

A sudden sense of loss hit her, like something was being ripped out of her chest. Would he look at her the same way after she told him?

"Is this about what you've been waiting to tell me?" he asked, his expression hopeful, but growing troubled.

She nodded, unable to speak, her throat tight with fear.

He stepped close, combing his fingers lightly through hers. "Come on, love. You've got me tied in a thousand knots wondering what this is about. I was so sure it was going to be good but now it's feeling wrong." He let out a sigh that shook his entire being. "It may be too soon to say this...but there's an uncommon bond between us. A connection like no other, as if I've known you my whole life." He tapped a finger over her heart. "And I can feel what's going on in there. Half the time I don't know where you begin and I end."

He grew quiet, his gaze penetrating deep. "I'm drowning in you, Fate."

Her knees went weak with longing. All she wanted to do was step into his arms and tell him she felt the same. But she'd gone leaden with dread. She was the only one who knew why they were both feeling this way, and as much as she wanted it to be the real thing, love didn't have anything to do with it.

When her silence dragged on, frustration skimmed over the vulnerability he'd allowed her to see. His face closed. "Say something," he said, his voice gruff.

Tears burned her eyes. "Finn, I've been looking for you for so long, trying to find you in the face of every guy I met, but I never *ever* found you…until now."

His brows shot up, incredulous. "This is a problem?"

She tore away from him, tilting her head to the sky. "God, how do I say this?"

He reached out, his voice pleading, "*Fate—*"

"You won't like what I have to tell you," she warned, her hand held up to keep him from coming any closer. "And you won't like me, because in some freakishly cosmic way, this is *my fault.*"

He stared at her with a look of utter bewilderment.

"You're not real, Finn!" she cried out. "You're a character I invented when I was twelve. You were my very first. I created you long before I wrote *Magick Brew*. And I never stopped writing about you…I couldn't. You are my greatest work and the story that should've been published. You've been a dear and constant friend to me for the last five years. I'm just sorry it took me so long to recognize you."

Suddenly, a snowflake falling to the ground would have been

loud. Finn stood rooted in place, his face frozen in disbelief.

She started talking quickly. Everything she'd held back spilled out unchecked. "I know all about your terrible childhood…because I made it up. After your mother died, your father started drinking, so much so that he lost his job and you had to start dumpster diving in the back alleys of restaurants to put food on the table. Then, when you were thirteen, your mother's father came and took you back with him to Scotland, where you discovered you were the descendant of a long line of Druids."

She could see the blood draining from his face. When at last he spoke, his voice came in a hoarse whisper. "I never told anyone about the bin howking. *Not a soul.*" His body went rigid, his expression dark as he shook his head. "*No,* I don't believe you."

"I know how crazy this sounds," she said, growing sick to her stomach as pain carved lines into his face. "I couldn't believe it either. But there were just too many clues."

"This isn't possible," he insisted.

She took one step. Her entire being reached out, wanting to comfort him.

He pointed his shoulder at her, staring into the stream, where it burbled cheerfully beneath the thick banks of undergrowth. A few agonizing minutes later, he turned to her, his hair in his eyes, his mouth a grim line. "Tell me what's in my pockets," he said, fixing his gaze on the ground, "other than what you've already seen."

"We don't need to—"

"Just tell me," he growled.

She let out a shaky sigh. "Okay, you have a clay pipe and a leather pouch full of holy blend, a flat round stone with a natural hole in its center that you found on the Isle of Skye, and a wooden flute your grandfather made for you. And…you carry a white satin ribbon your mother wore in her hair. It used to smell like her lilac shampoo."

She held her breath as Finn recognized the awful truth. His tortured gaze burned into her for a protracted moment, his mouth bending into a sorrowful line that knifed into her heart.

At last he moved, and without saying a word, he stormed past her.

As Fate watched him disappear within the multitude of birch trees, the whole world turned bleak and wintry.

CHAPTER 12

FINN HAD NO WAY TO PROTECT HIMSELF from the onslaught of emotions thrashing in his chest like wild animals clawing to get out. If he wasn't reeling with shock or disbelief, he was furious. His world had been ripped out from under him. He no longer knew who he was, or even what he was. His whole life was a lie, the offhand daydream of a bored twelve-year-old.

No matter how many times he ran it through his head, denial screamed in his veins, nerves and bones. How could he *not* be real? He breathed, he bled, he hungered, he loved. And what about his family? His friends? None of them existed?

He tightened the knots like he was strangling someone, tying down the last of the thatch onto Glenna's moldering roof. His hands stung with scratches made by the stiff straw and blisters covered his palms from pulling hard on the rope. He welcomed the pain, as well as the physical labor. He needed something to pour his rage into.

He jumped off the roof, his boots splattering mud everywhere. As he tromped over to the pail of mortar by the door, he slowed. Fate was inside with Glenna. He squatted next to the bucket, stirring the mixture with a stick while listening to their conversation.

"I don't know how skilled ye are with the darning needle. Me own work is solid, but not pretty, so I'll not be fussy about yer workmanship," Glenna said. "I hope this isn't more than is fair—it's just that most everything we have is worn through."

"No, this is fine. I'll do my best," Fate replied. There was a definite note of humility in her tone.

Finn picked up the heavy pail, glancing inside the hut as he slogged past the door. Glenna was thanking Fate with a hug. The look of surprise on Fate's face turned sad when she saw him pass by. He ducked his head down and kept walking.

He was spreading mortar over a sprawling vein of deep cracks when Glenna stepped outside. "I'm off to gather kindling in the woods, and then to market with me bundles," she said with a smile.

He set down the trowel. "How about I go to market with you? I can carry the load."

Glenna's eyes widened with wonder and appreciation. "I'll return for ye once I've finished me work," she said, and skipped off.

Finn watched her go, a wave of compassion washing back the gnawing anguish for a brief moment. She was so little, so alone and vulnerable. Taking out his knife, he stepped next to the hut's entrance and scratched several protective markings into the clay wall. As he stood back feeling a speck of satisfaction, an insidious question wormed its way into his thoughts. Was Glenna real? Was he wasting his efforts and concerns on a cardboard character only acting out human emotions?

But then who was he to judge?

Anger crashed back in, burning his gut like he'd swallowed acid. He closed the blade and shoved the knife back in his pocket. Grabbing the trowel, he swiped at the walls violently. He didn't know what to think anymore. Everything he'd learned throughout his entire life, all his beliefs, none of it meant anything. It was all made-up nonsense, meaningless words on paper—

"Are those Ogham markings?" Fate asked, jarring him from his thoughts.

He froze for a second, then caught himself and continued

filling the cracks. "You should know," he said without looking at her. She was quiet a moment. He could see her touching the wall out of the corner of his eye. He clenched his jaw to keep from telling her to leave him alone.

"If I remember right, these ones call upon the nearby birch, rowan and ash trees to act as protective wards," she said, her tone hesitant.

"It's alder, not ash, but you're right on the rest," he grumbled.

"I don't recognize the one at the bottom."

Still gritting his teeth, he took a deep breath. "It's my Druidic name." As soon as he said it, he felt foolish. Every test and initiation he'd gone through to be given a name that reflected his soul by the Order had never actually happened. She'd made that up too. There was nothing that belonged to him.

A lump of ice formed in the pit of his stomach as he realized an even more crushing truth. If he wasn't real, that meant he was soulless.

Suddenly she was beside him, her hand pressing on his arm in an attempt to stop his frenzied movements as he slapped mortar into a deep crevasse in the wall. His skin flushed with heat beneath her touch, quickening his pulse. He dropped the trowel in the bucket and stared into it. Every cell in his body responded to her presence, heightening his senses. Her pity flooded through him, mixing into his turmoil and clouding his mind with confusion. He hated this acute sensitivity he had to her every emotion.

"Finn, I'm so sorry," she said, her voice trembling.

The breeze played through her hair, flowing her scent over him. Pure heaven. He swallowed as the blood pumped through him hard and fast. Lifting his head, he met her gaze. Her face brightened, a blush of pink flushing her cheeks. Hope rounded her eyes as she opened her mouth to speak.

He silenced her with his finger to her lips. Helpless to look away or utter a word, he stared at the sensuous curve of her bottom lip. He wanted to blame her for this hell he was in, but now that she was next to him like this all he wanted to do was kiss her. How could he though? He was a mannequin, hollow and fake. Any right he had to declare his feelings for her as a man were gone forever.

A weak moan came from inside the hut.

Grateful for the interruption, Finn stepped around her and went inside. Crouching next to Glenna's mother, he felt her forehead and dipped deep into her mind with his senses. A horrible shiver ran up his arm, sapping the life from him as a cold, withering sensation traveled toward his heart. He jerked his hand away. "She's close to death," he said as Fate knelt beside him. "You have to use the Words of Making to save her."

Fate hesitated, worry stirred in her eyes. "But you said we have to be careful. I can't just write any old thing. What if it backfires again? With my luck I could turn her into a zombie… or a really healthy but deformed freak."

"We need the goblet," he said. "At least we know *it* works."

She pulled out the notepad. "Maybe I can write it up and bypass getting it from the veiled woman altogether."

"Aye, it's worth a try."

She wriggled her hips into a sitting position. His pulse raced in response, a fire spreading through him as she licked her lips and tapped the tiny pencil against her chin. Pushing the fever down, he drew in a ragged breath while she wrote. The little crease of concentration between her brows and tongue trailing along her top lip crumbled his wall of anger brick by brick.

"Okay," she said at last, looking pleased.

He let out a sigh of relief as she continued.

"Since I don't know what the goblet looks like, I've tried my best to describe its essence. Cross your fingers this works," she said, then read the passage aloud: *"Forged by the pale thin hands of swamp dwelling goblins many ages ago, a golden goblet came into being. The goblet bore such great form and beauty that it wept honeyed dewdrops of grace and healing for whatever lips kissed its gleaming warmth. It is my wish that this magic goblet vanish from the kingdom of goblins and appear here in my open hand in order to heal those in need."*

Finn listened, entranced by the poetic description, her voice a balm to his tortured psyche. Upon speaking the last word, a blue-green mist swirled round her hand and coalesced into a large golden goblet. Fate gasped with surprise, dropping it for the sudden heaviness. He lurched forward, saving it from hitting the ground.

He studied the goblet's braided spirals and its deep well inlaid with mother of pearl. Droplets of water beaded over the pale abalone and pooled within the cup. He looked at Fate, bewitched and in awe. Her thoughts, her words, had reached out into the ether and transported this work of art here into their hands. His heart opened and filled with admiration. He wondered if the words she'd used to describe him were anywhere near as beautiful.

For one fleeting second he was at peace with being her creation. But the bitter resentment skimming just below the surface punched through, shattering this fragile bit of acceptance. Everything had changed. He would never be Fate's equal. She was substance. He was a wisp of smoke.

CHAPTER 13

ON A ROUGH AND LITTLE-USED ROAD leading to Glenna's village raced a brightly colored horse-drawn caravan. The driver's seat was empty, yet the horses galloped as if driven on by the cruel whip of a harried driver. Inside the caravan, the veiled woman sat on her silk cushions. The horses were controlled by her will alone. She knew the golden goblet had surfaced into the world. She'd been hunting it for centuries but had always been ten steps behind the ever-elusive swamp goblins.

The passing of time and relentless search for what belonged to her people had robbed her of youthful vitality, shriveling her into something unspeakable. Only the goblet would restore her strength and youth. But now, someone else was drinking the restorative waters from that precious cup. This tortured her to no end. She didn't know whom she was dealing with or how long she had before the goblins reclaimed the goblet once again.

Determined to have it this time, she lashed her psychic whip and drove the exhausted horses on with even greater speed.

The angst Fate had caused Finn tormented her even more than the rage he radiated toward her. If she could take it all back and never say a word about his origins she'd do it in a heartbeat. But there was no unringing the bell. Something was now broken between them. Nothing could fix that.

As he tipped the goblet over the sick woman's cracked lips, she noticed his hands were scratched, the blood dry over the visible marks of his misery. She had offered to write up the repairs for him but he'd refused. Seeing his pain so plainly displayed hurt like nothing she'd ever known. If only she'd kept her secret.

Glenna's mother came to. She stared at Finn, then at Fate, her eyes filling with fright and confusion. "Wh-who are ye? Where's me daughter?"

Finn quickly explained the arrangement they'd made with Glenna. As she struggled to rise, he set the goblet down and helped her sit up. She glanced at the freshly cleaned and mended clothes, fluffy furs and woolen blankets Fate had conjured up earlier. Brushing her hand over the soft sheepskin rug in place of her straw bed, the woman beamed with delight.

"It seems only fit that ye call me Alma," she said, but a puzzled expression swiftly replaced her smile. "For someone in need of our measly fare, ye certainly work miracles." She eyed the golden goblet. "And drink from kingly cups!"

"Oh this old thing?" Fate said, gripping it by the stem and tipping it casually. Her wrist shook from the weight as precious drops fell onto the dirt floor. "It's a fake. We're traveling performers and this is one of our props. We thought you might be thirsty and…" She glanced around at all the washed cups and bowls stacked neatly on the ledge. "We couldn't find a cup…a cup clean enough for someone so sick…"

Alma's eyes lit up. "Storytellers are ye? There's a bit of the storyteller in me as well."

At that moment Glenna burst through the door in a panic. "There's a monster in the woods with wings as big as me roof and fangs as long as me—" She gasped, her hand flying to her mouth when she saw her mother sitting up and looking well. "What miracle is this?"

Alma held out her arms and Glenna ran into her embrace. There were tears and laughter and lots of questions flying about.

Once they settled down, Alma asked about the monster in the woods.

"Oh, that's our friend," Fate said, talking fast as daughter and mother looked horrified. "He's part of our small troupe. You must've seen him in his costume."

Glenna frowned with confusion. "It looked some real for a costume of cloth and stitches."

"Fate's a clever costume maker, among other things," Finn said, his reserved gaze flicking briefly to Fate.

As much as his remark was made to sound like a compliment, it cut deep. She understood the veiled meaning.

"Ye should invite him for dinner. There's much to celebrate," Glenna said, hopping to her feet. She turned to Finn. "Will ye still go to market with me? I'll be needing to get the makings for a fine meal."

"You'll stay with Alma?" he asked, directing his question to Fate.

She nodded, glancing away from the dull anger in his eyes.

He moved to the door. As soon as he swung it open the air rang with the jingling of bells and the thundering of hooves. With the goblet in her hand, Fate came up behind Glenna, looking in the direction of the noise. Two massive horses pulling a gypsy caravan emerged from the woods on a narrow, overgrown road. They skidded to a halt a few feet from the door. The massive beasts tossed their large heads, mouths frothing and nostrils flaring clouds of steam.

Finn turned Glenna around. "Go inside. You too, Fate."

She stepped forward, pulling the door shut after Glenna stepped past her. "No way. I'm staying."

The caravan door banged open. A knight in full armor jumped onto the muddy ground with a loud clank. Within two strides, he loomed over them and tore the goblet from Fate's grasp. Returning to the caravan, the knight handed it to a pair of grasping withered hands reaching from the shadows. Then Fate heard a pronounced sigh of satisfaction, followed by a sharp whispered command: *"Kill them all."*

Finn reacted by grabbing hold of Fate's hand and hauling her behind him at break-neck speed into the woods.

Nauseating terror coursed through her veins when she heard the clanking of the knight's armor and his heavy footfall getting closer. "He's gaining on us!"

"Just *keep* running," Finn insisted.

He suddenly changed direction. They were heading toward the descending sun. Branches thrashed against them. Fate could barely see where she was going for the tears in her eyes. She would've tripped by now if Finn weren't guiding the way. The sound of a sword slicing through the air just inches from her ear brought new speed to her limbs. She would've screamed, but she was too busy gasping for air.

Suddenly Finn was hollering for help.

Dismayed that he'd lost his nerve, she glanced at him for a split second. But there was a calculated look in his eyes. Relief kept her going when she realized he hadn't given up hope.

They fled across a field, but the ground was soggy and sucked their feet down. Each step became more and more labored. Fate was close to collapsing when she heard a loud thud. Finn slowed and she glanced over her shoulder. The knight was gone, but his helmet lay on the ground a few feet away. Then something slashed in front of her face, driving into the soil two inches from her feet.

Her head buzzed with shock as she stared at the knight's sword, the blade stabbing the earth and its jeweled hilt still wobbling. When she realized how close she'd come to having her face shaved off, her strength deserted her. Finn caught her before she fell. "What…just happened?" she panted.

"Look up," he said.

Sithias was coiled around the legs of the headless knight,

flapping his wings with laborious thrusts. The armor appeared to be completely empty, yet the knight's arms flailed and his torso twisted. Hissing with effort, Sithias climbed to a tremendous height before letting the knight fall. The armor smashed on the ground with bronze arms, legs and breastplate scattering in all directions.

He landed next to them. "Ugh, heavy metal. Awfully hard on the back," he said, rubbing his narrow back with the tip of his tail.

Fate felt a sigh of relief shudder through Finn as he rested his head against hers. She leaned into him, rocking with the tired heave of his chest.

"Sithias, we owe you one," he said, still catching his breath. "I wasn't even sure we were going in the right direction."

"No doubt I would've heard your caterwauling from wherever I wasss," Sithias assured him. "Thessse woodsss, if you can call them that, are sssparse indeed. I've never ssseen sssuch sssad excusesss for treesss."

Their voices faded away as Fate stared mutely at the glinting armor strewn amongst the bramble and grass. Another brush with death. What if her luck ran out next time? The cold hard truth hit her. She could actually die here and no one would ever hear from her again. She'd be added to the list of the permanently disappeared.

It hurt to think how devastated Eustace must be right now, not knowing if she was dead or alive. As much as he'd encouraged her to always test her independence, she knew how deeply protective he was—the very reason he'd never dated. He stayed in, even working from home, doing his best to fill the role of two parents and make up for a lack of siblings.

Tears burned her eyes. Her longing for the safety of home and the comforting ordinariness of their daily routines together suddenly became so unbearable she had to block it from her mind, or she'd fall to pieces. She looked at Sithias, tuning back into what he was saying.

"It appearsss we were dealing with a ghosssthand," he informed them. "Do either of you know who would be powerful enough to raissse one?"

"It was the veiled lady. She sent the knight after us," Finn said. "And now she has the golden goblet." He then explained how Fate had written the goblet into their possession and how it had healed Glenna's mother.

Fate felt him stiffen all of sudden. He let go of her abruptly. After letting his guard down, his defensive posture was back and it drove a hole in her already aching heart.

"You're white as a ghost," he said as he stepped away from her. "You should go back to the book. We'll make sure Glenna's safe."

His tone left no room for argument. Not that she had the energy or nerve to do anything but leave with her tail tucked between her legs. As she trudged back to camp, she'd never felt more alone or miserable. Not only had she blown it with Finn by telling him something no one should ever know, she was also wussing out in the middle of a real adventure.

She kicked at a buried rock, stubbing her toe instead. As she hopped on one leg biting back the pain shooting up her foot, she wondered why she was such a loser. She should be dazzling the guy of her dreams with her steely magnetism and ass-kicking skills.

But she was the opposite of all that: stupid and spineless.

Just outside Glenna's hut, the veiled woman stood in her caravan, stroking the golden goblet and watching the healing water pool inside the cup. When there was enough liquid to drink, she lifted her veils and gulped it back.

A warm tingling spread from her throat into her chest. She welcomed the painful throb of life flowing through her, gasping as her blue-veined hands plumped with youthful suppleness.

The goblet had already filled again, and she swallowed more of the sweet water. Strength and energy surged throughout her body. She ran across the room, ripping back the curtain that had long covered a large mirror. Staring at her concealed form, she pulled away each silken layer.

For countless ages she'd kept her hideously wizened body hidden from sight, but as the last veil fell to the floor, her reflection revealed a woman at the peak of her beauty. Her cat-shaped eyes flashed like black onyx against dark skin the color of polished mahogany. She touched her face to confirm what she saw in the mirror, feeling the fullness of her lips. Smiling, she glanced at the bronze statues of dancing women lined against the draped walls. There would be no need to bring those beauties to life anymore. She alone could now lure whomever she needed into her caravan. But her smile faded when she saw that her hair was still a coarse dead gray. Lifting the goblet to her lips, she let the water run down the sides of her mouth in her haste to guzzle more.

She turned back to the mirror, waiting for her hair to return to life, for this was where her ancestors dwelled. Within each strand, she carried the life force of an ancient race of mystics long forgotten by others. She was Sabirah, the sacred vessel of her people, awaiting the time when she could return to the Temple of the Winged Serpent, where she would bring her people back into the world by using the objects of the altar she'd reclaimed from plunderers who'd stolen them so long ago.

But the voices of her ancestors had grown dim over the ages until they spoke no more. Lost without their wisdom and guidance, she began her obsessive search for the healing goblet to revive her worn body.

Sabirah watched the inky darkness return to her hair. The voices began to whisper in her mind and her ebony locks writhed like a sea of snakes, caressing her arms and legs. She luxuriated in the touch of her lost tribe and listened. At first their voices were discordant, but they soon spoke as one inside her mind. *"Leave no trail. Kill all who have knowledge of the goblet,"* they commanded.

Donning her leather armor, she rushed out of the caravan and kicked the door of the hut open. The woman and child inside screamed when they saw her. Lifting her sword, Sabirah lunged forward, shrieking a war cry that sounded like an army of fierce voices.

A force, bright and sharp, threw her back against the caravan. She narrowed her eyes on the powerful Ogham inscriptions scratched in the mud walls. Cursing the Druid who had put them there, Sabirah stormed back to the caravan to retrieve a box. She returned to the gleaming marks and took out a cut branch.

"Oak of hatred, spread your dark poison into this place," she whispered, blowing the curse over the wood. She jammed the stick into the wards and broke it off. Stepping back, she watched the pale light of the wards extinguish as a shadow bled over the hut and surrounding earth.

Dropping what was left of the branch, she drew her sword, ready to slay the easy prey inside when she heard someone shouting. Sabirah turned to see a golden-haired young man racing toward her.

"Hey! Over here!" Finn yelled as he jumped over the creek and rushed forward. He saw the woman stop to look at him. He had no idea what he would do once he got there. He was unarmed against her sword. The most he could hope to do was lead her away from Glenna, maybe turn the tables on her somehow.

He was only thirty feet away from the hut when a nauseating wave of darkness crashed over him. His head started spinning, his legs went weak. Reaching out for something to grab hold of, his hand passed through air and he stumbled. Tilting forward, his knees rammed into rock and mud. Pain spiked through his kneecaps and down his shins. He swallowed the pain, pushing himself to get back up, but his muscles had gone soft. It was all he could do to stay upright.

"Ah, the loyal Druid returns. But alas, he feels the poison in the earth as if in his own veins," the woman said as she strode over to him. "That's the weakness of you earth lovers. You can never stay strong for that which you fight to protect."

Struggling to catch his breath, Finn looked up at a frightening beauty with a wild mane of hair snaking unnaturally in the air. He wondered if he was hallucinating.

She leaned down, brushing her lips against his ear, her dark tendrils coiling round his neck. "Stop resisting, your strength and powers will increase a hundredfold if you would but surrender to the darkness as Mugloth did," she whispered.

Finn's head filled with a noisy buzz, yet her words pierced the din and stuck like the thorn of a thistle in a shadowy corner of his mind. As she straightened, he followed her movement, his tongue too thick to speak, his body paralyzed. Through his blurring vision he watched her turn back in the direction of the hut, the blade of her sword leading the way. His mind screamed to move, to get up. Instead, he tipped over, his chin grinding into the rough sand of a shallow puddle.

As a large shadow passed over, he thought death had come for him. Then he heard the beating of wings. Was this the angel of death? Using every ounce of will he had, Finn rolled his eyes upward. The woman had dropped to her knees only a few feet away. Her hair spiraled skyward, stretching toward a white fuzzy figure flapping in place just above her. That's when he realized it was Sithias.

"Aradif," Finn heard her say, "I am greatly humbled by your presence." She continued kneeling like she was showing *respect…to Sithias!*

With his tail coiled round her sword, the snake glided to the ground. "Rissse," he commanded, gesturing with a grand sweep of the sword's long blade.

Certain he was delirious, Finn squinted at the unbelievable scene.

The woman remained on her knees, her hair reaching for the snake in an almost longing way. "May I speak, Aradif?"

"You may," Sithias said.

"It is not by chance that my ancestors and our Guiding Star should return all in one glorious day. Must I go to your ancient Temple, or may we build the altar here to begin the Rebirthing Ritual of your Tribe?"

"Hmmm," Sithias replied. "And how many day's ride isss it to the Temple?"

"Our homeland is far Aradif. It would take at least three moons to reach the sea and another two to span the great water that lies between this land and ours."

There was a long pause on Sithias's part. Finn tried to make sense of what he was witnessing, but a fog had filled his mind. Some force emanating from the ground had poisoned him. A seething darkness flooded through his body, drowning his thoughts, his memories, even the raw anguish Fate had opened up in him. There was a time when he would've fought to the bitter end against an invasion this menacing. But what did he have to fight for? Nothing.

So he closed his eyes and allowed it to take him.

For a brief moment, Sithias swelled with the power he held

over the woman kneeling before him. He had no clue as to why she revered him, but whatever the reason, he'd use it to his advantage. "Unfortunately, that isss exactly what mussst be done," he said with an air of authority. "The ritual mussst be performed on our sssacred landsss, not on thisss foreign sssoil." He spat on the ground with distaste for good measure.

She hung her head with a sigh, though her hair stretched toward him like the tentacles of an octopus. Shuddering, Sithias slithered backwards with a grimace.

She looked up at him. "It must be as you say it, Aradif. Please forgive my hesitation. Weariness presses on my soul and I would point out that once your Tribe is reborn, we could easily conquer these weaklings and begin anew, here in this land."

Sithias shook his head. "No, my people dessserve to return to their homeland." He waved his tail dismissively. "Now go. You have a long journey ahead of you."

Bowing her head, she rose to her feet and moved to climb into the caravan.

"Before you go," Sithias said, "you will leave the healing goblet with me."

She shot him the cautious look of someone who suspected she was being tricked. "What might you need the goblet for? You are immortal."

"For him," Sithias said, pointing his tail at Finn.

"Him?" She choked on the word. "Why would you give it to this…this *Earth* lover and deprive those who worship you and the sea of stars you come from?"

Sithias held his head high. "My mercy isss broad and mysteriousss, and not for you to judge. Be comforted in knowing that I will return the goblet to my Tribe during the Rebirthing Ritual."

Her face sharpened and her hair thrashed with fury. For a split second, Sithias thought she would refuse. A moment later, she gave him the goblet, then turned and climbed inside the caravan. The horses reared and whinnied as if they'd been lashed by an invisible whip and galloped away.

Once she was well out of sight, he began to breathe again. Glenna and Alma came tiptoeing out of the hut when they saw that the fierce woman was gone, though they stared every bit as warily at Sithias as they made their way over to Finn.

Glenna propped his head onto her small lap. "He's in a bad way." She looked up at Sithias with round, worried eyes. "And where's Fate? I hope she's come to no harm."

"She's recovering from a bad fright." Sithias slithered close and put the goblet in her hand.

"What's this?" she asked.

"I'll explain later," Sithias said. "Finn needs to drink from—"

All of a sudden the ground quaked violently. Alma lost her footing. Sithias swayed to stay upright. With a loud crack, the earth split open, yawning wide. A foul odor filled the air as slime oozed up from the deep. Swamp water spilled over the edges, mottled heads crested the surface—heads that peered at them with bulging eyes of pale green. When they saw the goblet in Glenna's hand, three of the goblins lurched from the murk with such speed she had no time to react. They snatched the goblet and dove back into the swamp.

Too stunned to move, Sithias watched in dismay as the goblet sank out of sight.

A few goblins lingered behind, all staring at Glenna with a strange gleam in their eyes. "We'll have our payment now," one of the goblins gurgled.

Sithias slithered to the edge, snaking his head close to it. "Payment for what?"

The little creature drew back in revulsion. "For drinking from the cup," it said. Without taking its eyes off the winged snake, it aimed a spindly finger at Alma. "This one glows with the healing water. Payment is due."

"What kind of payment?" Sithias pressed.

"A queen is payment enough. We'll take *her.*" The goblin pointed at Glenna.

Sithias hissed menacingly. "You can't have her."

The goblin didn't budge. "Then the one who drank will die."

Glenna's eyes filled with tears. "No, if it means saving me mum, I'll go without a fight."

"Oh no ye won't!" cried Alma. "The only way ye'll go is over me dead hands ringin' their slimy necks."

Glenna cast her mother a sorrowful glance as she moved to the edge of the swamp. "Mum, don't make it any harder than 'tis."

Alma lunged forward, wrapping her arms around her daughter's waist, staring fiercely at the goblins. "You'll be taking me too."

As soon as the goblins nodded their acceptance, a blue-green light wisped around both mother and daughter. Blank-faced and bedazzled by the spellbinding glow, the two floated out to the middle and sank into the swamp. With their pale eyes still riveted on Sithias, the goblins slipped into the slime, the earth rumbling as the ground sealed shut.

"Oh my," Sithias fretted as he waved goodbye with his tail. He could only hope it was for the best. His main concern was Finn. Coiling around his limp body, he lifted off and flew him back to Fate.

She was wearing a path back and forth in front of the *Book of Fables* when he landed and laid Finn gently at her feet. When she saw him, her hands flew to her heart. Dropping down beside him, she put her head to his chest, listening for his heartbeat. Her drawn expression relaxed only slightly when she lifted her head.

Sithias gulped as she looked up at him with watery eyes

swimming with questions. "She did sssomething to him," he said, not knowing what else to say.

"The veiled woman?"

"I'm not certain. She had no veilsss," he said while turning to the *Book of Fables* and flipping through its pages to the end of *The Goblin Queen*. He read quietly. "Ah yesss, it wasss the veiled woman. It saysss here, her name isss Sssabirah. She drove a branch from the cursssed oak into the Ogham markingsss he carved into Glenna'sss hut. There'sss no explanation, but I think it poisssoned him jussst asss it poisssoned the land."

Fear drained the color from Fate's face. "It has to be because his Druidic name was carved into the hut."

"Oh dear. Well, doess it help to know that the fable now saysss Glenna and her mother prefer their royal ssstationsss to that of poverty, even if it isss in a ssswamp?"

"No, I don't care," she cried, her tears falling on Finn's pallid face.

"Quite right misss. I suggest we move into the next fable. Maybe the effect will wane if we take Finn far from thisss poisssoned land."

"Yes, that could work." She looked up at him, desperate hope filling her eyes. "He'll be fine. Right, Sithias?"

The snake smiled, nodding vigorously to keep her from seeing the doubt troubling him deep down inside.

The Heart of a Troll

The chroniclers of old tell of an Elder race, the ancestors of all living things, whose blood flowed with magic and whose bones held within them the wisdom of Earth's most ancient knowledge. These mighty beings were the first giants. They lived peacefully for many ages, but when mankind began to spread over the world, the Elder race receded into nature. They became masters of illusion, able to change shape and blend with the land, until they came to be a lasting part of the earth. Yet it is not of these magnificent beings this story speaks. This is a tale of the lowly demise of those giants who over the ages dwindled in size and magnitude until they were nothing more than what humans called trolls or ogres. Even though they retained much of their forebears' powerful magic, they were generally loathed and feared.

One such creature was a tree troll named Grysla. She was as tall as a redwood cedar and rarely ever recognized by humans, because of her resemblance to a dead uprooted tree. Sadly, Grysla was the last of her kind. She had lost her mate and child to the torches of an angry mob of villagers who blamed the trolls for a blight on their crops. On that horrible day her family had been burned, while Grysla had been chopped to pieces. Unbeknownst to the villagers, a tree troll could grow back whole and complete.

Grief pushed Grysla to wander far from home to the cold lands of the Twisted Bone Forest. It was in those high mountains that she fell into a deep winter's sleep. She slept for more than a year until one day the shrill cry of a child's voice woke her.

Grysla broke from the ice and fixed her eyes upon the valley below to a river's edge, where a young boy clung to a log. Torn by fierce memories, she leaped from the cliffs. With huge loping strides, she thundered across the valley, not knowing what she'd do when she arrived. But strong currents took the boy just as the giant plunged her great hands into the water.

Near the river's reedy shore, a little girl named Tove watched helplessly as the river tore her brother, Leif, away. She sobbed, for now the orphan was truly alone. When Grysla discovered the tiny human tucked within the tall grass, her eyes widened in surprise. The child blinked up at the gnarled face whose weathered features curved upward in a sad, gentle fashion. After studying each other for a speck of time, Grysla held out her hand and Tove climbed into the giant's craggy palm.

Further downstream, Leif managed to pull himself free of the raging river and raced back only to discover that Tove was gone. The tall grass where she had sat was crushed into the shape of a massive footprint. Frightened for his sister, Leif struck out after her.

After sixteen years of fruitless searching, he grew into a man weathered in the ways of hunting and all the hardships life could muster against him. Along the way, he sought out troll hunters who helped him hone a mean talent for slaying the hideous giants. His weapon of choice became the arbalest, which he armed with wooden-tipped arrows carved from a cursed oak tree. The piece of oak had commanded a hefty price, but was well worth it, for when its sharpened tip pierced a troll's hide, its poison took root and spread swiftly.

One day in the dead of winter, Leif entered a tavern in a remote village. The place was full of music and merriment, and many tongues wagged with outlandish stories. One such tale caught Leif's ear. The story was that of a fae creature who some thought to be part human. It was said that she was as quick as a squirrel and could vanish from sight in the wink of an eye. And it was also whispered with the thrill of fear in the storyteller's eye that the sprite was not alone, that a rare few had seen something gigantic shadowing her, something that shook the ground and tilted the trees.

This was the first Leif had ever heard of a troll shadowing a girl, whether she be fae or not. With hope in his heart, he left at first light, picked up the troll's trail and followed it for days.

When at last he found fresh tracks, he crouched behind a snowdrift and waited. After much time, He was about to leave when something darted out of nowhere. A sprite of some sort whose runed skin gleamed with a luminous olive hue. She stood still, turning in his direction and sniffing the air. When he saw her face, he saw his long-passed mother in her features.

Leif came out of hiding, calling Tove's name in joyous recognition. As he waved to her, a tall, long dead tree tilted unnaturally and loomed large behind his sister. It took him a few seconds to realize it was the troll he'd been tracking. Filled with hatred and fear for his sister, he drew his prized arrow from his quiver, the one with sixteen cuts of the knife to mark each of Tove's missed birthdays. Taking careful aim with his crossbow, he squeezed the trigger. The poison arrow shot true and pierced the troll's heart.

Bellowing like a wounded elk, the creature crashed to the ground. Tove crouched like a wild animal ready to pounce and locked her gaze on Leif. The green eyes he remembered had gone black with fury. He feared she would attack at any moment, but the troll lurched upward, staggering and growling with a murderous rage. The poison had taken effect.

Grysla's crazed eyes fixed on them both. She knew not where she was or who they were, only that she feared them. She called out to her family. Tove answered, but Grysla did not hear. Her mind was trapped in the past, shrieking with grief over the murder of her family. All she saw were evil humans around her. The troll swept her massive arm at Tove and sent her flying into nearby trees. Drawing his sword, Leif dodged the giant's pounding fists, leaped forward and hacked off one hand, then the next. Grysla raged with pain and stamped at Leif with her mammoth feet. He jumped aside and hewed a leg off at the knee. She toppled over, breaking through low-lying trees, and fell in a shower of snow. The forest fell silent, save for the troll's labored breathing.

Leif started to climb onto her massive chest, ready to sever her head, but Tove barred his way. He reassured his sister, saying he would tend to her now. Tove didn't know him. She riled against the harsh, garbled noise of this murdering stranger. Then she looked into Grysla's tortured eyes, seeing only the kind, loving mother who had raised her.

Tove murmured the soft, clipped notes of troll speak. The tree troll turned her head away with a dreadful moan. Tove persisted, until at last, Grysla heard her voice. But the troll could not look at her daughter. The arrow's poison was making her see Tove only as a monstrous human. Also, her severed limbs were growing back too swiftly. As soon as she was whole, she knew she would lose control and kill Tove.

Only one thing could stop the inevitable. She explained to Tove what must be done. The girl wept and argued hard against it, but Grysla made her promise. At last Tove nodded. Her face went blank as she drew out a dagger and stabbed into Grysla's breast. The tree troll's cry of pain echoed out over the still forest as Tove carved out her mother's beating heart with the arrow pierced clean through.

Leif staggered back as Tove jumped off the roaring troll, whose limbs had grown back swift and sure. The troll rolled to her feet and attacked. Leif began fighting a losing battle against the crazed giant. But just when it seemed he would be crushed into the ground by a hammering fist, the troll froze. Its coarse hide petrified into granite.

Tove strode over to him, holding the smoking, skewered heart by the arrow. Leif smiled with relief. His sister had saved him by burning the troll's heart. She stared at him with her dark, disturbing eyes and let the heart slide off the arrow. The charred lump melted into the deep snow. As he sheathed his sword, she touched the marks he'd notched in the arrow's shaft and smiled back. Then she plunged the arrow into his chest.

Taking the dead troll hunter's sword, she raised it skyward and swore vengeance upon his kind. Before leaving the Twisted Bone Forest to begin her lifelong vendetta, Tove cast one last look at Grysla's grotesque statue, careful to remember instead, the gentle tree troll who had forgiven mankind enough to care for one small human in need.

CHAPTER 14

REMNANTS OF THE VIOLENT BATTLE and blood-soaked snow shattered into a chaotic whirlwind of glimmering letters, now blurring into white nothingness. The story had ignited a burning need for revenge in Fate. She wanted to strike out at that evil woman who'd poisoned Finn with the same rage Tove had felt toward Leif. But that opportunity was long gone, left behind in the last fable.

As an unbearable coldness seeped in, Fate couldn't tell where she was or what she was looking at. All she could see were blue shadows and texture within an endless white. Then it hit her. She was lying in snow. Lifting her head up, she glanced around. The *Book of Fables* had dropped them into the middle of snow-covered mountains full of the strangest-looking crooked, twisted trees she'd ever seen. She glanced over at Sithias, who was at that moment wilting in the glacial chill. When she saw that Finn was lying next to her looking deathly pale, she reached for her notepad and wrote up a swift reprieve from the biting cold.

The warmth of a crackling fire roused Sithias from a sleep that had been much too close to permanent. Ruffling his feathers, he glanced around at the inside of a cozy log cabin. The *Book of Fables* leaned against a wall, its open pages gleaming in the flickering light. When he saw snowflakes flurrying outside the window, he shivered, remembering the deadly chill that had overtaken him.

Finn lay on a sheepskin rug next to him, bundled as tight as a mummy in layers of woolen blankets. He looked much worse than before.

Fate let out a relieved sigh. "Thank God. You're finally awake." She was hunched over Finn, her face drawn and her eyes swollen from crying. "He hasn't woken. I tried everything I could think of to cure him. I even wrote up the goblet like before, but it wouldn't appear."

Sithias thought for a moment, suddenly grateful for the bit of knowledge that had rubbed off on him after so many years of service to a sorceress. "More than likely the goblins put a powerful binding ssspell on the goblet, one that would not allow it to be stolen the sssame way twice."

"I also wrote up an all-purpose magical antidote, but all that did was stain his teeth green." She lifted Finn's top lip to show him.

Sithias shook his head. "Poor Finn."

"And this too..." She peeled back the blankets, lifting Finn's shirt to reveal a thick yellow paste smeared over his chest.

He lurched backwards as a sharp, eye-watering odor released itself into the air.

Fate pinched her nose. "It's a mustard plaster. My grandmother used to say when all else fails, do the mustard plaster."

Waving his tail in a futile effort to flap the smell away, he darted his tongue out to taste the air. "The mussstard doesss not ssstand alone." He cringed. "*Whew.* I'm noting garlic, and do I detect a bit of ssstinkweed asss well?"

Her face flushed with embarrassment. "It's supposed to scare off the ailment."

"Oh you'll most certainly ssscare *sssomething* away." He tasted the pungent air again. "And coal? What could you posssibly ussse coal for?"

She exposed Finn's blackened soles. "It's supposed to draw poisons out through the feet."

"Your grandmother again?"

"What can I say? She was better than any doctor in the county."

"Poor, poor Finn," Sithias said, referring more to the homespun tortures than his illness.

She nodded glumly as she pulled Finn's shirt back in place while Sithias tucked the blankets in around him to contain the nose-biting smell.

"I was hoping you might have some ideas that would help," she said after a moment.

She looked so lost and desperate. If he could offer a solution that would restore her happiness, he would. "Sssorry, misss, I'm at a losss. Asss with all magic, there isss alwaysss one very ssspecific sssolution. I think we ssshould return to Elsssina. She knowsss of the cursssed oak that poisssoned him and she'sss a very powerful sorceresss. She might be able to—"

"She tried to kill us!"

"Yesss, well there'sss that," Sithias admitted. "Don't dessspair, a sssolution will presssent itself. And Finn'sss ssstrong. He may pull out of thisss on hisss own—given time."

She sobbed into her hands. "What if he doesn't? What if he dies? I'll never forgive myself. I was so insensitive. I didn't recognize him when we first met. And now that he knows what he is, he *hates* me for it."

Sithias stared at her in bewilderment. The suppressed passion between them and stolen glances when the other wasn't looking was enviable. What he wouldn't do to have that kind of sweet turmoil in his own life. "Hate isss not the word for it. Love would be more like it."

She looked up, sniffing and wiping her sleeve across her red nose. "You think he loves me?"

"Oh yesss, you'd have to be blind asss a bat, and deaf too, not to notice." He swallowed dryly. "Not that you're any of *thossse* thingsss."

She threw up her hands. "I've always had terrible luck with boys. I guess because I was never interested enough to make much of an effort. Most of them bored me to death. Do you know I'm seventeen and I've never kissed a guy?"

"A beautiful young woman like you hasss never been kisssed?"

Fate blew her inflamed nose, loudly. "No."

Sithias kept his smile in place as she blinked at him with puffy eyes and a red, runny nose. "Yesss, hard to believe for sssuch a lovely, young…lady."

She buried her face in the mangled tissue, crying again. "I was always looking for Finn. He's the only one I've ever been interested in."

Confusion replaced his smile altogether. "I thought you two had jussst met recently."

She looked up with specks of tissue clinging to her wet cheeks. "Technically, I only just met him in person a few days ago. But really I've known him since I was twelve. In my head and heart that is."

Sithias shook his head, now thoroughly baffled. "I'm sssorry, I'm entirely lossst."

"Finn's not real. Not like you and me—well, I'm not sure you're real either. I mean, you're a character in a book too." Her eyes took on a paranoid look. "But then again, maybe none of this is real. I could be in a coma dreaming all of this."

He remained silent, watching her teeter on the edge of insanity, not sure what to say anymore.

She let out a deep, shaky sigh and explained everything from inventing Finn and his life story for the last five years to the moment she'd met him in the bookstore and their ultimate arrival on Elsina's floating island.

As Sithias listened, he began to understand. He was most intrigued. Her story brought to mind the disdainful Pygmalion, who'd found fault with every woman he'd encountered. Only his own carved image of the perfect, yet unattainable woman could meet his high expectations. Fluttering his wings excitedly, he said, "Ah, now I sssee why you feel ssso ssstrongly for him. That's *fassscinating.* Finn isss your Galatea, and you are hisss Pygmalion. Now it all makesss perfect sensssse."

"How do you know that story? It's a Greek myth from *my* world."

"That may be, but I assure you, it happened in thisss world, where the godsss and goddessesss of Hellasss abound and carven imagesss of ivory are brought to life by their touch alone." He fell quiet as he regarded her with increased admiration. "Finn isss quite the credit to you and your imagination. How proud you musssst be."

She shook her head slowly, her chin quivering. "How can I be proud when I know he hates me? I've torn down his world and everything he ever believed in. It's all gone. He has nothing to hold onto. How could anyone ever recover from something that earth-shattering?"

"One day at a time?" Sithias offered. "He'sss here now, and he'sss real, in ssspite of hisss originsss. He's made of the gold you ssshaped him from, and with patience, I'm certain he'll come to accept you and hisss extraordinary emergence into the world. After all, it ssseems fate hasss brought you two together."

She winced like his words had burned her. "Want to know one of the many wonderfully depressing definitions of 'fate'?" She didn't wait for him to answer. "'To predetermine something, usually with negative results.'"

"Oh, did I sssay fate?" Sithias said with great haste. "Surely I meant to sssay providence had a part in thisss."

"Providence. I like the sound of that," she said, yawning. Pulling a blanket around her shoulders, she looked at him beneath drooping lids and gave him a sleepy smile.

Her vulnerability tugged at his heart. He smiled back, nudging her gently with his tail to get her to lie down. "Get sssome sssleep, misss."

She nodded, snuggling in close to Finn. Within seconds she fell fast asleep.

Coiling into a comfortable spiral, Sithias turned his gaze to the flames dancing in the fireplace. He was growing too fond of the girl. Being that they'd started out as enemies, he had to be careful. After all, she held his life in the balance with the mere stroke of her pen. But how could he remain on guard around someone so innocent in the ways of the world? If anything, he felt protective of her and worried over her well-being. Having read the other fables, he knew the trouble they were headed into. He had to warn her and help her prepare for what was to come. If she didn't start toughening up, she stood little chance of surviving. And he needed her to live. She was the key to getting what he'd come for on this journey in the first place.

The next morning, Fate woke to sunlight pouring in through the cabin's windows. Wriggling further under the blankets to escape the light, she reached out for Finn. Her hand met flat blankets. She threw off the covers and sat up, her heart pounding with relief and anticipation as she looked around for him. Where was he? She stood, letting the blankets fall around her feet, then tiptoed over to the bathroom and tapped on the door. "Finn?"

When there was no answer, she pushed the door open. The bathroom was empty. With a growing sense of alarm, she returned to the messy pile of blankets, lifting them as if she expected him to be buried underneath. "Don't be ridiculous," she muttered under her breath.

His boots sat by the fire. He wouldn't go outside without

them, so that was a relief at least. Where was he hiding? Then she noticed the black footprints and dried mustard crumbles leading to the front door. She followed them, dread mounting in the pit of her stomach.

An arctic wind blasted past her into the cabin when she opened the door. Squinting at the blaring white landscape stretching out before her, she saw a deep furrow in the snow where Finn had struck out into the snow barefoot. The path curved its way up over the hill, disappearing amongst a clump of crooked trees.

A flood of desperate questions rushed through her mind. When did he leave? How long has he been out there without shoes—without a coat? Worse yet, what would she find when she went looking for him?

Shaking more from fear than the chill, she slammed the door. "Sithias!"

The snake's head popped out from under his blanket. "Huh? What?"

Fate fumbled with her notepad, dropping the thin pencil and trying again until she managed to scrawl down what she needed. Sithias slithered over to her, blinking the sleep from his eyes with a bewildered expression. "Where'sss Finn?"

"Gone," she said, her voice tight. Even though she stammered while reading, she was dressed—within an instant—in a puffy, white fur-lined hooded parka, snow pants and big furry boots attached to a pair of snowshoes.

"I won't come back without him," she said, mustering a brave tone to cover the creep of terror taking over.

He nodded. "Lightning ssspeed, misss."

"That's it! Lightning speed—that's what I need." She wrote down her idea. *"I wish to be where Finn is right now,"* she said, closing her eyes.

"You're ssstill here."

Fate swore under her breath and wrote down another line. *"Finn is now here with me."*

When he didn't appear, her hopes evaporated. "What's wrong? Why can't I make this happen? I thought the Words of Making were all powerful."

"You would think ssso. The poissson mussst be interfering in sssome way."

Fear closed around her heart. "What if it's not working because he's…dead?"

"No, we mussstn't go thinking the worssst. I'm certain it'sss the poissson, and you bessst not wassste another moment. Go find him."

Taking some comfort in his words, she nodded and tramped out into the cold.

The glare off the snow pierced Finn's eyes like needles. Bitter cold stung his skin, though the burning in his feet had waned, save for the occasional sharp stab in his toes. His hands throbbed from cutting them on the sharp thorns of the strange, twisted trees rising up out of the deep drifts. Injuries made before he'd woken to find himself walking aimlessly without his boots and a jacket to protect him from the freezing cold. He was baffled as to how he'd come to be there in such a helpless state. He couldn't make any sense out of it. His thinking was muddled, and a fog filled his mind, one that concealed his most recent memories and whatever events had led up to this moment. Thankfully, he remembered his roots.

His leg broke through the ice crust again. Too tired to go on, he pulled out of the frigid hole and stopped there. He was lost with nowhere to go. Yet he was oddly resigned to the situation. Something told him that whatever he'd left behind was far worse than his present predicament.

He let out a tired sigh, producing a big white puff, just like the ones his grandfather used to make with his pipe. As the memory flickered in his mind, something disturbed the white glare of the forest and moved toward him.

His grandfather came into view, a wise old face with green eyes that spoke of a deep knowledge of ancient things. With a smile crinkling his features, he reached into his medicine bag, pinching tobacco and filling the well of his clay pipe. "Do you remember the holy blend, Finn?" his grandfather asked before putting a flame to the pipe's bowl.

Nodding, Finn breathed in the aromatic smoke. "Mmhmm. Golden Bough gathered on the sixth night of the moon, sweet cicely, celandine and woodruff anointed with the oil of amber."

Looking pleased, his grandfather handed him the pipe. The bowl, with its intricate weave of oak leaves and mistletoe carved into it, warmed his palm as he drew the smoke into his lungs. A welcome heat spread through his chest, down to his toes.

"Did you know it is Alban Arthuan, the day of the long night?" his grandfather asked. "Do you remember how to prepare?"

Finn's mind cleared somewhat. "I should strengthen my mind and spirit with the smoke of the holy blend and use it to call for guidance from the winter spirits."

His grandfather squeezed his shoulder. "Do this, and you'll have no trouble making it to the light of Alban Eiler."

"Thanks, Granda."

His grandfather's smiling face blinked out of sight.

Finn puffed on the pipe, sending a call for help to the winter spirits within each wisp of smoke he blew into the air.

He didn't have to wait long.

The sun was at its highest when a small white shadow

materialized against a distant snowdrift. Moving closer, the shadow kept to the snowy mounds before ducking in behind a curved ridge of ice. Out poked a black dot of a nose, followed by slanted eyes and thick furry ears. Keeping still as a block of ice, the snow fox stared at Finn. Then it trotted across the snow, running playful circles around him, scampering away and back again, taunting him to follow. Chuckling at the bouncing ball of fur, he struggled to his feet and trailed behind it.

Fate followed Finn's meandering path, seeing deep imprints where he'd fallen along the way. She was encouraged when she saw that the trail continued quite far, winding over the hills and out of sight. At least she knew he was still alive. Heartened by this, she picked up the pace and had covered a fair distance, when she suddenly stopped dead in her tracks. There were blood drops on the snow and huge paw prints. Finn was being hunted.

Fear crashed in. She had to move faster.

Pulling off her gloves with her teeth, she drew the notepad from her pocket. A shadow crossed over her, a hawk soaring overhead. Seeing the bird sweep over the hills gave her an idea. She wrote it down.

"I can now fly through the air and find Finn long before he freezes to death or comes to any harm," she read aloud.

She expected to feel lighter but nothing changed in that respect. She flapped her arms, only to remain grounded. "Up, up and away?" she muttered, raising one arm like Superman. She decided to jump up. Not that she thought that would work either. But much to her amazement, she continued climbing into the air.

Rising like a balloon, she thrashed her arms, grabbing for something to hang onto. As she rose higher she tipped head over heels, struggling to level out. This wasn't flying, this was floating and flailing. Would she keep climbing like this until the air grew too thin to breathe? Now she was scared. She twisted awkwardly, a move that made her roll round and round like a log in the water.

Splaying her arms and legs out stopped the rolling. She was facing down, watching the shrinking landscape. "I want down!" she screamed.

She plummeted, the spikes of the crooked trees coming into view way too fast. Her muscles went rigid with terror as she tilted her chin upward, fighting the pull of gravity. She shot skyward, building speed as she kept her neck stretched and eyes fixed on the blue expanse. Tilting her head down and to the right, her body followed in that direction. She laughed nervously. Apparently her head was the steering wheel. As relief flooded through her, she relaxed, letting her arms hang loosely at her sides, which brought her back to a slow glide. She quickly realized she could accelerate by stiffening and holding herself in the position of a human rocket.

After the initial fright and thrill of learning to fly, she turned her attention back to finding Finn. She flew low so she could stay close to his path, careful to avoid being gouged by deadly thorns. As she flew over the unusual landscape, she could see why it was called the Twisted Bone Forest. The skeletal trees were bone white and as crooked as if they'd been formed by the winds of tornadoes. Sprinkled amongst the sea of ill-formed trees, were small islands of green pines, the only color the white panorama had to offer.

Finn's path continued over a steep hill, down to a frozen river curving along the valley bottom. She flew past the river, only to discover that the path had ended. She turned back and landed. Hard ice crunched underfoot as she came to a jagged hole. Sprays of blood stained its edges. Nauseating fear coursed through her, weakening her legs so much she fell to her knees.

The hole was large enough for him to fall through and be pulled away by the rapid river churning beneath the ice.

Her heart shattered into pieces, like the ice that had broken under him.

"The trail is looking fresh," a man's gruff voice said from behind her. "Made after sunrise."

She jumped to her feet, nearly falling over as she wheeled round to see who was speaking.

"You look to have seen a ghost," he said in broken English, his Norse accent thick. He shifted the weight of his heavy pack and crossbow, staring at her with mild curiosity.

"I was hoping to find my…my friend, and I found this hole."

The man strode over to the punctured ice. "Not hole. Footprint," he said as his gaze traveled to another large break in the ice a good twenty feet upstream from where they stood.

She didn't grasp what he meant right away. "You mean those holes were made by a, a—"

"Troll." His voice dripped with malice. "The most vile and heinous creature ever to be spit from Niflheim."

She shook her head. "You don't think the troll step—" Her throat closed, choking off her voice.

"What? Step on your friend? No, I wouldn't say so."

A wave of relief swept over her.

The man strode upstream toward the next hole. "Ah no, I'd say it took your friend to its filthy nest for good meal." He spat out a foul gob of tobacco juice and moved on.

Fighting the urge to gag, Fate stepped around the steaming splotch and chased after him. "To feed him dinner?"

The man stopped and laughed. "Ha! No, to *eat* him!" He looked at her like she was completely daft. "What? You think a troll will cook up nice plate of lutefisk for your friend and serve it with flagon of ale to boot?"

He pulled out an arrow marked with notches.

She counted sixteen. So this was Leif. He fit her mind's eye image. He was attractive in a rugged sort of way, though she hadn't expected his crude, brutish manners.

"Man eaters, these things." He continued as he fingered the notches on the arrow, a deep scowl etched on his face. "I've seen them rip grown men apart. Their dens are filled with bones of humans."

"No. I don't believe you," she argued, clinging to one thought only. There had been no mention of tree trolls eating anyone in *this* fable.

Shrugging, he slipped the arrow next to a sheathed sword strapped on his belt. "It's not for me to make you believe." He turned, continuing up the river to yet another hole the size of a car.

She followed, breaking into a trot to keep up. "I'm going with you. If a troll took my friend, I want to be there when you find him."

He came to such an abrupt halt, she almost rammed into him. The cold, territorial look in his eyes made her stand rigid. "I be liking the pretty damsels, but not when hunting." His ruddy expression relaxed, his blue eyes raking over her face with brazen desire. "You would like I come round after dark? Maybe tell you what is found and warm your bed?"

She glared at him, astonished and creeped out. "I'd rather eat overly mayonnaised coleslaw with wizened grape mummies lurking in every bite!"

"Is that no?"

"*Yes,* that's no!"

"Suit yourself, little Freya." He turned without further ado and trudged up the hill.

She glowered at his back, then shot into the air, watching his form shrink to the size of an ant. "Jackass," she muttered.

Her thoughts turned to Finn as she hovered high overhead.

A sickening, empty ache spread through her, knowing he was lost and injured, or possibly worse. Stiffening every muscle in her body 'til it hurt, she sped through the sky, the tears freezing on her skin as she fixed her gaze on the snow blurring by below. She would find him or die trying.

CHAPTER 15

VISIONS OF GNASHING FANGS and tearing claws jarred Finn awake. Knifing pain throbbed across his chest, and his feet stung like he'd walked on broken glass. Gritting his teeth, he sat up, the smallest movements driving the pain even deeper into his chest. Afraid to look, he glanced down all the same, nearly passing out from the sight. Four long gashes exposed breastbone beneath shredded, bleeding flesh.

Drawing in a shaky breath to calm the panic threatening to overtake him, he focused on his surroundings. He was in an immense cave. A fire blazed next to him, the light flickering over walls covered in peculiar rune marks and pictographs. How had he come to be here? The last thing he remembered was standing by a frozen river.

The second he pictured the river, his heart hammered with the memory of a foul-smelling creature—all snarls, teeth and muscle—lunging at him, ripping into him. Cold sweat iced his back and forehead. He should be dead.

Forcing back the terror of the attack, he slumped, his body a limp rag. As his breathing steadied, he became aware of a presence. He turned his head, seeing a girl, no more than nineteen, crouching nearby in the dim light. Her face and arms were marked with the same runes as those on the cave walls. A wild tangle of silvery webs held her long ebony hair back from elfin features and she wore a sleeveless tunic with breeches tucked into thigh-high moccasins.

She seemed otherworldly—less human and more sprite—in the way her eyes smoldered with shifting colors of green.

Finn managed a pained, half-hearted smile. "I suppose I have you to thank for saving me from the jaws of death."

Her smooth brow knitted into a frown, as if his voice grated on her ears. Then she nudged her chin and pointed a finger at the bottom of his bed.

He followed the line of her slender arm, jolting with fright. "Holy hell!" The animal that had attacked him was lying over his shins. It took him several seconds to realize the thing was dead.

She lifted the furs covering him so he could see that his feet were buried deep in the animal's intestines. When the animal's rank, musky stench escaped, nausea gripped hold. "Oh that's bloody gross! And the *reek*, it's enough to gag a maggot!"

He started jerking his legs out of the carcass but she pinned them down, making it clear by her grave expression he was not to move. Too faint to fight her, he allowed his stinging feet to remain inserted within the animal's warm, squishy innards. Bilious convulsions rocked him, shooting hot flares across his chest.

She pulled a dagger from a sheath strapped round her thigh and cut out the beast's dark quivering liver. It steamed in the cold air as she placed the warm organ in his frostbitten hands. Finn stared open-mouthed and mute.

He gagged, gulping back bile. "Here, take it back. I'll chunder if you don't."

She shook her head, gesturing for him to eat it.

"No bloody way."

Making a growling noise, she pushed the meat against his sealed lips. He turned his head, but she grabbed him by the jaw and squeezed hard. When he opened his mouth to yell, she stuffed the liver in his mouth. He glared at her with pure hatred, but when he saw the unwavering set of her jaw, he knew he would lose against this willful creature. Nibbling off a small piece, he somehow managed to choke it down without throwing up. She continued pushing it in his mouth until he ate enough to satisfy her.

He had to admit, he felt stronger. And now that his stomach was settling, waves of exhaustion overcame him. He wanted to succumb to sleep, allow the world to recede, but a nagging sense of loss wouldn't let him relax so easily. Something important was missing, and whatever that something was, it had left a hole in his heart that made him sad.

Finn was alone the next time he awoke. His feet had been cleaned of the dead animal's blood and entrails, and they didn't sting nearly as much. The wounds on his chest, though mighty sore, were bandaged. The animal's skin had been scraped, stretched and left to dry by the fire. Its foul stench still marked the air, but with much less punch, though now and then, he thought he caught a whiff of…mustard?

Several slabs of skewered meat were roasting over the fire, which he guessed were the animal's final remains. Bile burned the back of his throat as his stomach lurched in response.

All of a sudden, the ground shook. He was sure it was an earthquake, until he saw a great hulking form lumbering into the cave, carrying the girl on its back. The giant resembled a tree, and he could only imagine how tall it truly was, because it stooped low to fit within the large cavern. A stiff mane of twisted, root-like nubs formed its enormous head. Worn, jagged points, which looked like broken branches, covered its hunched back. The creature's rough hide was a faded gray, spotted with lichen and tufts of moss growing within gnarled crooks and crannies.

The giant's eyes had the same shifting colors as the girl, but unlike her guarded gaze, there was only softness and wide-eyed curiosity. The ground continued shaking and rubble fell from the walls as the giant settled along the edge of the cave.

The girl sprang off the creature's shoulder, landing as light as a bird and strode toward Finn. Lifting a stick from the fire, she blew out its flame and broke it down to a shorter length. She then grabbed his arm and began marking his skin with the charred end.

He jerked his arm away. "Hey, *hey* there! That's still hot!"

She ignored his outburst, holding onto his wrist—she was surprisingly strong for such a slight girl—and continued writing a series of runes on him. After she was done with his left arm, she started on the other. When she was finished, she set the stick aside, speaking to him in clipped almost musical sounding notes.

He calmed down as she spoke to him in combination with sign language, making descriptive gestures and scribing the runes in the air. He grew more mesmerized by the second. Somehow she was using this foreign communication to form vivid images in his mind, which became literal translations.

She explained this was the magic of the ancient language of the Elder race, passed down through the rune marks. When drawn on the skin, they sank deep into the soul, allowing communication with and control over the earth, the animals and the elements.

He could tell the Elder race language ran along similar veins as the Dark Speech, but it seemed to be older, more of a root language to the Dark Speech than anything else.

Eager to test the intrinsic power of the runes marked on his arms, he stammered troll speak back to her, awkwardly signing with his hands. It was an effort at first, but after a while he got better at voicing the new sounds and the signing became more fluid. Within a few short hours they were communicating easily, delving into long conversations that took them deep into the night.

Finn learned the giant was a tree troll named Grysla. Her voice was deep and gruff, like a bear's, yet when she signed the runes and gestured pictures in the air, her huge arms moved as gracefully as branches swaying in the wind. With sadness in her smoky green eyes, Grysla shared her family's tragedy and how the gift of her human daughter had healed the hatred she once had for humans. So she raised Tove in the ancient knowledge of the Elder race in the hopes that her daughter would someday help humans and trolls understand one another.

As she recounted her story, the tree troll's memories materialized in his mind. He witnessed the injustice and experienced her sorrow. Unlike the Dark Speech, this form of communication was not an invasive connection. The Elder language linked hearts gently and intimately.

When the sun rose in the hush of the morning, Finn woke, peaceful and reenergized, unaware of when he'd fallen asleep. They ate a breakfast of dried berries and jerky. Then Grysla and Tove asked to hear his story.

He signed, speaking in their language. "I don't know how I came to be here in your snowy mountains." Shaking his head, he frowned, frustrated with his inability to remember. "I can recall my life much further back," he offered. Then talked of how his grandfather had taken him to Scotland when he was thirteen and how he'd learned of his Druidic lineage. He shared a few of the mystical adventures he'd had before he was ordained within the Order, only a few months ago when he'd turned nineteen. But anything beyond his time in Scotland was shrouded in a thick fog.

This troubled him greatly.

The old tree troll and her daughter exchanged a knowing glance. Tove leaned into the light of the fire. "We received many messages from the animals in the forest about a lost spirit. They called you the Shining One, and they wanted our help to save you." She paused, her gestures fluid as she transferred images of the snow fox, hawks, rabbits and a prowling wolverine, which Finn recognized as the vicious predator that had nearly torn him to shreds.

He smiled wryly. "I think we know which one wasn't out to save me."

Tove looked puzzled. "Do you not understand that the devil bear sacrificed himself to warm the ice-rot from your feet and renew your strength with his flesh?" She went on to explain how the laws of nature had dictated the circumstances, such as the predator hunting its prey. Even though she'd speared the animal to save him, the spirit of the devil bear had been willing to die for him, the Shining One.

Her insight humbled him. Placing his hand over his stinging wounds, he silently thanked the wolverine for its sacrifice. After a moment he smiled, but with confusion. "What's all this about the Shining One?"

Grysla answered, her voice a deep rumble, her gnarled fingers fluttering as she marked the runes. "The animals named you the Shining One because your spirit is much brighter and larger than other humans." Her gentle eyes softened. "But they saw a far greater danger for you than that of freezing to death. Your bright spirit is dimming because of a darkness growing inside you."

Finn turned his gaze to the fire and swallowed. *What the hell happened to me?*

CHAPTER 16

FATE FOUGHT TO CLOSE THE DOOR against the glacial winds and snow blustering into the cabin. Out of breath and bone-tired, she drew back her fur-lined hood and kicked off her boots.

Sithias tsk-tsked and shook his head. "I wasss beginning to worry, misss. You're much later than usual."

She was grateful he didn't mention she'd returned without Finn yet again. Shedding her parka, she rushed to the fireside, trembling violently with her hands held close to the flames.

"You shouldn't ssstay out passst dark," the snake admonished, "you could freeze to death out there."

Her teeth chattered so violently she could barely speak. "If th-that j-jerk, Leif can d-do it, so can I."

"He'sss been hardened by yearsss of exposure to sssevere weather, but you, misss, have not," he said as he slithered to the bathroom to run her a hot bath. A nightly routine they'd fallen into.

"What ch-choice do I have?" she said. "F-Finn's out there s-somewhere, lost and injured."

He returned to the room and coiled up beside her. "Now I thought we agreed he'sss more than likely been ressscued by Grysssla. Leif would've found hisss body by now if the worssst had happened. Ssso you mussst remain hopeful."

"Why isn't there any mention of him in the fable? Or us even? The story hasn't changed a bit since we got here!" Still shivering, she glared hard at the flames to fend off tears of frustration.

"From what I've ssseen, the fable remainsss the sssame until sssomething pivotal happensss to bring about a different end," he explained. "Now go sssoak in the bath until you've warmed up through and through."

She trudged to the bathroom, closed the door and stripped down. The steaming water was near to overflowing. Turning off the tap, she climbed in, her tight, shivering muscles relaxing as soon as the heat wrapped around her body.

She sank beneath the water, where silence engulfed her. The moment she closed her eyes, she saw nothing but miles of snow and those sharp, distorted trees. After spending every day of the last grueling three weeks, four days and eighteen and a half hours scouring the vast Twisted Bone Forest for any sign of Finn, the landscape had imprinted on her brain.

Her stomach contracted into a tight knot, a clenching pain squeezed her chest.

She broke the water's surface as a sob made her gasp for air. What if she was on a wild goose chase, hoping against hope he was still alive? Nothing could blot out that blood-stained hole in the ice and the rushing river beneath it. In her worst moments, she pictured his broken body sweeping along icy currents to some distant place, far from where she searched.

She sank back under the water, feeling guilty for luxuriating in such pleasurable warmth when he might have died in freezing water.

She sat up, hard and fast, the sobs wrenching through her chest convulsively.

"Misss?" Sithias said from the other side of the door. "You're doing it again. You know thisss isssn't productive. Come out and have sssome hot chocolate."

His voice somewhat pulled her out of the gloom. She watched the last of her tears ripple the water drop by drop as the gnawing ache in her chest waned to a dull throb. Then she reached for the soap.

A few minutes later, she padded barefoot into the main room, pink from the heat and wrapped in a fluffy robe.

"That'ss better. It's good to sssee the glow of warmth in your face," he said, looking up from his work, where he was busily writing with his tail coiled round a pen. To fend off the boredom of being cooped up in the cabin for weeks, he'd returned to his playwriting.

She sat down on the sheepskin rug next to him.

Setting his pen aside, he took the brush from her motionless hand and gently combed the tangles through her wet hair while flapping his wings to help it dry. When he was done, he pointed at the cup of hot chocolate sitting on the hearth. "Drink up, and tell me about your day."

Fate sipped on the frothy milk. "There's nothing to tell."

"Surely you were able to find more of Grysssla's tracksss?"

"Of course, I always find her tracks, but they never lead anywhere. It's like she's purposely trying to throw me off. The Yeti's got nothing on her when it comes to being elusive."

"Maybe it'sss not you she'sss avoiding, but the troll hunter."

She shrugged. "Maybe, but I've given up on tracking her. I've started following Leif. He's been circling the same area for days now. At first I figured he was closing in on Grysla, but I'm pretty sure it's some sort of mound he's interested in."

"Well, thisss troll hunter of yoursss may be onto sssomething. It's pure conjecture, mind you, but troll moundssss are purported to hold great treasuresss. Of coursse, diggingsss have proved to be fruitless venturesss. It's sssaid that trollsss can make gold look like rocksss and rocksss look like gold. One never knowsss what he hasss in hand until he isss far from the magic of the troll mound."

She frowned. "He's not *my* troll hunter. He's a hideous belching man who spits disgusting gobs of tobacco everywhere he goes and farts tunes for his own personal amusement. He's repulsive, Sithias. Even the word *repulsive* finds him repulsive."

Shaking his head, the snake tsk-tsked again. "And that'sss *saying* sssomething. Poor misss, what a nightmare."

"It has been," she muttered, tears pricking her eyes once more.

"I finished the play about the princesss and the time keeper," he offered hastily. "Would you like to hear it?"

"Yes," she sighed, trying to muster a smile for him. "*Please,* tell me a story. Just so long as it has a happy ending."

Sithias froze with a worried look. "Right...well, it'sss definitely a work in progresss."

Thankful for the distraction, she curled into a comfortable ball, ready to be carried away by his story. But exhaustion won the fight to stay awake. She was asleep before he finished reading the first page.

Fate struck out at sunrise the next day in search of the troll hunter. After a good night's rest, she was ready to enlist his help in a more direct manner. Knowing exactly where to look, she flew straight there, scanning for his dark shape against the snowy vastness.

Keeping his back to her so he wouldn't see her flying, she floated down out of the sky, landing right behind him. "Have you found that troll yet?" she asked, smirking when he jumped, lost his balance and fell over.

Scowling and thrashing like a turtle stuck on its back, he bellowed, "For Thor's sake and all holy hell! Sneaking'll get you shot!"

She laughed. "If you're so quick on the draw, how come I'm not a pin cushion already?"

"Oh, I've got mind to shoot!" He got to his feet with a lot of grunting, his crossbow in hand. "What did I tell you, girl? No bothering me on the hunt!"

She matched his serious expression. As much as she detested his company, she needed to make this work. "Listen, Leif—"

"Ah, you know my name," he said, giving her a sly smile. "You've been asking after me, eh?"

She rolled her eyes. "No, I happen to know all about you and what you're looking for."

He sniffed with pride. "It's no secret I am hunter of trolls."

"I'm not referring to trolls," she said, unable to hide her smugness. "I know you've been searching for your sister, Tove, for the last sixteen years."

His ruddy face blanched. In fact, he looked so stunned she could've knocked him back down with a nudge of her finger.

"Odin above," he whispered faintly. "It's been long since I heard her name outside my head!" His brows furrowed into a suspicious frown. "Who are you, eh? A Norn come to turn my fate?"

The irony of his question made her smile. If he wanted to think she was one of the Norns spinning the golden threads of his fate, it might very well work to her advantage to be one. "Well yes, that's exactly right." And then she went on to tell him of the violent encounter he would have with Tove if he stayed hell-bent on killing the troll who'd raised his sister like a daughter.

The flush of anger on his face darkened into purple rage. "*Wha-what?*" His voice boomed and echoed against the mountain range. There was murder in his eyes. "That foul creature was no mother to my Tove!"

Unnerved by his fury, she kept her eyes trained on his downturned crossbow. "Your sister's not a child anymore," she reminded him. "She's old enough to run an arrow through your heart for killing her mother. And as for the troll, her name's Grysla, and she only took Tove because she thought she had no family. She couldn't leave her to die."

Leif looked on the verge of popping a vein. "Curse you, Norn, and your evil words!" he yelled, raising his crossbow and pulling the trigger without hesitation.

Fate leaped into the air just as the arrow pierced her voluminous fur boots, barely missing flesh. Climbing high out of reach, she glared down at him, his red face upturned, shouting curses and shaking his fist at her.

"Oh stuff it where the sun don't shine," she grumbled and bolted across the sky.

CHAPTER 17

F*INN, WHERE ARE YOU?*

His heart leaped at the sound of the voice calling his name and the mysterious girl emerging from the swirling mist. Afraid the elusive sylph would disappear like so many times before, he pulled her into a crushing embrace, brushing his face along her neck, the softest place in the world. The scent of her hair was intoxicating as he slowly traced his mouth along the slender line of her throat, with the heightened anticipation of her lips touching his at long last.

When his mouth reached hers, the kiss felt wrong somehow.

The dream shattered. Her face vanished, replaced by Tove's, her olive skin glowing in the light of the fire and glossy dark hair splayed over his bed of furs. A fiery green lit her eyes as she pulled Finn back into the kiss. The heat and inviting press of her body should've made him forget everything else. But his ardor had cooled. He sat up, clutching at the ache in his chest.

Tove rose, resting her head against his back. "What troubles you?"

Guilt and confusion tangled together as he tried to hold onto the image of the mystery girl's face. But the mist had thickened, fogging over his mind until he could no longer picture her clearly. Yet the yearning lingered, as it always did whenever he had that dream. And he'd been having it more and more of late.

He turned to Tove, drawing her into his arms. "Nothing, pet. Just another dream."

She entwined her limbs around his, teasing him into lying down with her. As tempting as she was, he resisted. All he wanted to do was rush out into the snow and find that vitally missing piece of his life. The question was, where to go? And whom would he be searching for, a misty ghost who haunted his dreams and left him feeling madly discontented with what he already had?

Don't be a fool, boyo, he scolded himself. *Life doesn't get any better than this.*

He wasn't sure how long he'd been part of Grysla's family, but it already felt like a lifetime. From the moment he'd learned the Elder language, a rare and profound kinship had evolved between the three of them, especially with Tove.

When his strength had returned, she'd permanently inked the Elder race runes into his skin. They were a gift beyond measure, endowing him with unnatural strength and speed, heightened senses, rapid healing and greater resistance to the darkness that had taken root inside him. Countless hours had been spent with her while she'd tattooed his arms, down the length of his neck and spine and finally, three special runes on his left temple—the family knot.

Since then he'd come to understand the shifting colors of her eyes, another byproduct of the ancient runes once they were embedded in the skin. When they would chase each other over the snowy hills like fleeting ghosts, her eyes glowed bright green. Or when they hunted with bows drawn taut, her eyes shifted into dark orbs, yet calmed to an earthy sage when she taught him the mysteries of the earth magics.

She was fiercely passionate and uninhibited in the most innocent of ways, letting him know her feelings by slipping into his bed one night. He found her mesmerizing, and like any red-blooded male, he'd responded in kind. But when that moment of no return arrived, his heart had tugged hard on the reins.

He could never shake the feeling he was kissing someone else when he was kissing Tove. For whatever reason, she could not quench his thirst for the touch of another. So he refused to give into base desires. He wouldn't play games with her. The bond between them deserved better than that. So he'd told her he needed time.

Still, she slept in his bed, for which he endured many a torturous night thereafter, battling with conflicting desires, while the warmth of her body made him ache all the more for that brown-eyed beauty of his dreams.

"Sleep," she murmured, burrowing deep beneath the furs.

He tipped the covers back, kissing her on the forehead. "Can't, sweet imp. I need a walk."

He pulled on the fur-lined boots and coat she'd made for him from the wolverine's hide. Both were incredibly warm and beautifully stitched with swirling patterns of colored threads.

The air outside the cave was crisp and the moon hung in the twinkling sky like a giant paper lantern. Closing his eyes, he pushed his senses outward the way Tove had taught him. Not just through the earth but into every particle of the air where he could hear the hum of the stars, the breathing wind, even the stirring of life within the dormant seeds buried deep beneath the cover of snow.

When he opened his eyes, his heightened vision zeroed in on Grysla, where she sat, blending with the bare crooked trees. He crossed the expanse, silent as walking on wool. Hearing his footfall all the same, she turned her gnarled head and smiled.

Finn fell backwards into a snowdrift and stared up at the stars. "Guess the moon's keeping you awake too."

Her head tilted with those kind, wise eyes, telling him she knew better.

"Now don't go looking at me that way. I've been sipping that gloriously rank bog water like clockwork, so no worries there," he said, referring to the healing broths she'd made for him in an attempt to dispel the darkness. But the most her curatives could do was slow its spread.

Her eyes widened, encouraging him to tell her what was really bothering him.

"Really, I'm fine," he insisted. "And I'm sure I'll be fit as a fiddle after the runic ritual tomorrow night."

Grysla swept her hand to her heart, making the sign for sadness.

Sighing, he tucked his arms behind his head. "There's no hiding from you." He threw her a halfhearted grin.

The giant propped her great arms on her knees and leaned forward, ready to listen.

"I've been having disturbing dreams. Not the usual nightmares of death and mayhem, mind you. These…are different. They're the kind that fill you with absolute bliss but leave you heartbroken and confused."

A shooting star streaked across the black glittering sky.

He rose on one elbow. "I think the dreams are trying to show me what I haven't been able to remember. I'm more certain than ever that I left something behind—well, someone—very important."

Grysla's furrowed face softened as her gruff voice broke the silence of the frosty night. "The darkness in you is like water drowning your new memories." She made a wavy sign for flood. "In time, it will also flood over your oldest memories until you've forgotten who you are, and all that remains is the dark influence."

He sat up, his body rigid with dread. As much as the source of this darkness was a mystery to him, he knew Grysla spoke the truth. She had merely voiced his fears out loud.

"I shouldn't stay here any longer," he said after a time. "I'm a danger to you and Tove."

Grysla swept her massive hand in a circle, then pointed at Finn's heart. "There is hope, Shining One, but only if you heed your dreams by watching for the signs and following them."

He stared out at the windswept hills. "I will. But you have to promise me one thing. If the poison turns my soul, you'll—"

The tree troll stopped him with the sign for peaceful silence. She stared at him, her eyes sorrowful. Then she gave him a solemn nod, promising she would do what he asked.

A full moon illuminated a clear path through the snow as Finn, Tove and Grysla walked to a perfectly circular mound where nothing grew. The tree troll hummed a low melody as they spread out around the bottom. Finn and Tove joined in with their flutes. He'd carved the Elder race runes beside the Druidic inscriptions scored along the length of his alder flute.

As the rune notes marked the air, the wind song beckoned. Loose snow swirled at the top of the mound, thickening and churning upwards into a white cyclone that rose high into the ink-black sky. The rune notes pitched, lifting every snowflake until the bare earth revealed a carved spiral beginning at the bottom and ending at the top center of the mound.

When the wind song ended, the spiraling column plumed like a fountain, showering sheets of snow around the sides of the earthen rise.

Grysla sparked a fire at its center with a gruff word and a flick of her hand. Then she gestured to them to follow the spiral's path up to the fire. They did so, slowly and reverently.

Kneeling beside the fire, Tove held a stick in the flames until its sharp point glowed scarlet, steaming in the frosty air. Finn shed his coat, revealing his bare chest and the four red welts the wolverine had given him. Hesitating for the briefest of moments, Tove seared the purging rune into his flesh.

Scorching pain burned into Fate as if she was the one being branded. She woke, grabbing her chest, her heart thudding so hard she gasped for air. Glancing around to ensure she was in the cabin, her gaze went to the window, where the moon glowed over the forest hills like daylight. The same moon she'd seen in her dream.

It had seemed so real. Too real to ignore.

She flung the covers off and bundled up in her snowsuit.

Sithias poked his head up out of the covers from where he slept. "Where are you going, misss?"

"I dreamt of Finn," she said, marching to door. "He's at the troll mound."

Moonlight blanketed the milky hills with its cold brilliance, casting crooked tree shadows onto the sparkling snow. As she flew over the Twisted Bone Forest, Fate's heart skipped a beat when she saw a bright, flickering blaze in the distance.

As she drew nearer to the fire, she spotted Finn immediately. He was alive and well. Bewilderment obliterated her initial relief. What had kept him from returning to her? Surely he wouldn't have allowed her to go on thinking the worst for weeks. Uncertainty kept her from going straight to him. She slowed, seeing that he was with someone. She hovered, trying to make sense of the intimate exchange taking place.

Unaffected by the frigid temperature, Finn kneeled bare-chested in front of a sable-haired girl. Tove's name rose at the back of her polarized mind. She was stunning, a wild, beautiful daughter of nature. He had his hands on her shoulders, a look of intense passion on his face. Was she the reason he hadn't come back? Fate's chest burned with prickling heat. She suddenly realized she'd seen that look in his eyes before, but hadn't recognized it for what it was.

Tove salved the fresh burn on his chest, her fingers caressing tenderly. This obviously wasn't the first time she'd touched him that way. Fate wanted to look away, but she couldn't, her gaze trailed unwillingly over Finn's muscled torso to the symbols inked along his spine and down the length of his arms… those arms pulling Tove into his embrace.

The moment they kissed, Fate's heart imploded, becoming a black hole that sucked every last shred of happiness from her soul. She was in shock, unable to move, unable to feel anything but paralyzing grief.

But after a few minutes, raw fury burned through the pain. All this time she'd been freezing her ass off searching every inch of these mountains for him and always terrified he'd turn up dead. He'd been safe—with *her*.

Tangled, agonizing knots of rage and heartache doubled her over. Muffling a gut-wrenching sob in her glove, she shot straight up. After reaching a dizzying height, she tumbled downward, disoriented by the stars and snowy landscape blurring together. For a split second, she considered falling on the trees below. Being impaled would be less painful than this. But self-preservation kicked in before she hit the spiked trees.

Wiping away the tears, she glanced back at the fire, worried they might've noticed her chaotic plunge. She didn't want any delays. Not when she planned to get back and move into the next fable without Finn. Yet she lingered, staring at the excruciating scene as if maybe she might wake from this nightmare.

As she turned to leave, she noticed movement in the mound's shadow. Someone was crouched behind a snowdrift. She knew it was Leif when she saw him aim his crossbow, not at Finn and Tove, but at the tree troll, sitting unnoticed amongst the crooked trees near the base of the mound.

Fate knew she had to intervene. Otherwise, that stubborn blockhead would ruin the end of the fable for her. She swooped down, intending to knock the crossbow from his grip, but pulled back when Tove twisted round in Leif's direction. Fate held still, seeing that Finn was scanning the sky as if he knew she was there. Then Tove tugged on his arm, pointing at the snowdrift Leif hid behind.

The next few seconds slowed into brilliant clarity as Finn ran down the mound with shocking speed, his face a mask of rage. His movements were catlike as he sprang at Leif. In reaction, the hunter unleashed his arrow. Fate plunged across space, ramming into Finn, the arrow whistling past their heads.

Before she could dart away, he grabbed hold of her. They rolled down the slope in a tangle of limbs, their tumble ending at the bottom of the mound. When she found herself lying on top of him, she scrambled off. Finn stayed still, staring at her, first with a look of surprise and then a frown of confusion.

She staggered backward as he rose to his feet, his eyes burning with unnatural hues of shifting green. Tears stung her eyes. He had changed in ways that scared her.

His steps were slow and deliberate. "Who are you?"

Unable to believe her ears, Fate wiped her eyes dry with her sleeve and glared at him.

"She's a Norn, that one, and no good!" Leif bellowed.

Finn's eyes went black. He turned, lunging at the big man, knocking him on his back, punching his face hard and fast. Leif went limp. Grabbing his crossbow and sword, Finn tossed them so far they were lost in the deep drifts.

Tove circled round the bleeding troll hunter, her eyes dark and dangerous.

Fate edged further back, stopping when the ground shook under her feet. Grysla had closed the space between them in one step. The gnarled giant was of such intimidating size and staring so intently, Fate wanted to bolt. But memories of the Green Man's crushing grip kept her glued in place. The odds were too good she'd be snatched out of the air.

Finn's expression softened as he strode toward her. "Thank you for what you did."

She stood rigid, casting her gaze downward. "You're welcome." She turned to go.

Catching her by the wrist, he pulled her a few inches closer, pushing her fur-lined hood off her head. As his eyes traveled over her face, they turned a bright fervid green. "Do I know you?" he whispered breathlessly. "There's something… remarkably familiar about you."

She was about to answer when Tove stepped next to him, a possessive hand over his bare chest and a threatening look in her eyes.

Yanking her wrist free of his grip, Fate shook her head. "No, I don't know *you*." He started to speak but she cut him off. "Can I go now?" she said, nudging her chin at the tree troll looming over her.

The moment he nodded, she launched into the night sky, certain she must have imagined the flash of panic in his eyes when she left.

Sithias slithered over to where Fate slept, her lids squeezed tight, her features convulsed in a frown of misery. He could only guess at the horrible dreams tormenting her. He knew it had everything to do with whatever had taken place last night. She'd returned absolutely grief-stricken, too spent and devastated to do anything but crawl under the blankets and murmur that she'd found Finn alive. Unwilling to tell him more than that, she'd collapsed into a fitful sleep.

Setting down a mug of chicken soup next to her bed, he tapped gently on her shoulder. "Misss, you need to eat, ressstore your ssstrength."

She jolted awake, wild-eyed and disoriented. *"Finn,"*

she croaked.

"There, there. It's jussst me."

As soon as she looked at him, tears streamed down her face. "Oh, Sithias, he's completely changed," she said, crying into her hands.

Dying to know what she meant by that, he handed her a tissue and waited patiently as she sat up and blew her nose. He put the mug in her hands before she could start crying again. "Eat up. There'sss not much that chicken sssoup isssn't able to fix."

She seemed ready to take a sip from the spoon when her eyes took on a haunted look. "His body's all tattooed with weird markings. Doesn't he know that's so mainstream now? And his eyes. They changed colors. Grysla's and Tove's eyes did that dark to glowy thing too. It was like being in some cheesy vampire movie."

Curious as to what a cheesy vampire movie entailed, the snake wanted to ask but thought better of it and nudged the spoon closer to her lips. "Why didn't he come back with you, misss?"

She set the mug down, her shoulders drooping.

Glancing at the untouched soup, he sighed in defeat as her brown eyes overflowed with tears.

"He's in love with Tove, and he doesn't remember me at all." Her face crumpled as a deep, gasping sob tore from her chest.

Saddened by her pain, Sithias dabbed a few tears from his own eyes. Knowing there was nothing he could do to take her sorrow away, he sat silently by her side, stroking her hair with the tip of his tail.

Fate stared at the pages of the *Book of Fables*. The inked words of the fable stared back, declaring a new ending at last.

Finn had brought about peace between Leif, Tove and Grysla by acting as intermediary between the three. She could now move onto the next fable. Except that every time she thought about leaving him behind, another piece of her shattered heart chipped away. She turned to Sithias. "Maybe we should wait just a little longer."

The snake crossed the room, dragging his large pile of plays he'd bound together with twine. "Now, now, misss. We can't ssstay in this missserable wasssteland forever. It'sss been ten daysss sssince you last sssaw him, and four sssince the fable changed into a wonderfully sssublime end."

He was right. She needed to accept that Finn was content with his new life. She had to stop hoping he'd suddenly remember who she was and come running back. Even if his memory did return, what made her think he'd want anything to do with her anyhow? Was she forgetting he hated her before the poisoning?

The time had come to move on.

She put her attention on the illustration of a winged, serpentine dragon entwined around the letter I. "Did you model for that?"

Sithias gave her an indulgent, yet mildly annoyed smile. "Of coursse not. I'm much more handsssome," he said, coiling his tail round her waist. "Now, read on."

Her heart screamed no. "It's for the best," she whispered to herself. Taking a deep breath, she opened her mouth to speak the first word out loud when a sudden rumbling stopped her.

As another quake shook the cabin, hope filled the crater in her chest. She ran to the window. Grysla's large form crested the hill with Finn on one gnarled shoulder and Tove on the other. "He's here!" she said. Grabbing her coat, she slipped into her boots and ran out the door.

Finn jumped down, landing in front of her. He seemed

nervous, unable to meet her eye. "I…uh…" He glanced back at the giant, who nudged her chin with encouragement, though Tove kept a cold, distant gaze on the horizon. "Could I have a moment with you inside?" he asked.

"A moment?" Fate's hopes sank. "Sure."

When they entered the cabin, he took one look at Sithias with undiluted loathing. "I hate snakes," he said.

"Oh not *thisss* again," Sithias said, slithering off to the bathroom.

"It's okay. He's a friend, believe it or not," she explained.

"Sorry, the snake threw me off." He shifted from one foot to the other. "There's something I need to say to you."

Whatever it was, he looked uncomfortable enough to make her think she'd better brace for the worst. "Okay."

He stared at the floor. "I know this is going to sound like I'm a full-on nutter, but I haven't been able to get those bonnie browns of yours out of my head." He raised his gaze, a faint smile touching his lips when he saw her obvious surprise. "I don't know how or why, but I know you're important to me in some way." Relief smoothed his brow. "There, I said it. I've been working up the nerve for days."

"Oh." She was in shock. "I guess we should talk," she said at last. "My name's Fate, by the way."

"I'm Finn."

She smiled. "I know. Sorry I lied when you first asked me if we knew each other."

"Why did you?"

Heat rushed to her cheeks. "I was upset when you didn't remember me."

He looked apologetic, but kept silent.

They sat by the fire while she explained how they'd been traveling through the fables together after meeting at the bookstore, why a snake was with them, and how Sabirah had poisoned him. By that time, Sithias had come out of hiding.

She could tell he was waiting for her to drop the bomb by letting Finn know he wasn't real. But she didn't. She shouldn't have told him before. She wasn't going to make that mistake again.

"We were just about to move onto the next fable." She forced down any thought of him joining her and stood up. "So I guess you'll be wanting to get back to Tove and Grysla."

Finn shadowed her as she strode over to the *Book of Fables*. Catching her by the hand, he said, "No, I'll be going with you, Fate."

She searched his face. "Are you sure?" She sensed resistance, but he nodded all the same.

"Aye, I'm sure. I'll just go say my goodbyes."

She moved to the window after he walked outside.

Sithias joined her, where she stood in the shadows. "Isss it really wissse to watch thisss?"

"I have to," she said, squeezing her fists tight as the scene unfolded.

Tove leaned close to Finn, staring into his eyes like someone who knew his very soul. Whispering something in his ear, she traced her finger over the runes on his temple. He looked thoroughly entranced.

As the moment dragged on forever, Fate felt every torturous second.

Then Tove drew back ever so slightly. Her face was but a hair's width from Finn's, until her lips brushed his for the briefest second before pulling away entirely.

Fate stopped breathing when she saw him go rigid with a grief-stricken expression. Guilt gnawed at her. Was it wrong to want to take him away if leaving left him heartbroken?

Tove stood stone-still and majestic as she whistled two eerie notes. The wind obeyed with sudden force, streaking her dark hair against the crisp blue sky. Fate had never seen anything more arresting than this otherworldly girl whose eyes blazed with a fierce yet tender love.

An awful feeling of inferiority filled her constricted chest. Tove was everything she was not. Strong, confident, gorgeous and mysterious. Plainly she and Finn shared something profound, something Fate feared she would never have with him.

The swirling snow thickened around Tove, engulfing her. Then the flurry swept into the hills with astounding speed, taking her in its wake.

Finn looked lost without her.

The tree troll leaned down toward him. He looked up at Grysla, his stricken gaze so severe Fate worried he would decide to stay after all. They signed to each other, a silent yet deeply connected exchange. At last Grysla made a farewell gesture. There was sadness in her affectionate smile. The giant strode away, her heavy steps shaking the ground until her lumbering form dipped below the hills and vanished from sight.

"I can't do this," Fate said as she hurried over to the *Book of Fables*. Why had she tortured herself with watching their goodbye? Seeing Finn so lovestruck would forever torment her. Any musings she'd had of a future with him were gone now. He belonged here with Tove.

Sithias slid up next to her. "What can't you do?"

"Take him with us," she said, fixing her gaze on the next fable. Her heart was hammering so hard her legs wobbled beneath her. Grabbing hold of the snake for support, she forced back the little voice in her head urging her to stop and think before she acted.

"Misss, you're being rash," Sithias chimed in with the voice of warning. "Don't do sssomething you'll regret."

Frigid air blew into the cabin as Finn entered. She kept her eyes on the page. If she looked at him, she'd weaken and change her mind.

“Fate?” he said, the sound of his footsteps quickening across the room.

Squaring her shoulders, she choked out the first word of the fable. The magnetic pull of the story as it burst into being was instantaneous, and so very merciful in the way it emptied her mind of the misery she felt at leaving Finn behind.

The Dragon Empress

In the dim beginning of history there were unspeakable matings between humans and creatures of magic, which brought forbidden lives into the world. These abominations hid themselves and, more oft than not, bore disturbing evils in their tainted blood. They were to be feared if ever one was unfortunate enough to trespass into their domain, yet trespass is precisely where this story begins.

King Balor was the first to encounter such a race. After his victory in the North Endlund country, he chose to cross the River Torle and cut through Mount Fargrum in his haste to return home to Asgar. It was whispered there was a hidden place within these mountains, where women bore the offspring of dragons, where a race unlike any other ruled with the cold, reptilian minds of serpents.

King Balor dismissed this rumor as myth and forged ahead into uncharted territory. When his army reached what should have been an impassable ravine, there was instead a mysterious stone bridge, which crossed over into a road cut deep within the mountain. While passing through darkness, the soldiers spoke fearfully of dragon-born savages, yet when they emerged once again into the light, they were surprised to find a valley, where the land flourished beneath the long shadow of a resplendent castle.

The gates opened to them with an invitation to attend a grand feast. When Empress Moria stepped onto her balcony to welcome her guests, this fierce beauty whose eyes burned with a ruby flame transfixed King Balor.

He married Empress Moria at once and delivered her to Asgar. When they reached the outskirts of his kingdom, she dropped acorns of a cursed oak onto the soil. The seeds took root unnaturally fast and grew into a widespread belt of virulent oaks, which snagged unfortunates who were left to rot in their branches as hideous warnings to turn back. Having sown these hateful seeds of enchantment, no one would enter or leave Asgar from that time on.

Moria continued to unravel the kingdom's strength. Her unholy union with the king produced a son, Tynan, born with the same pale, dark beauty and entrancing eyes as his mother. The empress kept her son jealously close while the besotted king relinquished his rule to her authority little by little. She groomed her son in the art of war and molded him into the perfect heir prince. His strengths became that of a warrior with the heart of a diplomat. Tynan was a gift she gave to Balor and his people, a gift she would one day take back.

The kingdom fell into ruin and decay over the years, but Asgar's subjects perceived only prosperity, where they believed no one grew sick or died. They were bound within Moria's spell and did not see the crumbling castle or what ghastly fare filled their pantries and dinner tables. Splendor and bountiful harvests were all they could see. Moria's web of illusion was truly powerful…to all but one.

The king's counselor, the old Druidh priest, O'Deldar, had intimate knowledge of those born of unclean blood, for unclean blood ran through his veins as well. It was this very sameness that spurred him to use his powerful magic to see through Moria's spell. When he saw the horrors beneath her illusion, he made plans to liberate Asgar and hid them well from her. Now after seventeen years, the time was ripe to harvest the seeds he had sown from the day of her arrival.

During the Beltane festival, the horns of Asgar sounded a warning of intruders. The glint of spears bristled along the rampart walls as the royal guard fell in line to watch a fleet of ships cutting through the water. Tynan raised his spyglass. The lead ship's banner bore a gray falcon, and a young woman stood on the vessel's bow. Moria snatched it from him. When she saw what sped toward her, she shattered the spyglass and vowed to make the interlopers pay for their trespass with their lives.

O'Deldar greeted the fleet and announced to the furious queen that Princess Kaura of the Eldunough Islands had come to honor her betrothal to King Balor's first son. No one knew, not even Kaura, that she was the priest's very own daughter. When she stepped off the gangplank, the sun touched her hair with a red gold flame. Everyone stared in awe at this fair, mystical vision robed in a silvery cloak with eyes as gray as forest pools. Tynan lost his heart to her the moment they met. As well, Kaura felt the same deep love for him.

During the festival, the people of Asgar warmed to the princess as flowers will turn toward the sun, leaving Moria to wither in her shadow. Later when the sun sank into the dark ocean and flames blazed high upon the great bonfire, Tynan announced to the people he would marry Kaura the very next day.

Moria flew into a rage. The time had come to awaken her son's ancient bloodline. Taking a shard of her Serpen ancestor's dragon scale, she broke it and kept one half. The other, she slipped under Tynan's skin while he slept. Then she stayed in his bedchamber, waiting for the inevitable change to take place.

In the early morning a black dragon burst from the tower walls and flew away with Tynan's spirit slumbering deep inside. Moria used her half of the shard to see through the dragon's eyes and sent the beast to Kaura's fleet. The attack was swift and brutal. The dragon's venomous fire engulfed the ships and left no survivors.

When she took the dragon on a killing rampage throughout the surrounding townships of Asgar, picking off children, the feeble and the elderly, O'Deldar rushed to rouse the latent power inside his daughter. It awoke with a terrible suddenness, and Kaura's fragile form violently gave way to that of a giant falcon. The bird of prey launched into the sky and began the hunt for her mortal enemy. The falcon dove at the dragon's neck. The serpent reared his horned head and roared as talons ripped through hard scales, cutting deep to the bone.

The near-mortal blow woke Tynan. The dragon twisted, sweeping his spiked tail at the falcon's heart. Tynan felt Kaura's pain like it was his own and knew her dismay when she sensed she was battling her true love. The falcon released her grip as blood stained her soft breast.

But Moria's bloodlust was unquenchable. She wanted a battle to the death. The beasts circled each other, the falcon spreading her colossal wings and the dragon bearing his poisonous fangs while the trapped spirits of the two lovers cried out for each other. The dragon lunged and sank his fangs into the falcon's neck. Helpless to save her, Tynan wept as Kaura's life faded.

The bird fell to the ground. The battle was over, leaving Moria triumphant but overly confident, because there was still a spark of life in the falcon. Rising one last time, she raked her talons through the serpent's soft underbelly.

The dragon's dying roar could be heard from the lowest valley of Asgar to the highest peaks of Mount Fargrum. Moria never wept for her son. His birth and death had served her purpose. The Dragon Empress could return to her home at last. She had ruined the king who had trespassed into the hidden lands of her people. Moria left the people of Asgar to wake from her spell into an unimaginable nightmare, with a broken king and no heir to rebuild the kingdom.

As for O'Deldar, he had sacrificed everything to save his king, but if a king does not wish to be saved, then even a wise old counselor is obliged to leave. Where he went, no one truly knows. Some say he left on the back of a giant falcon, while others say he vanished in a mist that rolled in from the sea. Whether it was by way of bird or magic, O'Deldar was never seen again.

♠

CHAPTER 18

FATE'S RAGE TANGLED TOGETHER with Moria's. She could relate to her feelings of trespass. But even though Tove was the interloper in her own personal story, Finn's betrayal hurt the most. She'd thought his heart belonged solely to her. After all, wasn't there a "Made by Fate" tag stitched to it?

The last images of the fable burst into a cloud of letters. As they swirled back onto the pages, becoming mere words on paper, O'Deldar's name sparked bright at the base of her brain, fading slowly like a flashbulb's afterimage.

Struggling through layers of dizziness, she began to awaken to her new surroundings. The sounds of birds pierced the fog in her head. Just as she turned away from the book to see where she was, something knocked her to the ground. Winded and disoriented, she stared up at a sky filled with circling vultures and a host of screeching ravens and seagulls skimming the outlying treetops.

Before she could grasp what had happened, beady eyes lost within a fleshy face crowded in on her, blocking her view. "What have we here?" the man rasped. "Not just a magical book worth a king's ransom, but a soft young wench too." His fetid breath made her gag as he raked a rough hand over her cheekbone and down her neck.

Suddenly, he went hurtling sideways. She sat up, seeing that someone had tackled him to the ground. It was Finn!

"Leave her be!" he growled. Leaping to his feet, he grabbed the man by the collar, punching his face with unbridled rage.

Fate stared at him in shock. Was he really here or was

she imagining him? As blood sprayed from the man's mouth, she cringed, accepting his startling presence as real. Unsure about how she felt about that, she stood and started over to him, stopping when three other men pulled him backwards, each pummeling him from all sides.

Afraid for him, she cried out. But her fear was unwarranted. Finn's returning blow sent one of the plunderers flying into a thick tree trunk.

All of a sudden, the tree's branches snaked down around the man, lifting him into its sprawling canopy. Fate staggered back in disbelief, unable to look away as the tree slowly and cruelly impaled him with hundreds of writhing branches.

Stifling a scream, she absorbed the full horror of her surroundings. Stretching as far as the eye could see to either side, stood a dense belt of giant oaks. The rising sun glared at their backs, casting their twisted limbs in stark contrast. But it wasn't the trees themselves that gripped her with terror—it was the countless number of rotting corpses dangling like torn rag dolls from their branches. A veritable banquet for the droves of winged scavengers swarming over the carcasses, pulling strings of meat off bones, picking at empty eye sockets.

The wind changed, wafting the sickening stench of death over her. She dropped to her knees, retching.

Hearing muffled screams at her back, she turned to see Sithias coiled round the fat man's head and shoulders. The snake hauled him kicking and thrashing high into the air. Holding his position for a moment, he flapped in place above the trees as if he might save the man from an awful demise. But he let go, allowing him to fall into the grappling oaks, where countless branches skewered him alive.

Shrinking from the sight, she turned the moment Finn plowed both fists into the chest of one of the attackers, sending him hurtling through the air. He slammed into another oak, back cracking and a look of paralyzed fright on his grizzled face as a branch pierced his chest, hoisting him into the ghastly graveyard in the sky.

When Finn turned to the last surviving raider with a murderous glint in his black eyes and lips stretched in disgust, the man dropped to his knees, holding his hands in surrender. "P-please sir, s-spare me!"

In a seeming blur, he was next to the marauder, hauling him to his feet, shoving him toward the oaks. "Would you have spared any of *us*, had the tables been turned?"

The man's heels left trenches in the dirt. "*Yes!* We're robbers, n-not killers!"

Finn's voice lowered into a snarl. "And what of the young maiden? She would've been safe with her virtue intact?"

"I-I—yes, of *course!*"

He slammed him up against the tree. The sweaty man quaked, rolling his eyes upward. The oak's gnarled branches twisted toward them, suddenly repelling when they came close to Finn.

Sithias landed next to Fate. "Did you sssee that?"

She nodded in astonishment. While she was grateful for being saved from those awful men, Finn's unforgiving rage, coupled with such astounding strength and speed, was frightening. She knew he'd changed, but not to the core.

"Finn, let him go! There's been enough killing!" she yelled, running toward him.

He held still, glancing over his shoulder at her.

She saw his face twist with fear as a branch lashed out at her. Without seeing him move, he somehow closed the space between them, grabbing her so hard by the waist the air squeezed out of her lungs. As she struggled to breathe, pain sliced across her arm. Looking down at the laceration, the branch made another grab for her as Finn carried her away.

The limb twisted inward, catching the surprised thief who was too slow making his escape, it raised him into the canopy to join his fellow conspirators.

His tormented cries echoed out over the forest.

Shaking as he set her down, Fate covered her ears.

After what seemed like endless screaming, Finn forced her trembling hands down from her head. She resisted, wanting to hide from it all.

Nudging her chin to look at him, he stared at her, his eyes now a peaceful green, but questioning. "I sense you're angry with me, even scared."

Fate turned her gaze to the ground. "You've changed so much. I'm not used to it." She glanced up. "And the way you went after those men."

His brow creased into a scowl. "They were going to throw me to the oaks—Sithias too, had they been able to catch either of us." The green of his eyes vanished to black. "And they would've done despicable things to *you*."

Sithias slithered up next to them. "He'sss right, misss. We had to defend ourselvesss."

Fate glared at the snake. "Defend, yes, but you dropped that man into the trees like chum to sharks. He didn't stand a chance."

Sithias sagged. "I know. I wasss *cold-blooded*…well, I am cold-blooded, but—"

"And you," Fate said, turning her heated gaze on Finn. "You were so…*vicious*. You were out to kill."

He looked surprised. "I don't know what I was like when we were together before, but I clearly understand the relationship between predator and prey, and those men were killers. I swore never to be a victim again after Tove taught me to fight, hunt *and* kill if necessary."

"So, you're saying she taught you to be a brutal predator?"

"Listen, when we've got a moment, I'll tell you the miraculous things that happened while we were apart. Maybe that'll help you come to terms with it all."

"*Yah*, that's it, I want to hear all about you and Tove." She stormed off in the opposite direction, still ranting, "I'd rather have all the hair on my head tweezed out one at a time, thank you very much."

Sithias caught up with her, his expression uncomfortable. "I suggessst we get oursssselvesss to Asssgar—"

"By the way, how'd he get here?" she fumed under her breath. "You did this, didn't you?"

Dropping his head low, he glanced at her guiltily. "I lassoed him secondsss before you ssstarted reading."

"Why?"

"Becaussse you would've been missserable without him."

She eyed Finn, where she'd left him standing several yards away, his expression bewildered. "If you haven't noticed, I'm miserable *with* him," she whispered.

His wings flopped in a shrug. "Sssuch is the curssse of love."

Pulling her notepad from the pocket of her parka, she muttered, "You are *so* in trouble."

In the blink of an eye, they arrived on a grassy hill overlooking a rolling lush valley that swept to the edge of the sea, where a pale castle gleamed in the summer sun's early morning light. The regal citadel was heavily fortified on three sides by a wide moat and sheer cliffs protecting its back. Colorful pennants fluttered along the turrets and garlands of flowers lined the gates, denoting the Beltane festival. As did the numbers of happy, brightly dressed people flowing through the castle gates on wagons filled with food and wares.

Sithias stared at the splendor with a puzzled expression.

"It doesn't appear asss though the citizenry hasss been pauperized. All those wagonsss are carrying rather generousss suppliesss."

Finn closed his eyes. "There's powerful magic at work here. Moria's illusion extends to the borders of Asgar." His expression turned grim, his eyes darkening as he stared at the castle. "I can't see through her veil, but if I probe deep enough I can feel the undercurrent of hatred and even smell a tinge of rot and decay."

Uncomfortable knots of uncertainty pulled tight in Fate's stomach. He'd been sensitive before, but not this strongly. He was so different now. She could handle the new spidey senses and super powers easily enough. It was the ruthlessness that scared her the most. The Finn she'd created had valued life above all else. What had Tove done to him?

She glanced back, catching him looking at her, his gaze probing. Kicking at the grass with the tip of her boot, she glanced downward, hiding her face behind her hair.

"At the moment, I could care lesss," Sithias said. "I'm sssimply grateful for warmer weather. And what perfect timing—we're here for the Beltane fessstival. If we presssent ourssselves asss traveling performersss, we'll fit right in."

"I like it," Fate said, stepping over to where Sithias smiled up at the sun. His grin was infectious and the heat of the sun and lush meadowland was definitely uplifting after enduring the freezer box they'd spent the last month in. "Only I don't think you'd fit in even if this was a festival for snakes." She pointed at his wings.

Sithias slumped. "You could be right. Oh, why did Elsssina have to get ssso wing-happy?"

Jotting down a few words in her notepad, she whispered them aloud. Within seconds a glamour necklace appeared in her hand. She dangled it in front of him proudly. "Try this. If my writing skills are worth the money they pay me, it should work. But if it doesn't, we'll have to stick you in a cage and charge tickets to gawkers who want to see the freaky bird snake."

He looked revolted. "If I'm going to be put on disssplay, I prefer *sssnake* bird. The wingsss are more of a decorative feature, though gratifyingly utilitarian."

"Agreed," she said as Sithias dipped his head through the necklace.

Just when she thought the glamour might be a dud, Sithias transformed into a freakishly tall, skinny young man with bone-pale skin, long flaxen hair and a goatee that curled into a point. He wore a linen toga over a white body suit with a golden circlet of leaves crowning his head and a harp hanging at his side. Though his eyes remained amber and he'd kept his wings.

She cupped a hand over her mouth to keep from laughing. He couldn't control his new body and moved like a marionette puppet, tilting to and fro with long limbs flipping off in all directions. "Sithias! You're human! And you look...*interesting*."

He puffed out his chest. "A ssstoryteller mussst look the part." He looked almost dignified until he twisted his ankle, nearly toppling over.

"Any reason you kept the wings?"

"All part of the ensssemble." His proud expression went blank, like he'd forgotten something. Putting his back to her, he peeked under his toga. "*Oh my...*" he said, "I have gentleman vegetablesss!"

Finn stepped up next to him. "Having the twig and berries doesn't make you any more human. You're still a snake under it all." He shoved his shoulder into Sithias, nearly knocking him off his wobbly legs. "But you're timing's good, mate. It appears we have company."

Some of the people traveling to the castle were veering off their path to get a closer look at the giant book and winged man. With no time to address Finn's rudeness toward Sithias, Fate wrote hastily. By the time the curious onlookers climbed the hill, she had the *Book of Fables* tucked inside a mule-drawn caravan with carved giant storybooks on each side.

Sithias became the center of attention, waxing poetic and reciting a short story.

Finn drew up behind her, saying, "We should also change our clothes to suit the occasion."

The heat of his breath against her ear sent a tingling ripple up her spine. Resenting the ease in which he hijacked her feelings, she hurried round to the other side of the caravan to clear her head and conjure something suitably medieval.

Having shed his furry, arctic weather wear, Finn was down to his boxers when she looked up from her notepad. A plume of heat swept up her neck, burning her face. Embarrassed she'd been caught staring at his muscled chest, she shifted her gaze to the sky, remembering the agony of watching Tove salve his burn. The rune she'd branded him with was now a smooth scar over four disturbing welts. She longed to ask why he looked like a tiger had used him as a scratching post but felt far too estranged to do so.

Shrugging, he bent to pick up the clothes she tossed at his feet. "Sorry, I was positively sweltering, and modesty wasn't an issue with Tove and Grysla."

Anger flared in her chest. "Like I care." Putting her back to him, she climbed into the caravan to change.

Ten minutes later and a little less edgy, she emerged from the caravan dressed in a simple blue tunic dress over a cream-colored linen chemise.

He was waiting for her just outside the steps, grinning and holding out his arms to show he was dressed. "Does this please m'lady?"

She hovered within the door, her eyes sweeping over him with restraint. She'd supplied him with a linen Jacobite shirt under a brown leather tunic and tweed woolen breeches, tucked into tall leather boots. Everything fit him perfectly and, yes, he looked *more* than pleasing. Next time, she'd give him a jester's costume.

"It'll do," she said coolly, and stepped down.

He gathered up his arctic wear. "I'll just put these inside. Wouldn't want to lose them."

Her gaze darted to the fur bundle. "Souvenirs from the Twisted Bone Forest? A fridge magnet might've sufficed."

"A precious gift is what it is," he said, his voice tight as he traced a finger over the artful stitching.

Unable to bear the painful look of regret on his face, she hurried to join Sithias.

"We have an audience already," Sithias said as the crowd dispersed. "And I've been told we should get down there possst hassste before all the good spotsss are gone. Asss I'm sure you know, location isss everything."

They climbed into the driver's seat. Fate made sure Sithias sat in the middle between them. Finn didn't seem bothered; he simply directed the mules past the palisades enclosing the jousting fields and archery stations, over the drawbridge and through the castle gates.

The outer bailey overflowed with people milling about, pitching food and shop pavilions, and theatre platforms. The crowds parted as they moved deeper into the bustling enclosure, while a host of court jesters and minstrels on stilts paraded past—some juggling balls, others playing flutes or singing. Everywhere, young women adorned with flowers weaved through the crowds, casting flirtatious glances at their handsome young pursuers. The very air seemed to buzz with excitement and merriment, building with anticipation of the day's special events.

They passed by a group of men raising a tall tree stripped of its branches, except for the very top foliage. Garlands of flowers wrapped its slender trunk and long silken ribbons dangled from the top ring of greenery.

Sithias flung his long skinny arm out and pointed. "Ah, look, the Maytree."

Grinning, Finn elbowed him with a roguish wink. "Where the lusty passions of the day begin and build to a fever's pitch, only to cool when the bonfire's embers die in the wee hours of the morn."

"Yesss indeed, *ssspring fever*, when wantonnesss runsss amuck," Sithias said in a conspiratorial tone.

Fate watched this unexpected display of male comradery with total confusion. "What are you two going on about?"

They both looked at her and laughed.

"What?" she said, feeling like the butt of a joke.

Finn pulled the reins and leaned forward to see past Sithias. "Beltane's a celebration of the fertility of *all* living things, not just what is green and growing from the earth. Nine months from now, there'll be a baby boom in the kingdom." He raised an eyebrow, watching to see if she understood.

As she realized his meaning, she blushed. "Oh."

Sithias smiled at her. "No need to be embarrasssed." He turned, whispering to Finn. "Her mind doesssn't run in sssuch directionsss. After all, she'sss never even been *kisssed*."

"*Sithias*..." she said, feeling her face flare with even greater warmth.

Finn's expression softened into thoughtful surprise.

"Oh, I'm sssorry, misss," Sithias said, though she doubted his sincerity. He stood up, perusing where they'd stopped the caravan. "Ah yesss, I think thisss will do rather nicely." He clamored past Fate with elbows and knees coming close to knocking her from the seat, stumbled down the steps and landed in a tangled heap.

She jumped down beside him and helped him up. His humble smile and quivering wings effectively cooled her ire.

Smiling, she shook her head. "I hate to say it, but you suck at being human."

He straightened as best he could, though he still teetered like a drunken sailor. "I sssimply need a little practice," he said, and plucked a string of discordant notes on his harp as if this made him more appealing.

She grimaced. "Being human isn't the only thing you need to practice."

He pulled a pout—easy to do now that he had lips. "I assure you, I have alwaysss been musssically inclined. But what I'd really like isss to sssee what I *look* like. I'm positively burssssting. Would you be ssso kind asss to conjure up a mirror for me?"

Fate did as he asked.

He stood riveted in front of the full-length mirror, striking one ungainly pose after another. Pushing his lips down, he drew his brows up into a pitiful crease. Then he clapped. "That'sss sadnesss! Did you sssee it?" He then continued to make faces for other emotions.

Finn walked over to her. "There's no telling how long he'll be admiring himself, so how about we take a look around and get a lay of the land?"

Her heart gave a little flutter of excitement at his nearness, urging her to take another step to close the gap between them. But she couldn't. She didn't know him anymore. And even if she did, Tove was there standing in her way. "Uh, yeah. But we should probably split up. We can cover more ground that way."

He swallowed, confusion flickering in his eyes. "How will we know if one of us runs into trouble? I think we're best to stick together."

"You have a point," she admitted reluctantly. She didn't want it to be just the two of them though. Strolling side by side with Finn through a festival charged with sexual energy was a form of torture she'd really rather avoid.

"Come on, Sithias, let's go," she said, turning in his direction. When he didn't answer she walked over, frowning when he wouldn't budge his gaze from the mirror.

"You two run along, I will be quite fine," he said, exaggerating the movements of his mouth.

She continued scowling, hoping he'd cave in and tear himself away. No such luck. Forced to give up the silent power struggle, she turned away. As she did so, Sithias gave her a wink of encouragement. Narrowing her eyes, she looked again but he'd returned to making faces as if there'd been no interruption.

"You are *so* not getting any honeyed ham tonight," she fumed, her voice low.

Putting her back to him, she joined Finn and headed into the thick crowd.

CHAPTER 19

MUSIC AND LAUGHTER COULD BE HEARD at every turn as Finn led the way through the bustling throng. He soaked up the energy of the crowd's high spirits, allowing their good cheer to ease the persistent ache in his chest. Leaving Tove and Grysla had been the hardest thing he'd ever done. And as much as he welcomed the sultry summer heat, he already missed the striking beauty of the Twisted Bone Forest. If he hadn't recognized Fate as the girl from his dreams and known without a doubt he was meant to be with her, he would've been content to stay in those mountains for the rest of his life.

But there was no denying the feelings Fate stirred in him. Around her, his blood pumped hard. Every inch of him came alive when she looked his way. He may not know her beyond the dreams he'd had and what she'd told him of their brief past together, but she was as familiar to him as if she'd been imprinted on his soul. All he had to do was get her to realize the undeniable connection they had with each other. For the life of him, he couldn't understand why she was keeping her distance. Her fiery temperament was proving to be a challenge and a compelling one at that.

Biting back a smile, he glanced over his shoulder at her. Seeing she'd lagged behind, he backtracked, caught her by the hand and pulled her toward the center where the Maytree pierced the turquoise sky. The perfect place to begin getting to know each other.

He picked up two ribbons, placing one of the silken strands in her hand. "Later today, when the sun is at its highest, the young bucks and maidens will gather in equal numbers to dance around the tree. The music will play and they'll entwine the ribbons around the pole as they circle one way and then the other. This entwining symbolizes the lovers joining together. In ancient times—*these times*—this dance is as sacred as marriage."

She blushed, glancing everywhere else except at him. "I, uh…I hope you're not trying to get me to dance around this tree with you," she said. "I'm pretty much all feet."

"I just wanted you to know this is a reverent ceremony, not something lowly like you might have thought from our joking earlier," he said, worried she was thinking his intentions were less than honorable.

Dropping the ribbon, she kept her gaze downcast, her thick lashes veiling her uneasiness. Or was it disappointment? She was completely guileless and unpracticed in the art of hiding her emotions, yet he had a hell of a time pinpointing exactly what she was feeling at any given moment. One second she was all fire, the next ice.

Why was she so on edge? He started to broach the subject, when the garrison horns blared loudly. The festivities came to an abrupt halt as heads turned to watch the royal guard rushing to the sea wall.

"That must be Kaura's fleet," he whispered, turning his gaze back to her.

Fate was gone. Glancing around in a panic, he saw her moving through the still crowd. He pushed past those in his way, excusing himself, while keeping his eyes trained on her. When he caught up with her, he grabbed her arm. "Where are you going?"

"O'Deldar..." she muttered, straining against his grasp. The blank look on her face unsettled him.

"You mean, the king's counselor?" he asked, loosening his

grip. He waved a hand in front of her eyes. She stared straight through him like he was invisible. He wasn't sure what was going on but one thing was for sure, she'd checked out. All the turmoil she'd been radiating just moments before was gone. Some force or influence had taken over.

Before he could find out more, Fate wriggled free and ran through an archway leading into the castle's inner bailey. All he could think to do was shadow her closely and keep her safe until he figured out how to deal with whatever had taken control.

Pausing long enough to look for guards posted inside, she raced across the open quadrangle, through a stately garden past a pond inhabited by two black swans. Finn hid beside her under the shade of a tree near the main gatehouse, following when she darted along the wall and dipped into a dark corridor leading to a turnpike staircase within a turret. When they reached the top step, she froze in front of him.

Pressing his back to the curved wall, he peeked up around to see what had stopped her. Ten guards stood on the rampart with their backs to them, all focused on the fleet filling the ocean's horizon. Standing at the front was a regal, dark-haired woman clothed in finery befitting a queen. A young guy stood next to her, holding a spyglass.

These two royal figures could only be Empress Moria and Prince Tynan.

Finn's muscles coiled with tension. Knowing how Moria dealt with trespassers, they'd be killed on the spot if discovered.

The sound of breaking glass jarred his nerves. No doubt it was Moria smashing her spyglass. The guards would be dispersing any second. He had to get Fate out of there.

Clasping his hand over her mouth and gripping her by the waist, he carried her kicking and squirming to the bottom of the spiraled steps. When he let go, she backed away from him, a wild, feverish look in her eye as she spun around, searching.

"You want to see O'Deldar?" he whispered.

Her gaze fixed on him as soon he spoke the priest's name. For whatever reason, she would not rest until she found O'Deldar. Maybe the Druid could help figure out what was wrong with her.

"You can use the Words of Making to get us to him—"

She was already writing in her notepad and muttering the words.

Before he could tell her to make sure she included him, his surroundings melted away into shapeless gray hues before rearranging into a dusty chamber lined with shelves of scrolls, leather-bound books, jars of herbs and medicinal supplies.

O'Deldar stood with his back to a wall of oriel windows, staring into a bowl balanced on a granite pedestal. The old Druid looked up at them. He was a small man, dark-skinned and dark-eyed with long salt-and-pepper hair and a beard that softened his angular features. Even though he wore nothing more than a coarse gray robe, he emanated an air of majesty.

When he spoke, his voice was gentle and even, though his gaze penetrated to the core. "Tell me, do you expect me to pretend you've simply stumbled into my chambers by chance, or would you agree it's best we get down to the business of why you are here?"

Finn glanced at Fate, expecting her to say something but she stood rigid and even more wild-eyed than before. "We may have business with you," he hedged, when she didn't respond.

"Have a seat," he said, directing them to comfortable chairs before taking a seat opposite them.

Finn guided Fate to sit. She gripped the arms of the chair like she might jump and run any second. It wasn't fear he sensed in her. If he had to put a name to it, it would be hunger.

O'Deldar watched her as well. "Fate, I know you've come for the Rod of Aeternitas."

Finn's confusion increased, especially when the rigidity in her posture eased and she nodded like an automaton. He suddenly wondered if O'Deldar was doing this to her.

"Do you know what the Rod can do?" the priest asked.

Her body went stiff again. She looked like she wanted to speak, but her mouth remained a closed, tight line.

Finn moved toward her. "Fate, what's wrong?"

"She's under a powerful spell," O'Deldar explained. "A spell that brought her from very far away and sent her here for the Rod."

"Who did this?"

"The same person who stole the Orb from me. Brune Inkwell."

Finn remained mystified. "I don't know that name."

"She smells bad," Fate said, wrinkling her nose. "Very bad, like sour milk curdled over moose sausages…and rotten eggs."

They both looked at her. She still had that faraway look in her eyes and was covering her nose, her back pressed to the chair as if the smell was in the room.

"Strange, she's remembering," O'Deldar said, his wise face growing puzzled. "She shouldn't be able to remember anything under such a spell, but this odor she's speaking of must have roused her out of it somewhat."

Finn's eyes narrowed with suspicion. "How is it you know about this so-called spell? How do I know *you* didn't cast a spell over her?"

"It is the Orb of Aeternitas that holds her, and it is the Rod of Aeternitas that tells me so." He pulled a necklace from out of the collar of his robe, revealing a thin golden bar marked with tiny symbols.

Seeing it, Fate lurched at the priest, her hands clawing for the ornament at his neck. Before she could reach him, O'Deldar waved his hand, uttering something that forced her back in her chair like she'd been pushed and pinned to it.

Finn reared back in horror as she thrashed her head, growling like someone possessed. "What the bloody hell did you just do to her?"

"I only held her back," O'Deldar explained. "The spell is pushing her into this delirium." He stood over her with his thumb pressed on her forehead while muttering a chant.

After a few seconds she fell limp, slumping over in the chair.

Fearing the worst, Finn checked her breathing. Relief washed through him. She was alive and appeared to be sound asleep. Gathering her into his arms, he glared at the priest. "Will she still be crazed when she wakes up?"

O'Deldar gave him a regretful smile. "If she is not near me and the Rod, she will be what you know her to be. But the spell will always force her to retrieve the Rod."

"What's so bloody important about it?"

"Sit," O'Deldar said, directing him back to his seat.

Finn did so reluctantly, keeping Fate on his lap, her head resting on his shoulder.

The priest sat next to him. "To tell you of the Rod without first telling you of the Orb is like trying to explain how a flower spreads its pollen without the aid of butterflies and bees. The Orb is a small puzzle ball—golden and about the size of a cherry. A rather unassuming piece at first glance, unless you have the mind to look more closely. Then you'll see the interlocking hexagrams comprised of magical numbers and symbols, all of which represent ancient alchemical formulas and celestial forces powerful enough to bestow life and death." His tone marked the gravity of the subject. "The Orb's powers are limited to a small sphere of space, but the Rod, when used to unlock the hexagrams, will unleash its influence to extend throughout the world—granting its owner immortality and godlike powers."

Finn's grip tightened on Fate. "I get it. This is no small thing. So what happens if she doesn't get the Rod? Will things go sideways for her?"

"She will kill herself trying to do what she must." The priest moved to the table and reached for a glass vial. "Give her this. It will make her feel she's accomplished her task."

Finn held it up, watching as tiny gold flecks swirled in clear liquid. "What is it?"

"Spelled water mixed with gold shavings from the Rod. A decoy of sorts to trick the spell upon her into believing it has finished its work. But the potion won't last forever. I will leave it to you to see her home as soon as possible."

Finn debated whether to give it to her or not. He looked at the priest. If he couldn't trust a fellow Druid, whom could he trust? Besides, he didn't know how else to help her. Uncorking the vial, he lifted it to Fate's lips and poured the contents in her mouth.

Fate nuzzled against her father's chest, listening to the comforting beat of his heart and steady rise and fall of his breathing. She knew she was dreaming. She hadn't cuddled with Eustace while he read her stories since she was eight or nine. If only she could stay asleep and stay in that safe place just a little longer before reality crashed back in. But she couldn't keep from waking up. Strangely though, the feeling of his arms around her persisted. Lifting her head, she looked at Finn in surprise. "Wh-what happened?" She gasped. "Why am I sitting on you?"

"You fainted," he said.

She jumped off his lap. "No, I didn't. I'm not one of those wimpy fainters." She swayed dizzily and Finn caught her arm, pulling her over to sit in the chair next to him. Trembling, she sat down, glancing at the wall of scrolls, the menagerie of old-world items filling the table and the glittering sea outside the bank of windows. "Wait, how did I get here?" She recounted her last steps. The last thing she remembered was being in the courtyard amongst all the festivities. She shot the old man in the robe a sharp look. "*Who* are you?"

"I am O'Deldar."

She nodded, accepting that he looked like a Druid priest. But she wanted explanations, starting with how she'd gotten there without any memory of it. "What's going on here? Why did I black out?"

O'Deldar waved his hand. "Forget these concerns, Fate."

His voice filled her head, erasing immediate worries as a cool, calming sensation washed through her, soothing her nerves.

"We must address Finn's troubles," he told her.

She looked at Finn, then back at O'Deldar. "What do you mean?"

His dark eyes focused on Finn. "I see you've been poisoned by the cursed oak. You have tempered the blackness with the Elder race runes, but that has not stopped the spread."

Fate tensed. The cryptic tone in the priest's voice filled her with fear. She hadn't thought of the poisoning since she'd found out Finn was alive. She'd assumed he'd been healed but O'Deldar was talking like he had some sort of incurable disease.

"I know. I can feel it," Finn said, a deep dread in his eyes.

O'Deldar looked apologetic. "Unfortunately, there's nothing I can do. You must seek out the poison's origin and destroy it." His gaze passed over Finn's crown and down to his feet. "Hmmm, it's most strange. Your spirit shines more brightly than most. It has the radiance and purity of a newborn babe. Usually as the years wear away at us, our light fades, another reason the darkness is held at bay. Even so, I must warn you that this will not protect you for long. You will eventually become the darkness that is devouring you, and when that happens you will be the enemy of light and all that is good in this world."

A wall of silence came crashing down, filling the room

with tension.

"You know of Mugloth?" O'Deldar asked after a moment.

Finn frowned, shaking his head.

"I do," Fate said. Sithias had urged her to have a look through each fable when he saw that the cursed oak was the one constant thread throughout each story. Mugloth was a character from the eighth fable. "My friend read about him in a story," she added, careful to keep her knowledge of the *Book of Fables* secret.

"Then you know Mugloth is the source of this poisoning." O'Deldar paused. He seemed to be choosing his words carefully. "Finn, the time is coming when you will be forced to make a choice no one should ever have to make. But all will not be lost if you trust in your heart to know what must be done for the good of all."

Cold fear pricked at Fate. "How is it you know these things?"

"You could say I am an oracle of sorts. I *see* things," O'Deldar said.

"Then you should be able to tell us what's going to happen," she pressed. "You can tell us what to watch out for."

"If I tell you too much this early on, I risk distracting you from what you are each destined to do. Trust me when I say this—avoidance of pain does not always ensure a happy ending, and it's up to you to bring good fortune to this story and every other."

Startled by his choice of words, she wondered just how much the old Druid knew about the *Book of Fables*. "What makes you think we can change anything here for the better?"

"It is no secret the destinies of this world are being dictated by your travels through the *Book of Fables*."

She grabbed Finn's leg.

Having grown quiet, he started a little, then leaned forward, asking, "Are you saying that everything within these stories is real?"

O'Deldar's gaze shifted to the seascape. "What you know

as myths and legends in your world are, in truth, records of a time when our world was one with yours. But as eons passed, magic was banished—pushed aside by religious philosophies and science. Since then a great fiery divide in time and space has separated our two worlds. Ours stayed as it is today, while yours pushed ahead with its more limited, narrow views."

"And how does the *Book of Fables* fit into all of this?" Finn asked.

The priest frowned. "That cursed book is a source of great misery to this world. Before the Elder race receded into the earth, one of their chroniclers created the book as a record of Oldwilde—"

"Hah! I knew the book belonged to a chronicler!" Fate burst out. "Sorry," she mumbled when she received serious stares.

"I suspect there's much more to the book than meets the eye, but I have yet to discover what that may be," continued O'Deldar.

"What is Oldwilde?" Finn asked.

"The continent on which we live. Oldwilde was part of the First Earth, before the Elder race cracked it into pieces and shifted the land masses to different parts of the world."

"Is there a Middle-earth too?" Fate asked.

"No."

She fell silent and fidgeted under his solemn gaze.

"So what you're saying is that the *Book of Fables* is telling stories about *real people* here in Oldwilde?" Finn said, a frown of concern on his face.

Fate gulped. "And us trying to escape the book is changing all those lives?"

O'Deldar raised his dark brows and nodded. "Yes, in essence that's exactly right."

His answer sat like a boulder in her stomach.

"Not to worry, young ones. You have no other choice. Wodrid saw to that when he spelled the book with the curse to trap unwary readers and force them to change the endings into their mirror opposites as their only means of escape. Ever since that fork-tongued sorcerer got his hands on the book and took it into your world, Oldwilde's destiny has been swayed by the ignorance of many unfortunate readers. It's why I failed to *see* Moria's entrance into Asgar eighteen years ago. The future is less clear when a reader from the *Book of Fables* is involved. And since the last reader came through and changed our once glorious days into what you see now, we've been living in the gloom of unending misfortune."

"Well, the *Book of Fables* is here now," Finn said. "We could destroy it."

O'Deldar shook his head. "It is a ghost image of the book that's here in Oldwilde. The actual book still resides in your world, and nothing there can harm it. It must be returned to Oldwilde if it is to be destroyed."

"How can we bring it here if the book's the only way in?" Fate asked.

"There are other ways to cross the divide between our worlds. *If* you know how to find them," he said intently, as if speaking only to her. "But that is another concern for another time." He rose and beckoned them toward the bowl on the pedestal. "Come, let us attend to more pressing matters and see if we might devise a plan to put an end to the misery here in Asgar." He then passed his hand over the water's glassy surface, stirring up a thick mist that took on the shape of the castle and the busy movements of the people in and around it.

Having seen the merriment earlier, and now the festivities taking place in miniature inside the magic bowl, Fate found it hard to believe anyone in Asgar was miserable. But she'd read the fable. Everyone in the kingdom was in for a very rude awakening. That in and of itself was bad enough, but to be told that her actions could either make or break countless numbers of innocent lives made everything that much worse. The burden of responsibility had fallen squarely on her shoulders, and she found it heavy.

CHAPTER 20

NO ONE NOTICED when Fate and Finn returned to the festival like glimmering wraiths appearing out of nowhere. Distractions of every sort took place among the throng of high-spirited celebrants. Jostled at every turn, they moved through the lively crowd in the direction of the caravan to inform Sithias of O'Deldar's plan to defeat Moria. But there was no getting near his stage. Too many people surrounded him as he recited one of his plays and strummed his harp.

Fate waved to get his attention. He grinned and nodded, but she could tell he had no intention of halting his performance any time soon.

"Leave him be," Finn said, his voice tight. Their meeting with O'Deldar had obviously left him in a dark mood.

Grabbing her hand, he pulled her past a group of musicians and jovial dancers. She followed, avoiding the frolicking as best she could until two girls her age bumped into him. As they blushed and giggled, a grin chased away the troubled lines of his face. Then one of them whispered in his ear and left him with a sprig of heather.

As the girls skipped off, Fate tried to act nonchalant. "What'd she say?"

He twirled the sprig between his finger and thumb. "She invited me to dance around the Maytree."

Her mouth fell open. "Are you going to?"

He tucked the heather into his vest pocket. "I haven't decided yet," he said, his expression withdrawn again.

Her pulse quickened. Was he thinking of Tove and wishing he could entangle his ribbon with hers? She pushed the thought away. Her girlish insecurities didn't count right now. They had more important matters to worry about, the main one being the poison.

Finn zeroed in on a pavilion serving ale and pulled her inside its dim interior where the thick haze of pipe smoke hung in the air. She waited near the entrance while he walked up to the barkeep. A few minutes later he returned with two foaming mugs. Handing her one of them, he downed his ale, gulping loudly. Letting out a satisfied sigh, he wiped the foam from his lips.

"That should take the sting off things a bit," he said with a half-hearted grin.

Fate stared at him, horrified. "What's with you? Do you want to end up like your dad?"

His smile vanished, his gaze guarded and suspicious. "How do you know about my da?"

Heat rushed to her face. She needed to be more careful. Revealing too much about his life story would prompt unwelcome questions like before. "Uh…well, you complained about his drinking a lot before you were poisoned and forgot you knew me and, of course, everything we talked about."

He studied her face, looking only partially convinced. "Well…my da's circumstances were different than mine. He couldn't cope after he lost my mum." His lids drooped as he gave her a sleepy wink, a sign he was already feeling the alcohol. "Don't worry about me, I've been known to tip a few back a time or two with Granda. It was harmless and we had a great old time together."

His brooding yet cavalier attitude was beginning to get on her nerves. "Listen, we should really talk about what O'Deldar said—about the poison—"

“I don’t want to talk about it now,” he said, his tone gruff. “This is a day of celebration, and celebrate is exactly what I intend to do. At least until tonight when we have to deal with Moria. Lucky for us that’s hours from now.”

“You’ve really changed,” she muttered.

“So you keep saying. But if our history together is as short as you’ve led me to believe, there’s no way you could’ve known me all that well. So maybe I haven’t changed all that much.” He shrugged. “I feel pretty much the same.”

Fate remained silent. There was nothing she could say. Not unless she was ready to tell him how she knew him down to the tiniest detail. Explaining that he was a figment of her imagination come to life, on top of what O’Deldar had told him, was the worst thing she could do right now. Besides the nasty reaction he would have all over again, there’d be the added complication of the drinking, his frightening strength and speed, and the brutality he’d shown toward those robbers. No way. She wasn’t saying a word.

“Are you going to drink that?” he asked, reaching for her untouched ale without waiting for an answer.

His Adam’s apple bobbed up and down as he gulped back every drop. Slamming the empty mug down on a nearby table and startling the happy drunk sitting there, he gave her a lazy, intoxicated smile. “Tell me, why were those big browns haunting my dreams night after night?” His eyes lit up as his gaze drifted down to her mouth. “And those lips. It drove me crazy not knowing who you were, but needing you the way a man lost in the desert thirsts for water.”

This wholly unexpected confession shot a blazing, hopeful thrill through her. But then her mind raced back to what she’d witnessed between him and Tove, and confusion set in. Had she misinterpreted their relationship to one another? She narrowed her eyes. No, there was no mistaking the intimacy she’d seen them share.

"If Sithias hadn't told me you'd never been kissed, I would've thought you and I had exactly that kind of connection."

"No, not like that," she said, unable to meet his intense gaze. The air between them seemed to warm to an unbearable level. She could feel the sweat beading on her brow.

At last he lifted her chin with his finger. "We were…close?"

"In a way, but—"

He cut her off by touching his finger to her lips. "Then we're meant to be close again."

They spent the next few hours watching a few plays, some archery contests and a jousting tournament. Finn stayed near Fate, keeping his hand on her waist. Touching her even in this small way satisfied his increasing thirst to be close to her. During the jousting, while she covered her eyes with her hands right before the inevitable unhorsing of each loser, he took the opportunity to really look at her in the hopes of coaxing into the forefront of his mind his lost memories of their brief time together. But it was no use. No matter how hard he tried, he couldn't retrieve a single detail of their past encounter. Only the strong sense of knowing that he belonged with her persisted.

Later, when the sun reached its peak, the sweltering heat drove them to find some shade. On the way, a group of teenaged girls grabbed Fate and pulled her toward the Maytree, saying they needed one more dancer. She glanced back at Finn, her eyes round and imploring. Smiling, he ducked out of sight behind a horse and rider trotting by. Keeping an eye on her from afar, he watched the girls as they coaxed her with good humor while braiding flowers in her hair.

Holding hands, the girls herded Fate into a half circle around the tree while six boys in their early to late teens moved in to complete the circle. Finn tapped one of them on the shoulder. "Hey, mate. Some bonnie lass was asking after you over by—"

"Was it the Baron's daughter?" the teen asked eagerly, turning an excited gaze to the crowd surrounding them.

"Sure was. You're a lucky man," Finn said as the boy broke into a run, leaving his place in the line up for grabs.

Finn stepped into the circle, winking at Fate, who stood opposite him with ribbon in hand and panic in her eyes. Glaring at him, she mouthed some sort of silent plea, which he ignored.

As he picked up the ribbon lying near his feet, the music started, a rich medley of fiddles, flutes and tambourines. He followed along as the other dancers moved in one direction and then the other. Chuckling softly, he watched as Fate fell in step with legs of wood.

At first it seemed as though they were merely going back and forth, until the girls weaved past him and the other boys, brushing by as soft as feathers. The beat of the music increased, as did their pace. All the girls, except Fate, laughed with careless abandon. The boys stared back at them, the gleam of desire plain in their eyes.

Finn watched Fate. She was biting her bottom lip in concentration, her gaze fixed intently on the movements of the other dancers. When he circled round, his shoulder grazed hers. He felt a bolt of electricity pass between them. She must have felt it too, because her head shot up and she locked eyes with him. The instant blush of color in her cheeks stirred something primal in him. He thought she'd look away, as she so often did, but her lips curved into a playful smile. His heart hammered in his chest. She twirled out of reach, circling the tree until they met on the other side. This time he leaned close to her upturned face, feeling the heat of her breath and the touch of her lips against his cheek as she whisked past him.

The intertwining dance continued on this way, building the chase between each young man and woman while ribbons laced together. The heady scent of lavender, roses and lilac filled the air, as did the music's earthy rhythms. Finn only had eyes for Fate as she lost herself in the dance, swaying to the beat and staring back at him with a passion that burned as hot as his own.

At last the music hit a final crescendo and ebbed just as the dance turned in the opposite direction. Once again, the girls wended their way between the boys, slowly unraveling their ribbons from their initial entanglement until they were all going in one direction—though now the order was mixed, male and female standing side by side.

When the motion around the tree came to a standstill, Finn could no longer keep a lid on his emotions and crushed Fate against his chest, twirling her around. "You are *miraculously* breathtaking when you let your hair down."

She laughed as he set her down gently, keeping her in his arms. Her smile was mischievous when she looked up at him. "Does this mean we've tied the knot?"

He lifted one of her curls to his nose, inhaling the perfume of the flowers woven into her hair. "Technically, it's not official unless the ceremony's consummated before next Beltane. Until then, we're bound by an unspoken promise to be truly wed."

Uneasy excitement played over her features as she looked at him, her eyes wide and searching. A mixture of emotions sparked off her like the burning embers of a campfire, singeing him first with hope and passion, then all of a sudden scorching him with distrust. This increasing connection he had with her—experiencing her feelings as if they were his own—didn't do anything to help him know what she was thinking. Frustration set in as her tension grew more pronounced.

Guessing he must've said the wrong thing, he loosened his hold, trying to get her to face him. "Don't get me wrong. I'd *never* expect that from you."

Her eyes flashed with anger. "Because of Tove? You'd rather she was here instead of me?"

He let his hands slip from her waist as his heart tore in two. "Tove and I shared something I can't begin to describe. We were as close as any two people can get—but she's not *you*."

She stepped back, putting a painful chasm between them. "But you love her, don't you?"

"Is that the reason you tried to leave me behind in the last fable?"

"Oh, you noticed that?" she muttered.

"I guess you were being considerate, but you have to trust me when I say that what I share with you outshines everything else. It's as if you're part of me…or I'm a part of you."

He thought his honest confession would please her. Instead, her eyes welled with tears.

He sucked in a deep breath. The tightening in his chest hurt. Maybe it was best she remain unhappy with him. He shouldn't have given into his feelings in the first place. Not when the poison was changing him in ways she found frightening. Looking back, he had to admit inflicting justice on those robbers was probably much more satisfying than it should've been.

He needed to be more self-disciplined around her. Of course that was easier said than done. His overpowering desire to be with her had turned him into something needful and greedy. "I'm sorry," he said, defeat weighing him down. "I've been selfish. I don't know what I was thinking declaring my feelings like I've every right to. I'm doomed *and* a danger to you."

Fate's watery stare rounded with concern. He sensed her defenses coming down.

She stretched out her hand. "No, don't go thinking that way.

We'll find a way to stop the poison before it's too late. I *promise.*"

The conviction in her voice gave him hope. He reached across the space between them, taking the hand she offered. "Hearing you say that makes me believe I might actually have a chance."

She stepped close, timidly, wrapping her arms around his waist and resting her head against his chest. Surprised, he stopped breathing, afraid to move lest he scare her away. He wished he could freeze this moment. Make it last forever. Carefully, he circled his arms around her, turning his face into the softness of her neck.

They stayed that way for one fleeting moment of bliss, while the multitudes of rollicking people flowed past them like the rapid currents of a river flowing around a tiny island.

CHAPTER 21

FATE STARED AT HER REFLECTION in disbelief. She'd been fitted in a gown of rich brown taffeta. She ran her fingers over the intricately beaded bodice. It hugged her curves nicely. A fairy godmother couldn't have done a better job, though she would've preferred a quick wave of the wand to having a group of strange women plop her in a steaming bath, scrub her skin, slather her hair with oils and even towel her off and dress her in layers of unnecessary undergarments. Yet she'd endured it all—even the cinching of the rib-crushing corset—without protest to ensure that O'Deldar's generosity would not be held under scrutiny. Their plan involved an evening at the masqued ball so they could get close to Moria.

Hiding a pleased smile, she looked over her bare shoulder to check out the backside of the dress.

"Hold still please, miss," one of the handmaids scolded as she added the final touches. Two tortoise shell combs crowned the cascade of curls framing her face. A twinkling amber necklace graced the elegant neckline of her gown, and matching earrings mirrored the color of her eyes.

Thanking her helpers for the miracle they'd managed to pull off, Fate slipped on the long velvet gloves they handed her.

A knock on the door of her suite had one of the maids scurrying to open it.

In walked Finn. He was dressed in a white linen shirt, a gold and black brocade overcoat, and suede breeches tucked inside black boots trimmed with gold buttons. He looked so devastatingly striking, Fate's heart climbed into her throat, rendering her speechless.

He stared back, his eyes wide and mouth open. She couldn't tell if he liked what he saw or not and the longer he stood in silence, the more uncomfortable she became. She wasn't one to obsess about her looks but at this very moment her appearance meant everything. So much so, her anxiety turned into the heckling voice of the late Blackwell—*she thinks she's a princess but she's really the Duchess of Dowdy.*

"You're beautiful, beyond words," he said finally, his voice cracking.

"You too," she said as the maids drew back with tearful smiles.

Flustered and unable to stop the Kamikaze butterflies crashing in her stomach, she reached for her beaded mask to hide her nervousness. "Shall we?"

Clicking the heels of his boots together, Finn smiled and offered his arm. With her gloved hand resting on his forearm, they walked out and joined a dignified group strolling down the castle's long hallway. After turning a corner, they passed through a garland-trimmed archway leading into the great hall, where the gilded walls and marbled floors glowed from an overabundance of candles. Stretching down one side of the hall was an incredibly long table set with elaborate fruit bowls, baked breads molded into fanciful forms, bowls of vegetables gleaming with butter and herbs, and large platters laden with peacock and venison, swordfish and suckling pig.

Once the nobles took their proper seats, Finn pulled out a chair for her toward the end of the massive table. As she arranged her skirt and sat down, they both caught the eye of O'Deldar farther up. The priest acknowledged them with a slight tilt of his head before turning back to his conversation.

Fate settled in, delighting in the scenery and admiring costumes that artfully mimicked fairy and sea folk, angels, goblins, devils and jesters. While other opulently dressed guests milled around an ice sculpture of Poseidon surrounded by scaly fish with mouths spouting white wine, minstrels strolled about playing flutes, violins and harp lutes.

When the hour struck five, the trumpets blared as the king and empress made their grand entrance. All heads turned to see Empress Moria, radiant in a gown of raspberry gauze and a necklace encrusted with black diamonds and ruby rosettes. Braided ropes of her dark hair formed an exotic sculpture, like serpents writhing above her glittering crown. A black velvet mask shadowed her eyes, but the candlelight still caught their scarlet glint.

Silence filled the ballroom as the empress stepped onto the dais, her movements smooth and sinuous. The large, red-bearded King Balor gleamed in his suit of copper brocade but he looked almost hazy and vague next to his wife. Once seated at the royal table, Moria announced Prince Tynan and their honored guest, Princess Kaura of the Eldunough Islands.

Another wave of gasps and whispers rippled out over the ballroom when the royal couple appeared. Prince Tynan cut a fine silhouette in a tailored coat of ebony silk and an intricate dragon mask. But it was the lady on his arm whom everyone watched with breathless wonder. Dressed in a gown of shimmering pale gray, Princess Kaura seemed to float into the hall like a cloud of mist, her hair cascading down her back in a fountain of liquid gold and her mysterious gray eyes hidden behind a silver mask.

Once the royal family began dining on the sumptuous fare, the guests were free to join in. When Fate reached for a basket of soft steaming bread, Finn stopped her hand, reminding her that it was all an elaborate illusion. As much as her mouth watered from the sight of so many enticing dishes, she followed his lead and allowed the enchanted food to pass her by.

Pretending to sip on some wine, Finn set the glass down and leaned close to her. "Look how King Balor has his back to his queen. He can't wipe the fool's grin for the princess off his face. Moria looks ready to spit venom."

She nodded. The story was unfolding before her eyes. The princess appeared powerfully magnetic, much more so than Moria, but in a way that drew one's attention like a breathtaking sunset or a majestic mountain peak. While Moria's presence fostered obsession, Kaura's ignited inspiration.

The muscles in Finn's arm tensed into hard bands. Fate turned to look at him. His eyes were closed behind his black Colombina mask, his jaw set tight.

"What is it?" she asked.

His eyes opened. They were dark and disturbing. "I can see the serpent inside Moria. There's nothing but black rot in her heart. She finds these people loathsome." When he looked at Fate his eyes lightened, only to turn dark again when his gaze returned to the empress. "There's something inside her—some sort of demon. It's what lights the red fire in her eyes. We have to stop her. She means to crush this empire to dust."

Fate looked at the empress, unable to see the demon he spoke of.

A troupe of performers paraded past and began entertaining the guests and royal party for the next hour. Surprisingly, the last and most highly acclaimed performer of the night was Sithias. After several encores, he ended off with a tragic comedy. Everyone cheered, showering him with flowers and gold coins.

She started toward Sithias, but admirers were swarming around him.

Finn took her hand, flashing a dashing smile as he did so. "Would you care to dance?"

Her heart fluttered against her breastbone like a frightened bird in a cage as she followed him onto the dance floor and fell in step with the other dancers to a somewhat stilted waltz. She was playing a fool's game by loving someone whose heart was divided and who couldn't remember he hated her for inventing him. But she clung to the fact that Finn had chosen to leave Tove to be with *her*. And as far as his origins were concerned, she could only hope he *never* remembered.

"You're a hard one to figure out, lass. One minute you're as soft and warm as a feather bed, and the next as impenetrable as granite." He tapped a finger over her heart. "Tell me, love, what's going on in there?"

His touch made her knees go weak. "I—"

"May I have this dance?" asked a young man whose face was hidden behind a baroque lion mask.

The look Finn gave him was sharp and Fate thought he'd say no. But he surprised her by bowing out without a word. Feeling trapped, she watched him disappear behind a sea of people. As her new partner talked about how much he enjoyed the leg of mutton stuffed with garlic, she did her best to smile and act like she was interested. But when he turned the subject of food to roasted blackbirds and a list of other poor birds she'd never consider eating, she simply nodded while scanning the masked faces for Finn. Was it too much to ask for one peaceful moment to get comfortable with each other without something always getting in the way?

When the dance ended, she tried to escape but an endless line of suitors hedged her in and kept her whirling around the dance floor for the next hour. As much as she wanted to make an abrupt, probably rude exit, she couldn't risk offending the wrong person. Maybe she'd have to pull a faint. Odds were good that having a touch of the vapors was perfectly acceptable in a time of tight corsets.

"May I have this next dance?" someone asked from behind her.

"I'm sorry, but I do believe I'm feeling faint and must sit

down," she said breathily as she turned with all the fragility she could muster up. When she saw Finn standing there, heat flooded her face.

He gave her an amused smile. "I thought you said you weren't one of those wimpy fainters."

"I am if it'll end this torture." She frowned. "Where have you *been?*"

"Waiting in line. It seems someone's taken an interest in orchestrating your dance card to save you from being devoured by these hungry wolves all at once."

She rolled her eyes. "Good God, *someone* has a twisted sense of kindness."

"How about we sneak out 'til it's time for the bonfire?"

"*Yes*, me and my sore feet thank you," she said as they waltzed off the dance floor.

Taking the nearest stairwell leading to the outer bailey, they joined the lesser gentry who were boisterously celebrating with music, dance and wine. Removing her mask, she kicked off her satin slippers. The cool grass soothed the ache in her feet, but she was still much too warm and wanted to be barefoot. Hiking up her skirt, she started rolling one of the thick stockings down the length of her thigh when Finn tugged the skirt back down in place.

"You have an audience," he said, directing a protective scowl at some leering faces nearby. He scooped her up off her feet with a devilish smile. "It's best I let them know you're with me, temptress."

She gave a little gasp, then laughed and wrapped her arms around his neck. He carried her effortlessly to the nearest turret, up the stairs to the south rampart, taking a seat on the parapet and keeping her on his lap.

Wanting to see his face, she slipped off his mask. His tousled bangs fell into his eyes. As she brushed them off his forehead, she saw that his gaze had turned to the ocean. Resting her head on his shoulder, she stared out at the water, where the sinking sun spilled its radiance over the calm sea and the horizon blazed with the last of its fully ripened light. For once, everything was perfect.

"We don't have long before the fires are lit," he said, his tone grave. "Listen, when Moria comes out to light the bonfire, I want you to find Sithias and go back to the caravan."

Not so perfect.

She sat straight and looked at him. "That's not the plan. I'm back-up, remember? And I still think writing up a Gloom dragon to fly her into the Gray Waste of Hades is way better than O'Deldar's idea."

"Too risky. Do I need to remind you of the Green Man debacle?"

"I'm staying."

He frowned. "No, I can't have you there."

"Why?"

"You know what I intend to do to Moria, and I'm telling you it'll be hideous in comparison to throwing those men to the oaks."

They'd gone over the plan in great detail with O'Deldar. She'd argued against the method in which the two of them had decided to stop Moria, but after much discussion, she'd agreed in the end. "No…I'm staying," she said, gulping back her apprehension.

He pulled her close, his embrace tight and desperate. "Fate, you need to know—the poison…its been stirring up revolting thoughts that leave me feeling ugly as sin. It's growing inside me like a seed of rage that thrives on punishing others in the most unspeakable of ways."

"I won't leave, I can't," she whispered, her lips brushing lightly against his neck.

His hands slid along her back until they reached her neck. She shivered feverishly under his touch. He tilted her chin back with his thumbs, staring longingly at her parted lips. Barely able to breathe, she closed her eyes, feeling his warm mouth exploring the line of her jaw.

Suddenly his lips pressed hungrily against hers.

She was wholly unprepared for the sweet taste of his mouth and the hot waves crashing through her body. Coiling her fingers through his hair, she pulled him close, kissing him deeply, wildly.

He pulled away after a few seconds. "Wait, slow down."

She trembled all over. His kiss eclipsed every pale imagining she'd ever had.

"You have no idea how much I want this, but it's not the place, or the time," he said, his breath ragged with desire and his eyes flaming bright green.

"It's Beltane, and we're promised…it feels right," she whispered back.

"By all that's holy, it surely does, but not here—not now."

Urged on by the thundering beat of his heart against hers, she pressed against him. But his conflicted gaze had already moved to the orange sliver of light slicing thin across the dark horizon. "No, it's time to deal with Moria."

Feeling like he'd just thrown her in frigid water, she stared at him, angry and frustrated. "I don't care about any of that."

He set her off his lap and stood up. "One of us needs to keep a cool head." His tone had changed.

An icy trickle of fear slid down her spine. Within a heartbeat, Finn had transformed. He seemed taller, radiating a dangerous, concentrated energy that scorched away who he was, leaving him unrecognizable—a stranger who stared blindly past her with the cold, emotionless eyes of a killer.

CHAPTER 22

WHEN THEY ARRIVED back inside the castle, the royal guests had crowded onto a wide terrace overlooking the outer bailey, while those of dubious title gathered below. Moria stood at the tip of the balcony, which extended over a giant pile of timbers almost as tall as the terrace itself.

"If you're going to stay, stand here at the very back," Finn whispered to Fate, his hands gripping her shoulders to keep her at arm's length.

She held her mouth in a tight line as she nodded, fear and anger in her eyes.

Resisting the urge to pull her into his arms again, he let go and pushed his way through the guests pressing in close to the front. Having Fate anywhere near him made it impossible to concentrate on what must be done. When he reached the terrace's balustrade, he could see Moria holding a torch to light the bonfire below. Scanning the crowd, he found O'Deldar. The sage acknowledged him with an unwavering gaze of encouragement before turning to escort Tynan and Kaura away. The Druid priest had played his part: remove the heir prince before the chaos began.

An expectant hush fell over the hot sultry night until the only sound was that of the waves crashing against the moonlit shore. Moria seemed to glow as she delivered a lofty speech on the holy day of light. Her words inspired everyone under her spell, but rang hollow in Finn's ears.

Closing his eyes, he sampled the atmosphere with his

extraordinary senses. In his mind's eye, he could see dark slithering specters emanating from the dragon empress, reaching out, feeding on the adulation of those she meant to destroy.

Justifiable hatred surged through him like an electric jolt. Wanting to get closer, he shouldered his way through the guests gathering close to the front of the terrace. Those nearest him drew back as if afraid. He stopped several yards from Moria and whistled two rune notes ever so softly. He smiled with satisfaction when he saw the breeze he'd summoned sweep over the sweltering faces of those nearby. Licking his lips, he whistled another rune note—a more powerful one—and felt the immediate tension of forces unleash from the North.

The breeze transformed into a sudden, icy gale and rushed at Moria. As she gripped the railing for support, Finn knew the bitter chill had slowed her serpent's blood.

Fate grabbed Sithias by the arm and hauled him toward the front of the balcony. Curling his wings back, he tried not to disturb anyone as they wedged themselves past others who were also trying to get a better view, but his harp twanged and heads turned.

"Misss, what isss ssso terribly presssing that we need to be rudely pushing our way to the front?"

"I can't see from back there."

"Didn't Finn sssay sssomething about ssstaying at the back?" He stroked his goatee with a baffled expression. "If I remember correctly, he sssaid it wasss of the utmossst importance. Why isss that?"

She stopped and looked at him. "Are you serious?" She stood on her toes and whispered in his ear, "Finn's going to destroy Moria. You *do* remember the plan, don't you?"

He looked alarmed. "Why would he want to dessstroy sssuch a beautiful rossse?"

She rolled her eyes in frustration. "Snap out of it. You're under Moria's spell. Remember how she plans to ruin the kingdom by first turning Tynan into a dragon tonight?"

"Oh…quite right."

A frigid wind raged over them. Everyone gasped.

Shivering, Sithias hugged his arms. "Oh, thisss isss awful. It feelsss like the Twisssted Bone Foressst all over again."

As much as Fate agreed, she pushed her way as close to the front as she could. Peering between the stubborn few ahead of her who wouldn't budge, she caught sight of the empress looking ashen-faced as the icy wind tore at her beautiful gown. Searching for Finn, she spotted him standing on the other side of the balcony. The ruthless line of his lips and the depthless stare in his jet-black eyes chilled her far more than the North wind he'd summoned.

Her insides twisted with dread as he moved toward Moria, slowly and purposely.

When the empress saw him reach inside his breast pocket, she signaled the guards. They closed around him as he pulled out his flute.

"Your highness," Finn said with a bow, "it would be my greatest pleasure to play a song to warm your heart, if not the air, while you light the Beltane fire."

The torch in Moria's hand guttered in the wintry wind as she scrutinized him. Fate worried she would somehow know Finn was the one who'd called the winds, but when she signaled the guards to stand down, she realized the empress didn't have a clue about his powers.

"This is highly unusual," Moria said, her voice silky despite the chill.

"A North wind as cold and strong as this during Beltane?" Finn said. "Indeed it is."

The empress gave him her nod of approval, then returned

her gaze to those waiting below. Finn began playing a soft, seductive melody. The notes seemed to gentle the wind, but the frosty air still bit the skin.

Someone bumped into Fate. She turned to see Sithias swaying drunkenly to the music. His dazed, amber eyes were fixed on Finn's flute. "What's wrong with you?" she asked.

"Sssuch entrancing musssic…" he muttered.

When Sithias started to dance toward the tip of the balcony, Fate held onto his arm, realizing Finn's music was influencing him as well. For all their planning, they'd forgotten one important detail. Sithias was a serpent too. She glanced at Moria, who seemed equally drunk; especially in the way she tossed the torch onto the bonfire as if she were throwing away garbage.

The torch landed on the timber below. Flames fanned by the brisk wind consumed the giant pile with an unnatural fury.

Everyone cheered and backed away from the sudden blaze and intense heat.

The empress turned to Finn with a look of longing. Her body—a vessel of pure sexuality—swayed to his music. Holding her fixed within his dark hypnotic gaze, he played each note as if his fingers caressed her ivory skin.

Fate's heart hammered chaotically. Why hadn't she listened to Finn? He'd been right, she didn't want to see this.

Moria's undulating movements roused an immediate primeval lust within Finn, an involuntary urge he resented—further fueling his loathing for the demon she truly was. Moria was used to transfixing men and stripping them of their senses. But he was the one with the power here. He had the vile serpent mesmerized. It was her turn to suffer for the evil she'd inflicted on so many others.

The darkness inside him swelled like never before, merging

with the energy of the Elder race runes embedded in his skin. As the two forces blended, he felt the thrill of a wild, dark power hissing and sparking past his lips.

He continued playing the beguiling tune, now adding a rune note to bend the wind to his will. All it took was a mere thought to plunge the gust downward to the base of the bonfire and stoke the fire from the bottom up. Without warning, the flames flared skyward into a raging inferno.

Onlookers stumbled back from the intense heat with cries of shock and surprise.

He narrowed his gaze on Moria, his fingers flicking rapidly over the holes of the flute. She danced wildly, flinging her head back and tearing at the neckline of her gown as if suffocated by it. Then her eyes fixed on the flames flickering well above the balustrade. He could tell she was drawn to the heat. Her cold, reptilian blood craved warmth, an instinct that pushed her closer until she stretched over the railing and hung over the scorching fire.

She was right where he wanted her.

Savoring the power he wielded, Finn waited for a fraction of time, then blew the final note. The blaze burst high in a wave of voracious flames, engulfing Moria and flooding across the balcony. As the molten tide flowed over those closest to the empress, chaos broke loose as blood-curdling screams echoed over the courtyard and human torches pitched themselves over the edge.

The sudden burst of flames, scalding heat and ensuing pandemonium galvanized Fate into action. She hauled Sithias backward but not fast enough. Half his wing went up in a flash. Knocking him to the floor, she smothered the fire with the skirt of her gown. As everyone rushed to escape the encroaching inferno, she grabbed him and they scrambled on all fours to one side of the balcony to avoid being trampled.

Disoriented and confused, Fate looked for Finn. He stood where she'd seen him earlier, a malicious gaze leveled on the empress who was thrashing and clawing within a solid blanket of flames. Her keening scream resounded over all others. As Moria crumpled to the floor, Finn blew two more rune notes. The servile wind strengthened, further fanning the deadly blaze.

Putting her back to the intense heat, Fate curled in on herself, covering her ears and clenching her eyes shut. After what seemed like an eternity of screaming, the last of Moria's tortured cries and dying rasps fell silent. Lifting her head, Fate glanced up as the frigid wind vanished and the fire receded with unnatural swiftness. King Balor trudged through the stillness, past the dead and wailing wounded, and knelt by the smoking husk of his queen. Sobs of despair and the reek of burned flesh drifted in the air, turning to nausea in Fate's stomach.

Sithias stumbled to his feet, looking more than a little bewildered and frightened. "Wh-what happened here? One minute I'm lissstening to Finn'sss musssic, and the next, everything'sss burnt to a crisssp."

Gulping back the bile burning her throat, Fate stood on shaky legs and held onto his trembling arm for support. "I'm sorry, Sithias. I can't believe we didn't remember you'd be just as affected by the music as Moria."

Finn drew up behind her, slipping his arm around her waist. His touch sent a cold shiver through her and she recoiled.

A flash of anger crossed his face. "We need to leave before the shock wears off and people start looking for someone to blame," he said, his voice gruff.

She followed, keeping her distance from him as they moved past those who'd been burned. The sight was surreal, full of weeping angels, sad court jesters and faeries with shredded, quivering wings. Guilt put a drag in her step as she thought about the scars they would bear from the terrible rain of fire Finn had brought down upon everyone. Had they first considered the safety of innocent bystanders, they might've come up with a different plan.

She stared at Finn's back, remembering O'Deldar's forewarning: *"You will eventually become the darkness that is devouring you, and when that happens you will be the enemy of light and all that is good in this world."*

They were wading through the melee in the hall when Fate realized Sithias had fallen behind. She found him cupping his hand over his mouth, staring at the banquet of food on the table. What had been bowls of fruit, vegetables and bread were lumps of worm-infested gruel, the suckling pig, a roasted torso of some unfortunate man.

Gooseflesh prickled over her skin as dizziness slammed into her. Her body heaved violently as she vomited until there was nothing left. Spitting out the last of the bitter acid, she lifted her head, seeing that Sithias had been overcome as well. His complexion had gone from pale to ghost-white.

She couldn't move, her brain felt numb and disconnected from her legs. When she saw that Finn was doubling back toward them, she pushed her body into action and staggered over to Sithias. Finn stopped, his posture stiff as he waited for them to catch up.

As she and Sithias stumbled through the great hall with Finn leading the way, the gilded walls gave way to dull, dilapidated surfaces, luxurious carpets grew shabby and threadbare and the vibrant tapestries on the walls faded into moth-eaten remnants before their very eyes.

By the time they reached the outer bailey, Moria's spell of enchantment had dissolved completely, revealing the hideous truth of everyone's existence beneath her glamorous veil. Many stood in mute disbelief, while others screamed and wailed—shocked by the tattered rags hanging from their emaciated bodies and the stacks of putrid corpses in place of their bountiful fare.

The kingdom was in ruin. The odor of squalor, decay and death hung in the air like a thick, noxious gas. Sithias vomited again, pressing Fate's gag button once more. With nothing left in her stomach, she dry-heaved, a bout that left her weak and unsteady. Finn hovered nearby, offering to help her walk the rest of the way, but she shook her head. She didn't want him near her. She was too mixed up. The blissful moments they'd shared together—the ribbon dance, the kiss—had all been part of Moria's illusion. None of it had been real or true, except the undeniable reality that Finn was a merciless executioner.

When they reached the caravan, O'Deldar emerged from the shadows. "You have accomplished much good here today," he said.

Sithias coughed and pinched his nose. "How can thisss be good? Thessse people have been *eating* their dead!"

O'Deldar nodded in agreement. "This is the price for ignoring their hearts. For many years they've known deep down everything was wrong, yet they refused to look beneath the surface. The effort will be tremendous, but they *will* rebuild Asgar into something real and wonderfully imperfect." His gaze shifted to Finn. "The dark power is a cruel temptress and she will exact a heavy price each time you call upon her."

The muscles in Finn's jaw tensed as his gaze flicked to Fate. "I know."

O'Deldar placed a hand on his shoulder. "Not to worry. In the end, you will do what's right."

"Even if doing what's right feels wrong?" Finn asked, his face grim and tortured.

When O'Deldar hesitated, Finn stormed over to the caravan,

climbing inside, where the *Book of Fables* awaited.

Fate stepped forward. "Well?" she said, her voice muffled behind her hand. "Are you going to answer the question?"

"As you walk this path of thorns laid before you, try not to focus on what's right or wrong. Choosing to fight and conquer that which causes fear and misery is all that's important."

She nodded. Strangely enough, she took some comfort in the priest's words.

Sithias tugged on her arm. "Misss, if we don't leave now, I fear this sssmell and thessse horrorsss will be forever etched on my brain and I'll never be able to eat again."

Fearing the same, she hurried after him. As she climbed the steps into the caravan, O'Deldar left her with one parting message, "Fate, when the blood is on your hands, remember what I said here tonight."

Stopping on the top step, she glanced back in alarm but he was gone.

Old Mother Grim

She was old, some say as old as the making of the world. Certainly, she was an ancient creature wise in the ways of sorcery and eluding the decay of time. No one knows how she came to be. Only that she was born of the most ghastly of nightmares.

It was whispered she made her lair on the edge of forests, rivers or lakes, where the in between exists and magic is at its strongest. There she would plant the acorn of a cursed oak and nourish it to swift maturity with a potion of human blood, cat's eyes and claws, and the crushed bones of mice.

She dwelled within the roots of the oak, waiting for the foggiest of nights to leave her dank burrow. With a cloak of mist gathered round her misshapen form, Old Mother Grim crept through the villages, sniffing at the cracks of doors for the sweet scent of baby's breath.

So it was in the peaceful village of Shytuckle that the people woke to the screams of frantic mothers running through the cobbled streets searching for their young ones. Everyone searched the village and surrounding hills until the wolves howled in the night, only to return heartsick and empty-handed.

When they barred the doors and windows shut, no one thought to ask the poor waif, who huddled in a pigsty on the edge of the village, what she had seen. She was only a child vagabond, a drifter who sometimes played with their children, giving them strange charms and entertaining with magic tricks. Had they noticed the tattered girl, they would have seen her fear, for she had witnessed a fog-shrouded creature drifting through the streets.

Several clear nights and a bright waxing moon kept the remaining children of Shytuckle safe…for a time. But when the moon waned and storm clouds gathered, an unnatural fog rolled down from the damp mountains to weave through the valley once again. No iron locks or barricaded doors could keep Old Mother Grim from what she hungered for. This time the waif saw the malformed creature leaving the village with two swaddled babes in her crooked arms and three small tots following like sleepwalkers in her misty trail.

When more children were discovered missing, the panicked villagers ran through the streets calling their names. This time the waif told them she had seen the child-stealer. Some stopped to listen, but when she described the mythic monster, the villagers scoffed and pushed her aside.

Before darkness fell, the villagers locked themselves inside the oratory with ten of the strongest men standing guard outside. Hours later, Old Mother Grim traveled silently within the folds of a massive fog rolling into Shytuckle.

The enticing fragrance of so many babies in one place drew her straight to the oratory. She swept the air with her broom of sticklewort dipped in snake venom. When the sickly green vapors of her sleep potion hit the men on guard, they dropped like felled trees. Old Mother Grim shuffled her great weight up the front steps, stared at the locked door and swept her clawed hand over the lock. The door unbolted and swung open. As fog and sleep potion poured inside, the women and older children collapsed where they stood.

Old Mother Grim stuffed the last five babes into a bloodstained bag, then crooked her bony finger and beckoned six sleepy tots. The spellbound children followed her like a row of ducklings. But they were not the only ones. The waif followed them to the oak tree on the edge of the forest and watched them climb down into the hollow.

When she ran back to Shytuckle, the waif woke the villagers and showed them where to find the children. Armed with pitchforks, axes and torches, the angry villagers made their way to the base of the ominous oak and reeled from the terrible stench wafting up from its roots.

Two men crawled into the dark hollow beneath the tree with torches. The others strained to hear the children's voices, but all they heard were the muffled cries of the men who scrambled out with pale faces, sick from the horrors they'd seen inside the foul burrow.

Chaos ensued. Some took axes and pitchforks to the tree, while others wailed with fists pounding the ground. The villagers wanted vengeance, but the monster that stole their children from them was nowhere to be seen. No one knew that Old Mother Grim had receded into the blood-soaked clay beneath the tree.

Every red, burning gaze turned to the waif, the only stranger in their midst. They called her a wolf in sheep's clothing. What better way for a monster to hide if not within the innocent guise of a lost child? The villagers tied the waif to a stake, set torches to the straw stacked at her feet and watched in numb silence, deaf to the poor girl's cries.

When the burning was done, they returned to Shytuckle. No one glanced back. Therefore, no one saw the hideous thing climbing up into the peculiar fog pooling around the oak's trunk. Had they done so, the nightmare might have ended there. But as fate would have it, Old Mother Grim was free to hunt and feed her hunger for centuries to come.

CHAPTER 23

THE SICKENING PORTRAIT of helpless children following Old Mother Grim to her blood-soaked lair, and the innocent waif burning, dissolved into rivers of letters that flowed back onto the book's pages. Heartsick and spent, Fate clutched at the ache in her chest, fearing she'd be forever haunted by those horrifying images.

And all this on the heels of watching Finn destroy Moria and seeing the unspeakable carnage beneath her web of illusion.

A gloom settled over her. She'd seen the frightening darkness in Finn, and wasn't sure she could ever look at him without seeing the inhuman stranger he'd become. All she wanted was to get back to Eustace and her old life. If wishes were horses, she'd be galloping home instead of being forced to face Finn in this dismal place with the stench of death clinging to her hair and clothes.

As exhaustion set in, her courage collapsed. Feeling ill, she bent at the waist, staring at the ground. Finn reached out to steady her, but the look of disgust she shot him made him pull away. Seeing the hurt in his eyes only made the queasiness worse. She was torn between wanting to say something to ease his pain and the urge to run as far away from him as she could get.

He saved her from making a choice. He was already backing away, an expression of absolute dejection on his face as he turned and strode off in the opposite direction.

Sithias hoisted his toga up over his long, skinny legs and tiptoed to keep his skimpy sandals from sinking deeper into the marshy ground as he made his way over to her. "You mussstn't judge him too harshly, misss. If anything, he needsss your sssupport, *now* more than ever."

"Unfortunately, you were too busy doing the snake dance with Moria to see how much he *enjoyed* what he did to her," she said a little too sharply. "Sorry. I don't mean to snap." She touched his burnt wing. "And I'm really sorry about this."

Sithias shrugged. "It'll mend. But you won't, unlesss you accept that he isss no longer the Finn you created."

"But that's just it. He's *not* the Finn I always dreamed of. *This* Finn is damaged, and his heart's torn between me and Tove."

He brushed a loose strand from her eyes, trying to tuck it behind her ear. When it wouldn't stay, he gave up. "I've ssseen how that young man looksss at you. You should never doubt hisss feelingsss. Asss for Tove, he chossse you. I know you're new to affairsss of the heart, not to mention the dizzying array of feelingsss that accompaniesss falling in love. In the end though, you mussst choossse whether you are falling on the ssside of love, or fear."

She bit her lip. "I'm afraid about so many things. What if we can't save him? What if he turns into the monster O'Deldar said he would?" She waited for the hard lump in her throat to subside. "What if he gets to know me and finds out he really doesn't like me and wants Tove instead?"

"We'll find a way to sssave him. And I'll eat my sssandals if Finn isss the kind of young man to play such dassstardly gamesss between two innocent girlsss. He knowsss hisss heart, and he'sss following it. You could learn from that. And with all that he'sss facing, he even managed to bring about a good end to *The Dragon Empresss.*" He stroked his goatee with an amused grin forming on his face. "I jussst read the lassst entry, and it'sss quite entertaining really. Apparently, the people thought

Moria'sss death brought about their terrible ssstate of affairsss… ssso they built a temple to deify her in hopesss of regaining their prossperity. Tynan married Kaura, and they gradually ressstored the kingdom to its former glory. Oh, and Finn will be forever known asss the Unholy Piper. They waged a bounty on hisss head—the heaviessst in Asssgar's hissstory. He'sss being hunted asss we ssspeak. Ssso you sssee? He dessservesss your gratitude, not your judgmentsss."

Fate's shoulders drooped. "You're right. I've been unfair and judgmental."

"That'sss the ssspirit," Sithias said, raising a fist dramatically. He dropped his arm. "The red in your hair doesssn't help either. Your temper burnsss twice asss hot."

She blew at the stubborn strand hanging in her eye. "It's not *that* red."

"It only takesss a pinch," he said, shivering and rubbing his arms. "Brrr, I wish I had a little of that fire. I'm catching a chill." He closed his eyes in concentration, using his glamour to make his scorched wings vanish and transform his skimpy toga into a forest green jerkin and tan breeches, topped off with a tweed hat.

She watched his face age to a distinguished man in his fifties. "Nice look. Why so much older?"

"I've been formulating a ssstory for usss ssso we'll be welcomed by the villagersss without sssuspicion. You are looking at Dr. Benjamin Weathersssby, traveling physician extraordinaire, who lossst hisss wife in childbirth a few short monthsss ago. You and Finn are my two eldessst children, and you've recently lossst your one-year-old brother and baby sssister to Old Mother Grim."

Realizing she hadn't actually put any real attention on their new surroundings, Fate looked out over a valley covered in a patchwork of wheat and cornfields with a small village of peculiar beehive-shaped stone huts clustered near the river's edge. There seemed to be no sign of life in Shytuckle, save for the small tufts of chimney smoke trailing up to a sky of swollen gray clouds sagging over the village. "That's good, Sithias. You came up with that while listening to all my woes?"

He sniffed and stroked his silvery goatee. "Yesss, well, I do have my momentsss." He eyeballed her attire with displeasure. "Of coursse, you'll need to change out of *that* malodorousss thing you're wearing, and write up a caravan sssuitable for a doctor traveling with hisss delicate inssstrumentsss of ssscience."

Offended by his rude remark about her beautiful gown, she looked down, shocked to see that it was nothing of the kind. The clock had struck midnight and her coach had turned back into a pumpkin. In this case her gown had returned to being the dingy shapeless garment it had always been beneath Moria's illusion. Grossed out, she hastily unpinned her notepad and wrote up being freshly bathed and shampooed, her teeth brushed, and fully dressed in a suitable change of clothing. Within seconds of reading the description aloud, her skin tingled with a cool, clean sensation as her grimy shift transformed into a simple rose tunic dress over a white chemise cloaked beneath a hooded wool cape. And for a little added comfort, she put her feet back into a pair of Doc Martens.

Turning her attention to the *Book of Fables* standing upright on the bog and peat like a stone megalith, she conjured two horses and a sturdy caravan with the book resting within, as well as the good doctor's delicate instruments of science.

"Now go talk to Finn," Sithias encouraged. "Show him your sssupport and be the ssstrong young woman of character I know you to be."

"Thanks, Sithias," she said and headed over to Finn, who stood a fair distance from the forest's edge.

As she drew near, a kind of sickly sigh wafted off the woods, not really a breeze or wind, but something like the foul breath of a dying gasp. The hairs rising on the back of her neck made her slow down. When she saw the oak, she stopped in her tracks. Dwarfing the surrounding trees, it looked very much like a weed in the garden, stubbornly rooted there with its thick bulbous trunk and sprawling limbs gobbling all the space around it. It was easy to imagine Old Mother Grim had planted the monstrous thing.

Finn was staring at the oak with a black look on his face.

"I brought you a change of clothes," she said.

He gave the slightest start, as if deep in thought, before turning to her. He looked as worn and frayed around the edges as the tattered shirt his once gleaming brocade overcoat had become. Golden stubble shadowed his jaw and his bronzed blond locks fell in careless waves over his rune-marked temple. Fate's heart fluttered out of control. His soul, though battered, was shining through, and the dark visitor was nowhere in sight.

He must've seen the recognition and acceptance in her eyes, because he pulled her into his arms. "I'm so sorry you had to see me that way," he said, his voice thick with sorrow.

He held her too tight, his body trembling as his breathing came in ragged, uneven bursts. Hearing a faint sob, she didn't know what to do. There was nothing she could say that would make this better, and he knew it.

His body went suddenly rigid and he let go of her.

Feeling cast adrift, she wobbled in place, startled by the sudden deadpan look in his eyes.

"I'll help you with Old Mother Grim, but afterwards, I'll be taking my leave and moving on alone."

Icy pain seized her heart. "You're just going to up and *go?*"

When he stared at her blank-faced, she couldn't stop tears from filling her eyes. *"Answer me."*

His features furrowed into determined lines. "It's best for you if I do. I lost myself back in Asgar. The darkness took over.

And the worst of it is I *enjoyed* the glorious rush of it all. I can't trust myself anymore. I'm afraid I'll hurt you."

"You don't think it would hurt me more if you just left?"

"You know what O'Deldar said."

"Yes, but I also know you can't do this without me. We have to follow this through to the eighth fable. Mugloth is the key to curing your poisoning."

"I don't know if I'll last that long. I'm changing and there's nothing I can do to stop it. And I can't take the way you looked at me after Moria…so *repulsed*."

"There's a definite ick factor to seeing you seduce a woman into burning herself alive, but I'm dealing."

She could see him studying her face, measuring her every move. At last a visible degree of relief passed through him. Smiling, he scooped her up in his arms and whirled her around in circles. "You have no idea how much courage you fill me with." He set her down. "I was going abso-bloody-lutely mental when I thought I'd lost you—"

"*Shhh,*" she said. "Just kiss me."

They arrived in Shytuckle an hour later. A few women who were out tending to their daily chores met them with closed, fearful expressions, while the men glared with open hostility. Within minutes, the villagers withdrew into their dwellings, doors and shutters slamming shut.

There appeared to be no tavern or inn to speak of, so they drew the horses to a halt in front of Shytuckle's largest stone structure, standing sturdy and solid with a high peaked roofline and an arched entrance.

Finn jumped down, taking Fate by the waist. She slid down to the ground, pressed against him. "Stop that," she said, feeling an uncontrollable thrill pass through her, "you're driving me crazy."

"Look who's talking," Finn said with a mischievous grin.

Sithias shot them a look of annoyance. "An ounce of decorum *pleassse*. You're suppossed to be brother and sissster." With a huff, he surveyed the deserted street and shut doors from his perch high in the driver's seat. "Well, it appearsss asss though we won't be getting any ussseful information from the villagersss. It would certainly be helpful if we knew how many visssits the grim old monster hasss made thusss far."

"I saw a pigsty on the way in," Fate offered. "If the waif's there, she'd probably talk to us."

Finn gauged the sun's position behind the thickening clouds. "We need to get to it then. It looks like we're only a few hours from sundown."

Sithias moved to join them.

"You should stay," Finn said. "Someone needs to be here if the villagers start getting nosy about us."

Sithias threw up his arms. "Oh sure. Leave me all alone with the burn-you-at-the-ssstake-for-being-a-ssstranger-in-Shytuckle villagersss!"

"Just holler for help. I'm sure we can make it back before they singe a hair on your chinny-chin-chin," Fate said with a chuckle.

Finn laughed at his horrified expression as he grabbed her hand.

She looked back at Sithias over her shoulder, throwing him a reassuring smile. "You'll be fine."

They reached the pigsty within a few minutes. It was nothing more than a lopsided hut looking ready to tip over in the slightest breeze. A wobbly fence surrounded three rotund pigs laying in the muck.

Finn stopped her from going further. "Allow me to be the gentleman and check to see if our wee waif is inside."

"By all means."

"Oh, you might want to have some food ready in case I need to bribe her out."

She nodded, despite how wrong it felt to conjure food next to the rank odor wafting off the pigsty. Ten smelly minutes later, Finn emerged from the hut with the ragged child.

Seeing the wretched girl struck Fate with an instant pang of sympathy. She was so little, no more than six years old with filthy rags hanging from her tiny frame. Despite the layers of grime, her pale-brown hair remained a stubborn cloud of frizz framing impish features. For one so young, her brown downcast eyes were far too alert and vigilant.

"Fate, this is Gerdie," Finn said. "She has much to tell us, but I thought we'd have lunch first."

Fate said hello, but the girl had seen the basket of food. She stared at it like a hungry dog, licking her cracked lips, unable to tear her eyes away long enough to acknowledge Fate. They headed far from the pigsty and situated Gerdie downwind of them before settling on a grassy knoll amidst some grazing sheep. As soon as the sandwiches were out of the basket, her small hand darted out to grab one. After gulping down two, she set another sandwich on top of her frayed bundle with a sheepish look.

"Thanks. That's more food than I've had in years." She burped and gave them both a lopsided grin.

Finn chuckled. "You're welcome." He looked at Fate. "It seems we came to the right person. Gerdie was telling me she's seen Old Mother Grim before."

The girl nodded. "A long time ago, when me, my big sister and grandmother first came here. I was real young then, only five or six."

"You don't look any older than that now," Fate said, surprised by the grownup comment.

"Oh, right," Gerdie said. "Time moves slow when you're roamin' from one place to another."

Fate regarded the girl with a growing sense of sadness. She couldn't imagine having to fend for herself at such a young, helpless age.

"Gerdie, you said Old Mother Grim's been to the village twice already," Finn said, his gaze turning to the distant hills, where thin shreds of mist were pooling into clouds of fog.

"And she'll be comin' back tonight as soon as the sun's down and the fog's thick as barley pottage mixed with carrots, potatoes and pigeon." She smacked her lips together with a dreamy expression.

"We've got maybe two hours to prepare. You said your grandmother nearly destroyed Old Mother Grim, right?" he asked.

Gerdie nodded sadly, dropping her gaze to the grassy mound. "She gave the old monster a mighty wallop, enough to keep her lickin' her wounds for a time, but in the end Old Mother Grim went on with her evil ways and Oma paid for it."

"What do you mean?" Fate asked.

"Bein' that Oma was a healer and a dabbler in the magic arts, the villagers of Woodknoll burned her at the stake thinkin' she was the monster who took their children."

Fate glanced at Finn. They both knew Gerdie would meet the same ugly end if they didn't stop Old Mother Grim. "Sorry to hear that," she said.

"It was a long time ago," Gerdie muttered.

Fate stared at her; the poor little thing really had lost all perspective of time.

"You said you had your grandmother's notes? Can we see them?" Finn asked.

She untied her bundle, revealing sticks with runes carved into them, several smooth rocks, a ragged-edged notebook and a withered carrot. She handed the notebook to Finn. "Everythin' you're lookin' for is written in here. Hope you can read, cuz I can't."

Fate leaned close to him as he thumbed through the book. Every page was stained and filled with lengthy handwritten notes and sketches of plants, stones, peculiar symbols and various body parts with diagrams overlaying them. He closed the book and looked at her. "She had some Druidic knowledge, but there's a strange mixture of other magic and healing arts here I don't recognize. Are you sure we'll be able to pull this off?"

Gerdie patted Finn's hand like an adult comforting a child. "If there's one thing I'm sure of, there's no such thing as sure in this world. We'll be lucky if we survive goin' up against Old Mother Grim. But I don't care anymore. There's only one thing worse than dyin' here and that's livin' here forever and ever."

CHAPTER 24

SHYTUCKLE'S ENTIRE POPULATION was standing around the caravan when they returned. Sithias had his doctor's bag out and was up in the driver's seat next to an old man. The villagers watched while he examined the man's open mouth then moved to the man's nose, pulling back each nostril with a tongue depressor.

"Ah ha! I sssee the problem here," Sithias said in an authoritative tone. "There ssseemsss to be far too much nossse hair growing in there. It'sss no wonder you can't tasssste your food. You can't sssmell it, sssir. Trim it all back and you'll be tasssting every delectable herb in your wife'sss pottage from the very firssst bite."

The man's face lit up like he'd experienced a miracle. When Sithias saw that 'his children' had returned, he dismissed his patient and held up his hand like he was giving a toast. "Everyone of Shytuckle, I'd like you all to meet my ssson and daughter—" He stopped mid-sentence as his gaze landed on the bedraggled waif standing next to them. "And uh—"

"Your next patient," Fate called out.

She scooted Gerdie past the villagers and shuffled her off to the back of the caravan. Leaving her with Finn, she went inside first to conjure a wall of curtains to hide the *Book of Fables*, and then to prepare a hot bath. While the young girl splashed in the tub behind a privacy screen, Finn looked through her grandmother's notebook. He was focused on a particular page when Sithias, radiating absolute annoyance, stepped inside the caravan.

"Would it have killed you to ssstop and sssay hello to thossse people?" he said. "It wasssn't exactly easssy getting them to warm up to me. I'll have you know I had to look into a few too many unsssightly orificesss to gain their trussst."

"Sorry," Fate said. "We're in a hurry. The sun's going down."

He stamped his leg and flapped his long arms, a motion that resembled an angry stork. "Oh really, the sssun'sss going down? And to think I didn't know that. Of coursse I did! And that'sss why I've got an invitation from the villagersss to join them in the oratory tonight. We've got front-row ssseatsss to the main event." He glanced at the screen Gerdie was bathing behind. "And what'sss that urchin doing here?"

Fate stepped close, patting his arm and leading him over to have a look at Gerdie's notebook. "Calm down, Sithias. You did well, but we've still got a lot more work to do before we can go locking ourselves up with the villagers. Thanks to Gerdie, we now know what to do."

He looked doubtful.

Finn glanced up from the notebook. "There's a spell here to bind the oak tree in its sleeping state. Apparently, it's been grown to protect Old Mother Grim during the day while she sleeps. Usually the tree snoozes at night, but if it senses she's in danger, it'll wake up, and on the wrong side of the bed. We'll need to use this spell to keep it napping while we trap its master." He reached out and pulled Fate close. "I've got a shopping list for you, love."

She sat down next to him on the bench, trying to put some space between them so she could think clearly, but he slid her closer, keeping his arm around her waist. His touch distracted her so much she hadn't registered what she was writing until the last item.

"What's the dove for?" she asked.

"We'll be needin' the blood of a dove," Gerdie explained as

she stepped out from behind the screen wearing the olive wool dress Fate had provided. With the grime scrubbed off her elfin features, they could now tell the difference between a few freckles spotting her nose and what had been specks of dirt. She blinked with confusion when she saw Finn cuddling with Fate. "I thought you were brother and sister."

"Uh…" Fate said with a blank face.

Finn laughed. "Guess the cat's out of the bag on that one. No, we're *far* from being related." He gave Fate a wolfish grin. "To my great pleasure."

She blushed.

Gerdie shrugged. "Don't matter to me."

"Unlesss you're tired of everyone elsssse having all the fun," Sithias muttered.

Fate frowned at both Finn and Sithias. "About the dove?"

"No need to worry," Gerdie assured, her child's voice edged with a maternal tone. "We'll only be needin' a drop and nothin' more." Pushing up her sleeves, she sat down at the table. "We've got a lot of work ahead—two bindin' spells to cast, charms to make, plus the talisman that'll bring the elements crashin' down on the old hag, if all goes right."

They huddled around the table while Gerdie and Finn discussed the details of what needed to be accomplished within the next hour. Thanks to Fate's instantaneous conjuring, they had two binding circles—one of stones and the other of braided rope of rowan, mistletoe and holly—placed around the oak's perimeter, plus all the protective charms they would need to keep themselves and the villagers from falling prey to Old Mother Grim's sleeping potion. Surprisingly, Gerdie responded to Fate's ability like it was about as common as dirt. She was obviously used to magic.

But there was one more item they needed, and no amount of writing could describe it accurately. "If I can write up all this other stuff, I should be able to do the same for the clay," Fate argued.

Throughout their discussion, Finn's mood had grown more serious and dismal. Only his eyes softened when he looked at her. "Have you ever been touched by evil? Do you really *know* what it is?"

"No, but I heard from a source I totally trust that evil likes to monologue a lot, and it tastes a little chalky."

He didn't look amused.

"Okay, I don't *know* what evil is," she mumbled.

"Then you can't expect to know how to write about it. We have no other choice. The clay has to be taken from the ground near the oak's roots."

Fate's eyes darted from one face to the other. "But what if Old Mother Grim's still there when we arrive?"

Finn flipped back a few pages and read a passage from the notebook. "It says here, Old Mother Grim is as timely as the sun's coming and going. As soon as the twilight hour has passed and the night is as black as ink, the creature crawls out from under the roots of her evil oak to begin prowling for innocent victims. Her body is heavy and sluggish, yet when she joins with the fog, it seems she glides swiftly upon the currents of its moist breath as easily as a canoe on a river."

As Fate listened to the description her heart thudded with dread. "Oh, that's reassuring. Wherever there's fog, Ol' Snaggletooth's sailing through it like she's on jet skis. I don't like it."

"There's nothin' to like about any of this," Gerdie said, unnerving Fate with an unflappable gaze from where she peered up over the edge of the table.

Fate started to object but the girl's mature tone and expression stopped her short, a trait she found unnerving. Apparently Gerdie's well-honed survival skills had forced her to grow up faster than the average six-year-old.

"Just do what you gotta do and get back here as soon as you can," Gerdie continued, "'cuz old grim guts is no doubt climbin' out of her rotten hole as we speak."

Fate's throat tightened with fear. The thought of stepping anywhere near that oak and the horrors that lay beneath its roots terrified her.

Finn squeezed her waist. "I'll be with you."

"Maybe *I* should go with you, misss," Sithias said, obvious dread in his eyes.

Surprised by his brave offer, she had to wonder why.

Finn stood. "No, *I'm* going with her." He turned to Fate. "And I think we should fly there. That way we'll be able to lay eyes on the old witch from a safe distance."

"Yeah, I don't like the idea of popping out of thin air if she's anywhere near the tree," she agreed.

The night was complete in its darkness when they stepped out into the cold, damp air. She had one foot on the steps when Sithias stopped her. "Watch yourssself now," he whispered. "You'll need to be ssstrong for both of you."

She searched his anxious expression. "What is it?"

"I senssse a dangerousss shift in Finn. Sssomething about him isss making my ssscalesss quiver."

"You don't have any scales right now," she reminded him.

"Thisss is no time for sssemanticsss," he said, his hushed whisper more sibilant than usual. "Jussst be careful. There'sss a randy sssort of gleam in hisss eyesss that'sss never been there before."

"But earlier, you were his cheerleader, pompoms and everything."

"I ssstill am, but watch for the poison'sss influence." He gave her a less than confident smile and raised his voice for Finn's benefit. "I'll be watching the time and expect you both back in fifteen minutesss or lesss." He shook a finger at Finn like a father whose daughter he was dating. "Don't make me have to come looking for you. *Ssseriously,* I really don't want to go up there."

"Like you would," Finn said from where he stood in the dusky light.

As Sithias let go of her hand, she gulped back the fear mounting in her chest, forcing a smile on her face before turning to leave with Finn.

The valley and distant forest below appeared flat and featureless without the light of the moon. They flew slowly and close to the ground while Finn adjusted to flight. Fate held onto his hand to keep him steady, but she didn't have to for long. He was swift to catch on after she wrote up his ability to fly, and far more stable than her first time flying.

He smiled wide and called out, "Well I'm hooked—flying *rocks!"* He swooped upward, spinning into somersaults and testing his speed.

Smiling at his boyish antics, she was glad to see he could still be so lighthearted. She loved that about him. Nothing ever seemed to get him down for long, even in the direst of circumstances. Though part of that could be because he'd forgotten a key element to his earlier misery. She decided it didn't matter. She'd enjoy his good mood as long as it lasted. And as far as Sithias's worries were concerned, she chalked it up to him being overly cautious.

Swooping up from behind, Finn curled his arms around her, pulling her close. The cool breeze washed over them as they sailed through the air. A euphoric thrill passed through her, and she would have lost her bearings had he not held her in his firm grasp.

They slowed to a stop, hovering in the air. Adding her own buoyancy so he wouldn't have to carry her, she ran her hand over the chiseled contours of his face. When she reached the irresistible curve of his mouth, he kissed her fingers, sending tingles up her arm. Sliding her hands into his thick hair, she pulled his lips to hers. He responded with unbridled passion, his fingers digging hard into her back with such fervor, it hurt.

She pulled back, heart racing and breathing hard.

His eyes gleamed a bright green, but his pupils were enlarging, swallowing the irises. He buried his face against her neck, kissing and biting 'til she shivered with a bewildering mixture of desire and alarm.

"Finn…stop."

His hot breath came hard and fast against her skin. His hand slid to her thigh, his fingers clenching the material of her dress, lifting her skirt. A bolt of fear shuddered through her. She shoved him back with all the strength she could gather.

"Stop," she said.

He drifted backwards, his gaze downcast. He held every muscle taut, and for a moment, she feared he might pounce on her. But when he looked at her, self-loathing twisted his face.

"Forgive me," he said, his voice edged with regret.

He continued to drift farther away. Afraid he might leave with his newfound wings, she dove against him, wrapping her arms around his waist.

"It's okay," she said. "I overreacted."

His hands were on her shoulders, shoving her back at arm's length. "No, you didn't. I was losing control." The muscles in his jaw tensed and his eyes narrowed. "It's gotten worse since I killed Moria. There's something savage inside me and each time I give into it, I feel chunks of my soul being devoured. I'm losing myself."

His silence stretched out for an eternity.

"Fate," he said, his voice becoming a determined growl, "I *can't* be anywhere near you when there's nothing left of me but the darkness."

Tears stung her eyes as she shook her head. "If you're trying to say you're leaving me *again,* I'll just follow. You're stuck with me, buster. Just think of me as barnacle…or one of those suckerfish. Better yet, duct tape."

He remained quiet. His gaze hardened as he stared past her into the dim night.

"Don't do this, Finn."

When his gaze flicked back to her, there was an unsettling, crazed glint in his eyes. "I said I'd help you with Old Mother Grim, and I will, but afterwards I have to put an end to this."

His words closed over her heart like a cold fist. Before she could say another word, he shot forward, following the incline of the hill leading to the forest. She sped after him as he flew through thickening patches of mist, losing him entirely when she hit a solid wall of fog. She climbed above it, looking down at the fog bank, a tumbling tidal wave that would soon flood the valley and engulf the streets of Shytuckle.

Fate hovered over the dense sea of mist, searching with growing panic for any sign of Finn. She listened, but the silence was eerie in its totality. The hairs on the back of her arms and neck stirred. She glanced down and knew with dead certainty that something dreadful lurked somewhere within the fog.

Icy fear shot through her limbs. She rose higher, feeling only a little safer as she scanned the rolling cloud below for what she knew it concealed. Then she saw it. A deepening shadow, where the fog parted and rippled like the deep waters of the ocean when something as large and powerful as a great white shark is skimming just beneath the surface. Old Mother Grim was moving toward the village.

A hand clamped over her mouth. It took a few terror-filled seconds to realize it was Finn before she relaxed.

He let go and took her hand. "Come with me. The tree's over

here," he whispered.

They landed a few yards away from the gnarled giant and crept toward the trunk through the shredding mist. Fate glanced up into the branches spreading over them like an ugly inkblot.

The two large binding circles of stone and braided wood she'd written up earlier at the caravan were in place around the tree, their radius as wide as the sprawling canopy. Finn stepped over the stone circle, gesturing for her to follow. "Come on. We need to pass through both circles to get the clay closest to the trunk."

Fate couldn't go any farther. "You know this is the part in the horror movie where the audience is saying don't go in, right?"

"You're not alone," he assured, and pulled her along.

As soon as she crossed the stone circle and stepped inside the circle of braided wood, her skin went cold and clammy. The perceptible shift in energy was jarring. Chills slithered up her spine as they crept over the mist-covered ground in search of protruding roots. Her foot found them first. She tripped and landed face-down in the damp soil next to where a depression in the ground deepened into a gaping cavity beneath the tree's rootball.

Finn knelt and lifted her up. "Are you hurt?"

The putrid odor of death clung to the dank night air. She had nearly fallen into Old Mother Grim's lair.

She swallowed back the bile erupting in her throat. "No, but I think I'm going to be sick."

"Hold your breath," he told her. It was too dark to see his face, but he seemed so unaffected by it all. She couldn't fathom how he was able to distance himself so easily.

"I can't do this," she said backing away. "*You* get the clay."

He went stiff, his hands curling into fists at his sides. "No. That's not a good idea."

She was about to argue that he wasn't the one ready to puke

his guts out but something in his voice stopped her.

Dropping to her knees, she hastily dug up the tainted clay and filled the small pouch she'd brought along. The moment she stood, a wave of nausea hit her. She doubled over, convulsing in pain with nothing to vomit. She'd expelled the contents of her stomach just before they'd left Asgar and hadn't had enough of an appetite to eat since they'd arrived. Finn crouched next to her, holding her hair back and keeping her upright.

When the retching finally stopped, she gasped for air and her lungs filled with stinging bolts of fear and misery. Grisly images flashed before her eyes: small grasping hands, gnashing, yellow teeth and dying gasps drowned in gushing blood.

Her terrorized scream echoed into the night.

Finn lifted her up and flew back toward Shytuckle. She thrashed and twisted in his arms, her cries unceasing. Unable to fly with her in such a state, he descended into a wheat field. Desperate to console her, he held tight, rocking her in his arms.

He hated himself for making her dig up the clay. His need to shield himself from the overwhelming presence of the oak had kept him from manning up to the job. After he'd stepped inside the binding circles the darkness had expanded in him, snaking out through his soles into the foul earth to connect with its spawn. It had taken every ounce of strength and concentration he had to cut off the vile energy and keep it contained.

But Fate was in real trouble now, and there was only one way to free her from the endless nightmare playing in her head.

Closing his eyes, he probed her tortured mind, opening to her terror and the ghosts of all those murdered children. The awful gloom seeped deep into his core, riddling him with an unbearable pain.

Fate collapsed against him, sobbing softly.

"You're safe now," he said through clenched teeth.

She opened her eyes at the sound of his voice. Her nerve endings were still raw, making it hard to stop the shaking. "Finn…I…I can't face that monster."

"You leave that to me," he said, his voice wooden.

She leaned back to see his face. The fierce look in his eyes as he stared past her made her glance in the same direction. Every muscle seized with terror when she saw the massive fog bank spilling down the hill with ominous speed toward them.

"We have to get back. She's almost on top of us," he said. Holding onto her, he stood up and leaped into the sky.

The wind at their backs seemed charged with evil intent as they skimmed above the river, disturbing thin wisps of mist curling over the water's shimmering surface, racing over Shytuckle's quiet rooftops before coming to a smooth landing beside the caravan.

When he set her down, he wouldn't meet her gaze. She sensed guilt and shame, but there was something else brewing beneath the surface. Something menacing.

"They're waiting for you," he said in a curt tone.

His decision to shut her out of his life was still firmly in place. She wanted to talk him out of it, change his mind. But she could see stubborn resolve in his rigid stance as visibly as heat waves radiating off a sun-baked sidewalk.

Too wrung out to rise to the challenge, she entered the caravan and dropped the pouch of tainted clay on the table.

Sithias whirled around. "Oh, I'm ssso glad to sssee you back sssafe and—" He clapped his hand over his nose. "Ew, that clay smellsss *atrociousss*—like…" He coughed and gagged. "I sssimply *do not* have wordsss to describe it."

"It smells like death," Gerdie said. She gestured to him. "Now, take it out of the pouch and put it in that there bowl."

Sithas went stiff. "I will *not!*"

Gerdie picked up the blackthorn dagger and pointed it at him. "Unless you want blood everywhere, you'd better get over your prissy self and do it."

Sithias opened and closed his mouth in shock. "Are—are you threatening me?"

"It's for the bird, you nutter."

Wilting with relief, Sithias muttered a mild protest under his breath but picked up the tip of the pouch between his finger and thumb anyway. The clay slipped out, plopping in the bowl with a sickening squish.

Staggering back, he dry heaved convulsively. After recovering, he glared at Gerdie. "Happy?"

The arguing continued on from there, with Gerdie tossing out orders and Sithias following them with grumbling retorts.

Gerdie gathered the dove in her hands. Fate couldn't watch when she pierced the bird's breast for the few drops of blood she needed to add to the clay. She'd seen enough blood to last her a lifetime. Turning her attention to the door, she wondered why Finn hadn't followed her inside.

Just as she decided to check on him, he stepped in and leaned against the wall. While Gerdie set fire to the cedar under the ball of clay, Fate watched him. Tension tightened his features, cording taut lines along the muscles of his arms. He looked ready to bolt at any second.

She suddenly regretted using the Words of Making to give him the ability to fly. Of course, the power could be removed. Couldn't it? There was no way of knowing unless she actually tried, but not without telling him first. And then she'd have to explain why. Best to let it go. After all, Tove had given him his speed, strength and elemental powers without taking them back.

"There, that should do it," Gerdie said, smiling with satisfaction as the flames died out. "The talisman now has the power to call upon the forces of nature to put things back in their proper order."

Finn picked up one of the many protective charms lying in the basket on the table. He strode over to Fate and tied it around her neck. It consisted of several crusty herb-covered twigs tied together in the shape of a crude pitchfork and smelled of mold, dirt, stinkweed and garlic.

Pinching her nose, she questioned him with a look.

His expression was controlled. "I need you to be safe."

The chill coming off him pushed her anxiety to the edge of anger. She grabbed a charm and shoved it in his hand. "Shouldn't be a problem. This stench would have a skunk running for the hills."

"It's not to keep Old Mother Grim away. It's to keep us awake when she tries to put us all asleep," he explained.

"I know," she answered, her tone sharp, "but it'll keep *you* away, won't it?"

She regretted her words immediately. She hadn't meant it the way it sounded, but he'd taken it in the worst possible way. Self-reproach fractured his carefully composed expression. But he was quick to reassemble his features into stone. Now there'd be no talking him out of leaving.

Sithias watched the volatile exchange with alarm. "I agree, there will be no romance in the air with thessse hideousss sssmelling thingsss dangling under our nosesss, let alone sssleeping." He gave Fate an encouraging wink as he picked up the basket of charms, holding them at arm's length as he headed for the door.

Gerdie grinned. "The smell is part of the charm's charm," she said, marking a starburst-shaped rune into the lump of clay before wrapping it in cloth and tucking it under her arm.

"There'sss nothing charming about it," Sithias muttered. "And I'm certain the villagersss will agree."

Gerdie's lopsided grin vanished. "Now listen up," she said. Her grave tone had everyone's attention. "This here's important. The only way this talisman'll have any power over the old canker is if she's lookin' at it." She held up the dagger. "When her eyes are fixed on it, stab the dagger into the rune, and go deep into the clay. I'd like to be the one who sticks it to her, but it don't matter who does the deed, so long as it gets done."

The room fell quiet. There was nothing more to say. They were about to face the most unspeakable of monsters—from within and without.

CHAPTER 25

TENDRILS OF MIST threaded between the stone huts as they walked the short distance between the caravan and the oratory. Finn lagged several steps behind as Fate, Gerdie and Sithias approached the men standing guard outside the building.

"I should conjure up some swords or something," he heard Fate whisper when she saw they were armed with nothing more than farm tools as weapons.

Gerdie shook her head. "Nothin' but powerful magic and a whole lot of luck is gonna stop vulture face now."

"Oh, *that'sss* reassuring," Sithias muttered. Clearing his throat, he lifted his chin and smiled at the harried looking men as he explained why they should wear the protective charms he offered. They appeared doubtful when the smelly sticks were passed around, but they wore them all the same.

Finn caught Fate by the arm as they neared the front doors of the chapel. "I'll stay out here with the men."

She shook her head. The instant terror in her eyes tore at him. "*No,* please stay with me."

He swallowed hard, clamping down on his need to ease her suffering. He didn't want to refuse her, but he'd made up his mind to keep his distance after he'd lost control earlier. The way she'd opened to him while they'd drifted together through the air, kissing him with such wild abandon had awoken something frightening inside him. The urge to possess her had flared hot in him like never before. If she hadn't stopped when she did, he didn't want to think about the damage he might have wreaked.

She put a hand on his chest, her touch penetrated deep into his heart. "Please stay."

If he had any decency, he'd tell her to go inside without him. "For a while," he conceded.

Upon entering the chapel, the thick wooden doors closed behind them with a heavy thud as two men hoisted a large, thick beam across them. The fear inside was palpable. Several men stood with anxious, gritty expressions along the periphery of the large room, each posted in front of a boarded window. The women sat with the hollow expressions of mothers who'd either lost a child or feared losing the warm bundle in their arms. The older children sat as still as their parents, while the toddlers, who could not grasp the danger they were in, squealed with glee and raced across the stone floor.

Sithias held up the basket of charms. "If I could have everyone'sss attention. We've made thessse protective charmsss for you to wear."

"How's one of them charms going to protect us from marauding, underhanded thieves?" one of the men said, while others nodded in agreement. "I've seen them smelly sticks before and they never once stopped our youngsters from being stolen out from under our noses."

Sithias stared in surprise. "You think it'sss maraudersss?"

"What else do you think stole our babies?" the man said with a snort. "Ghosties?"

Gerdie yanked on his sleeve. Sithias bent down as she spoke in a hushed tone. "They never believed me about Old Mother Grim, and they didn't like me givin' their kids charms neither. Just say it's for good luck."

Sithias stood straight. "Did I sssay protective charmsss? I meant *good luck* charmsss."

Faces turned hopeful, and everyone surrounded him with outreached hands. The anxiety lifted somewhat, but after an hour of boredom, mixed with the noise of restless children, the mood grew strained again. Finn could hardly stand the tension building in the room as he sat next to Fate and the others in silence, each of them waiting for the impending doom.

Gerdie's patience ran out first. She jumped to her feet and joined the fidgety youngsters, distracting them for a short time with a few magic tricks. She pulled pebbles out of their ears, which she juggled and turned into fleeting butterflies that vanished into puffs of smoke. For a girl so young, she handled the toddlers in a practiced, levelheaded manner. Unfortunately, her tricks only served to excite, rather than quiet them.

"I guess the charms are working," Fate said, her voice low. "If Old Mother Grim was going to do something, she probably would've done it by now."

"Don't be fooled, she's out there," Finn said. He'd been feeling her formidable presence for some time. His skin prickled as if she lurked directly behind him, fouling his air with her fetid breath. Strangely, he wasn't afraid. He looked forward to making her suffer for her unspeakable crimes. When he thought of the innocent lives she'd taken, vengeance swelled and collided with the dark power coiled tight inside him, ready to strike snake-quick when the time came to destroy the abomination. He looked at the others. "Be ready for anything."

Fear flickered across Sithias and Gerdie's faces. Fate sat still beside him, their arms touching as she glanced down at her hands and gripped her legs. As much as she was keeping a tight lid on her dread, he felt the quake running through her. He exhaled slowly, resisting the reflex to put his arm around her.

Gerdie sat down next to Sithias, her small brown eyes darting round the room. "You're right. She knows we've got protection against her sleepin' potion. I figure she'll wait us out 'til we're so tuckered out we're half-witted with sleep."

Sithias sighed. "It appearsss we're in for a very long night. I sssuggessst some ssstory time to sssettle down these ssspirited youngstersss. As much asss squealsss of laughter can be musssic to the earsss, I don't think my nervesss can take any more."

Fate leaned forward, her desperation for a distraction from the stress showing on her face. "One of your stories would be so great right now."

"Well, misss," Sithias said with an apologetic look, "I think you're bessst sssuited for the little onesss. I'm sure my talesss would sssail right over their tiny headsss. Too much romance, political intrigue and frou-frou, if you know what I mean."

"Yeah," she said, disappointed. "But I'm not sure—"

"I think we'll all go barking mad if we have to sit all edgy on the edge of our seats any longer," Finn said. "Go ahead, tell us a tall tale. Or better yet, take us away to some place that'll remind us of sweet, fresh smells, like that of heather and pine… of home."

"You mean Scotland?" she asked.

He smiled faintly. "Aye."

"Do you still remember it?"

He frowned, trying to see through the thickening shadow of the internal darkness slowly blotting out everything he loved. "Of course," he said, not wanting to admit that his dearest memories were losing their clarity.

Fate nodded, unable to hide her doubt and sadness. "I have some stories about Scotland I can tell."

"Why not Hellas?" Sithias suggested, a panicked look on his face. "You can't go wrong with all thossse godsss and goddessesss."

"No," she said, scolding him with her eyes. "It's the perfect time for a Scottish tale."

Puzzled by the tense exchange between them, Finn watched

her take a seat on the steps near the altar, while the smaller children settled in around her feet. Even the adults and the older children looked eager for a respite from the fear-laced boredom.

She glanced over at Finn, the ghost of a smile on her lips. Something passed between them. That mysterious tie connecting them shivered with a mixture of hope and apprehension pouring straight from her heart. He stared back, anxious to know what she was thinking. He could see she had no intention of keeping secrets. Her face was an open book.

Keeping her gaze fixed on him, she started telling a story about a curious boy with a love for life. A boy who found his roots in Scotland and learned he was the descendant of a long line of mysterious Druids. He listened intently with an increasing sense of discovery as she dusted off the relics of his life and brought them into the sunlight, new and shiny and beautiful. As delighted as he was to be walking down memory lane, it baffled him as to how she knew so many tiny details, especially when she described his wise grandfather's quirky antics.

He chuckled softly, his spirits lifting as the children squirmed with laughter. For just a moment, he was home in Scotland seeing the arching backs of the fells strewn with heather, the ridge of blue mountains feathered with morning mists. Then as Fate described the boy's encounter with the wolf wraiths of Black Spout Woods, the youngsters grew quiet, leaning forward with chins on small hands.

The deeper she traveled into his past, the more a thread of suspicion worked loose in him, tangling into a ball of troubling questions. How could she know all these things about him? The shadows in the hushed room seemed to spread and the air grew heavy. An ache like an old wound throbbed in his chest and a bewildering sense of betrayal opened wide as she described the great moose king, Lord Rakimnal, who guided the boy to the sacred grove of the Olde Ones, where they bestowed him with the tongue of the Dark Speech.

Raw anguish poured through the gash, drowning him with the forgotten knowledge that he was not the man he thought he was. He was a figment of Fate's imagination, a meaningless toy, nothing more than an amusement. How could she keep this from him, not just once but *twice?* Emptied and blasted to the core, he narrowed his eyes on her.

She stopped in mid-sentence, her face paling as she slowly stood.

Sithias rose from his seat, tapping incessantly on Finn's shoulder. He glared up at him. *"What?"*

"Look," Sithias said, pointing.

Thick streams of sickly-green mist flowed through the cracks of a boarded window. The curling tendrils moved with unnatural deliberateness, splitting into filmy tentacles snaking out around the women holding babies and the toddlers sitting on the floor. As the sleeping potion came near the charms they wore, the feelers recoiled violently and evaporated.

A few seconds later, shouts and screams came from the men outside. Sickening cracks and thuds sounded against the outside walls, followed by a dreadful silence.

Finn jumped to his feet. "Get the children to the back of the building!" He caught Fate staring at him. When their gaze locked, she stiffened, the light in her eyes extinguished. Too hollowed out to care, he turned and ran to the front entrance with the other men.

The black look of poison Finn threw her sliced deeper than any knife could, confirming for her the question of whether his memories had returned or not. That hadn't been her intention. All she'd wanted to do was remind him of who he was and where he came from. Restore his foundation and give him something to hang onto. She'd known it was risky but she couldn't bear seeing him lose pieces of himself any longer.

Sithias had tried to warn her. She should've listened.

Sithias hurried over to her, looking as terrified as the little girl he was clutching in his arms. "Misss, come with usss," he said, pulling her attention back to more immediate concerns.

Fate picked up the child closest to her, a boy no more than two, and ran to the back of the large room with the other women and children.

"Shouldn't you be up front with the men?" Gerdie asked Sithias.

"Who saysss?" he asked in surprise. "I'm a *sssnake*, not a man."

Confused, Gerdie looked at Fate, who simply shook her head. "It's a long and weird story. I'll tell you la—"

All at once, a deep and penetrating force reverberated throughout the oratory. The very air throbbed and tightened around them. The pressure intensified, culminating into one momentary release—a frightening free-fall—before the entrance doors exploded inward, deadly splinters shooting out like a barrage of arrows.

Fate flew backwards, slammed against the back wall and fell to the floor. The roof caved, stones rained down and a cloud of choking dust billowed in.

Cries and screams filled the blinding ruin.

Somehow, Fate had managed to hang onto the boy. He was shaking and crying in her arms. She sat up, disoriented and bruised, trying to see something—anything—but the dust and grit watered her eyes, making it impossible to see clearly. *"Finn!"* she called out, knowing he'd been standing in the blast zone.

He didn't answer.

"Gerdie? Sithias!" she cried.

Gerdie scrambled forward. "You okay?" she asked.

"Yeah, for the most part. What about you?" She could hardly see Gerdie's nod through the chalky murk. Leaning against the wall, Fate made a feeble attempt to comfort the boy in her arms by patting his back. "I don't see Finn or Sithias."

"Sithias should be here," Gerdie said. "He was standin' right next to me."

Fate felt around the floor with her free hand hoping to find him nearby. Ragged splinters of wood and shattered stone were all that met her touch. She was almost thankful for the clouds of dust still falling from the pulverized ceiling; she didn't want to see the misery hiding behind them.

Gerdie gripped Fate's arm. "Feel that?" she whispered.

Fate froze, gulping back the panic in her throat. She felt it too—the onset of something terrible and powerful pressing forward.

Tentacles of cold mist snaked through the ashy whiteness. Tortured, drawn-out cries of pain came from the wounded men lying somewhere in its midst. Sudden death stopped their screams in the instant of several hideous, bone-crunching cracks. Terror iced through Fate's veins, paralyzing her the moment she glimpsed the shambling, hulking shape of Old Mother Grim emerging from the thinning mist and dust.

Dragging her clubbed feet beneath her cumbersome weight, the ragged creature shuffled to a halt, leaning on her thick-handled broom of sticklewort 'til it bowed to the point of breaking. Her large drooping breasts hung like half-full bags of flour over an engorged belly, yet her arms were bone-thin and grotesquely long.

A cry rose in Fate's throat as she realized Old Mother Grim's primitive garb was a mottled patchwork of little human shapes stitched crudely together. She stifled a horrified sob against the whimpering boy's shoulder and squeezed him tight to her chest.

The same foul graveyard stench Fate had dug up from the oak's roots wafted off the creature, mingling uneasily with the freshly laundered scent of her own clothes. Nausea churned in her belly, spiking a needle-sharp pain right to her brain.

Craning her small, shriveled head, Old Mother Grim fixed her blood-red gaze on the boy in Fate's arms. His protective charm had fallen off. Extending her bony arm, the creature reached out, her splintered talons just inches from his face.

The boy screamed, broke free from Fate's embrace and leaped off her lap.

Old Mother Grim's eyes snapped on the boy and she spoke. Her cracked, blood-encrusted lips formed the garbled sounds of some primeval language. The strength of her spell-cast words gripped him in her thrall. In the blink of an eye, he went from sheer hysteria to utter calm, and stepped beside the monster as if she were his protector.

Gerdie jumped up, a crazed look in her eyes. "Hey, you ugly old crone! Look over here, I've got somethin' for ya!"

Old Mother Grim's head twisted in Gerdie's direction. The second the creature looked at the lump of clay in her hand, she stabbed the blackthorn dagger into the rune mark. An impossible amount of blood gushed from the talisman, spilling in thick splotches over the stone floor. "That's for *Oma* and every kid you took under *my* watch!" she screamed, her face contorted by a rage too long-lived for one so young. She dropped the clay, a cold smile twisting her mouth. The lump splashed in the blood, splattering her skirt.

Old Mother Grim's vulturine face betrayed something akin to recognition as a shrill, unearthly shriek tore from her gaping mouth. Thunder rumbled in the distant mountains and a sudden savage wind swept through the broken building. Old Mother Grim shrank back as if she feared something riding in the gale. She stood there, still as a rock for a brief moment, then snatched up the little boy and vanished in a billowing cloak of fog.

Lunging for him, Fate fell through the emptiness. She

scrambled to her feet, frightened for the boy she'd failed to protect. The adrenaline pumping through her body diluted the guilt pushing to the surface. She didn't know how, but she'd get him back safe and sound no matter what.

Her gaze landed on the bodies littered throughout the rubble and dying eddies of dust. In her panic to find Finn she slipped in the puddle of blood Gerdie had made. Stumbling to regain her balance, she waded through the debris, dread tightening her lungs as she searched frantically. Her breath returned only when she discovered he wasn't lying amongst the dead and injured.

She turned back, seeing that Gerdie was leaning over Sithias. Tripping in her rush to get over to him, she saw the girl he'd been carrying patting his bloody chest. Fate's legs buckled out from under her upon seeing a thick splinter of wood sticking out of him. She fell to her knees beside him, tears flooding her eyes. She couldn't lose him too.

His amber eyes fluttered open. "Ssseemsss I've been ssskewered like a shish kabob. But no need to worry, misss, we sssnakesss have nine livesss," he said, managing a weak smile.

Sniffing back the tears, she couldn't help smiling. "You're getting that mixed up with cats, silly."

"Well, I'll jussst have to be a cat then," he said groggily. His human form gave way to that of a white tiger. Then he let out a gruff sigh and fainted.

Gerdie and the little girl gasped, drawing back from the tiger in surprise. Sudden wails from those survivors who'd discovered the dead and wounded, interrupted Fate's attempt to explain. Thinking it best to escape the chaos unfolding around them, she unhooked her notepad and wrote herself, Sithias and Gerdie back into the caravan.

Gerdie dropped the bloody blackthorn dagger. "What in

the world?"

Her nerves shot, Fate began talking fast. "Sithias is really a giant snake with wings, but he's been wearing a glamour to look human and it can turn him into anything else he wants. He must be delirious right now, but he's perfectly harmless. I promise. Can you help him? Get that stake out and patch him up?"

Gerdie nodded blankly. "I'll be needin' some supplies."

Fate conjured the clean cloths, thread and needle, iodine and tweezers she asked for. Pacing while Gerdie went to work, she couldn't shake a growing sense of urgency. "Where could Finn be?" she asked, not so much to Gerdie, but to the world at large.

"He's gone to the tree," Gerdie said, tearing a square of cloth into narrow strips.

"What?" Fate stared at her in disbelief.

"That was the plan all along," she said, tugging gently on the large splinter.

Wincing as more blood gushed from the wound, Fate gulped and turned away.

"It's all there in Oma's notes," Gerdie continued. "Once Old Mother Grim's weakened, we knew she'd go back to the oak and burrow in like a tick to shield herself from the elements. Let the tree take the brunt of the attack until she gets her strength back—just like before."

"I should've been told about this. He can't do this alone." Angry, Fate headed for the door.

Gerdie was suddenly beside her. "You can't go. Finn told me to keep you here." She reached out squirrel-quick, tore Fate's notepad from the waist of her dress and held it behind her back. "He said you wouldn't go without it."

Fate glared at the little girl, wearing the implacable expression of a bouncer. "Hand it over."

Sticking out her chin, Gerdie shook her head. "I promised Finn."

"I'm bigger than you," Fate warned.

"You won't hurt me."

"Fine. Keep it, I don't need it," she said, not feeling nearly as confident as she sounded. She pushed through the door and was just about to leap into the air when she looked back. "Just do what you can to make Sithias better. And when you're done, drive the caravan up to the tree."

Without waiting for Gerdie's protest, she shot up into the darkness and vanished from sight.

The sky over Shytuckle was eerily clear and the valley was free of the sinister fog. But as Fate flew up over the rise in the direction of the forest, she saw storm clouds amassing into an enormous churning whirlpool of seething darkness over the oak tree.

As she sped through the air, it seemed like the massive thunderhead rumbled and growled with fury. The closer she got, the stronger the wind became, making it difficult to gain any real speed. But as more of the oak tree came into view, she instinctively slowed, trying to make sense of what she was seeing before getting too close.

The tree had awakened, looking like a black clot against the horizon with twisting veins thrashing at something near the base of its trunk. She floated closer, hearing a shrill, spine-tingling sound—the same eldritch shriek Old Mother Grim had made when Gerdie stabbed the clay talisman. This time it wasn't vengeful magic making her shriek. It was her protector, the massive oak.

One thick branch wrapped around her swollen belly while others ripped her long, bony arms from her body as easily as plucking legs off a bug. Fate watched in horror as this monstrous justice took place. She gagged as the oak tore out one of Old Mother Grim's short, gelatinous legs. None of this added up. Why was the tree destroying its master?

Her answer came when a bolt of lightning illuminated the entire scene. Finn stood within the center of the tree's splayed branches, his face a mask of grim ecstasy, arms gyrating like an insane conductor orchestrating a cacophonous symphony. His movements controlled the tree's sadistic actions.

Fate soared high, circling wide before descending. Careful to avoid the thrashing branches, she drifted down just behind him. As he ripped out another limb, Old Mother Grim's shrieks reached an unbearable pitch. She covered her ears, wishing he would just end it.

"You shouldn't have come," he said without looking back at her.

She opened her mouth to speak, but he turned, holding up a hand to stop her. His eyes were ruthless black pools. "Maybe it's best you did," he said, letting his hand drop with a careless shrug. "It's time you saw what I truly am." Turning his unfeeling gaze back to Old Mother Grim, he tore open her swollen belly.

Twisting away from the grisly sight, Fate kept her eyes on the stubble of gray moss covering a branch near her head. But as Finn spoke, she couldn't keep herself from turning back to the gruesome spectacle.

"She was human once—eons ago," he said, his voice flat and matter-of-fact. "She was a mother of three. But her desire to cheat death led to an unthinkable sacrifice to an ancient evil. *She ate her own children.* And the insatiable witch *liked* it. Biting into soft pink flesh and tasting the sweet gooey center of pure innocence gives her the same rush of pleasure a miserably stuffed glutton gets from gorging on a dozen more raspberry turnovers."

He kept jerking his arm, directing the tree to continue yanking out all of Old Mother Grim's entrails. Anyone else would have died by now, but she clung stubbornly to life, shrieking in protest. Coughing on the bile burning her throat, Fate pressed her hands harder against her ears.

Finn turned, his face grim with self-hatred. "I've seen and done things, Fate, unspeakable things that can never be unseen or undone. The truth is, I'm just like her. I'm a monster who enjoys ripping other monsters apart. But I won't stop there. I've acquired a ravenous appetite for dispensing punishment. And the time will come when it won't matter who or what I torture and slaughter."

He grew quiet for a moment. Fate could see tears glittering in his eyes, yet even as he turned away, his face turned to stone. "Take a good hard look. I'm a walking nightmare."

She could hardly disagree as he yanked his fists apart to make the tree rip Old Mother Grim's torso in half. The part still attached to the head continued its keening wail of pain and would not be silenced. Then Finn brought his fist down. The tree drove her head and shredded torso deep into the ground.

Merciful silence came at last, save for the howling wind and thundering sky.

A powerful gust of wind blasted past them, nearly knocking Fate out of the tree. She grabbed at a branch to keep from falling and it twisted beneath her grip. Letting go with a shudder, she found her balance. "No, this isn't you," she cried out. "It's your connection to this evil oak that's making the poison stronger. It's turning you into something you're not."

"Oh don't go blaming the tree, love," he said. "That's too easy."

She shook her head. "I know you, Finn. I know you to the very core."

A cruel smile warped his expression. "Aye, like the boy in your story?"

She was afraid to say anything.

"No more games now. You know I remember." He nodded

with an almost gleeful expression. "Your stories really did the trick. At first I figured I must've shared them with you when we first met. But you knew details I was forbidden to speak of outside the Order. Then it all came back to me. You made me up." He stood still, watching her reaction carefully. "You know, I was never so miserable as the day I found out I was nothing more than a bunch of words on paper—that my entire life was a lie, a meaningless fantasy made up by a silly lass infatuated with an idea she called Finn McKeen." His voice dipped to a soft murmur before ending in a low growl. "Aye, I really quite hated you for it…I loathed you."

Fate froze, feeling like a deer shot in the heart by a hunter's long-range rifle. The rancor in his voice poured acid into her veins.

A flash of lightning lit the malice in his eyes. "Surprised? Guess you would be, since you fashioned me to be the golden boy—the good friend, the constant companion, the strong protector." He crossed the broad limbs between them with ease, stopping with his face only inches from hers. His arm snaked around her waist, pulling her roughly against him. "The tender lover," he whispered into her ear.

A sickening spasm of fear shuddered through Fate. She pushed to get away, but his arms were hard unyielding bands of steel.

His chest shook with mocking laughter. "But I'm thinking you like your lovers rough and forceful, being the closet thrill-seeker you are," he said, his voice now a guttural snarl. "Isn't that why you've been winding me up for so long?"

He radiated rage, scorching her with it. "Well here we are, you with your dream lover, and me eager to fill the role."

With one arm clamped around her, he used the other to tear

at the neck of her dress. The cotton chemise shredded like tissue under his violent tug. She grabbed the torn material, trying to hide her bare shoulders from his feral gaze.

"Don't," she pleaded, her voice but a shaky whisper as she clamped her eyes shut, a vulnerable act of pure terror. She felt paralyzed, her heart slamming in her chest. Vicious winds raked across her exposed skin, icing the tears streaming down her face. Every muscle within her tensed with fright, bracing for the unthinkable. But she remained untouched.

Was he toying with her? Cold sweat trickled down her back as she opened her eyes.

Finn was still standing in front of her, his body shaking, his head down. She hadn't felt the release, but he'd let go of her. His arms were folded, or so she thought. A streak of lightning revealed the glint of metal in his hand, a dark sheen of blood covered his forearm.

"Finn, stop!" she cried.

His head jerked up, torturous pain had replaced the heartless black of his eyes. He kept cutting into his arm, struggling to speak, "Fate. *Leave now.* Before…it's too late."

She grabbed at his injured arm, slick with too much blood. "No, give me the knife!"

He pushed her away with his knife hand, his eyes threatening to shift to black again. "The pain…it's the only thing stopping me," he growled, returning the blade to his arm. *Go!* I don't know how much longer I can resist!"

Fate choked on the tears coming hard and fast. Watching him cutting himself was unbearable. "We can fight this together!"

Shame etched deep lines in his paling face. "Do you have any idea what I was about to do?" An indescribable sorrow filled his eyes. "I'm done for. There's no saving me. You *have* to let me go down with these monsters."

The wind battered in from every side, whipping stinging strands of hair into her eyes. "No, I can't."

"You have no choice!" He paused for one endless moment, staring at her with red, grief-stricken eyes. Then he shoved her so hard, she went tumbling through the air.

CHAPTER 26

TIME SEEMED TO STAND STILL as Fate hurled past writhing branches. Thunder shook the heavens and blinding lightning ripped them open, striking the oak where Finn stood. Her shock was so great she never thought to use her power to fly. Flaring sky and dark earth spun across her vision before she slammed to the ground a good twenty yards away.

The impact hammered the air from her lungs. Struggling to breathe, she staggered to her feet. "Finn!" she cried out weakly. Hugging her sore ribs, she fought to gather her bearings.

The burning oak convulsed like some tentacled sea creature in the throes of death. She staggered forward, recoiling as another bolt of lightning struck the tree. The thick trunk split and a horrible peeling resounded through the night as half of it crashed to the ground in flames.

Where was Finn?

She ran as close to the blaze as she could. At last she found him, sprawled unconscious beneath the fallen part of the tree. Another bolt struck the oak's standing half. A terrible cracking pierced the raging wind and fiery sparks showered down as the last of the tree toppled, blocking her way completely.

She flew up, skirting around the blistering heat. When she located a narrow opening, she dove in, crawling on hands and knees beneath a ceiling of flames. Finn was just within her reach when she heard a soft whimpering. It was the young boy who'd been snatched from her grasp in the oratory.

Guilt stung at her. She'd completely forgotten him. Sliding forward on her belly, she grabbed the boy's leg. Startled into hysteria, he screamed, thrashed and thumped her on the nose. Cursing from the pain, Fate yanked him out and pulled him to safety. But when she moved to crawl back in, a portion of the tree had crumbled, setting the low-lying branches afire.

Finn lay helpless within the inferno. There was no way in.

She leaped into the air, circling frantically. "Finn, get up!" she screamed.

He didn't move.

A loud rumbling came from deep within the earth. The ground split into a gaping maw ready to swallow the felled oak. She hovered above the incredible sight as the gnarled branches scrabbled across the dirt. Floating lower, she waited for them to sweep past Finn but the crumbling edges of the huge pit gave way beneath him.

She dove down, catching hold of his arm before he fell. Digging in her heels, she yelled, "Finn! *Please,* wake up, I'm not strong enough to hold you!"

The riven oak scraped by, dropping into the abyss, its flaming bulk vanishing into the shadowy depths.

Fate's muscles burned from the strain, her grip weakening. Even when she used her full weight to pull on him, she couldn't get more than his arm up over the edge. He suddenly slid farther down, his weight landing her on her knees. She tried not cry but the tears came and she wondered why the hell she hadn't given herself super-human strength along with the power to fly.

Her hands slipped along his forearm to his wrist. Holding on with renewed intensity, a burst of adrenaline pumped through her, giving her just enough strength to haul his chest up over the brink.

"I got his other arm!" Gerdie yelled, wrenching on his cut

forearm, her hands sliding ineffectually because of the blood gushing from his wound.

Spurred on by Gerdie's show of support, Fate summoned the last of her energy. Yanking on his shirt, she pulled him back a few more feet until only his legs hung down. Heaving one last time, she lugged him fully away from the hole, then tumbled backward onto solid ground, utterly exhausted from the effort.

She was still catching her breath when the sky opened and dumped a torrent of rain. Drenched before she could even scramble to her feet, Fate took Finn by the legs and dragged him to the caravan as the softening earth caved in and buried the oak's charred remains.

Once she had Finn inside, she laid him next to Sithias. He'd returned to human form, and his shoulder was bandaged. Fate could see he was sleeping peacefully. Gerdie had done well—not just once, but twice.

"I'll take us back to Shytuckle," Gerdie offered.

Too spent to speak, Fate nodded, collapsing in a chair as Gerdie closed the door of the caravan to go around to the driver's seat.

Sitting up in alarm, Fate shouted out to her. "Gerdie! Stop the horses!" Jumping back into the rain, she scanned the dim landscape until she spotted a small pale form several yards away. The little boy she'd forgotten yet again was huddled near the chasm. She scooped him up and brought him inside.

After they made their way back to Shytuckle to return the boy to his grateful mother, there was little else to do. The time had come to move on, so they followed the road leading out of the village, and traveled alongside the river for a good ways—each girl silent within her own thoughts.

The rain had eased to a fine mist when they pulled the caravan to a halt. They were both cold and weary, but there would be no rest for Fate until she checked on Finn.

His face was pale and drawn, his breathing shallow. The inflamed cut he'd made along his left forearm was bleeding, though less than when he'd first sliced into it. Her mind recoiled from the painful memory. Never had she been so completely torn as in that moment—loving him body and soul, while at the same time being terrified of him. She knew the same was true for him. His self-inflicted wound was evidence of his struggle. A lesser man would've given in to the dark influence, and she loved him all the more for the strength he'd shown.

As she ran her fingers through his damp hair, they slid over a warm slippery spot near his temple. Alarmed, she drew back her hand.

More blood. Her palm was covered in it.

"Gerdie!" she called out.

The young girl rushed over. Her skillful hands parted Finn's hair, revealing a gruesome gash slicing across half his skull, still bleeding and matted with coagulated blood.

Gerdie drew in a sharp breath. "No wonder he's been out cold for so long."

Fate's knees quaked—not from the sight of blood, but from the paralyzing fear creeping through her. Seeing him this way, so human and frail despite his displays of extraordinary power and strength, brought home how close he'd come to dying out there. Which is exactly what he'd said he wanted.

She grabbed the bedpost for support.

The poison was working against him. Finn was losing the battle. Or had he already lost? She wouldn't know until he woke. Would he be the menacing stranger again, or would he still be Finn? She prayed he could hold the darkness at bay long enough to face Mugloth in the last fable.

Gerdie went to work, calling for more boiled water, cloths and herbal concoctions. Grateful for something to do, Fate conjured the items as quickly as she ordered them.

An hour later, Finn's head wound was cleaned, stitched and bandaged, as well as his arm.

"Thanks, Gerdie—for everything," Fate said as she tucked the covers under his chin. Lingering, she traced her fingers over the square line of his jaw. Her gaze moved to his smooth brow, thick lashes and the gentle upward curve of his lips. It was hard to believe such cruelness had come from such an angelic face.

She caught Gerdie watching her with an expression that far surpassed her age. "You two are uncommonly close, strangely so. It ain't just puppy love."

Fate smiled faintly. "You have no idea just *how* strangely connected we are." As tired as she was, she really needed to talk and decided to tell Gerdie everything. She barely knew the girl, yet she felt a certain closeness, like she would to a sister if she had one.

Sitting on the end of Finn's bed with her knees brought up under her chin and wool dress tight around her legs, Gerdie listened intently. Fate sat down on Sithias's bed and told her about meeting Finn at the bookstore, how she'd discovered he was one of her fictional characters after they'd entered the *Book of Fables*, as well as his poisoning and how it was changing him. She was too absorbed in the telling to notice the excitement building in Gerdie until the girl jumped to her feet.

"I knew you had it here as soon as I saw you doin' the Words of Makin'. Can I see it? I gotta see it with my own eyes!"

"The book?" Fate asked.

Gerdie's wispy mop bounced as she nodded her head.

Fate strode over to the curtains hiding the *Book of Fables* and drew them back.

Gerdie fell still. "I gave up hope of ever seein' it again." She grinned. "My ticket home's finally here!"

Fate was stunned. "You've seen it before?"

Gerdie stared at the giant book's worn wooden cover and intricate lock. "I curse the day I did. That book, plus my big sister Brune, are what got me stuck in this neverendin' mess."

Feeling the blood drain from her face, Fate grabbed a chair and sat down. "B-Brune Inkwell? *Brune's* your sister? She put you in here? For how long?"

Gerdie looked at her with concern. "You okay?"

"She put you in the book? Did she do it with a spell?" Fate said, her pulse now roaring in her ears.

"No, nothin' like that. It was Brune's doin' though. Oma caught her openin' the book when she shouldn't have. Brune was gonna read me one of the stories, but Oma tried to pull us both away. Brune bein' as stubborn as she was, started readin'. And you know what happens when you read out loud from that book." Gerdie's face lit up. "It was real nice when we first got here. You wouldn't 'ave recognized it. The fables were magical places like nothin' I'd ever seen before—all sunny and beautiful, with happy people and happy stories."

Her wistful smile faded. "Until we came along. And you know what I'm talkin' about. Because of the book's rules for gettin' out, we had to turn each fable into a horrible endin'. Believe me, there's nothin' worse than havin' to bring misery everywhere you go."

Fate's shock gave way to distrust. She narrowed her gaze on Gerdie, realizing the adult mannerisms she'd found so disturbing were because she'd been catching glimpses of an old soul inhabiting that little body. She didn't know whether to feel sorry for her or creeped out. It certainly didn't sit well with her that Gerdie had been party to whatever had to be done to bring about the horrifying endings Fate was now struggling to rectify.

Plus she was Brune's sister.

"What's wrong?" Gerdie asked, the woman in her voice now apparent in the child's tone.

Fate stared back into those attentive eyes, searching for a sinister presence. But all she could see was a caring one. The mistrust simmering below the surface fizzled out. Gerdie may not be what she appeared to be, but she certainly wasn't evil in miniature either. Not after witnessing her rage against Old Mother Grim and everything she'd done for Sithias and Finn.

"I'm still trying to wrap my head around it all," Fate said. "So how long have you been here?"

Gerdie did some counting on her fingers, which only frustrated her. She gave up with a bemused shrug. "I couldn't tell you, except to say I'm old, very old."

"Spock old?" Fate grimaced. "Or *Yoda* old?"

"Sorry, don't know those fellas or how old they are."

Fate shook her head, sad for Gerdie. She really was deprived.

"Let's just say I'm older than anyone has a right to in a body this young. And I've spent most of that time movin' from village to village tryin' to save as many young'uns as I could with protective charms whenever Old Mother Grim showed up. I suppose I could've left and gone further, maybe back to the snake queen's kingdom, but I guess I had some silly notion that the day I left would be when Brune came back for me."

Fate swallowed dryly, sad for the little girl who'd been left behind and forced to survive all alone. And to be trapped, not just in the book but also in a body that didn't mature along with her. "I can't believe she moved onto the other fables and left you in this hell!"

Resentment soured Gerdie's young face. "When we first entered the book, we all knew what needed to be done to get out. We were okay with it at first—seein' that we were only dabblin' in the lives of storybook characters and all. But after a time everythin' started feelin' too real. When we got to this fable and there was nothin' but simple people livin' peaceful lives, Brune used her Words of Makin' to bring Old Mother

Grim out of some book she remembered readin'. It was too much for Oma and she tried to undo it. Nothin' worked though. Once the monster was made, she took on a life of her own and dug her claws in deep."

Fate didn't doubt it, not after what had happened when she'd written the Green Man into existence.

Gerdie continued, "After Old Mother Grim made her first kill and brought darkness to the land, Brune tried to get us to move onto the next fable. But Oma couldn't leave without destroyin' the child eater, which woulda kept us trapped here. And Brune, she wasn't havin' any of that."

Gerdie's movements became stiff as she picked up the bloody towels and threw them in the water bucket. "When I told you the villagers turned on Oma and burned her at the stake…" Her mouth closed in a tight quivering line. For a second, she looked as though she'd break into tears, but she sniffed, scrubbing the towels with a vengeance. "It was Brune who got them to do it."

"Your sister's pure evil!"

"I know, she got the hunger for power. It all started when she stole that Orb thingy off a priest."

Fate sat up straight. "What priest?"

"He was the king's counselor. Can't recall his name…"

"Was it O'Deldar?" As Fate asked the question, her spine tingled with an overpowering, restless energy.

"Sounds about right," Gerdie said. "We brought that story to a nasty end by stealin' his Orb from him and puttin' a spell on his king to make him trespass into the snake queen's territory. But Brune, she got downright obsessed with the Orb. She figured out how to do things with it. Unnatural things, like killin' animals and bringin' them back to life. But they were never right afterwards. They were just movin' carcasses. And she figured out how to make plants grow from seed to full size in a blink. That would've been good, except the fruit was always rotten on the inside. Then when she started wreakin' havoc on the weather, Oma said to stop, that playin' God would only invite the devil into the game."

A glowing pendant flashed in Fate's mind, causing a mixture of concerns, one being Finn. Had Brune used the Orb to make him? If so, that meant there was something about him that could go wrong. A chill ran through her. Maybe the poison wasn't the only thing to blame for what he was becoming.

"Do you think Brune used the Orb to create Finn?" Fate asked.

Gerdie looked reluctant to answer. "Once she got it, she *always* used the Orb to cast spells."

"But how could she have known about Finn?"

"She wouldn't have needed to. I remember a spell called Eyes of Eros. Anyone who knows magic knows it's best used on top of love spells or summonin' spells, cuz it sees the heart's deepest desire and causes a restlessness in whoever's bein' spelled. That person's forced to leave a perfectly happy life and find that part that's missin'. But if you combine that kind of spell with the Orb, you risk conjurin' up a doozy of a surprise."

It was all making sense to Fate now—why she'd left the book signing to go to the bookstore, and why Finn was exactly as she'd imagined. As her fear increased, she grasped for a solution. "If Finn *was* made by the Orb, and let's say there's something wrong with him, is there a way to fix him?"

"The Rod might do it," Gerdie said. "Brune was spittin' mad when she couldn't get the Rod after stealin' the Orb. She knew it was why the Orb's magic kept backfirin'. It isn't complete without the Rod."

A thin gold bar engraved with the key to unlocking the mysteries of the universe blazed in Fate's mind. The image blinded her to everything else as her hand went to her neck with the expectation of finding it there. When she didn't feel it, she lurched at Gerdie, grabbing her by the shoulders. "Where is the Rod? Did you take it?"

"You've got that same hungry look in your eyes that Brune had." Gerdie shrank back. "She spelled you, didn't she? She sent you to get the Rod!"

Fate shook her violently. *"Tell me.* Where's the Rod of Aeternitis?"

"With the priest," Gerdie said, her voice a frightened whisper.

Fate let go and paced the length of the caravan. She was consumed by a sudden, desperate craving, one that dominated her body, mind and spirit.

Without warning, the caravan rocked violently. Fate fell, hitting her head on the table. Knifing pain throbbed on one side of her skull. As she sat up, the sounds of angry voices and pounding outside the walls brought her back to her surroundings. A trap door in her mind slammed shut on the Rod, wiping it from her thoughts completely.

Rubbing the sore spot on the left side of her head and wondering why she was on the floor, Fate rose to her feet. She shook her head, clearing out the cobwebs, and headed toward the angry insistent voices outside the door.

Just as she was about to open it, Gerdie yanked on her arm. "Don't open that! It's the villagers. They've come to do us in."

Fate looked at her like she was insane. "We're heroes, remember?"

Gerdie backed away from the door. "Don't be so sure. They sound awful mad. You'd best get us out of here."

The caravan suddenly rocked back and forth in jarring waves. Frightened and bewildered, Fate decided Gerdie was right, but didn't understand why. She rushed over to the big book. If something had gone wrong, the answer would be in the fable.

Prying back the heavy cover, she turned the thick pages until she found what she was looking for. "Here it is. The villagers think we brought Old Mother Grim to Shytuckle. You're right, Gerdie, they've come to punish us. It says here, once the caravan burns to the ground, happiness reigns throughout the land once more." She looked at Gerdie with relief. "We've still got our happy ending, so long as we skedaddle."

Gerdie had her hand on the floor where thick smoke was flowing up through the cracks. "Better be quick. They're burnin' us from below and it'll be fast. I smell lard."

Sithias groaned from his bed. He lifted his head, blinking through sleepy eyes. "Would sssomeone pleassse sssettle the boat. I'm feeling ssseasssick." He flopped back down with a pained expression, stayed that way for a moment, then sat up ramrod straight. "What in the world isss going on?"

Fate started toward him, jumping back as the floor buckled under the weight of the heavy table in the middle of the caravan. A wall of flames blasted from the hole burning up through the floorboards. Then the door busted open and the mob flung rocks at them. One hit Gerdie in the back of the head, dropping her to the floor.

"Grab Finn's hand!" Fate yelled at Sithias as she dragged Gerdie's limp body by the arm and skirted around the edges toward him.

Flinching as rocks zinged past him, Sithias reached across the span between beds and grabbed Finn's hand. Forming the last link of the chain, Fate took hold of Sithias. Smoke billowed up from the rampaging fire, obscuring her view of the page left open to the seventh fable. She couldn't read a thing, all she remembered was the title.

So under the circumstances, Fate did the only thing she could do, and shouted it out at the top of her lungs.

The Lightning Sword

Long ago, in the morning of the world, there arose from the cosmos great beings of immense power and magnitude. Born from chaos, these unpredictable beings helped to shape the earth, sea and sky. As time passed they came to be known as gods with many different names. They cared little for mortal affairs unless it suited their purposes, and woe betide the human who was noticed, as he was toyed with for sheer pleasure.

As with all things great and small, these gods faded back into the stars, undone by either their own deeds or those of humankind. But they did not depart without leaving behind fragments of their power in which to slip back to this world for yet another chance to unleash their might.

In this tale, such a fragment was the lightning sword, carved of deep blue marble streaked with crystal veins like lightning bolts frozen in time. How the lightning sword came to be sunk deep in a well of still water is unknown, but there it lay for thousands of years until something else shared its resting place. Something that saw the sword for what it truly was, and sought to put it into the hands of unsuspecting mortals.

Beldereth, a mighty kingdom long ruled by men, lacked the gentle hand of women to lend its governance proper balance. King Lortaun had the great misfortune to fall in love with his queen. This was unheard of, for the men of Beldereth believed a woman to be nothing more than the inert soil in which a man cast his seed, and altogether useless if she bore no sons. But Lortaun grew to love Heda, who came to him with grace and wisdom from a land where women were men's equal. They conducted their love in secret, but when she bore three daughters and no son, the royal court ordered the king to take another wife. But the day Lortaun married another was the day Heda died of a broken heart.

Stricken with grief, Lortaun banished his new queen.

In the autumn of his life, the king's thoughts turned to a successor. His young brother, Prince Rudwor, was next in line to the throne. This troubled the king, for Rudwor was lazy and entirely careless about politics, while his three daughters possessed both Heda's good judgment and his leadership abilities. Leaving the throne to a woman was unthinkable, yet this is exactly what Lortaun intended to do.

The day came when the king decreed his daughters would inherit the throne by order of birth, with Prince Rudwor last in line. The assemblage of stern, white-browed statesmen shook their fists and opposed this despicable proposition. In contrast, Rudwor sat quietly by, relieved to be lifted of the burden of kingship.

And so an insidious plot against the king's heirs took root that very day. The second daughter, Valesca, was the first victim. For two years, she was given a tiny drop of henbane mixed with black hellebore in her morning tea until she slowly grew crazed and dim witted. Another year passed peacefully until the eldest daughter Scylea's horse ran headlong across the fields and leaped off the black cliffs of Razgard with her as its helpless passenger.

Shortly after Scylea's death, a servant discovered a chest containing evil items in Rudwor's chambers. Inside were the heinous tools of a dark sorcerer: henbane tincture, the poisonous hellebore blossoms and a stone horse with Scylea's golden locks wrapped around its broken form. There was also a figure carved from a cursed oak in the likeness of Bremusa, Lortaun's youngest. Fearing what might happen to her if the carving was destroyed, the king kept it in his care.

When word spread of Rudwor's suspected guilt, the royal court demanded his execution. Lortaun knew his enemies had positioned Rudwor as their scapegoat, meaning to remove the royal bloodline altogether and establish their own king. To save Rudwor's life, while also appeasing the public outrage against him, the king exiled his brother to Duenthorn, a bleak, lawless region in the East, filled with ruthless bands of murderers, thieves and outlaws known as the Bane. He doubted Rudwor would survive, but it offered him a chance, whereas being beheaded offered none.

Lortaun climbed to the oracle set high in the mountain of Alderath to consult the scryer, a magical sea beast whose premonitions and wise counsel had granted the royal family much good fortune. The king's ancestors had captured the creature and forced it to dwell within the Well of Eyes. For centuries, promises of freedom were exchanged for its invaluable foresight. As time passed, it was never a concern how the imprisoned scryer felt about being torn from the wild, free sea and housed within the confines of the well. A consideration that would have proved prudent for those further down the branches of the family tree.

The sea creature's piercing blue eyes fixed upon Lortaun, ever waiting for news of its release. When the king expressed only his selfish concerns, the scryer dropped its gaze to the glassy water and peered into the king's future. Sinking beneath the water, the creature reappeared with an unusual stone sword. It laid the weapon before Lortaun and whispered these fateful words into the king's mind: "Send your wooden daughter with the undeserving, then seek the goddess of war to protect all women. With this sword, she will cast out all who despise her. When their armies return to destroy you, take blade to your daughter's throat in the name of Murauda. Do not fear, your daughter will be reborn. She will wage vengeance upon your enemies like no human can. But be warned, great grandson of my captor, it is better to have a thousand known enemies outside your gate than to have even one that is unknown within."

Upon Lortaun's return to Beldereth, he had the undeserving Rudwor take Valesca with him to Duenthorn. He then had a temple erected in honor of Murauda, the goddess of war. As predicted, a temple for a female deity in Beldereth disintegrated the royal court. When the assemblage of old statesmen left, they took Lortaun's army with them.

The king took it upon himself to raise young Bremusa in the

art of war. She grew to be a great warrior by the age of seventeen, and Beldereth became a haven for all women who'd suffered at the hands of men. Indeed, it seemed Beldereth flourished under the protection of Murauda, for the kingdom became the strongest nation in the land, protected by a formidable army of women.

Over the same span of time, the assemblage of calculating old men, formed unholy alliances with Beldereth's most ancient and abhorrent enemies, while their dark sorcerer, Gorm, gathered the forces of the North to wield an endless savage winter upon Beldereth.

The siege came before sunrise, when all of Beldereth was low in spirit from enduring three grueling years of winter. Lortaun woke to the sounds of battle horns and the rock giants of Mount Helgunth beating at the gates. He was unprepared for what met his eyes. A massive sea of soldiers blotted out the snow. Beldereth's downfall was inevitable.

The king remembered the scryer's words and told Bremusa of the sacrifice he'd been instructed to make. His brave daughter handed Lortaun her dagger and led him to the temple. Kneeling at the base of Murauda's gigantic statue, she guided her weeping father's hand to her throat and forced the blade into her flesh. As her blood poured over Murauda's stone feet, Lortaun wept and a powerful storm raged in. The temple ceiling cracked and opened to the heavens. Savage winds rushed in, thunder rumbled and a bolt of lightning struck Murauda's effigy, shattering her image into jagged shards. Yet the marble sword remained intact and fell onto Bremusa's body.

Upon the sword's touch, she drew breath. Her skin took on an unearthly radiance and her eyes blazed with the brilliant light of the stars. An inner fire emanated from her heart, illuminating her armor with a blinding luster. Grasping the hilt of the lightning sword, she rose to her feet, growing in magnitude to the height of three men. Then Bremusa knighted her warriors, as well as the inexperienced women and girls in the kingdom, imbuing them with the powers of thunder, lightning and wind. She touched all aids of war with her sword, enabling horse and chariot to take to the sky and carry her army upon the wind's currents.

Bremusa's enthralled army rumbled over the vast body of her enemy, raining flaming arrows and spears down upon the unsuspecting army below. When they descended to the battlefield, bodies were rent asunder by a single blow of their swords, and bones were shattered by the fierce war cries of the newly empowered Beldereth army. No sword, arrow or battleaxe could touch Bremusa's warriors. They were as swift and shifting as the wind itself.

When they were done, a lake of blood stained the snow. But the assemblage of plotting old men stood a safe distance away, cowering in the shadow of Bremusa's army. They were delivered to King Lortaun, who ordered their immediate execution. Yet when Bremusa raised her sword over them, her hand would not obey. Even when she ordered her warriors to kill them, her body was pushed to defend the contemptible men.

With wicked smiles, Gorm and the conspirators revealed talismans made of the same cursed oak Bremusa's wooden image had been carved from. Gorm commanded Lortaun to surrender her wooden likeness, because he needed it to bind Bremusa completely to their will. When the king refused, Gorm torched his body with a bolt of red flames.

Bremusa never defended Lortaun. His daughter was not the one who watched…it was Murauda.

Poor King Lortaun died on that dreadful day, never realizing that the vengeful sea creature trapped within the Well of Eyes had orchestrated its captor's ultimate downfall. But he should have known. The scryer's warning had been quite clear. It is better to have a thousand known enemies outside your gate than to have even one that is unknown within.

CHAPTER 27

ARCTIC WINDS HOWLED like savage beasts, raking everything in its path with claws of ice.

Shivering convulsively, Gerdie tightened into a ball, almost surrendering again to the deep plunge into oblivion, where she hadn't been aware of the bone-marrow chill and the dull ache at the bottom of her skull. But she'd weathered enough storms to know if she closed her eyes in frigid temperatures without finding shelter first, she wouldn't wake up again. As she forced her eyes open, a pitiful whine joined the roaring wind. *"I'm all alone!"*

She pushed up on one elbow. Squinting against the pelting snow, she could only see what was directly nearby. Finn was lying next to her, still unconscious, and the whiner was huddled close to her on the other side.

"Oh thank g-goodnesss. One of you isss awake!" Sithias said, his shoulders hunched and teeth chattering.

As she tilted into a sitting position, pain jabbed her temples and her stomach dipped in a sickening manner. She held still, waiting for the queasiness to pass. "Ooh, I forgot what a gut-wrenchin'ordeal it was to go from one fable to the next."

"You're ill b-becaussse the ungrateful sssimpletonsss of Shytuckle know how to throw rocksss and make f-fire."

"Right. That explains the goose egg," she said, rubbing the bump on the back of her head. The wind shifted, smacking ice and snow in her face as she tried to see through the blurring white. "Where's Fate?"

“Isssn’t she lying on the other ssside of Finn?” Sithias asked, fear pitching his voice even higher.

Gerdie leaned on Finn, stretching over him to look. “I don’t see her.”

Sithias stumbled to his feet, fighting with the vicious winds to keep his blanket wrapped around his shoulders as he circled around her and Finn. *“Sh-she’sss gone!”* he cried out in panic. “Fate’sss not here! Where isss she? What are we g-going to do? What am *I* going to do? Snakesss d-don’t do well in the cold you know. These c-clothesss are keeping me from icing through, but they won’t d-do for much longer.”

Furious gusts suddenly flapped the pages of the *Book of Fables* beside him, slamming it shut and startling him. Losing his balance, he flailed, giving the wind free rein to grab his blanket and carry it away. The book toppled into a deep drift, blasting him in the face with a plume of snow.

“She must’ve wandered off,” Gerdie muttered. She stood up, studying the snow for footprints leading away from them. As far as she could see there weren’t any, other than Sithias’s haphazard tracks. “Hmm, it looks like she never made it here.”

“Th-that’sss what I’ve been sssaying!” Sithias squawked. Fully iced with snow, he moved close to her, stooping low to sob on her shoulder and snuggle close, gleaning whatever heat he could from her. “She m-mussst be trapped in sssome sssort of magical limbo. Now we’ll be ssstuck in thisss dreadful icebox forever—if we don’t f-freeze to death firssst.”

Finn sat up slowly, groggy but concerned. “Fate’s not here?”

“Nooo, she’sss not!” Sithias cried.

“So long as she’s alive, she *has* to be part of this fable ‘cuz she read us into it,” Gerdie explained. “I think this is like the time my sister ended up in the castle of Asgar, and me and Oma found ourselves plunked in some village a day’s walk away. We were pretty sure we weren’t gettin’ out of that fable since my sister was the reader the same as Fate is in this go around. We're all part of the same fable, you can be certain of that. Sooner or later we'll meet up with her."

"We'll all *die* if it'sss later than s-sooner," Sithias whined.

Finn was now fully awake. "Are you saying you were trapped inside the *Book of Fables* like Fate and me?"

She nodded, hugging her arms and jumping up and down to get her blood circulating. "Yup, I traveled through all the f-fables up 'til my sister left me behind in *Old Mother Grim.*"

Sithias stood straight, frowning in alarm. "Your sssister sssoundsss like a d-dreadful perssson. How did you manage to sssurvive?"

"How about I tell ya later? My lips are goin' numb."

Finn stood up and immediately doubled over, grabbing his head. "Uh…I've got a raging pounder."

Gerdie stepped up close, holding his arm to steady him. "You took a real hard knock on the noggin." While he was still stooped over, she peeled back the bandage to check his head wound. "Huh, it's healin' over fast, much faster than—"

He ripped off the blood-stained bandage, watching the spot of red whip in the wind and vanish in the blustering snow. As his eyes shifted to her, a scowl formed on his face. "I remember getting hit by lightning, and being glad for it. Why didn't you stop Fate from coming? I should be plucking a harp right about now or, more likely, sniffing the reek of brimstone. She could've been killed. Whereas I *should've* been!"

She let go of his arm, his harsh tone driving the chill deep to her core. "Didn't know you had a death wish. And there was no stoppin' that girl. She's as stubborn as a mule, *and* she can f-fly."

Stepping off the blanket he'd been wrapped in, he faced the glacial tempest. "Where is she?" He glared at her, his irises expanding, becoming black pools, the way they had when he'd talked about Old Mother Grim in the oratory. A telltale sign of hatred now marked for her. "Did you have something to do with her disappearance?" he said, his voice a low growl.

Frightened, Gerdie glanced over at Sithias for help. He was chasing after Finn's blanket flying away on the wind.

There was nothing she could do but face his accusing stare. "N-no, I didn't even know you had the book until Fate showed me. Course you were knocked out silly, so you wouldn't know that. B-besides, there can only be one reader at a time. None of us are goin' anywhere without Fate. Haven't you f-figured that out by now?"

He didn't look convinced. "Well, if she's the reader, how come the book came with us instead of her?"

"That's a g-good question," she admitted, trying hard not to shake, lest it be mistaken for fear. "When m-my sister was the reader, it went with her to Asgar. I don't know why it came with us. Maybe it's c-confused by me bein' here."

Sithias returned with the blanket stretched tight around his thin frame. "I'm dying," he announced. He threw Finn a mournful glance. "Have you f-forgotten I'm a cold-blooded sssnake under thisss human guissse? Not to mention, I've been *seriousssly* wounded!"

Finn's stormy eyes slid impatiently to him. "You won't freeze any faster than either of us will when you're in human form. But if you're really that cold, make yourself into an animal that lives in this kind of weather."

Sithias's face lit up. "Oh, well that'sss not a bad idea at all."

"H-how about a r-reindeer? Then you c-can c-carry us," Gerdie suggested, her teeth knocking together so hard she had to be careful not to bite her tongue.

Sithias looked appalled. "I will *not* be your beassst of burden."

"Well if thisss isssn't humiliating, I don't know what isss," Sithias grumbled as he trudged through the deep snow, despite how easily his long reindeer legs traversed the drifts. He had a slight limp in his front leg where he'd been wounded near his front quarter—formerly his shoulder—but his newfound strength compensated for it. Nonetheless, complaining was required to maintain a necessary level of dignity. Not to mention, he was feeling rather foolish for not having been the one to come up with the idea of shifting into a hardy fur-covered animal. He tossed his enormous antlers in disdain for good measure. "I'd better not pop a ssstitch!"

Gerdie's legs trembled against his sides as she leaned forward, yelling to be heard over the increasing roar of the wind. "You're warmer aren't you?"

"One can't help but work up a bit of heat when you're a lowly *pack mule.*"

She pressed herself flat to his back, shudders running through her small body as she patted the side of his muscular neck. "Th-thank you."

"You're welcome," he said, flicking his furry ears irritably. Not because he had to carry her—he was happy to do it—but because there was nothing he could do to stop her shivering. She was a tough little thing. He admired her refusal to grouse about freezing to death.

Finn landed next to them, appearing in a cloud of whirling snow, as if out of the ether. His hair and brows were crusted with ice, yet he seemed only slightly chilled by the frigid winds slicing into them from every direction. "There's nothing here but an endless frozen wasteland—no sign of life at all," he said. "I think you're right. We're probably in…what did you call it?"

"Duenthorn," Sithias said. "Which meansss we follow the sssun asss it setsss in the Wessst, sssince the fable indicated Duenthorn wasss eassst of Beldereth."

"Maybe I should fly ahead to be sure we're heading in the right direction," Finn suggested.

"I'd say yesss, but asss much asss thisss painsss me to sssay, I think you'd bessst sssit on my back with Gerdie and keep her warm." he shifted his weight and huffed. "She'sss in danger of freezing, or losing sssome toesss and fingersss at the very leassst."

Hearing this, she poked her head up out of the blanket again. "Sithias, I d-didn't know you cared."

He stamped his hoof and rolled his eyes. "Hmf, I don't. Your conssstant shaking isss extremely annoying."

They continued on their journey, leaving the *Book of Fables* behind in the snow bank where it was swiftly covered in snow. Finn had marked its location with a stack of large stones, which would no doubt be buried just as thoroughly, but it was the best he could do given the circumstances.

He sat on Sithias's back begrudgingly, his coat open and Gerdie huddled against his torso. He would've preferred bundling her in the arctic wear Tove had made him so he could fly ahead and scout, but the clothing had been left behind in the last fable. No doubt lost for good. Not that it mattered anymore. There wasn't much that mattered anymore.

He glared at the angular rocks slicing through the snowdrifts like daggers. He felt at home here, with the fierce, bone-chilling winds shaping the land into an unforgiving, hostile place, a perfect mirror to the poison obliterating his soft edges, sharpening him into a deadly barb. Even now, he wanted to lash out at the small girl sitting in front of him. She was to blame for letting Fate come after him. If Gerdie had deterred Fate as planned, he would've died without her having to see the ugliness he'd been hiding.

Whenever he thought about the moment he'd lost control and forced himself on her, his chest burned as painfully as if he'd guzzled bleach. If only Fate hadn't been there. If only Gerdie hadn't failed. He could snap the girl's neck for that.

It would be easy…a simple twist of the head. Done swiftly, she'd never feel the moment of death.

Horrorstruck by the unbidden thought, he shoved the murderous urge back down into the shadow place from whence it came. But there was too much anger and resentment brewing there. The compulsion to kill could not be contained, erupting once more, shuddering through him even as he fought to hold it back.

Gerdie turned her head to one side. "You okay?"

He swallowed. "Aye."

"That bump on your head may be healin' good and fast, but it'll make you feel out of sorts all the same."

"I'm *fine.*"

Gerdie twisted round, looking up at him. Fear filled her eyes. Without a word, she turned, looking straight ahead, stiff and hugging her knees close.

Shame gnawed a hole in his stomach when he saw her reaction, but that seductive voice of reason he'd been hearing of late whispered in his mind: *When will you stop torturing yourself with useless guilt? Don't you know that such sniveling is beneath you? The man you keep longing to be never existed. You're chasing after a ghost of your former self, clinging to an illusion…blind to your true nature.*

His scowl deepened as the wind battered his face with ice. If his true nature was what had driven him to brutalize Fate, he wanted only to die. Agony ripped open his chest as her frightened face flashed in his mind, vivid and brilliant. He shrank from the memory, unable to stop seeing his hand tearing at her clothes and hearing the malicious words he'd said. Aye, he'd been angry with her, but how was it possible his resentment could overpower the love he felt for her? All he'd ever wanted was to be close to her. But not like that…never like that.

Suppose you could hold her in your arms again. Would she look on you with anything but fear and disgust? The whisper became a growl. *How can she love you when all she wanted was to remind you of the soulless puppet she created? She's not worthy of your remorse. You're nothing more than a plaything to her…and for that, she deserved to be punished.*

Finn's insides balled up into agonizing knots. The voice made sense in a twisted sort of way. What if it was true? What if all he'd ever been to her was an amusing distraction?

We promise, if you see her for what she truly is you'll no longer thirst for her touch or the sound of her voice. Turn to your true nature. The justice you mete out on the damned will sate you more than she ever could. You'll be filled with a greater glory. The power inside you awaits. Give into it, and you alone, can smite like the divine hand of God, unstained by the blood you spill.

As Finn surrendered, the unbearable tightness in his gut loosened. Honeyed darkness poured through him thick and sticky, coating over his agony, filling the hole in his heart with an all-consuming passion for retribution.

He smiled grimly at the dark, knife-shaped rocks barely visible through the blinding snow, regarding them with admiration, so imposing in their strength and oddly beautiful. This was where he belonged, the perfect setting for a righteous crusade that would go down on the pages of—

Chaos broke loose around them, shattering Finn's thoughts. Dark figures burst up from the snow with primitive cries and guttural growls. Before he could react, a brutal blow from the side knocked him into a drift. His ribs felt crushed, but a delicious rush of fury overrode the pain. He sprang to his feet, ready to tear limbs from his attackers.

A large form exploded from a nearby drift, blocking out half the wind-blurred landscape. Finn swung his fist but before it struck flesh, a thick club came down hard and heavy upon his crown. A bone-crunching sound filled his skull and sparks of light blasted before his eyes.

Then, sweet oblivion.

❦

Finn woke to a throbbing brain. The jostling made it worse as he bumped against the back of the man carrying him. The blood dripping from his head splattered over stone. He tried pushing his muddled senses outward to get a feel for where he was, but his aching body chained him down.

He glanced over at Gerdie. Her hands were tied and she was being shoved alongside him, while some rough characters heaved on the ropes binding Sithias, who bucked and strained against them.

They were in an underground cavern lit by fire pits and torches anchored on greasy rock walls. A rank smell came off a row of stretched animal skins left to dry, while some were being scraped clean by tangle-haired women who turned their worn faces toward them. A group of soiled, grubby children squatted on the floor, playing with animal entrails. They stopped what they were doing and looked at Gerdie like it was Christmas morning.

Men dressed in crude furs and decorated with fang necklaces and bone breastplates stood around a pit, arguing and shoving each other while watching two snarling badgers tangled in a vicious fight. A woman screamed and struggled as several men dragged her into a dark corner, but as the newcomers moved in their midst, every one of them abandoned their unsavory activities.

The stench of sweat, smoke and putrid meat wafted off the motley, weather-beaten tribe and hung thick in the air. Every eye glittered with distrust or greed and most definitely hunger, especially when their gaze landed on the large white reindeer.

The man carrying Finn dropped him on the ground. "Get up, scum!" he snarled, driving his foot into Finn's bruised ribs when he didn't move immediately.

Biting back the pain, he staggered to his feet, facing him with a defiant grin. "Take it easy, sunshine. I was hoping you'd help me up, since you were so good as to carry me all this way."

The man stood a foot taller and was built like a bull. His thick features furrowed into a glower. "Shut yer gob!" he bellowed, punctuating the order with a fist to Finn's gut.

Finn caved at the waist, feeling the pain burn deep. He imagined his fist going through the man's face and out the back of his skull but decided he'd wait for his energy to return more fully, in case the whole tribe descended on him.

Fear flickered over the man's face when Finn lifted his head and smiled wickedly. His captor shoved him into the throng, navigating them through the unmoving, foul-smelling crowd. Some of them rammed shoulders with him and others pushed Gerdie 'til she stumbled and nearly fell. Guffaws and derisive hoots followed them as they made their way to the back of the cavern, where a large bearded man lay on a pile of furs. This appeared to be the chieftain. He was the only one wearing a regal lion's mane headdress embellished with an impressive set of bullhorns.

When Gerdie and Finn were several yards from the leader, their captors yanked on their bound arms and kicked in the backs of their knees, forcing them to kneel.

While surveying his two prisoners, the chieftain took a piece of raw meat from one of the young women lounging at his side and swallowed it whole. The girls were less grimy than many of the other women and still had the bloom of youth upon them. In fact, the chieftain himself was not nearly as unkempt as the rest of his grubby band. Apparently his high-ranking position offered the rewards of a regular bath and a comparatively clean harem.

The chieftain's gaze narrowed on Finn. A restless intelligence moved behind his probing gaze. "And who are you who dares to trespass into Bane territory?" he demanded, his voice booming throughout the cavern.

When Finn remained silent, his captor punched him in the kidney. The pain stabbed deep, making him stumble. Without a word, he gathered his composure, lingering on the notion that his torturer would soon have his head torn from his neck—a hole in the head was too neat.

"My name's Finn McKeen," he said at last.

The chieftain stared at him blank-faced. "Never heard of you. What were you outcast to Duenthorn for?"

"Murder," Finn said. Since he'd been unconscious through the reading of the fable, he only knew what Sithias had told him, but guessed what the Bane needed to hear.

Gerdie's mouth fell open as she turned to Finn.

"How many?" the chieftain asked, his gaze skimming over his rune-marked temple with veiled interest.

"Five."

First there was silence. Then the chieftain laughed, a deep belly laugh that had the whole band joining in with cackles and heckling screeches.

"Is that all? You mean to tell me you've been exiled to the most heinous piece of earth this world has to offer for just *five murders?* Usually you've got to do more damage than that, eh?" he boasted to his tribe, laughing again.

"Eighty would *almost* do it!" a heckler yelled from the back, as others shouted out even more ridiculous numbers.

The chieftain looked at Finn. "Well if you didn't want to be thrown back to the snow, you should've thought to do better than that, young sapling. I suppose that reindeer will spare you a night by the fire. That's if you survive to see sunrise." His half-veiled eyes slid to Gerdie. "The nipper's on the scrawny side, but we'll fatten her up so she grows into an able-bodied wench."

Gerdie glared, sidling closer to Finn. "Do somethin'," she murmured, turning a worried glance back at Sithias, who'd been hemmed in by a group of menacing children with sharp sticks.

"I say we gut 'im now," someone yelled.

Grunts and jeers swelled up from the motley horde, while those standing closest to Finn chanted, "Gut 'im! Gut 'im! Gut 'im!"

Urged on by the bloodlust building in the mob, Finn yelled, "I challenge any of you to a fight!" He turned his heated gaze on the brute who'd gotten in one too many undefended blows. "If I had my pick, it'd be you, *doll*. Starting with a Glasgow kiss."

The rapacious glare Finn gave him had the man stiffening. And his challenge had the crowd chanting, "Fight! Fight! Fight!"

The chieftain's expression darkened. Most everyone saw his changed demeanor and the chanting died down, but a heckler in the back of the crowd still carried on.

Rising like an irritable bear fresh out of hibernation, the chieftain scanned the crush of grimy faces for the noisemaker. When his eyes landed on him, he threw his dagger into the tribe's midst. Sudden silence descended as everyone turned to see his chosen target. A sinewy man with a rake of scars down one side of his face stood stock still, his body rigid and quaking as he mutely pulled the dagger from his shoulder.

Swallowing up space with his great height and girth, the chieftain signaled his men. "I decide when there'll be a fight. Take the prisoners to my den."

Finn's torturer boxed him alongside the head and grabbed his arm. "You heard 'im, scum. *Move it!*"

Finn strained against his ropes, skin burning as the knots loosened. Before his captor realized what he was doing, his wrist slipped free and he grabbed the man by the neck. "That's it *sweetmeat,* I've had quite enough of you."

Before he could react, Finn head-butted him. The pain drilling into his forehead fueled his fury. Seeing red, he lurched forward, biting down on the end of the stunned man's nose and tearing it off. He let go of his screaming victim and spit out the bloody lump. Disgusted by the metallic tang of blood, Finn sneered, wiping his mouth with the back of his hand. "Huh…not so sweet after all."

Gerdie watched in horror. Short of foaming at the mouth like a rabid dog, it was plain to see Finn had gone off the deep end.

She dodged out of the way as several men pounced on him all at once. He whipped one of them forward, propelling him into the crowd, and kicked another one back with a blow to his chest. The rowdy bunch pushed and shoved, but most kept clear of him—all staring half in fear, half in rage.

"Come on," Finn goaded, his eyes crazed and gleaming bright green. "Who's next? I'll give every one of you a royal gubbing!"

The chieftain closed in behind him with surprising speed, snaking his thick trunk of an arm around his neck and squeezing hard. Finn wrenched on his brawny arm, but the chieftain lifted him off his feet, cutting off his oxygen. Kicking and twisting for nearly a minute, Finn's eyes rolled back in his head and he fell limp.

Letting him drop to the ground, the chieftain strode away. Without looking back he called to his men, "Grab his sorry bones and bring the lass." He paused for a split second. "And after the beast's been butchered, bring me those handsome antlers."

Frightened for Sithias, Gerdie rushed toward him, but someone grabbed her by the scruff of her dress, hauling her into the air. As she was carried away the mob descended on Sithias like a flock of vultures. All she could see were his antlers and a battery of sticks raining down on him.

CHAPTER 28

"PUT ME DOWN!" GERDIE SCREAMED into her captor's ear as he carried her through a maze of dark, drafty passages. "You touch my reindeer and I'll kill y—"

Clamping his rough, filthy hand over her mouth, he scowled at her with his one good eye and pushed past a curtain of fur hides covering the opening of a den. Once inside, he released his grip, letting her drop like a sack of potatoes. Jabbing an oily finger at her as she scrambled backward, he growled, "You need a lesson on behavin', runt." Hearing a noise out in the passage, he glanced nervously over his shoulder then back at her. "I'll be dealin' with you later."

Gerdie let out a relieved sigh when he turned and left. Rising up on her feet, she looked around in surprise. This did not look like the den of a barbarian. A collection of candelabras lit the chamber and a fire crackled at its center. Persian rugs softened the rough walls and hung behind bookshelves filled with leather-bound books and finely appointed bric-a-brac. Layers of sheepskin rugs covered the cold stone floor. A polar bear rug—complete with head and gaping fanged mouth—lay on top. Silk cushions were scattered around the fire and more were piled on a large mattress draped with gossamer.

However, it was the young woman sitting by the fire who captured Gerdie's attention. Her delicate features spoke of fine breeding, but she was clearly lost in a world of her own imagining, playing out some sort of drama with a wooden doll. Gerdie tiptoed over and knelt next to her to study the carven figure in her hand. A knowing came over her. This was Valesca, the daughter who'd been poisoned and pushed to insanity, which meant the doll must be the carving of Bremusa.

Two men pushed through the flaps, dragging Finn's limp form between them. They hoisted him into a chair and tied him to it with careful, painstaking knots. The chieftain followed them in, tugged on the ropes to ensure they were secure and ordered the men to leave. Yanking the fur flaps back in place, he turned to Gerdie. "Now then, tell me about your friend here. Why's he so dead set on getting himself killed?" he said, his tone hushed.

Confused by his friendly manner, Gerdie watched as he removed his headdress and rubbed his big hand over a shiny bald head ringed with long brown braids. He placed it next to Valesca, who stared at the gold fur and ebony horns of the headdress as if it had just fallen from the sky. When she smiled up at him, he stroked her auburn hair with affection.

His gaze returned to Gerdie then flicked to the entrance. "I haven't got much time. The natives will be wanting to draw and quarter this young lad as soon their appetites are sated with fresh meat, so I need to decide whether he's worth sparing."

Gerdie studied the chieftain's broad features. His face had lost the severity he'd shown earlier, revealing a gentle, disarming quality in his expression and kind eyes, the color of lightly toasted biscuits. "Uh…it's kind of a long story, but the short of it is he's been poisoned. It's been turnin' his innards dark for a while now."

The chieftain looked at Finn, his gaze thoughtful as he studied his slumped form. "I can see that. Whatever this poison is, it packs a powerful punch. The lad's uncommonly strong—and fast."

"Oh, it's not the poison that makes him strong. It's the runes on his skin. The poison just makes him mean."

The chieftain scratched his chin. "Runes, eh?"

"Yeah, they're an old language—"

"I know what they are," he interrupted. "I've just never seen the runes of the Elder race on a human before. I was told I would one day, but I'd nearly forgotten 'til now."

Gerdie remained quiet, not knowing if this was good or bad.

"I think it's time we woke the young scrapper," he said, grabbing a water pitcher and dumping its contents over Finn's face.

A face full of icy water was as shocking as a bare-knuckled punch. Immediate rage shot through Finn's rattled nerves and had him lunging at the perpetrator. When he couldn't move his arms and legs, his temper exploded in a frenzied attempt to break his bonds. *"What the bloody hell?"* he shouted, his furious gaze falling on the big bald man standing over him. It took a second to realize it was the chieftain.

"Calm down, laddie," he said with an easy smile that caught Finn off-guard. "No one's after you—well, Dreg's going to be wanting a nose for a nose, and then some for what you did. But you're safe for the moment."

"Bring it on," Finn fumed.

"You'd like that, wouldn't you? A chance to unleash that bottled rage onto such deserving characters as the Bane? Don't get me wrong—it wouldn't be any skin off my teeth. The Bane are nothing more than dishonest curs, the whole lot of them. They'd slit the throats of their own children if it meant getting the Chieftain's seat." He sat down opposite him and leaned forward. "You wouldn't believe what I've had to do to keep them fearing me. Biting someone's nose off is child's play compared to what I've done to get my seat, and keep it."

Finn gripped the arms of the chair, his pulse pounding. "And your point is?"

Shrugging, the chieftain settled back in his chair. "We've all got a dark side, lad. And sometimes it's necessary to use it, but we don't have to let it rule us. I may be the reigning King of Hell outside this room, but when I'm in here with my niece, I shed that monster and remember who I truly am."

Finn laughed, a grim sounding bark. If only it were that easy. Yet a part of him he thought was gone, grasped for the lifeline being tossed to him.

Gerdie stood, angling away from the addled girl talking gibberish, staring at the chieftain wide-eyed. "Are you Prince Rudwor?"

A shadow crossed over his face. "How is it you know my name?" Standing, he unsheathed his sword, his suspicious gaze darting between her and Finn. "Ah, I see how it is. You've been sent to end the royal bloodline for good, have you?"

Gerdie held up her arms in alarm. "We're nothin' but messengers. It was King Lortaun who sent us," she said, her gaze shifting to Finn as she covered for them both. "Beldereth was attacked, but Bremusa used the power of the lightnin' sword to defeat them."

Rudwor stood still. "Lightning sword? What is this thing?"

"It came from the scryer in the Well of Eyes."

Lowering his sword, Rudwor narrowed his eyes and looked at Finn. "'Twas the scryer who told me I'd meet a young man with the Elder race runes on his skin, and that he would be the one to lead me back to the throne of Beldereth."

Finn lowered his gaze, concealing his surprise.

"That's right," Gerdie said, going on to explain what had happened in Beldereth and how Bremusa had received all of Murauda's powers. "You gotta return to Beldereth with Valesca's doll. It controls Bremusa and her army. With that doll, you'll be king."

Hearing this, Valesca screamed at the top of her lungs.

Finn strained against the ropes, the noise grating on the raw edges of his nerves.

Kneeling down, Rudwor wrapped a burly arm around his niece's thin frame. As he made soft shushing noises her screeching quieted into a whimper. He lifted a sad gaze to Gerdie and swallowed. "If you're here to resurrect this would-be king, then my brother must be dead."

"Gorm tortured him to get the doll." She hesitated a moment. "He died without telling him where it was."

Rudwor's chest caved with grief. "No, he would never tell. My brother was a better man than I could ever hope to be." He took a deep breath and straightened. "He won't have died for naught. You've given me reason to finally wedge myself from this ill-begotten kingdom of mine." He clapped his big hands together, looking both determined and troubled. "Only one problem. We need to leave without calling attention to ourselves. And let me assure you, any attention from the Bane is never good—"

"Hey! We're ready to skin that mangy cur!" One of the Bane yelled from behind the flaps. "Hand 'im over!"

Rudwor stomped to the entrance. "I'm not done with him yet!" He smashed a vase against the wall and ruffled the flaps. "I'll burn out your eyes, cut out your tongues and eat 'em raw!" He put his ear to the flap, listening to their response outside. Satisfied, he lumbered back and moved to cut Finn's ropes, stopping at the last second with his blade poised. "If I cut you loose, do I have your word you'll work with me, not against me?"

Finn stared at him, resisting the grounding influence the self-possessed man was having over him. He couldn't give into hope. Not after what he'd done. He was a monster unworthy of freedom and he deserved whatever grim death the Bane wanted to dish out. "No, just leave me be."

Rudwor's expression grew fearsome. "You'll not stay here, young sapling. It may have been foretold you'd be the one to lead me back to the throne, but something tells me this goes both ways. Maybe I'm here to help lead you back to yourself. Sometimes it takes one monster to understand another."

Finn sneered. "You think you can save me? Don't you think I've tried? You have no *idea* what I'm capable of." Rudwor stared back with recognition in his eyes, as if looking straight at the demon hiding inside him. Unable to bear the scrutiny any longer, Finn turned his head, glaring at his ropes. "I've done unforgivable things," he muttered through gritted teeth.

"Well, if that's how you feel," Rudwor said. He lifted his sword and brought it down.

Finn clenched his eyes shut, bracing for the slice of steel through his chest. Instead the ropes fell from one arm. Angry that he hadn't finished it for him, he glowered at the huge man. "You really shouldn't have done that."

Rudwor cut the rest of his bonds. "I won't be your executioner, lad. This isn't the time or the place for you to meet your maker. I've got a sense about you, and it tells me you've got more good in your little toe than all the Bane combined," he said, undaunted by Finn's scowl.

Finn shook with silent laughter. "I've already met my maker, thank you." As he tried to hold Rudwor's unwavering gaze, he shifted uncomfortably and said, "All right. But mark my words, you'll most likely live to regret this."

A grin transformed Rudwor's stern expression. "No I won't. You don't know what *I'm* capable of," he said, slapping Finn's shoulder, nearly knocking him off his feet.

"Okay," Gerdie said, stepping up between them, "now that we've got that settled, you gotta get our reindeer back."

Rudwor glanced down at her with a guilty shrug. "He's dinner by now."

Just then a white mouse with brown wings hastily darted into the chamber and landed on Gerdie's shoulder. "Sssorry to disssappoint," the mouse squeaked, gasping for air. "But I'm very much alive. No thanksss to any of you."

"Oh thank goodness, you're alive!" she said, smiling with relief. "And so cute!"

Wringing its tiny paws together, the mouse twitched nervously. "Thisss is no time for flattery, nor will it win my forgivenesss. Thossse barbariansss wanted to *eat* me! And when I changed they went berssserk. I wasss nearly sssquashed!"

"And who or what would this be?" Rudwor asked, perplexed.

"I would be Sithiasss," he said, wiggling his pink nose and fluttering his wings. "I'm the reindeer you so callousssly threw to thossse wolvesss!"

Rudwor raised his brows in confusion. "This mouse is daft. He thinks he's a reindeer. Or maybe I'm the nutter. After all, I'm talking to a mouse—with wings no less."

A guttural shout from outside the chamber startled Sithias. He dashed into Gerdie's hair, hiding as Rudwor rushed to the entrance and poked his head through the fur flaps.

Finn tensed, ready for a fight as he listened to the muffled, heated exchange between Rudwor and his men standing on the other side.

"You can skin them both after I'm done—*if* there's anything left!" Rudwor bellowed. He drew his head back inside. "They want the meat of the scrawny wench and the nose biter in place of the missing reindeer." He looked at Finn. "We're going to have to claw our way out of here."

The sudden heady rush of battle fever pulsated through Finn's veins. "Let's dance," he said, taking a step forward.

Gerdie tugged on his arm, holding Fate's notepad up to him. "I think I can get us outta here."

All his suspicions and resentments toward Gerdie rose to the forefront. “What are you doing with that? First the big book, and now this?”

She blinked nervously. “Don’t be mad. I only have it cuz you told me to take it from Fate so she wouldn’t follow you to Old Mother Grim’s tree.”

“Why didn’t you give it back to her?” he said, fear chipping away at the ice that had formed around his heart where Fate was concerned. “She’s lost out there without any way of helping herself!”

“I know, but I forgot I had it ‘til now,” she said, looking crestfallen.

Sithias poked his nose out through her hair. “Don’t blame her, a lot’sss happened sssince then.”

Rudwor shoved a sword in Finn’s hand. “Don’t mean to interrupt the family feud, but can it wait?”

“Hold on,” Finn said, turning back to Gerdie. “Do you really think you can do anything with it?”

“I should be able to. I saw Oma do it,” she said. “Only problem is, I never learned to spell.”

“I can help with that,” Sithias squeaked as he scurried down her arm, jumped off and morphed back into human form.

“Whoa!” Rudwor said, staggering back a few steps from the sudden transformation. “What’s this?”

“It’s a long and weird story,” Gerdie said, before turning to Finn and holding out the notepad. “*You* should be able to use the Words of Makin’ just the same as Oma and Fate.”

He shook his head, remembering he wasn’t real like them. “I tried it once. It didn’t work for me.”

“What’s all this fuss over books and writing when we’re about to be skinned and boiled?” Rudwor said, having recovered from his shock.

“Gerdie knows magic,” Finn explained. “She can write a spell in this notebook that’ll get us back to Beldereth without us even having to leave the room."

"Aye, and I'm brown as leather because Duenthorn's a tropical paradise," Rudwor said, frowning and looking at each of them. "You're serious." He heaved an impatient sigh. "Well do it quickly, little witch. Hell's about to come pouring through that door."

Finn nudged his chin at Sithias. "Help her write it out. And *fast,* mate." Gripping the hilt of his sword, he swiped the air to test the blade's weight.

"Pray for a miracle," Sithias said, a frightened look of doubt on his face as he helped Gerdie guide Valesca to the back wall of the den.

Rudwor signaled Finn to take a position opposite him on the other side of the entrance.

They were barely in place when several men burst into the chamber with murder in their eyes.

Finn slammed his shoulder into the one nearest him, knocking him back into four others making their way inside. Adrenaline coursed through him as he streaked forward faster than they could recover. Surprise froze on their grizzled faces as his blade slashed across one man's windpipe, sliced through the breastbone of another, stabbed the belly of the next and severed the arm of the fourth. Pivoting on one foot, he glanced over his shoulder ready to swing again. Through the spray of ichor, he saw Rudwor run his sword clean through the fifth one. As the chieftain extracted the red blade, he seemed magnified in size, a giant radiating a savage energy, his eyes wild and shining with a bloodlust Finn knew all too well.

They locked eyes, both laughing maniacally in recognition of each other's demons. A singular moment interrupted by more men careening blindly through the flap, crashing into Finn's back. Stumbling forward, he hit the bed, breaking his fall by catching his sword in the mattress. A plume of downy feathers shot up from the gash like a flurry of snowflakes.

Suddenly time slowed. He registered every minute detail: Valesca's screams stretching out, Gerdie's voice speaking their names, the angry growls of the Bane horde swarming into the room and a cloud of feathers frozen in the air. Spinning round, Finn dove into the mob with his sword raised. When he brought his blade down on the skull before him, he hit something other than bone. Red flames arced up the length of the sword and the hilt glowed with scalding heat under his hands. Before he could let go, jolts of electricity seized his muscles, juddering in his teeth, nerves and bones. Then time shifted back to normal, and in one split second, his sword had shattered, an explosion that sent him hurtling backward.

CHAPTER 29

A MASSIVE STORM CLOUD HELD FATE and her fellow knights firm within the ether as they watched the battle far below them. The swirling blackness growled with thunder, spitting fiery bolts at the tiny soldiers scurrying like ants entangled in a desperate fight to the death.

Dressed in full armor, Fate gripped her helmet under one arm so she could view the battlefield without hindrance. She could see how one army pushed forward with greater might and bloodlust than the other. Something deep inside her flinched as bodies were run through with swords and blood spilled bright red over white snow. She'd been told this weakening human emotion would leave after she made her first kill. But Murauda hadn't yet allowed her newly knighted warriors to engage in battle. She insisted they weren't ready and must learn by first studying how the senior warriors fought.

Sitting on the sidelines was excruciating. The forces of wind and lightning coursed through her veins, enlivening every cell, rebuilding the matrix of all her tissue, muscle and bone into stronger, denser matter. The elemental energies pulsed beneath her skin, throbbed behind her eyes and pounded in her ears. She was still adjusting to her heightened senses, seeing rich color in everything. At first she'd been entranced by the tiniest details, staring at the lustrous texture of her leather saddle, the sheen of her armor and the racing clouds reflected in its silver surface. Sounds were acute and ran together, becoming a confusing clamor in her head before she learned to sift through the onslaught and focus in on one thing at a time—the breathing of her horse, Murauda's velvet voice. As thrilling as the transformation was, without an outlet, this new power was building to a feverish pitch, urging her to lunge into the fray and unleash her untested might.

Clamping down on the white-hot ball of nervous energy burning in her chest, Fate's restless gaze anchored on the war goddess. Her deep blue cloak flapped in the wind as her keen gaze flickered over the clash of sword and shield below. The white stallion she rode stood steady, the wind beneath his hooves swelling like waves.

Fate could tell the goddess had already chosen the army she would bring to victory by the way her gauntleted hand slid to the hilt of her weapon. Murauda unsheathed the lightning sword and raised it high with a war cry that was most likely heard for miles. Her seasoned warriors roared in answer, their mounts rearing as they leaped from the storm cloud. Fate squeezed the leather reins, shaking as she forced herself to keep from spurring her horse onward along the wind currents to ride with them down the steep, death-defying grade.

Upon touching solid ground, the knights drove their horses into the warring armies, swinging battleaxes and swords. The war goddess slashed her way into the heart of the battle, lighting afire whatever her blade touched. Dismounting from her giant stallion, she towered above the tallest men on the field. Despite her tremendous size, Murauda moved with unnatural speed and grace, slicing through lines of men with one powerful sweep of her sword while eluding an onslaught of arrows, spears and blades. She was like a phantom, vanishing in one spot and reappearing in another.

Unable to sit still, Fate twisted round in her saddle, her adamantine silver armor bending like a malleable second skin as she glanced at the other newly knighted warriors. Each of their faces mirrored the same wild fervor she felt. If they weren't forbidden to speak to each other, she'd have asked if they had experienced the same cyclone of marbled blue flames, which she had during her induction only hours before. Or the silver lightning that had shot through the fiery curtain and scorched the air with the smell of ozone. She still remembered her lungs searing with hot sparks, the fire in her bloodstream and the molten heat exploding in her chest. Every nerve ending had flared with unbelievable pain. In shock, she'd glanced down to see the red smolder of her beating heart glowing bright through bone, muscle and clothing. That's when the pain had vanished, replaced by the sound of Murauda's bold heartbeat joining in rhythm with her own. Together they became a booming roar of living fire surging through her veins, burning away all memories of her former existence. Never had she felt more intensely alive or invincible.

On their way to the battleground, they'd come upon a woman and her two daughters, whom Murauda chose for her army. When the husband and son fought to save them, the war goddess massacred both. The mother and girls had wept angry tears until Murauda touched them with her sword, removing all grief and resentment. And tiny crackling bolts had licked over their skin, but there'd been no engulfing blue flames or red glowing hearts. Even now Fate could see the faint luminescence of her own heart through the breastplate of her armor, something that was missing in all the other warriors, except Murauda.

Anguished cries pulled Fate's attention back to the carnage below. Murauda's warriors had nearly wiped out the losing army. Many of the men had turned tail and were running for their lives, but her warriors pursued them, shattering their bones and armor with the sheer force of their shrieking war cries, or spearing them from great distances, leaving the soldiers standing like limp vines propped on sticks.

As Fate scanned the bloody wasteland of twisted, broken bodies, a part of her shuddered and wept. She pushed it down, having been told the weak must be weeded out to allow the strong, bold and unflinching to survive. Just as the strong killed the inferior in battle, so it was that every warrior must kill the weakling within.

The victorious army shouted words of praise and knelt before Murauda for helping them destroy their enemy. Another temple to the war goddess would soon be raised. Murauda turned away, riding toward the defeated kingdom, where she would take more women for her army. After harvesting her rewards, she set the castle and surrounding villages ablaze.

The war goddess took to the smoke-filled sky and joined her fledgling warriors. Her presence was like a balm to their burning furor, but only for as long as she was near. Without so much as a glance back at the war-torn field below, the air riders followed her back to Beldereth, a journey made swift by the strong winds of rolling thunderheads.

A different battle was already taking place when Fate and her fellow warriors returned to Beldereth's great hall. The rotting corpse of King Lortaun hung on a spit near his vacant throne, while the assemblage of old, white-haired men dressed in scholarly robes of royal-purple gathered opposite the dead king. They were each clutching the oak talismans hanging round their necks, the only thing keeping Murauda and her warriors from slicing them to pieces. Their sorcerer Gorm, a bald man with dark piercing eyes and a pointed beard, faced a golden-haired boy a little older than Fate.

There were others. A huge bear of a man dressed in primitive garb and a frightened young woman clinging to him with a wooden doll clenched in her hand. There was also a little girl with a head of frizzy brown hair. A white cat paced nervously at her feet.

Fate returned her gaze to the boy, who was really more man than boy. He was unshaven, lean and muscular, with strange runes marking his temple. His movements were smooth and predatory as he glared with depthless black eyes at the sorcerer. As she watched, the young man's smiling face and luminous green eyes flashed vividly in her mind. The second she tried to grasp hold of the compelling image, it shifted out of focus and vanished. But the brief glimpse had nicked her heart, a tiny scratch that stung and surprised her. Who was he? Someone from her previous life?

She was suddenly torn, split in half. Two parts of her battled, one to unearth the past, the other to stomp it back into the ground. The warrior won. Unification with Murauda was all that mattered.

Gorm unleashed a bolt of fiery light from his staff. The young man dodged the ensorcelled flames with shocking speed, at the same time harnessing some sort of wind magic to deflect the fire and send it back to the sorcerer. Fate guessed he must be some sort of mage with mastery over air.

Gorm absorbed the lethal energy, but was visibly weakened. As the mage circled round, glaring fearlessly at his opponent, his face contorted with a feral grin as he reached in his pocket and pulled out a simple wooden flute. Blowing two piercing notes, he advanced on the sorcerer, whipping the flute back and forth like a sword.

Gripping his staff in both hands, Gorm held it horizontally, drawing energy from the ground in rippling crimson waves. Before the sorcerer could take aim, the mage was in front of him, his movements lightning-quick as he sliced the staff in half with a sharp blade of air flaring from his flute.

The sorcerer staggered back in shock while hastily conjuring a ball of red energy in his palm. The mage was too fast, lashing out with his air blade, swift and precise.

Gorm's severed hand fell at his feet.

Witnessing such prowess agitated the pent-up energy in Fate. She could barely contain her desire to run out there and challenge the mage to a fight. He was a worthy foe, as well as a mystery. How did he capture the power of air and make it work for him? Especially since it didn't appear to run through him the way lightning, thunder and air coursed through her.

Unable to take her eyes off him, she found herself walking forward, then realized it was Murauda's will moving her body. For whatever reason, the goddess desired to experience this particular battle through Fate's eyes. She sensed this impulse throughout her entire being.

"Fight him," Murauda's voice resounded in her mind. This was not a command. This was a dare. Fate looked at the goddess standing head and shoulders above all others in the great hall. The giantess nodded, giving her permission to proceed.

That was all Fate needed to unleash the fierce energy she'd been forced to suppress all day. Glaring at the mage through the slats of her helmet's visor, she charged at him, sword drawn and shield lifted, its surface vibrating with wind.

The power surging through her poured into her sword, igniting the blade with a tangle of lightning bolts. The second she was within striking distance, she targeted his chest and plunged her sword. The deadly point drew within a hair's width of piercing his flesh when he all but vanished, darting out of the way in a seeming blur. The weight of the fiery blade carried her motion downward, striking the marble floor and cracking the stone on impact.

She recovered instantly. Pivoting on one foot, she rushed at him, slashing her sword in deadly arcs. He faced her, his body coiled to spring out of the way once again. Frustration fueled her onward. This was her chance to prove herself and all he was doing was side stepping her. Fury boiled to overflowing when she realized she'd have to force a satisfying fight. Embracing the bloodlust coursing through her veins, she filled her lungs with exquisite rage and roared.

Finn barely had time to buffer the shock wave with his own shield of air. Even so, the blast sent him flying back several yards. Without waiting for him to rise, the knight grabbed the battleaxe strapped to her thigh and flung it. The axe whipped through the air, whistling past his left ear as he dipped low and rolled to one side.

Leaping to his feet, he crouched, ready to evade the next attack. He had no wish to kill the warrior. Sithias had told him Murauda's knights were innocent women and girls trapped within an unbreakable thrall. But he wasn't sure how long he could go without injuring her, especially since she was hell-bent on killing him.

The knight charged, her blazing sword cutting tight lines in the air, leaving a stream of tracers in her wake as Finn blew two new rune notes into his flute, creating a scimitar-shaped wind blade. She rammed into him, her armor bludgeoning one side of his body with a strength equal to his own. Their blades clashed and tangled together, his unbending stream of wind deflecting her crackling flames in a spray of fiery sparks.

He sidestepped her advance, wrapped his leg behind hers and shoved her back. She crashed to the floor. Her helmet fell off and a wild spray of russet curls cascaded over the marble. When he saw it was Fate, his heart nearly stopped, a mixture of shock and relief rendering him momentarily speechless.

She was breathtaking to behold. Her skin gleamed with an

unearthly luster, as if fire burned at her center. But the ferocity in her expression had scorched away every trace of the sweet tender girl he used to know. Nor was there any hint of recognition in her fierce gaze. He should've been grateful she didn't remember him and the unforgivable things he'd said and done. Yet he hungered for something from her, even if it was her hatred. At least then he'd know the girl he loved was still present. Having to look into the void in her eyes was torture.

"Fate!" he yelled, hoping she'd hear the sound of his voice from somewhere deep inside.

She sprang to her feet, her sword raised and arcing down at him. He angled the strike away. Swiftly, she parried, bringing her blade back to center, their swords colliding in a stream of spitting fire. Even as he strained against her supernatural strength, he puzzled over how the hell she'd been captured by Murauda and what he could do to break her out of the thrall. "Fate, I'm not your enemy," he said, keeping his voice low so only she could hear.

He felt her falter slightly, but only because she'd shifted her weight to drive her knee up into his ribs. Something sharp and hard punctured deep. He grabbed his side, staggering back from the bloody spike protruding from the leggings of her armor, the warm gush of blood seeping through his fingers.

She was unaffected by his injury. If anything, his weakened condition spurred her on as she barreled in for the kill. Finn blocked the near-fatal blow with his wind sword. Sparks glanced off the blades as he locked eyes with her.

"I won't fight you," he said. "I'll let you kill me before I'll hurt you again."

Fate woke as if from a dreamless sleep. Disoriented and filled with a terrible sense of urgency, she struggled through layers of dark heavy air charged with crackling light. Chinks appeared in the sizzling black, giving way to sprawling cracks expanding into gaps. Shifting bursts of wind hit her face as the gaps gave way to a flaming, sparking sword jutting skyward, Finn's face behind it and a huge hall of marble columns beyond.

Before she could ask him what was happening or where she was, her body moved of its own volition, forcing the sword she was holding downward with astonishing strength. Finn's shoulder dropped in a hard jerk. That's when she saw his flute in his hand and a visible stream of air shooting out of it in the shape of a curved blade. As her body twisted around full circle, she watched in horror as her arm involuntarily aimed the sword's blade at his neck. He lunged backward, but not before the razor-sharp point glanced his jaw. Sickened by the cut she'd made, she tried to release her grip on the sword but her hand was not her own. She was a puppet, helpless to stop her body from being used as an instrument of destruction.

What had taken over?

Finn staggered, regaining his footing with difficulty. He looked exhausted, beads of sweat rising on his forehead, dark hollows around his eyes. Then she saw how he gripped his side, a sanguine stain wetting his shirt, growing steadily bigger. Guilt ripped into her when she realized she was responsible for his injury. Yet he faced her with complete trust. "Fate, I know you're in there," he said, his voice faint.

She tried to say she could hear him but her vocal chords were locked.

A sudden rush of fury—funneled in from the tyrannical force controlling her—flowed through her arms, making her swing the sword. She wrestled for control.

"It's okay if you can't stop this," Finn continued, hastily. "Even if you do your very worst to me, I want you to know, *I love you.*"

His words seared into her soul. The chokehold on her body

released. She was free…for all but a heartbeat. *"Kill him,"* a voice boomed in her head.

In that second all the missing pieces fell into place and Fate knew who was in the driver's seat. Murauda was in her blood, muscles and bone, overriding her thoughts and governing her every move. But she would never hold dominion over her spirit. *"No!"* she screamed in her mind.

Murauda's will crashed down on her like a sledgehammer. The war goddess expanded within her, a brutal violation of mind and body. Never had Fate felt so tiny, crushed and confined. There was no fighting the invader catapulting her into a frontal assault on Finn.

As their blades clashed again, all Fate could do was stare helplessly into Finn's eyes as Murauda made her lunge at him. As they stood blade to blade, she was so scared for him. His face was growing paler by the second and the resistance he offered was weakening.

"I love you," he whispered, seeing past the shell of her body straight into her soul.

Fate strained against her bonds, every part of her reaching out toward him.

Incensed, Murauda's powerful will and energy surged through Fate's body so fast she could barely track her own movements. In one swift blur, her sword hooked Finn's blade from his grip and sent his flute flying. The puppet master pulled the strings and Fate's arm came down. Steel sliced the air, ready to carve him in half.

In that second, something exploded inside Fate, a detonation fueled by protective rage and pure indignation. Finn loved her. She was determined not to let anything get in the way of that. And screw this body snatching business. Somehow through her connection to the war goddess, Fate knew she could turn this powerful energy coursing through her to her advantage. Murauda didn't know it, but she had crossed into enemy territory.

Focusing inward, Fate embraced Murauda's energy and pulled it in, allowing it to build. Then she made it her own and redirected the sword's aim. The blade crashed down at Finn's feet, splitting the striated rock. "I'm back," she said, giving him a triumphant smile.

"Cutting it a might close, love," Finn said wearily, though his green eyes lit with relief.

She picked up his flute and tossed it over. "Ready to kick some immortal ass?" She barely had the words out when a furious roar echoed through the hall. Fate turned, raising her shield. Murauda's shock wave smashed against her arm, blasting her into Finn. Thrown backward, they hit the floor and slid several yards, coming to rest near a big man, a wild-eyed young woman and Gerdie, who was holding a trembling, amber-eyed white cat.

"Hey Gerdie...Sithias," Fate said as she scrambled to her feet.

Gerdie waved, her eyes round as she looked at Fate's armor. Sithias stayed in character and meowed. Then he suddenly went stiff, hissing with his hair raised on end as he looked over Fate's shoulder. She glanced back to see Murauda charging across the great hall toward them.

"Uh, we'll catch up later," Fate said, trying to sound brave, but she was suddenly very afraid. It was one thing to boot Murauda out of her body, another to face the pissed off twenty-foot tall deity head on.

Finn played a series of piercing notes on his flute. A fierce gale rushed in through the broken ceiling and churned at the center. Taken aback, Murauda slowed, glaring at the tornado forming in front of her. But it wasn't enough to keep her attention off Fate.

"Traitor!" the war goddess roared.

Fate held still under her wrathful gaze as she unsheathed her lightning sword, her giant strides rapidly closing the space between them. Instinctively, Fate took a few steps back, an automatic sense of helplessness welling up from within. Then she stopped, reminding herself she wasn't weak and powerless anymore. She didn't have to be the victim here. Sucking in a deep breath, she let out a scream that reverberated throughout the hall, a screech of bitter anger and resentment at being used.

Her war cry punched into Murauda, doubling her over, pitching her off her feet. When she hit the floor, the lightning sword fell from her grip. Fate leaped at it. Flying fast and low, she grabbed the sword, slowed down at first by its great size and weight. Holding it with both hands, she climbed to the highest peak of the hall to the gaping hole in the ceiling a hundred feet above everyone's heads.

From there she saw Finn direct the tornado on the old statesmen. It snatched them up like a vacuum sucking up specks of dirt, turning them into a roiling cone of blurred purple robes. At the same time the big primitive-looking man raced after the older girl with the wooden doll. She seemed to be under Gorm's influence, because she'd walked unnoticed over to the sorcerer, the carving in her hand extended out to him. That's when Fate remembered the carving of Bremusa and realized the girl must be Valesca. With a savage growl, the huge man flung his dagger, embedding the blade between Gorm's dark eyes.

Just as Fate returned her gaze back to Murauda, a thunderous, ear-piercing shriek slammed into her with the force of a semi truck. Stunned by the bone-throbbing pain, she fell to the floor, the jarring impact of the fall shooting another wave of pain through every inch of her body. Struggling to breathe, all she could think about was how she'd be dead right now if she hadn't been physically altered by Murauda's energy pumping through her.

Still dazed and in physical agony, Fate rolled onto her front, hunting for the lightning sword she'd dropped. Murauda was several yards away, bending to pick it up. As the space closed between sword and master, thin streams of lightning flowed between the hilt and her huge hand. Fate scrambled desperately toward it, knowing she didn't stand a chance the moment Murauda turned the lightning blade on her.

Just as Murauda's finger touched the sword, Finn's tornado swept in and swallowed the war goddess whole. Her furious cry shook the hall, fracturing giant columns and rupturing the length of the marble floor. Fate lunged on the lightning sword, still crackling in response to Murauda's nearness.

"Use the sword to light the twister on fire!" Finn yelled above the cacophony.

Fate plunged the blade into the raging wind. Lightning poured from the sword, igniting the vortex into a spinning cone of blue flames. As jagged bolts of lightning streamed out in every direction, Fate ducked behind her shield, her mouth filling with the metallic tang of electrified air.

"It's time, Rudwor!" Finn shouted. "Throw it in!"

Surprised by the name, Fate turned as the big man flung the cursed effigy of Bremusa into the burning tornado. Ear-splitting, inhuman shrieks came from Murauda, cracking the walls.

Finn stumbled toward the fiery maelstrom. He was bent over and holding his side. Nearly half his shirt was soaked in blood. Icy fear gripped Fate's heart. She started toward him but he shook his head, gesturing for her to stay where she was. He looked away, his pallid features hardening with effort as he shouted in a language she didn't understand. Wholly unprepared for the preternatural volume of his voice, the deafening sound vibrated in her bones. The blazing cyclone responded to his command, ripping through the hall, ramming against the far wall and embedding Murauda and Beldereth's enemies within solid marble.

The scene was grotesque. Murauda's burnt, petrified face was partially buried in rock, forever captured in an enraged scream. As for the calculating old men, their bodies lay scattered around her face with only an arm or elbow protruding here, a leg or an occasional terror-stricken face there.

Silence followed. As Murauda's thrall lifted from the other warriors, they straggled out of order, staring at the horrific wall and then at Finn, the destroyer of the mightiest destroyer. A mixture of fear and respect shadowed their faces as they kneeled to their new king and his champion.

Fate joined in the awe, her mind in shock as she stared at Finn. She thought she'd witnessed the limit of his powers before, but this latest demonstration was one she couldn't even begin to comprehend. Her battered body still pulsed with danger, leaving her wide open to the disquiet building just below the surface of her troubled thoughts. Her Finn was back, but for how long?

His eyes met hers and held across the expanse of the great hall. Fate's heart beat faster, her worry falling away as she felt that invisible filament between them tighten. She fell into a run, wanting only to feel him near. Then the connection snapped, a sensation as physical as being stabbed in the heart. She was suddenly on her knees and bent in anguish, her chest hollowed out by a frightening emptiness. Terror blasted through her as she leaped into the air and shot across the great hall to where Finn lay collapsed on the floor in a bloody heap and still as death.

CHAPTER 30

"MISSS, DON'T YOU THINK IT'SSS TIME you brought your day to an end? I know you're usually at thisss from sssunup to sssundown, but the hour'sss quite late even for you," Sithias said, worrying his hands together. "You haven't even eaten sssupper yet."

An arrow whistled past his head.

Startled, Sithias tensed his legs to keep his knees from knocking together. "If you're trying to ssscare me, it'sss *not* working," he said, trying for an unflustered, noble expression by arching his brow and lifting his nose.

Another arrow shot out of the darkness, spearing the generous fold of his fancy velvet hat, snatching it off his head. Sithias stomped his foot and frowned. "I liked that hat!" Taking a breath to calm himself, he smoothed down the front of his silk doublet. "I'll forgive you for puncturing a hole in my *favorite* hat if you put that bow down and come insside right now. It may be ssspring, but the night air isss ssstill chilly."

Fate emerged into the light of his lantern, her bow in hand and quiver removed. Even now after two months of seeing her this way, he was still caught off guard by the unnatural pale gleam of fire under her skin and the luminous red glow emanating from her chest. The lingering effects of Murauda's lightning sword were thankfully fading day by day but not nearly fast enough for him. Fate remained changed and not just physically.

Sithias breathed a sigh of relief as she set down her bow and arrows on the grass but stopped halfway when she drew her sword. "Oh *pleassse.* What can you posssibly do with that? Your sssparring partnersss are all in bed for the night."

She moved with deadly elegance toward him, her blade slicing the air with swift precision. "I guess that leaves you then. Spar with me."

He rolled his eyes. "In all the time we've been in Beldereth have I *ever* sssparred with you?"

Fate swiped the blade next to his ear, fluttering his hair and jangling his nerves. "No," she replied, her obvious disappointment apparent in the way she stabbed her sword into the ground.

"Well I'm not about to ssstart now. My pen isss my sssword. And I'll have you know I've been ssslaying them in court with my clever prossse. Not that you're ever there to sssee."

"Party pooper," she muttered.

"Misss, thisss nonssstop ssstrenuousss activity isssn't healthy. Look at your armsss. They're getting mussscular. That'sss unsssightly on a young woman." He looked her up and down, not bothering to hide his distaste. "You look posssitively mannish."

"You *know* why I'm doing this. I have to be ready for Mugloth. I just never thought I'd have to wait this long."

Her shoulders dropped and for a second he saw the vulnerable girl he'd grown so very fond of. "I know, misss. But I'm sure it won't be much longer."

Picking up a cloth, she wiped the sweat from her brow. "Yeah, but it's the waiting that's killing me. I have absolutely no patience anymore. This energy inside me, it just keeps building up. I can't just sit around. I *have* to do something about it or I start coming unglued."

"You're not feeling that way now, are you?" he said, hunching his shoulders up in alarm. "The lassst time you came unglued, you disssappeared for three daysss and came back covered in—"

"You *promised* you wouldn't talk about that *ever* again."

He gulped. "I promised at the time, but—"

"No buts, Sithias."

Avoiding her stern expression, he dropped his gaze to a tiny wrinkle in his silk sleeve and went to work smoothing it out. But he was tired of skirting around the issue. Clearing his throat, he plucked up his courage and looked her straight in the eyes. "Misss, we can't keep ignoring that you went missing for three whole daysss without remembering a thing. And your clothesss, they were ssstained with sssomeone else'sss blood…*and* you came back with *that*," he said, pointing at the necklace with a thin bar of gold resting against the pulsating scarlet light of her heart.

Shame and confusion clouded her expression as she pulled the laces of her blouse tight to cover the necklace. "Are you trying to torture me? Don't you think I haven't run it through my mind a thousand different times? I don't know where I went, or what I did, or who this belongs to!"

Seeing the tears glittering in her eyes made him want to cry also. He pulled out his handkerchief and blew his nose. "I'm sssorry, misss. You're right, it'sss not worth talking about if there'sss nothing to remember." He managed a smile. "Ssso the glue'sss holding at leassst?"

Her lips formed the ghost of a smile. "For the moment."

Sithias shook his head, knowing the actual problem was really about how much she missed Finn. If he was here, everything would be very different. "Well, I sssee only one sssolution to thisss. Let'sss do a bit of sssparring." Heaving a sigh, he grabbed the hilt of her sword and struggled to pry it out of the ground.

Sunshine hit the stained glass windows, scattering sapphire

and ruby specks of light over Fate's bed. She woke with a feeling that something was different about the day, though there was nothing to indicate anything out of the ordinary. Since her talk with Sithias a few days before, she'd made plans to go riding and hunt for pheasant, a welcome departure from the intensive training she'd been putting herself through with Beldereth's most experienced warriors. She'd formed deep bonds with them and was looking forward to joining her new friends.

She jumped out of bed, reaching for her leather breeches and white cotton blouse. Pulling open the balcony doors, she let the sunlight warm her skin—glad the snow was gone at last. Sithias was right. She'd been pushing herself far too hard, but it was either that or spiral into a state of utter madness.

Even now she had to be careful. Quiet moments such as these were dangerous and inevitably turned her mind to the sublime moment Finn had spoken those three magic words to her. But the grievous wound she'd dealt him just before he'd declared his love would always mar that special memory. Her throat tightened with grief. If only she could erase the trauma of that terrifying feeling of emptiness when he'd fallen and his life's blood had spread over the marble floor.

Rudwor had worked fast to staunch the wound, calling for Lortaun's best healers to minister him. They did everything they could for Finn while he hovered for days at death's door. She'd stayed by his side while he'd slept—a deep sleep broken only by nightmares he never fully woke from.

Then one afternoon, she'd gone into his room after a brief respite, only to find him gone. Her grief-stricken wail had echoed through the halls, attracting servants from every quarter. They tried to explain, but she was inconsolable. When Sithias found out what had happened, he was the only one she would listen to.

Rudwor had taken Finn away to the Springs of Almsdeep

to help him fully heal. She was told they would return only when he was completely well. She'd been furious, and wanted to fly there, but everyone was forbidden from telling her where the springs were hidden. No one would explain why, which infuriated her to no end. Worse yet, when she'd tried to use her Words of Making to go to him, the location eluded her as if cloaked by some sort of magic. The temptation to take charge and write up Finn's swift recovery and return to her had been stronger than any desire she'd ever had to overcome. For this, she hated Rudwor. Not only had he taken Finn away from her, but she'd been forced to endure each day waiting for his return without knowing when that might be. The only thing that had kept her from meddling with the Words of Making was her colossal mistake with the Green Man. She feared the possibility of an unimaginable backlash more than the anguish of missing Finn.

With him gone, she'd been left with a horrible sense of loss, like something had been torn out of her. The world stopped spinning and time slowed to a torturous crawl. There was no joy in anything. Even the food she put in her mouth tasted like cardboard. She probably would've spent the last two months too depressed to get out of bed had it not been for the high voltage energy constantly surging through her, building into a frenzy that pushed her into an almost murderous rage.

Taking up the sword, plus every other instrument of war she could get her hands on was the only alternative to going all Lizzie Borden on everyone. Training was the only time she felt even a modicum of peace, not to mention the best possible preparation for when Finn returned and they moved onto the next fable. She must've read through it a hundred different times, searching for some sort of advantage for when they would finally face Mugloth. Unfortunately, the book never spelled out in advance all the dangers they'd encounter. There were always surprises. Even so, she lived for that day, because if all went well, their future together would be wide open.

Or would it? There was always that one niggling worry. Ever since Gerdie had told her of the Orb's imperfect power, she couldn't stop wondering if there was something innately wrong with Finn, that maybe the poison wasn't the only reason for his struggle against the darkness.

Fate fingered the necklace hidden beneath her blouse as she stepped out onto the balcony. She suspected the tiny gold bar might be the Rod Gerdie had spoken of. But for some reason, she couldn't bring herself to show it to her and ask. She couldn't shake the fear that Gerdie would want to take it from her, especially if she knew how it had come into her possession. It was bad enough Sithias had been in her room when she'd returned with the necklace in that gory state. She closed her eyes, wishing she could forget the blood-encrusted sword, her clothes spattered a deep red and hands coated like she'd dunked them in paint. At times she felt the awful stickiness between her fingers and she still couldn't look in the mirror without seeing arterial spray covering her face.

But no matter how much her gut twisted with shame, the pain wasn't enough to make her take off the necklace. From the moment she started wearing it, the maddening tension always building in her wasn't nearly as severe. The little gold bar had a soothing effect she desperately needed and wasn't willing to give up. She only wished its influence would lift the nagging guilt.

It was torture not knowing why she'd taken off for three entire days without any memory of where she'd gone or what had happened. Was she really capable of that kind of bloodshed? O'Deldar had told her there would be blood on her hands and that she should try not to focus on what's right or wrong as she walked down a path of nettles—or words to that effect. She shuddered, greatly disturbed by his prophetic message. How had he known? Had he seen some sort of black stain on her soul?

A deep sense of sadness overwhelmed her as Eustace came to mind. How could she ever face her father if she'd actually killed someone? He had worked so hard to shelter her, keep her innocent. There'd be no hiding it from him. All he'd have to do is take one look at her to know she was changed, and not just because her skin still gleamed with a weird fiery light and her heart glowed through her clothes like Iron Man's mini arc reactor. There was a time when having superhuman strength and supernatural looks would've been the coolest thing ever, but not if those powers were turning her into Mr. Hyde. She wondered how long the visible signs would last. The thought of never being able to return home gnawed at her. She missed Eustace. And it scared her that she couldn't remember his face as clearly as she used to.

Leaning against the railing, she gazed out at the green garden burgeoning with clouds of pink and white spring blossoms. As she surrendered her troubles to the beautiful scenery, her spirits began to lift little by little. Movement caught her eye. Two men strolled the garden's winding path—one large and barrel-chested, the other, not quite as tall, but young and lean. Her breath caught in her throat when the sunlight hit his bronzed, golden locks.

Fate gripped the railing, dizzy with disbelief. Then he turned as if she'd called out to him. A wide smile spread over Finn's upturned face. Her heart pounded wildly in response as he launched into the air and landed next to her on the terrace.

Grabbing hold of her by the waist, he drifted upward as he whirled her out over space. For a second she wondered if she was dreaming, but the feel of his arms around her was too real. She gave into the moment, drinking in the masculine scent of his skin and the warm odor of his leather coat. As she melted against him, a blissful calm came over her. When he set her back down on the balcony she placed her hands on each side of his face, taking in every detail—the robust color of his skin, his moist lips and the green of his irises flaming bright with excitement. There wasn't a trace of inner turmoil in his eyes. He seemed freed of the darkness he'd been fighting. By all appearances Rudwor's enforced convalescence had worked miracles.

"You're okay," she said, barely able to catch her breath.

"I am at that." His gaze roved over every curve of her face. "You goring me in the ribs was probably one of the best things that ever happened to me."

Guilt knifed her in the chest.

Seeing her reaction, he laughed. "I'll tell you all about it later tonight," he said, his voice low and husky. As his lips brushed against her cheek, she closed her eyes, expecting a kiss, but he let her go.

She opened her eyes in shock. "Tonight? Why not now? You can't leave—you just got here."

He leaped over the railing, landing below the balcony. "I've got a few things to arrange, love. Don't worry, I'm not going far," he said, looking up at her with a mischievous smile.

Too stunned to speak, she watched him rejoin Rudwor in the middle of the garden and stroll away in the opposite direction.

She left her bedchamber in a daze, walking the wide hallway aimlessly.

"You alright? You're lookin' flushed."

Stopping near the banister, Fate focused in on Gerdie coming up the stairs with Valesca. They hadn't seen much of each other over the last few months. Fate had been busy training, while Gerdie, having taken a strong liking to the addled princess, had been working with the healers, referring to her grandmother's notebook to combine magic with herbal treatments. They'd made some progress. Valesca seemed less absorbed with her imaginary world of late.

"I'm fine. Better than fine. *Finn's back,*" Fate said breathlessly, her excitement building as the reality of his return sank in.

Gerdie's eyes rounded with surprise. "How'd he look?" she asked as Fate moved past her and descended the stairs.

"He looked perfect," she murmured, hovering a few inches off the floor as she slowly floated in no particular direction.

When Fate entered the private garden, Finn's heart leaped into his throat. Dressed in an elegant gold satin gown, she outshone the brilliant copper flame of the sunset sky behind her. As much as he'd fought against it, he'd thought of her the entire time he'd been away, unable to keep from nurturing every recollection of her. But his memories paled miserably in the presence of this vision before him. And now with the goddess energy lighting her from within, she'd been transformed into an otherworldly creature he found even more entrancing. Which only made what he had to tell her so much harder than he'd expected.

He swallowed, pushing that part of his evening plans to the very end. It was important they first find comfortable ground. Stepping forward, he extended his arm to her. "I'll take it from here," he said to the servant who'd escorted her in.

Fate smiled nervously, her gaze flicking over the elaborate table set for two, the paper lanterns hanging from the trees and servants standing in attendance. "What's all this?"

"Just a little something to show how much I missed you," he said as he pulled out her chair. She slipped into her seat in one smooth graceful motion. His mouth went dry seeing how differently she moved, like a cat. Breathing deep to center himself, his nose filled with the scent of jasmine and vanilla feathering off her skin. He went hot all over, his mind hazing with desire. Before he knew it, he was pressing his mouth against her ear. "You look *amazing.*"

Shivering, she tilted her head back, exposing the slender curve of her neck, her lips parted in anticipation and eyes half closed.

A wild, all consuming need to possess her erupted from the depths of his being. He went rigid with fear as it clawed its way up out of the darkness into the light, this terrible shadow thing that fed on his strongest emotions and twisted them into the vilest of urges. Reeling backward and tripping, Finn regained his footing and walked stiff-legged to the opposite chair and sat down. Squeezing his eyes shut, he silently recited the mantra he'd been taught by the monks of Almsdeep. *The victor need not fight. The victor need not fight.*

The dark uproar receded, shrinking in size as he repeated the calming mantra.

"Finn? What's wrong?"

He opened his eyes to her troubled expression. "Nothing, love," he said, quickly averting his gaze to the treetops. He hated lying to her. Rudwor had warned him it was too soon to be alone with her. He should've listened but missing her had become a physical ache he could no longer bear. *God, I want to hold her.*

"This is nice, but you really didn't have to go to all this trouble," she said, her tone uncomfortable. "I would've been perfectly happy just spending the day with you."

Finn forced his gaze back to her. She sat facing the sunset. The autumn hue of the sky's light deepened the red-brown of her eyes while the wind caught in her hair, fluttering wavy strands near her inviting mouth. He was stricken by her beauty, made defenseless once again.

He had to do something or he'd lose control altogether. *Don't look into her eyes.* Dropping his gaze to her throat, he stared hard at her necklace, following the chain down to the slim gold bar resting over her radiant heart center. He gulped when he recognized it. "Is that the Rod of Aeternitis?"

Her hand moved to cover it. "What? Why would you call it that?"

"Because that's what it is. And the last time I saw it, O'Deldar was wearing it."

She blanched, a wild panic showing in her eyes. "Are you sure? I-I don't remember seeing it on him."

His mind raced. Why did she look so guilty? "Do you have any idea what the Rod is and the kind of power it will unleash in the Orb?"

"Gerdie told me that everything that was ever created by the Orb was incomplete without the Rod. Did you know that?" she said, heat flushing back into her cheeks like a sudden fever.

He frowned in confusion. "So you *do* know about the Rod?"

"I think that's the reason you haven't been able to overcome the poison's influence," she said, rushing over his question. "We can fix you with the Rod. We can make you whole."

He shook his head. She wasn't making any sense. Had Brune's spell taken over again? "Fate, do you know where you are?" he asked, searching her face for that telltale vacant look.

She frowned at him like he'd lost his mind. "Are you serious?"

The last time he'd seen her under the spell's influence, she'd been completely out to lunch. She was certainly present at the moment. "It's time you knew that Brune's had you under a spell this whole time. That's why you're *here*. She sent you into the *Book of Fables* to get that Rod."

"Are you making this up?" she said, expressing genuine surprise.

"Course not. The last time we saw O'Deldar, you went positively mental when he showed us the Rod. You weren't you. You nearly attacked him to get it, but he subdued you and gave you an antidote to Brune's spell. I know I should've told you but it seemed prudent at the time not to." A queasy feeling throbbed in his gut as he leaned forward. "How did you manage to get it from him?"

"Why didn't you tell me?" she snapped. "Don't you think I had a right to know that I'm being used? That I've been made to do awful, unforgivable things..." The anger in her eyes flared for only a second. A haunted look of guilt had moved in.

"Like what?" he asked, the sick knot in his stomach tightening. "Fate? Tell me how you got the Rod. I know O'Deldar didn't just hand it over."

Her face reddened as the rapid beat of her heart burned bright behind her breastbone. "I...I used my Words of Making," she said, pressing her lips together defensively.

He could tell she was lying but he didn't want to push it. She obviously wasn't ready to confess the truth yet. He understood that kind of angst.

"I suppose now you expect me to give it back," she said in a challenging tone.

"No, you have to keep it now. Whatever O'Deldar did to interrupt the spell isn't working anymore. He said you'd die trying to get the Rod."

Clutching at the necklace, she fell against the back of her chair, the stressed lines of her face smoothing with relief.

"When we get back to the bookstore, you *mustn't* give it to Brune," he warned. "O'Deldar was quite clear on that."

She nodded, narrowing her gaze on the horizon. "No worries there. Brune's not getting anything from me but a thorough ass kicking for everything she's put me through."

"Aye, she deserves it," he agreed, still unused to this new tough attitude.

One of the servants cleared his throat, indicating to Finn a tray of food he must've been holding off on serving during their tense conversation.

"Thanks, mate," Finn said, gesturing for him to set down the first course and signaling for the servants to let them eat in private.

Fate took a small bite of pheasant and set her fork down. "So is there a reason you couldn't spend the day with me after we've been apart for two months?"

"Uh, about that," he said, caught off guard by her directness. Another change he'd have to get used to. "I was hoping to talk about that later in the evening, but..."

She sat stiff as if bracing for bad news.

He shifted in his chair, feeling her tension flowing into him. The shield he'd learned to put around himself to keep from being a sponge for her emotions was thinning the longer he was near her. He quickly visualized the Sovereign Symbols he'd been given by the monks, breathing easier as the buffer rapidly fell back into place. Resting his elbows on the table, he smiled, though a bit forced, to help put her at ease. "There's so much I want to tell you, to help you understand."

"Understand what?" Her shining heart was beating fast, betraying her mounting anxiety.

"Why I need to limit my time around you for a while," he said, unable to keep the smile going. Just saying the words brought on the worst kind of sadness. But he couldn't go on fooling himself either. It was plain to see he needed more time to master everything he'd learned during his stay at Almsdeep. Once he was more practiced, he could then be around her without worry.

Pain raked across her face. "This is all because I made you remember where you came from, isn't it?"

"No," he was quick to say. The memory of that terrible night came slamming back. Shame clouded his mind, making him lose focus. "I'll admit the pure shock of finding out my origins all over again made it easier to give in to the darkness."

"That was never my intent," she said as tears filled her eyes. "You just seemed so lost at the time with your memory fading.

I only wanted to help you find a little peace in something familiar to you. I never meant to push you further into the poison's grip."

He smiled sadly. "I know, love. And I need you to know that every despicable thing I said and did that horrible night was *not me.* It was this thing inside me feeding on the despair I felt over not being real, not knowing what I was or where I belonged."

She stared at him with a desperate look that tore at him. "I know that wasn't you that night and I don't blame you for what happened. You *have* to know you're more real than what I ever imagined. And as for where you belong…you belong with me."

She reached across the table, touching the tips of his fingers with hers. An electric current raced between them. It was all he could do to keep from throwing the table aside and taking her in his arms.

"Finn," she said breathlessly, "you have no idea how painful it was for me to write about you everyday for all those years—the one person I wanted to be with more than anything. To fall more deeply in love with you, not be able to touch you, talk to you and have you respond to me? It was maddening."

He gripped the sides of the table, wrestling with the dark presence rearing its ugly black head again. He'd been waiting for her to open up to him for so long and now that she was baring her soul like never before, he couldn't risk a single move in her direction for fear of what he might do. His need to be with her, skin to skin, soul to soul was overpowering.

She held still, waiting for him to say something, *do* something. The hopeful, expectant look in her eyes killed him.

"God knows you should harbor only hatred toward me, and I'm grateful you don't," he said, his eyes closed as he pulled his awareness inward and focused on the speech he'd rehearsed a hundred times in his head. "And as far as my origins are concerned, it doesn't matter anymore. I'm here now, and it's what I do from this time forward that defines who and what I am. Rudwor has helped me realize that. My time with him has been a true gift. He's been like the father I always wished I'd had. He's been helping me deal with the guilt and shame that's been eating me alive. And without the guidance of the monks of Almsdeep, I wouldn't know how to hold back the darkness." He glanced up at the dusky sky, avoiding her gaze. "You have no idea how close I was to losing the battle. I was ready to stay with the Bane, to become one of them if they didn't kill me first. I felt it was all I deserved after what I did to you."

Feeling stronger now, he looked at her. She was staring down at her lap, her forehead creased with disappointment. He hated letting her down. But he'd rather have her angry with him than abused by his hands ever again. "I'm in a better place now. I've even learned to shield myself from sensing your every emotion. Well, pretty much. It's easier when I only have my own feelings to contend with, but I still fear losing control. *That must never happen again.* Right now as it stands, being too close to you is having an effect on me. My mind fogs and something wild claws its way out—something I'm not strong enough to tame. At least not yet. *That's* why we need space from each other until I've got a better grip on this. Then we can move onto *The Bloodthirsty Oak* and I'll do everything within my power to rid myself of this demon once and for all. Or die trying." He waited for her to respond but she remained silent and deflated. "Is any of this making sense to you?"

She straightened and faced him. It took a moment for her cold, remote gaze to set in. The light of her heart was subdued now, the beat steady. There was an eerie calmness that shouldn't be there.

His heart thudded with panic. "Please say something." She stood up, meeting his gaze head on but staring right through him. He'd seen that look before, the warrior stare when she'd been under Murauda's thrall. "I understand. I'll leave you alone," she said, her voice flat.

As she rounded the table, he stood up so fast his chair fell over. He caught her by the wrist. "Don't...don't leave like this."

Twisting her wrist, she wrenched free of his grasp and pushed him back with startling strength. "This is your choice, Finn, not mine. But you can't expect to have it both ways."

Too dumbstruck to speak, he pressed a fist over the pain in his chest, his heart shriveling with each stride she took away from him.

CHAPTER 31

THE NEXT FOUR WEEKS after Fate had drawn the line in the sand between them were excruciating. Every time she replayed that final moment in her mind—which was a lot—she crumbled inside. But what was she to do? Short of standing naked before Finn, she'd poured her heart out under the assumption he felt exactly the same. And what had he done? He'd shut down and rattled off a bunch of flimsy reasons they shouldn't be together, not even asking how she felt about it. She couldn't understand why he felt the need to protect her. She wasn't the weakling she used to be. Couldn't he see that?

Still, she regretted having closed the door on him, but what hurt most was that he'd left it closed. Several days after that disastrous night, he'd sent a note. She'd ripped it open, expecting a change of heart, or at least some hint that he missed her as much as she did him. But it had been an impersonal message saying he'd be ready to move onto the next fable after Rudwor's coronation in a month.

After that, Finn spent his days with Rudwor. At first she was miserable with grief, but as the days passed, anger set in, triggering the unbearable energy build up. She returned to her training like never before. The sparring, target shooting and hand-to-hand combat sharpened her mind and strengthened her body but did nothing to rebuild her broken heart. Whenever she saw Finn, either from afar or at the occasional dinner, his carefree attitude only increased her pain. By all outward appearances, he seemed quite content with the distance between them.

The night of the coronation arrived at long last. Fate wanted to wear something Finn would find utterly irresistible, so she fussed over every detail of her dress with Sithias's help. Together they designed a cream-colored gown that pooled around her like dollops of whipped cream. She had to rewrite the description of the bodice several times before he agreed the one stitched with lustrous pearls and scooped neckline would do the trick. Then he decided she needed to make her hair long to the waist and braid it loosely with a strand of fragrant gardenias. With that final touch, he gave her a teary-eyed nod of approval, deeming their creation heavenly. He especially liked how the gown downplayed her newly developed "mannish" qualities.

During the coronation, Finn stood next to Rudwor in full regalia—the traditional Beldereth black and gray tartan kilt and charcoal jacket trimmed in silver buttons embossed with the royal crest. Much to Fate's surprise, the new king awarded him the station of First Knight. Having known nothing of this, she watched them from her pew several rows back, uneasy with how Rudwor looked at him like a proud father.

She didn't like it. She didn't like any of it one bit.

A grand feast followed the coronation. She sat opposite Finn but three seats down. Keeping her gaze from meeting his, she made every attempt to converse merrily with whomever she could. She'd give him a taste of his own bitter medicine and freeze him out, but she drove herself crazy wondering if he even noticed.

When the dancing began, she gave up and glanced over at him. His chair was empty. When she saw him on the dance floor with Meara, a beautiful blue-eyed blonde who had been one of the many young women Murauda had knighted, an unbearable tightness squeezed the air from her lungs. Finn was holding Meara close and whispering in her ear.

It was plain to see he'd moved on, a certainty solidified by a constant stream of women keeping him dancing throughout the night. Fate knew there was a shortage of available men in Beldereth, but the women were drawn to him like moths to a flame and he didn't even bother to pretend he wanted her company. Even Sithias was being kept busy on the dance floor, but he at least found a moment to slip away and pull her out to join him.

"I can sssee the dessspair paling your lovely face, misss," he said. "You mussstn't let your emotionsss get the bessst of you now."

"Look at him, all irritatingly gorgeous and acting like I don't exist. It's his way of letting me know it's over."

"Did he sssay that to you?"

"He doesn't need to." When she saw that Sithias didn't believe her, she said, "I guess I always knew it would be this way, but I hoped maybe he'd choose me after I set him free."

Sithias's eyebrows shot up, puzzled.

"I used my Words of Making to release Finn from that Vulcan mind meld we have with each other. He needs to be the creator of his own life and choose who to love without being magically handcuffed to me."

"When did you do that?"

"The day he sent me that unfeeling memo letting me know his chosen departure date from Beldereth."

Understanding filled his eyes. "Oh, I sssee…"

Unable to face the truth any longer, Fate dropped her forehead against his shoulder. "I can't do this," she said, her voice faltering in her throat.

Before he could say another word, she ran from the ballroom.

When she arrived in her bedchamber, she let her beautiful dress fall in a crumpled heap, slipped into her nightgown and crawled onto the bed. The heavy scent from the gardenias braided in her hair choked in her throat. As she ripped them out, hot tears ran unchecked and sobs tore from her aching chest, until at long last, exhaustion forced a surrender to merciful sleep.

Finn stared at the whorls and knots of the heavy wooden door, suddenly frozen with uncertainty. He'd been working toward this moment all month, meditating, reading sacred texts and maintaining his purifying rituals without fail. Rudwor felt confident he was ready to test himself, see if he could Stay Whole, as the monks called it, in Fate's presence. But what if he failed? He turned his head slightly, seeing the feet of the warrior knights he'd posted on either side of the door. She'd be safe if the worst happened. They were eight of Beldereth's best.

As he knocked on the door, his heart raced. The seconds ticked by like minutes. He was just about to knock again when the door opened. Fate stood before him, an exquisite, tousled mess. The moonlight shining from the window at her back sifted through her thin nightgown, casting each perfect curve in soft silhouette. As she rubbed her sleepy eyes and looked up at him in surprise, he gripped the doorway and gulped. "Uh…" His mind went blank.

"Finn?" There was nothing guarded in her eyes, all her defenses were down.

"Why did you leave?" he asked, unable to raise his voice above a rough whisper.

The corners of her mouth curved down. "You have to ask?"

Digging his fingers into the wood, he followed the path of her long hair falling against the gentle rise and fall of her breasts. Every thought burned away as he lifted a silken lock to his nose and inhaled the intoxicating scent of gardenias lingering in her hair. A sudden fever rose beneath his skin and his body pulled tight.

Swallowing dryly, he let go and grabbed the other side of the doorway. It was all he could do to keep from descending on her in a rush of blind passion. "Fate," he managed to say, "I wanted to dance with you one last time."

She looked crestfallen. "One last time?"

"Did you forget we're leaving tomorrow to go into the last fable?" he asked, the angst of leaving Beldereth clearing his mind a little.

Her eyes widened with hope. "You still plan to go?"

Forcing his gaze to the window, he stared at the full moon grazing the distant mountain peaks. "I'd be lying if I said I haven't been dreading it. But what choice do I have?"

"You could stay," she said. "You seem to be fine now."

He dropped his gaze back to her. Helplessly drawn in, he bent his head and leaned toward her. "I've missed you so much."

The light of her heart had diminished to a faint glow over the last month, but it suddenly flared bright, pulsing fast as she stepped closer and touched her lips to his, feather light like the silken touch of butterfly wings. He lost himself once again.

"Stay with me tonight," she whispered.

He drew back in surprise. After their last encounter he'd expected some resistance on her part, especially since she'd avoided all contact with him at the ball. She was so open right now, too open. His confidence cracked. "I shouldn't."

She pried one of his hands free from the doorway. "Just *be* with me. Nothing more."

He stiffened, stricken by fear, yet unable to make himself leave.

She smiled. "Stop worrying, I'm not the helpless girl I was three months ago." Her expression grew serious, intent. "I have faith in you, Finn."

The conviction in her voice strengthened him more than she would ever know. Letting go of his anchor, he allowed her to pull him into the room. Without taking her eyes off his, she kicked the door closed behind her. As she padded toward the bed, she glanced over her shoulder. He went rigid as she settled within the downy softness of the pillows and featherbed.

She patted the mattress, gesturing for him to sit next to her. "I won't bite. Not much anyway," she said, a mischievous light in her eyes.

"Not funny," he muttered, clamping down hard and fast on the explosion of heat coursing through him. Taking a deep measured breath, he crossed the room slowly, repeating the tranquility mantra in his mind, but his concentration crumbled when he stepped on the gardenias scattered by the bed, their perfume releasing into the air. He took a step backward, stopping when she reached forward to grab his hand.

"Can I…can I see the scar? The one I gave you?" The playfulness had gone out of her voice.

"It's not all that pretty."

"Please, I want to see it." Shifting her weight, she raised onto her knees, unbuttoning his jacket with hands shaking.

He gritted his teeth, fighting the wave of mindless abandon washing over him. As she pulled his shirt back, her fingers skimmed over his skin. Trembling beneath her touch, he gripped the carved bedpost, squeezing 'til his fingers ached.

Hearing a little gasp, he glanced down. Shame warmed her face as she stared at the scar. It was fully healed but remained a thick, purplish welt. "I'm *so* sorry," she whispered.

"Don't worry yourself over it," he said. Brushing his hand over her hair, he kissed the top of her head, wanting only to ease her guilt. "Like I said, it's the best thing that could've happened to me. Same goes for the others."

Her gaze moved to the rake of four scars the wolverine had given him. "You never told me how those happened."

"You're right, I never did," he said, relaxing enough to sit down next to her. Talking was just the distraction he needed. She moved over, tucking her legs up under her nightgown and pulling the hem tight over her toes the way she probably had when she was a little girl. Feeling more comfortable, he settled against the pillows, stretching his legs out in front of him and hands behind his head as he described the wolverine attack and the underlying meaning of the animal's ultimate sacrifice.

Fate listened in rapt attention. When he was done with his story, she pointed at the faint scar Tove had branded into his skin the night she'd found him at the troll mound. "And this? Why did she burn that mark into you?"

"It's a purging rune," he said, thinking of Tove. For a brief moment he was back in the Twisted Bone Forest, remembering that simple, peaceful time. "It's burned into the skin to clear out whatever the body needs to be rid of, in order to heal—in my case, the poison. Of course, it didn't work on me." He lapsed into silence, that ever-present burden weighing him down.

"Do you still love her?"

The answer came to him in an instant but he hesitated. He didn't wish to hurt Fate. Then again, he couldn't lie to her either. She deserved his honesty. "Aye," he said at last, "I still love her, but not in the way I love you."

The light of her shining heart crept into her neck, betraying her escalating pulse. "How can you love us both?"

"I know that's not what you want to hear, but it isn't as simple as pushing a button to turn off my feelings for Tove. You have to understand, she threw me a lifeline when I was near death, and she brought me out of it a stronger and wiser person. I'll be forever grateful to her and Grysla for that."

"But you fell *in love* with Tove."

"Aye, I did. She's unlike anyone I've ever known. She's not of our world, yet she's connected to everything around her in a way that's extraordinary." Fate jumped to her feet and would've leaped off the end of the bed had he not instinctively grabbed her by the waist. She struggled against him as he pulled her back down to sit beside him. “Don't, Fate,” he said, folding his arms around her, touching his forehead to hers, “*you* gave me *everything*. Tove may have saved my life, but you *gave* me life. I am who I am because of you.”

She went still in his arms.

“Telling you this is long overdue,” he continued, “only because it's taken me a good while to come around to it. But now that I have, I know it's *why* we're so deeply connected. We're part of each other, two halves of a whole—”

“You still feel that way?” she said, tensing again.

“And why wouldn't I?”

“No reason,” she said too quickly, a sure sign she wasn't telling him everything.

He loosened his grip, pulling back to look at her. The disappointment in her eyes only confused him further. “What's wrong?”

“It's just…if you're drawn to me over the *incomparable* Tove, because as you say, I'm you and you're me, it makes all this a bit narcissistic. Don't you think?”

“It's not like that and you know it. Fate Floyd, writer extraordinaire, may have given me the stuff I'm made of, but I'm my own man now. As each day goes by, I become *more* than what you made me.” He paused, brushing the back of his hand along one side of her face, so beautiful in the milky light of the moon. “And I am someone who finds you absolutely captivating.”

She went limp as all the tension drained out of her. “You do?”

“I do,” he said, needing desperately to show her he meant every word, but he couldn't risk even a kiss without going to a dangerous place. Then it came to him. He opened the sealskin sporran at his waist and pulled out his mother's ribbon. “I want you to have this."

She shook her head. "No, I couldn't. I know how much it means to you."

"Aye, then you know it's like a piece of my heart. So don't say no." He wrapped the white satin ribbon around her wrist several times and tied it, sealing the knot with a kiss.

Smiling shyly, she rubbed the silky fabric against her cheek. "Does this mean we've tied the knot again?"

"Our knot's always been tied and never undone," he whispered, his throat tight with overwhelming joy. *She's mine.* Smiling, he pulled her close and leaned back into the pillows.

She eased her head down on his chest. "This is good."

"Aye," he agreed.

The morning sun blazed bright through the window, prodding Finn awake. He opened his eyes in a panic, fearful of what he might've done after losing consciousness. When he saw that Fate was still curled into him and sleeping peacefully, he relaxed, grateful he'd managed to Stay Whole through the night. He sank back into the pillow as the memory of what they'd shared flooded him with peace. So much had been healed between them. They'd united in heart and mind. And as tempting as it was to make love when words could no longer express their feelings for each other, he'd had to hold back. There was no way he could risk letting his guard down to that degree. Not yet. Fate had understood, but that hadn't kept the raw desire in her from overflowing. She'd been awash in it, a bittersweet form of torture for him. He'd had to call upon every discipline he'd learned from the monks to keep a tight rein on himself…and still did.

Thinking he'd probably pushed his luck as far as he should for the moment, he decided it best to leave and take a break from the draining task of having to stay constantly vigilant. Careful not to disturb her, he slowly slipped his arm out from under her head and eased himself off the bed. He froze when he saw the *Book of Fables* leaning against the wall. The night had kept it cloaked in shadow. Seeing it now in the light of day filled him with dread. It hadn't occurred to him that she'd already retrieved it from the wastelands of Duenthorn, but now the giant book loomed in the corner as an ominous reminder of the ultimate trial he would face in just a few short hours.

As he tucked in his shirt and buttoned his jacket, he looked back at Fate, his apprehension subsiding as his gaze lingered on the stunning disarray of her long curls, the angelic lines of her face and the inviting curves hidden beneath the thin veil of her white nightgown.

The fierce yearning he'd held back all night suddenly erupted, awakening the slumbering darkness with frightening speed. Feeling it uncoil like a serpent ready to strike, he staggered back and ran from the room.

"Do you really think all that'sss necessary?" Sithias asked. He was dressed in tweed traveling attire and carrying a leather tote bag filled to the brim with his newly written plays. "You look ready for all-out war."

"It's called armed to the teeth, and I want to be prepared for anything," Fate said as she slid the last of her six daggers in the strap around her thigh. Wearing her usual leather armor, she had her sword belted at her waist and a small crossbow and quiver strapped to her back. A hooded cloak concealed her arsenal, figuring it unwise to advertise her weapons to the inhabitants of the next fable immediately upon their arrival.

Sithias eyed the white ribbon around her wrist. "What'sss thisss?"

A plume of heat rushed into her cheeks. "It's from Finn."

"Ah, all isss well then. By the way, where isss he? I thought he'd be here by now."

"He must be saying goodbye to Rudwor." She was careful to keep her tone even. She didn't want him noting how anxious she was. After that amazing night with Finn, waking up alone had cut deep. She'd thought all the walls between them had crumbled. They'd talked about everything under the sun, moon and stars. Misunderstandings had been corrected, confessions both joyful and painful were shared, fears admitted, lessons imparted and dreams of the future made. As much as it had driven her mad with desire to lie next to him without so much as a kiss, she'd managed to control herself. Knowing he loved her and having him close had been enough. She'd trusted the time was very near when they could surrender all fear and melt into each other.

But now she wasn't as sure as she'd been last night.

A knock on the door had her pulse racing in anticipation. When Gerdie poked her head inside, disappointment caved in. "Sorry I'm late. I had a time settlin' Valesca down. She doesn't like goodbyes, poor dear." She glanced around the room. "Where's Finn?"

"Good quessstion," Sithias said, tapping his toe impatiently.

"Maybe I should go find him," Fate muttered, her uneasiness increasing as she headed for the door. Just as she touched the door handle, there was a knock. Relief mingled with renewed excitement. *Finally.* She couldn't take another lunch bag letdown. Her nerves were already on edge about leaving the safety of Beldereth and moving ahead into the unknown, without the added anxiety of wondering why Finn was taking so long.

She opened the door fully expecting to see him standing there. It was Rudwor's large form filling the doorframe instead. "Uh, come in," she said, her heart thudding out of control when she saw that Finn wasn't behind him.

"I came to see you off," Rudwor said, his deep, booming voice filling the room as he entered. His eyes fixed on the *Book of Fables*. "So this is the big bad book. Mind if I read the last two fables? My curiosity's been peaked, for obvious reasons."

"You'll be glad to read that Beldereth's future looks bright," she said, keeping her expression neutral to hide her panic and confusion. She'd never let Rudwor see her upset, no matter how flustered she was at the moment. She turned the book's thick pages to *The Lightning Sword*. As he read through the story, she paced, chewing her bottom lip.

"What's this?" he bellowed all at once. "Why didn't anyone tell me about this treachery?"

She jumped. His voice had a way of penetrating to the bone. "What treachery?"

"It says here the royal scryer manipulated *everything*." His face was red and turning purple. "The traitor turned on my brother!"

Fate met his furious gaze head on, unable to keep from shrugging carelessly. "*Sorry*, I guess it was an oversight." She glanced at Sithias, who was shaking his head in warning.

"An *oversight?*" Rudwor yelled. "You're lucky you belong to Finn, or I'd…" He threw up his arms and huffed. "The creature must be executed at once."

"Hold on a sec. Your family's been holding that poor creature prisoner in a tiny well for centuries. It's not a sea monkey, you know—which by the way, look nothing like their pictures." Realizing his frown had gone from annoyed to perplexed, she decided to stay on point. "So who could blame it for taking revenge? Your family *promised* to let it go home to the ocean if it kept its side of the bargain, which it did for a whole lot longer than you or I would've," she argued.

He held his breath, his face swelling before he finally exhaled. "I *cannot* free it."

She stepped forward, her hands on her hips. "No big surprise. It doesn't seem to be in your family's blood to set things free."

"You're talking about Finn."

"Where is he?"

"I told him to wait until I read the last fable for myself."

"Why?"

"Because I'm not certain he's ready for the challenge." He turned his back to her and returned his full attention to reading *The Bloodthirsty Oak*.

Fate stared daggers into his broad back, her temper reaching the boiling point with every passing second. But she held her tongue, more troubled by Finn's absence than Rudwor's interference. He could've at least showed up to tell her he wasn't ready to leave. She walked to the window, tapping her fingers on the glass and staring at the garden. A robin landed in a nearby tree. Seeing a worm wriggling in its beak, she turned away with a grimace and caught Gerdie and Sithias looking at her, both with worried expressions. She could tell they were thinking what was on her mind. Why wasn't Finn here? Then the answer hit her. She suddenly felt as if the floor had dropped out from beneath her. Last night had been goodbye.

Rudwor turned away from the book, looking grim. "Now I see the cause of so much grief in the world. I don't envy your quest."

"Then you can see I need Finn's help as much as he needs mine." The quaver in her voice betrayed her sudden lack of conviction.

"No, he'll be of no help to you. As soon as he's on that island, he'll be directly under Mugloth's influence. And then there's you, muddling his senses. All you'll do is get him killed." Rudwor moved toward the door. He had his hand on the doorhandle when he stopped to look at her. "I'm sure you can see the wisdom in this. And if you love him as much I think you do, you'll take your leave without a fuss."

Fate glared at the king. She was so angry she couldn't speak. She stormed over to the *Book of Fables* and turned the pages back to the end of *The Lightning Sword*. She skimmed over the final passage before turning her heated gaze back to Rudwor. "Now that your decision's made, you'd better read the last paragraph before you go."

He gave her a sharp look without budging. She figured he'd leave, but he surprised her by returning to the book and reading the passage aloud. "Beldereth enjoyed good fortune for a time, but King Lortaun's line was destined to be cursed by the scryer's prophesy. King Rudwor's champion, the First Knight was touched by an evil that was turning his heart black. Beldereth had an enemy inside its walls once again, an enemy that would leave the kingdom in ruins forevermore."

He stared in disbelief at the newly inked words on the aged paper. "How can this be? It didn't say that a moment ago."

"Your decision to have Finn stay has changed your destiny, and mine," Fate said. "We're all doomed now."

"No, you're not," a voice said from the doorway.

Everyone turned to see Finn. He stood with shoulders squared and stance wide, his gaze directed at Rudwor. There was a defiant look in his eyes, though measured with respect as he strode into the room.

Relief welled up in Fate. It was plain to see Finn had decided to join her.

Rudwor's whole demeanor softened. "You've decided to go have you?" he asked.

"Aye," Finn said. "It's time I stand on my own."

Smiling sadly, the king slapped his large hand on Finn's shoulder. "I know I shouldn't have pressed so hard for you to stay. I was being selfish. You've become the son I always wanted, and it pains me sorely to see you go."

Finn's eyes misted over.

Rudwor squeezed his shoulder. "Don't doubt your strength, Finn McKeen. And I'm not speaking of that outlandish power you displayed against Murauda. I'm speaking of something much more powerful, the unlimited power of your spirit and its undying strength to do what must be done. I suspect we've only seen the tip of it. Its full might is yet to be tapped and I'm certain your true strength will be far greater than any of us can imagine." His gentled gaze flicked to Fate, surprising her, especially when his expression didn't turn to irritation. "When you have something important to fight for, laddie, nothing can stop you. *Not a single thing.*"

His sincerity melted through her ire like the sun's heat on icy branches. For the first time she could see why Finn admired him so much and it broke her heart that he had to leave this man who'd become his father.

Rudwor enveloped him in a bear hug. After a moment, he let go, holding him at arm's length. "You have a home here, young sapling. Always." His tearful gaze flicked over Fate, Sithias and Gerdie. "You all do," he said, his voice cracking. With his head down, he turned and left.

Raw pain etched the lines of Finn's face as he stared at the space Rudwor had left empty. Sithias and Gerdie gathered close while Fate turned the page to *The Bloodthirsty Oak*. There was nothing to be said. There were no words for the pain of leaving or the fear of what awaited them. All they had was each other and that was enough, more than enough. Taking Finn's hand in hers, she began to read the last fable, which for better or worse would seal all their fates.

The Bloodthirsty Oak

In the first age of the world, the Earthmind grew the First Trees to be its voice to those who would listen. Known as the Grandfathers of all forests, these benevolent beings taught their earth magic secrets to the Druidhean and these wise sorcerers used this sacred wisdom to help guide mankind. And so it was that humans lived peacefully within nature's laws for untold ages. But as time wore on, many humans lost their way and broke the laws of nature.

These laws were not merely broken, but torn asunder on the small island of Innith Tine, home to a giant oak, the oldest of all Grandfathers. His trunk was as wide as a large house and his thick branches sprawled outward to the size of a small village. He could be seen from anywhere on the island, for he stood rooted on the highest hilltop overlooking a majestic forest of oaks.

Each spring the Druidhean made their annual pilgrimage to the hallowed grove of Innith Tine to celebrate Alban Eiler, a time when day and night are equal, when light and darkness stand face to face. The island's location had always been a guarded secret, but one spring when the Druidhean gathered there, they discovered a tiny fishing village on the island's shores where none had been the year before. The sorcerers entered the sacred catacombs beneath Grandfather Oak's roots to seek his wisdom. The ancient tree told them the villagers had been peaceful and respectful of the land thus far. Accepting this, the Druidhean carried on with their celebration. But before they left, they chose one among them to remain as Grove Guardian.

Mugloth was chosen for his healing abilities with herbs and his knowledge of cultivating crops and animal husbandry. The Order believed the villagers would welcome these skills and in turn be open to learning the sacred laws of nature. When the mysterious Druidh walked into their humble fishing village and taught them how to grow bountiful crops and heal with herbs in a way that respected the land, the village prospered under Mugloth's care. Soon after, the people took part in the annual celebrations to honor the earth and its changing seasons, and all was well. But when the fishermen set sail on the seas, word spread about their beautiful island of oaks. Each year more boats pulled ashore and more villages sprang up like weeds in a garden. As much as Mugloth traveled from village to village teaching the sacred laws, not everyone listened. There were those who cast greedy eyes upon the lush forest and took wanton axes to the trees.

Mugloth took council with his fellow Druidhean when they arrived to celebrate Alban Eiler. They grieved for the loss of so many trees and told him to have faith and keep teaching. For the next year Mugloth did as they advised, but the people were blinded by greed. He warned them that the forest was under his protection and risked punishment if they did not stop raping the land. But no one feared the gentle Druidh, and they resented being lectured on how to manage their island's bounty.

Miserable with grief, Mugloth withdrew into the catacombs. Grandfather Oak groaned a warning, telling him to be patient, all would be well in time, for he had many acorns and would grow a new forest. This did nothing to soothe Mugloth's fury. He could not understand why Grandfather Oak was not enraged. He knew the ancient tree felt the pain of each felled tree even more than he, but Grandfather Oak believed the people would see the error of their ways, though this was not to be. As the protective canopy of the forest dwindled, and with it the verdant carpet of moss, fern and flora, the villagers' souls became as barren as the island.

When more than half the forest was gone, and many of the birds and beasts with it, Mugloth could stand it no longer. Calling on the winds, he gathered forth a storm that crashed ships upon the rocks and destroyed the villages. Unfortunately, this led to more trees being cut down to rebuild homes and new ships. So Mugloth cursed their crops and poisoned the land. But this only brought more ships to the island, ships carrying food, which left with greater supplies of lumber.

When the Druidh returned to Innith Tine the following year, they were shocked to find that only a small grove remained. They found Mugloth brooding in the catacombs and accused him of failing in his duty as Grove Guardian. He described the wrath he had brought down upon the villagers. Judging his actions as rash and shortsighted, the Druidhean cast him out of the Order and banished him from his beloved island.

Taking his leave, Mugloth stomped through the barren land, cursing the Order and thrashing his staff against the stumps lining the path. He was so deep in thought he tripped and fell over a deer carcass. Its hide seemed to squirm and he drew back in horror as he realized it was covered in a blanket of flesh-eating ants. Studying the tiny creatures, he marveled at how the ruined land had forced them to bring down such giant prey. He stayed there and watched the ants for hours while the sun sank into the great watery horizon. As darkness fell over the island, an even greater darkness settled over his soul.

Mugloth began spinning a sinister spell around the ants. One that increased their numbers a thousand fold and sent them marching up the hill to feast on the Druidhean sleeping within the catacombs. When the ants had cleaned the meat from their bones, he sent his army into the villages. Most were eaten alive, while a few escaped to the ships. But Mugloth quickly conjured a storm, which crashed their ships against the island's rocky shore. Those who survived and swam ashore soon discovered even greater horrors awaited them.

When he returned to the catacombs, he felt the weight of Grandfather Oak's sadness. The great tree wept so hard, the earth shuddered and the catacombs caved inward, burying the bones of his fellow Druidh, while Mugloth barely escaped being buried alive.

This was the last betrayal for Mugloth. So he summoned the winds and thunderheads to destroy Grandfather Oak. The fierce winds pushed and shoved at the massive tree, but his roots clenched the earth and held fast. Mugloth shoved his staff skyward and pulled lightning from the black clouds. The bolts struck Grandfather Oak at the heart of his trunk. There was a sickening crack and a terrible groan as the ancient tree split in two.

Waving the storm aside, he approached the mighty tree. Grandfather Oak's voice cracked with anguish and compassion as he forgave Mugloth, promising to help him return to the sacred ways. But the darkness in Mugloth had a firm foothold.

He believed he had every right to take vengeance on the lawbreakers and vowed to make Grandfather Oak see this. So he climbed up the thick cloven trunk and wedged himself inside. Using his staff, Mugloth channeled all of his hatred and venomous thoughts into Grandfather Oak's wound.

The great tree was no match for the terrible darkness inside him. In that moment something horrible happened. As the break closed over the Druidh, man and tree became one and the same. The instant Mugloth imprisoned himself within living wood, Grandfather Oak transformed into a hellish monstrosity, which burrowed its hungry roots throughout the island, seeking vengeance by feeding on the remaining lawbreakers until its sap turned black with blood and reeked of death.

The doomed villagers eventually ended the feeding frenzies by sacrificing one of their own to the Bloodthirsty Oak each year on the day of Alban Eiler. As time wore on, everyone did what was necessary to survive. They gathered the evil oak's acorns and pieces of riven wood to use as barter with those passing by on the trade winds, while many a poor visitor was captured and sacrificed in place of their own. Countless centuries passed in this way, allowing the vengeance of one man to seed his hatred far and wide throughout the world.

CHAPTER 32

IT SEEMED A LIFETIME since Fate had gone from one fable to the next and she'd forgotten how intensely immersive the stories were. She felt Mugloth's hatred pressing in on her—a palpable force from which the very fabric of the air seemed made.

At last, the horrid images of the oak splintered into a furious swarm of letters that seemed to resist returning to the book's aged pages. The weighty feeling persisted even after the story's release. The thrust into Innith Tine was violent, knocking Fate off her feet.

Finding herself flat on her back, she opened her eyes to a blue sky of wispy clouds and a blur of gray gulls wheeling overhead. Sucking salt air into her jarred lungs, she turned her head, looking for the others. Sithias and Gerdie were nowhere to be seen but Finn was next to her on his knees, his head low.

Worrying about what had happened to them, she sat up in alarm, nauseated by the sudden motion. Had they been left behind in Beldereth? She started to get up but her stomach roiled and pitched. Forced to stay still, she waited a moment for her strength to return and the queasiness to subside. She glanced at Finn. His body was rigid, every muscle corded with tension. He seemed unable to move. At first she thought he was suffering from ill effects of the transition, but then she realized it was something else. Guessing he must be reacting to the bombardment of Mugloth's hatred during the reading, she hoped he wasn't about to become the vicious stranger again.

If he was, she needed to be ready. Her hand moved to the

daggers strapped around her thigh. She wasn't about to let the horrors of last time play out again.

Finn lifted his head, his face ashen and contorted with agony. "I can feel him."

Relieved to see he was still with her, she scrambled over and put her hands on his shoulders. His tensed muscles shook with restraint beneath her touch. "What do you want me to do?"

Clenching his jaw, he drove his fist into the sand. "Get away from me before I give into him. I don't want you anywhere near me when I do."

"*No,* we fight this together."

The muscles in his arms and back bunched with tension. He lifted his head slowly—his irises black and the whites of his eyes bloodshot. The savage darkness he'd been holding back for so long was brewing right beneath the surface, ready to burst free. Frightened, she let go. "Look," he said, his voice a low growl as he pointed beyond her shoulder.

Fate turned, her jaw dropping as she took in the barren landscape, ugly with nothing but stumps and scraggly bushes. As her gaze followed the rising terrain to the hilltop in the distance, she saw the gigantic oak tree, bare of leaf and as black as if it had been burned to charcoal. Its immense sprawling branches tangled upwards and seemed to grapple with the very sky. Icy fear spread through her as the awful reality set in. They hadn't arrived at the beginning of the fable when they could've dealt with Mugloth before he'd gone over to the dark side. The *Book of Fables* had dumped them at the very end.

"Now do you understand?" Finn said, interrupting her thoughts. "He's everywhere. His roots are all over the island, alive and crawling beneath us right now. There's no fighting that. And if you try, you'll just get yourself killed. I couldn't live with that."

The fear and pain in his eyes only heightened her fear.

He was giving up and she knew if he surrendered now, there'd be no getting him back. She had to do something to snap him out of it, and there was only one thing she could think of. As much as it killed her to do it, she had to bring out the fight in him.

Jumping to her feet, she kicked him hard in the chest. He flew backward and landed on his back. Before he could recover from the shock of her attack, she lunged and pinned him down with her full weight, grateful for the residual supernatural speed and strength left in her.

His shock wore off, replaced by instantaneous rage. He flipped her over his head and sprang to his feet. She rolled and rose to a kneeling position, a dagger gripped in each hand.

"What's this? You've already given up on me? This is how it's going to be? Kill, or be killed?" he said, his voice a growl and his face a dark mask.

Adrenaline surged through her. Had she pushed him over the edge? She couldn't tell. Clenching a fistful of sand, she allowed him to draw close before throwing it in his face. The wind blasted sand in his eyes and he staggered back. She took the opening and rammed into him with the point of her shoulder, throwing him to the ground, this time with the tip of one blade pressed at his throat and the other positioned over his heart.

"You won't do it," he seethed.

She pierced his skin. A drop of blood beaded against the blade. "Give me a reason not to."

He glared up at her. "Just *do it.* We'll both be better off," he said, the pain evident in his voice.

Why was he being so defeatist? It made her want to scream. Lucky for him she no longer had the power to break bones with a war cry. She pulled the razor-sharp blade across his neck—a shallow cut, always safer than a deep lance—and stopped at the jugular. A line of bright red blood sprang from the wound.

"You can either die by giving up, or you can die fighting. But if it's me you want to battle, I promise, you'll bite the big one here and now."

"I'm always ready for a good brawl," he said through gritted teeth.

Unsure of his meaning, she twisted the blade, at the same time hating herself for hurting him. "With who?"

He began shaking with laughter, his lips stretched in a grimace. "Not you, fireball. I'd rather face a hundred Mugloths than your wrath any day."

Fate kept the blade in place, searching for any sign of deception on his part. But his eyes were growing a bright green as he stared at her in astonishment. She barely had her blades sheathed when he wrapped his arms around her and rolled her over.

"You never cease to amaze me," he said, his voice husky. "You slashed straight through the gloom and pulled me out. How did you know to do that?"

"I didn't, but I wasn't going to just stand by and let you cave. I figured getting you angry was better than allowing the fear to take over."

His expression turned serious. "You're right. I needed a good slap." He stood up and pulled her to her feet. "It's strange. Seeing you this strong—it's like you've handed me a shield. I can still feel Mugloth trying to get at me but I don't feel nearly as vulnerable as before."

She dabbed his cut with the end of her sleeve. "Nearly is good, but still worrisome in that will-my-werewolf-boyfriend-bite-me sort of way."

He winced as she wiped his cut clean. "Trust me, I can handle it from here."

Sithias stumbled into them, winded and out of breath.

Relieved to see he'd arrived inside the fable safely, Fate

almost hugged him. But annoyance and renewed concern for Gerdie stopped her. "Where did you go? And where's Gerdie?" She glanced past him, happy to see her trotting toward them at a slow and steady pace. "I've got enough to worry about, without wondering where you two are!"

"I'm sssorry misss, but when we firssst arrived, you and Finn were taking ssso long to recover from the trip, we decided to explore the beach a little. And it'sss a good thing we did. Which isss what I need to tell you. We have to hide the *Book of Fablesss—now*. Before thossse fishermen round the point and sssee it."

"Where? I don't see anyone," she said, looking further down the long beach, where it curved out over the water into a thin spur.

"Trusst me, they'll be along shortly. They had jussst docked with a poor whale in tow when they caught sssight of Gerdie and me. They called out to usss but we sssort of ran away," he said, his gaze turning to the cut on Finn's neck. "What happened to you?"

Finn gave him a pained smile. "Fate happened."

Sithias shot her an anxious look.

"It's not what you're thinking," she said, knowing he was afraid she'd become unglued, as he so often put it. She glanced around for a place to conceal the *Book of Fables*. "Geez, there's no trees or bushes big enough to hide this thing." She shook her head. "They've really ruined the place."

Finn nodded sadly. "The island's little more than an open wound."

"You could make it invisssible again," Sithias suggested, seeing that the fishermen had rounded the point.

"No, somebody might come along and bump into it," she said. "I say we bury it here in the sand." Removing her notepad from the pocket of her cloak, she quickly wrote up a description of the book being buried. As soon as she read it aloud, the giant book descended, the ground rising where it burrowed beneath the surface, while an invisible wind smoothed over the sand like it was never there.

Gerdie joined them just as the last of the book disappeared beneath the sand. "Good timin'. I don't think we want any of those men catchin' sight of the book. They're a rough lookin' bunch."

They all turned toward the fishermen.

Carrying bloodied harpoons, the men walked up the beach to meet them. "Ahoy there!" one of them called out, his Celtic accent thick. There were five of them—each more weather-beaten than the next with rough, calloused hands and stiff manes of sea-sprayed hair.

Sithias waved back. "Ahoy!"

Ignoring him, the men eyeballed Fate with an uncomfortable amount of interest. Finn angled himself in front of her but she stepped around him, staring straight back at them until all but one dropped their gaze.

"And what brings ya to our little island, darlin'?" said the man who'd remained undaunted by her cold stare. His dark wavy hair framed the swarthy remains of once handsome features. She could tell he was used to getting what he wanted from women.

She narrowed her eyes on him, thinking fast for an answer. "We're interested in buying some oak. We heard this was the place to get it."

The man grinned, revealing a mouthful of tobacco-stained teeth. She swallowed back her revulsion as his eyes roved from her untamed curls tangling in the wind, down past her chin to places that made her flush with indignation. "Well, ye came to the right place fer that. But really, what brought ya here? I don't see any ships."

Finn slipped his arm around her waist, his grip tight

and possessive. "Our ship's anchored on the other side of the island, mate."

The man reluctantly pulled his gaze from her and looked at Finn. "Are there any more of ya?" he asked, his tone skeptical. "Back on this ship of yers?"

Finn's eyes shifted to darker shades of green and the muscles in his jaw twitched. "The usual captain and crew. And they'll be waiting for us as long as we need them to."

Sithias stepped forward, inserting a smile into the conversation. "Isss there an inn here on the island with sssome roomsss for rent?"

The man's gaze shifted dully to Sithias, flicking to Gerdie with even less interest, and back to Fate with an excited glint. "Just follow the shore. It'll lead to the village—and the inn."

"Thank you," Sithias said, with a wave goodbye.

When they were well away, Gerdie let out a relieved sigh. "Well, they sure seemed like slippery sorts."

Sithias glanced back to ensure the fishermen were returning to their catch of the day. "Yesss. I didn't like the look in their eyesss."

Finn's grip on her waist relaxed somewhat. "We've got to be careful. They're *all* dodgy here, right down to the nippers. Remember, they're only out to save themselves."

Sithias wrinkled his nose. "What isss that sssmell?"

They had arrived in the village, which clung like salt-encrusted barnacles to the craggy rocks jutting along the shoreline. Choppy waves crashed against black boulders, spraying sea-foam over a gray, lichen-covered boardwalk. A large group of women were gutting fish and tossing the refuse over the pier. Their glazed expressions were weathered by the elements, but the dullness in their eyes sharpened with keen interest the moment they spied the island's new visitors.

"Fish," Gerdie muttered with a sour look on her face.

Sithias waved a hand in front his nose. "Yesss indeed."

They walked farther along the rotting boardwalk, the wood creaking and sagging underfoot like it might give way at any moment. It was plain to see that the village reflected the same rough, worn-out exterior as its inhabitants. Before they reached the main collection of buildings, which looked more like crooked shacks leaning together, a group of disheveled children swarmed around them. Small grimy hands fawned at their clothes as they begged for money. Sithias tossed a coin far from the boardwalk to lure them away. They descended on the lone coin, shoving, hitting and biting each other like wild dogs fighting over a scrap of meat.

Fate watched, troubled by the disturbing scene. Then she realized one of them hadn't joined the fray. A small red-haired girl stood off to one side, staring at Fate with a sly smile on her face. Something in the look the child gave her put a knot in her stomach.

They moved on, finding the inn at the other end of the village. Their pace slowed when they saw the sign swinging sorrowfully in the breeze. It was faded, paint-chipped and half dangling from one hook of a rusty, wrought iron post.

"Someone's got a lot of nerve calling thisss the *Royal* Oak Inn," Sithias muttered. He glanced down the length of the weathered building. Most of the structure stretched out over the water, held up by a wobbly-looking pier. "I don't think we should sstay here. If the wind picksss up, we may find ourselvesss waking up in the sssea."

Gerdie screwed up her face. "The ever-present stink of fish bothers me more than anythin' else. It makes the old pigsty smell like a rose garden."

"Yeah, not exactly five stars, is it?" Fate said. "Decrepit probably isn't a sufficient enough word for what awaits us inside. I know it's a far cry from what we were used to in Beldereth, but let's try and make the best of it for the moment, shall we? We don't want to attract any undo attention. Not while we're trying to figure out exactly how we're going to turn this fable around for the better."

"I sssee no happy ending for thessse horrible people," Sithias said in a hushed tone. "They make my ssscales ssstand on end. Ever sssince we got here, I've felt like we're being watched and lissstened to. Even when there'sss no one in sssight."

"I think you mean the hair on your arms, but yeah, I know what you mean," Fate agreed. "There's a definite Children of the Corn vibe going on here." She'd had similar sensations—that prickly feeling on the back of her neck like she was being spied on. And a warning bell going off in her head to watch what she said because every word was being measured and judged. She wondered if it was Mugloth's presence they were sensing. Finn had said his roots were everywhere. If they were only becoming aware of it now, how must he be feeling? She glanced at him, unable to hide her concern. He'd been quiet all the way to the inn.

Finn caught her worried look and leaned close to whisper in her ear. "Don't fret, love. It was a little dicey for me on the way here, but I'm better now that my feet are off the island and on the pier. The roots mustn't have broken through the rocks."

"Good," she said with relief and pushed the door open, its creaking hinges announcing their presence.

Lard oil lamps filled the dim interior with a choking haze. It was times like these when Fate really missed electricity and such things as modern health code enforcement. Her thoughts touched briefly on enjoying some twenty-first-century conveniences and entertainment with Finn after all this was behind them. For once she was finally seeing the light at the end of the tunnel—a bright new path opening up in front of her. Unable to keep from smiling, she led the way past some empty tables to the back of the room. A plump man with a meager sprinkling of wispy gray hair stood drying some glass mugs behind an oak bar, its surface scratched and well-worn by its many patrons, who she guessed would be swigging back a pint or two by sunset.

"What can I do fer ya?" he asked, his loose jowls quivering as he spoke. It seemed like he should be surprised to see visitors, but he wasn't.

Fate started to speak but Sithias cut in.

"Allow me to handle this," he said, setting down his tote bag. Lifting his chin, he looked down his nose at the man as he removed his leather gloves. "We're looking for a couple of roomsss," he told him. "One for the ladiesss and one for usss gentlemen."

The innkeeper leaned forward, scrutinizing their appearance from head to toe, no doubt evaluating their worth. "Have ya got any gold pieces to rub together?"

Sithias slapped two gold coins down on the nicked surface of the bar. "Will these do?"

Fate leaned in and whispered, "Where's all this money coming from?"

Puffing out his chest, he whispered back, "Jussst a little sssomething from my adoring fansss in Asssgar. There were more beansss and pebblesss in the mix after Moria'sss illusion faded, but a few were actually gold."

The innkeeper bit down on each coin and grinned smugly. "These'll do nicely—for a few days anyway. It'll take two more if yer lookin' to stay twice that long." Tossing his tattered washrag over a shoulder, he ambled out from behind the bar and led them down a long narrow hallway. Out of breath by the time they arrived at the end, he opened two facing doors. Each filthy room housed a lumpy bed with a shabby throw, a dilapidated nightstand and a soot-stained oil lamp.

He pushed open the door between the two rooms and trudged in. "The tub's in there, with a stove and wood to heat the bath. And all the water you'll need is beneath yer feet," he said, opening a hatch in the floor to reveal waves crashing against the inn's rotting pylons below.

Appalled, Sithias stared down the hatch. "Sssea water? You expect usss to bathe in sssea water?"

The innkeeper shrugged. "Beats swimmin' in it. There's much less sand and seaweed gettin' stuck in those hard-to-reach places when ya bring it up into the tub," he said with a chuckle. Leaving Sithias with his face pinched up, he shuffled back up the hallway and vanished into the tavern's smoky shadows.

"Well, I *never,*" Sithias gasped.

Smiling at her fastidious friend, Fate shook her head as they moved into one of the rooms. "No worries, Sithias, you know I've got you covered with clean water and Mr. Bubbles."

Gerdie closed the door behind them. "Geez, stop goin' on about baths. We got other worries, like watchin' out for those villagers. They could make their move any time."

Sithias sat down on the bed, coughing and sneezing as a cloud of dust wafted up around him. "I'm forced to agree. It's obviousss by thisss profussse amount of dussst that they don't houssse any guestsss here. No doubt they throw their unsssuspecting victimsss to the Bloodthirsssty Oak before they can even sssettle in."

"One good thing is they only do the sacrifices on Alban Eiler," Gerdie said. "That could be days or weeks from now."

"It's today," Finn said.

Gerdie looked uncertain. "How can you be sure?"

"I can feel it on my skin and deep in my bones. On Alban Eiler the forces of light and dark are equally balanced. And right now the ether is teeming with colliding waves of hot and cold." He glanced at Fate, giving her an encouraging smile. "But the darkness has been waning while the light has been waxing so that when tomorrow arrives, light will overcome the darkness."

"Promise?" Fate said, returning his smile.

A knock on the door interrupted his reply.

She rolled her eyes. "Really? Already?"

"Should we answer?" Gerdie asked.

Finn stepped around Fate, his hand trailing over the small of her back, shooting a distracting tingle up her spine as he brushed past to open the door.

The innkeeper was standing outside in the hall. "Word spread that yer in the market fer some oak. If yer interested, there's a few merchants ready to show ya their goods."

"We'll be out in a minute," Finn said.

"I'll tell 'em," the innkeeper said in a syrupy tone.

Finn shut the door and leaned against it. "They're all out there—ready for an ambush."

"Oh, I knew it," Sithias said, his tone woeful. "And here we are sssticking out over the ocean, like lobstersss trapped in a cage."

"No, they don't know who they're up against," Finn said. He shot Fate a wink. "But we'll educate them with a show of strength they've never seen before, hey love?"

She nodded, gripping the hilt of her sword as pre-battle fever pumped through her veins.

"That'sss easssy for you two to sssay with your sssuper powersss. But what do you expect from usss?" Sithias balked, gesturing at himself and Gerdie with flailing arms. "I sssuppossse I could shout insultsss while teensssy-weensssy bitesss sssome anklesss."

Gerdie glared at him. "I can do serious damage if I really want to!"

"That won't be necessary," Fate said, trying to keep a straight face. "But thanks for the offer all the same. I think Finn and I can handle this."

"Aye," Finn agreed. "All we need you two to do is leave through the hatch and find a safe place to hide until we've sewed this up."

"We can do that," Sithias said, but he didn't seem relieved.

"What?" Fate asked.

"I can't shake the feeling that thossse awful people know what we're planning," he said, looking under the bed as if he expected to see someone hiding there.

"It's Mugloth's presence you're feeling. The whole island's rotten with his roots," Finn said, his expression grim.

Sithias looked at Fate, his amber eyes wide with worry. "Maybe you should ussse the Wordsss of Making to sssolve this one. After the missstake we made with the Green Man surely we know what to avoid now. Don't we?"

Fate gulped, glancing at Finn hopefully.

He shook his head. "I know what you're thinking. But we don't have the luxury of time to think this through. We have to consider every angle and how this could go very wrong if we aren't careful."

Disappointed, she dropped her gaze to the floor. "I suppose."

He nudged her on the chin to get her to look him. "After we've gone out there and shown these people we're not here to be sacrificial lambs, but the answer to their problems, we'll look into setting things right with the Words of Making. Agreed?"

The confidence shining in his eyes lifted her spirits. "Sounds good, let's do it."

Sithias and Gerdie crowded near the door as Finn stepped into the hall. "Sssee you sssoon, misss?" Sithias said, dread and worry apparent on his face as he reached for Gerdie's hand.

"Before you can say honeyed ham," Fate said, her smile faltering when she saw his chin trembling.

"Come on, you big baby," Gerdie said, dragging him over to the bathing room as he nervously muttered "honeyed ham" under his breath.

Fate waved goodbye, troubled by a sudden pang of anxiety as she watched them close the door.

Gripping his flute in one hand, Finn closed his eyes, allowing his awareness to trail out in front of him. He immediately sensed the presence of even more people waiting in the tavern. Their tension and impatience was palpable. He glanced back at Fate. "Ready?"

Drawing her sword, she gave him a nod. "Five by five."

"Huh?"

"Never mind, I just always wanted to say that," she whispered, her expression apologetic as a ravishing blush colored her cheeks.

His attention strayed to the night before when her face had been flushed just like that, but with desire. A lazy ripple ran through him. Even in the midst of danger, all he could think about was how much he wanted her. Concentrate he scolded himself. *Clear the road ahead first and then kiss the lass.* He turned abruptly and led the way down the hall.

A foul, fishy odor punched them in the nose as soon as they turned the corner into the dim tavern. The room was packed with grimy, contemptuous faces staring at them from the shadows.

"Now!" someone yelled.

They both stopped, instinctively watching for a frontal attack. Something heavy dropped down, slamming them both to their knees and knocking Finn's flute from his grip. He pushed upward, trying to gain leverage beneath the thick net of ropes enveloping them. Then the net tightened at their ankles, toppling them over, smacking them flat on their backs. Twisting round, he reached for his flute, mere inches out of reach. Exploding with fury, he thrashed, wrenching at the net and further entangling himself.

The air hammered out of him as he took a hard kick to the chest. Struggling to inhale, he strained to look in Fate's direction, seeing her stab a dagger in someone's calf. Blood spurted from the wound as she twisted the blade before pulling it out. Her aggressiveness was startling.

"Take those knives off 'er!" her victim shouted as he grabbed his leg in pain.

She targeted several Achilles heels before anyone could react. The men bellowed and toppled to the floor. Grabbing another dagger, she shoved it in Finn's grasp hilt-first. He drove it into the top of someone's foot just as a mob descended on him, knees and fists bashing against his back, flattening him face down, squashing the breath from his lungs. He couldn't move. The weight of six men pinned him down.

Someone drove a foot into Fate's stomach. Black rage erupted in Finn as she curled in on herself, gasping for air. He fought with renewed frenzy to get up, but the men holding him pummeled angry fists into his head and kidneys. Pain lashed across his backside, breaking him for the moment.

Lifting the net, they jerked Fate to her feet, yanking her arms behind her back to bind her wrists with rope before she could recover from being kicked in the gut. The lech they'd met earlier on the beach grabbed her by the hair and wrenched her head back. "Ooh, yer a hellcat, and a strong one too." He kept her head locked in place, his breath rattling. He was plainly excited by her inability to get away.

Incensed by the sight, Finn fumed, his body shaking with each painful breath. The internal darkness latched onto his fury, swelling inside, filling his mind with black thoughts. He wanted to *kill.* He could do it by just opening his mouth. He could use the Elder race language to bring down nature's full might on every one of them here and now, just as he had when he'd destroyed Murauda. As the murderous urge burned hot, something much stronger burst forth, dampening the fire. Love and the need to protect blasted through him, clearing his head long enough to realize that he'd be endangering Fate if he unleashed the elements while she was standing in the middle of the storm.

"Best see what else yer hidin' under there," the lech said.

Fate writhed against her bonds, her eyes blazing with hatred. Another man gripped her throat, digging his fingers in until she stopped resisting. Her eyes glistened with angry tears as the slimy fisherman slipped his hand slowly down over her waist to her thighs.

Finn thrashed violently, enraged that the scumbag was touching her. Fists cracked against his ribs, spine and skull. Jagged sparks filled his vision as pain spiked through his temple. He fell limp, his body riddled with the ache of so many beatings.

"Finn, stop fighting!" Fate cried out as his captors tightened the net over him. She looked at him with a silent plea in her eyes to surrender.

The fisherman threw Finn a smug smile before turning his attention back to Fate.

Swallowing back his fury, Finn held still, looking forward to the moment he could wrap his hands around the creep's throat.

"What have we here?" the fisherman said. He unbuckled the straps around her thighs, removing the daggers and arrows. The sword came off next. He looked her over, taking his time to enjoy the view. "Need to be thorough," he said, running his hand along the curve of her waist, then sliding upward to linger at her breast before he grabbed her crossbow.

A growl rose up in Finn, a wild snarl that came from the bowels of his being. "Get your bloody hands off her before I rip them off!" he roared, surging up from the floor, knocking the men holding onto the net off their feet. The fisherman staggered backward, his eyes wide with fear as Finn lunged at him. His hands were inches from the man's throat when the slack net tightened, jolting him back to crash to the floor once again.

They all descended on him at once, kicking and punching from every angle. Spasms of pain shuddered through every inch of his body. The sound of Fate's cries weakened him further as the men pummeled him. Twisting in her direction, he saw her lurch toward him. The fisherman yanked her hair and slapped her across the face, marking her cheek with a scarlet handprint.

"I'm going to kill you!" Finn shouted, his rage so heightened he no longer felt the fists pounding into muscle and bone. Strengthened by his need to protect her, he rose on his knees, his body shaking with the effort of straining against the tremendous weight of the net and the men tugging on it. Bringing one leg up, he launched himself into the ceiling, smashing into the wooden beams with those holding onto him. They fell away like crushed flies. Landing with a thud, he fixed his gaze on the fisherman and pulled back his fist, ready to bury it in the man's face. Instead, he was the one struck, a solid blow to the back of the head that rattled his skull and dropped him into nothing.

Fate screamed the moment she saw the chair cracking down over Finn's head. His dead fall to the floor shot her through with the worst kind of fear. Tears scorched her eyes as her heart pounded hard against her ribcage, threatening to punch a hole through her chest. Frantic with worry, she yelled his name over and over, wanting him to wake up and show her he was alive.

"Shut up!" the fisherman shouted, gripping her head and pulling her face close.

The sickening smell of bile on his breath and the pain in her scalp ignited a searing fury that momentarily burned through her grief. She looked at him through veiled lashes. "I'm sorry," she whispered, the words choking in her throat.

"Hmm. Now there's a good wench," he said, taking a step

closer, which is exactly what she wanted.

She drove her knee into his groin with the force of all her rage.

Pitching forward, he fell to his knees with his hands cupped between his legs. "You barmy shrew," he groaned.

"Enough!" a voice yelled just as the other men lunged at her.

All heads turned to a red-haired boy perched on top of the oak bar. The *Book of Fables* leaned against the wall behind him.

Fate stared at the giant book. This wasn't supposed to happen. She was a warrior of Beldereth and Finn was the destroyer of destroyers. They'd been fools for misjudging these seemingly dull-witted people. This was a fishing village. They were skilled at netting and killing large prey like the whale Sithias had seen, and even sharks. There'd been a proud display of trophy jaws hanging on the buildings. She'd forgotten the first rule of defense—*never* underestimate your enemy. Expect them to be as fully armed as you. And never assume you're better. Arrogance fells even the greatest of warriors.

"Bring her here," the boy demanded.

Someone shoved her from behind. Still in a daze, she stumbled and fell a few feet away from Finn. His face was turned the other way but she could see he was still breathing. Her relief was so great she laughed—a tearful hysterical laugh.

The fisherman, having recovered somewhat, gripped her by the arm and hauled her up. *"Move,"* he growled in her ear.

Tensing against his grip as he steered her over to the bar, she frowned at the boy. Who was he and why was everyone following his orders like he was king of the hill? There'd been no mention of a prepubescent tyrant in the fable.

He stood up on top of the bar, looking down his freckled nose at her. "I hear you've got a tiny spell book, and that you used it to hide this here giant book in the sand without liftin' a finger."

"I don't know what you're talking about," she said, inwardly alarmed and baffled.

The little red-haired girl she'd seen on the boardwalk stepped forward. "It's not nice to lie," she said, wagging her finger with that same disturbing smile on her face. Lifting her other arm, she swung Fate's notebook by the chain in circles.

Startled, Fate glared at her. The brat had picked her pocket earlier! A queasy uneasiness rose in her. How had they known about her notebook? They would've had to have been very close by when she'd hidden the *Book of Fables*, and she was pretty sure there was no hiding the orange pop of color on both their heads against that barren landscape.

"That's right, little sis. Lyin's *bad*," the boy said as he gestured for one of the men to lift the girl up onto the bar. Brother and sister stared down at her with high and mighty expressions. "Yer bad for lyin'. And you need to be punished."

Indignation erupted in Fate. "For *what?*" she yelled. "For wanting to do honest business and *paying* for our rooms?" She shot the old innkeeper a scathing look.

His fleshy chin jiggled with a quiet chuckle. His callous disregard increased the nauseating knot forming in the pit of her stomach.

"We know why yer really here," the boy said. He took the notebook from his sister and shook it at Fate. "And ya won't be conjurin' any defeat against us."

Fate gulped as cold sweat iced her back.

"Give it back, Rory!" his sister whined, pouting until he returned the notepad.

Rory kneeled, his eyes moving back and forth over Fate's face with an eerie boldness. "Ya think yer smarter than us, don't ya? Oh, the lovely Fate, with her fancy weapons and Words of Makin'. But ya weren't smart enough to figure out that we've been watchin' ya all this time and preparin' for this long awaited day."

The moment he said her name, her head buzzed with such

noisome static it nearly drowned out everything else he said. At the same time some vague realization hovered on the edge of her shock and disbelief.

"Are ya comin' round to it yet?" he asked. "No? Allow me then. *Finn's* been our eyes and ears, lettin' us know yer plans." He smirked. "Not to mention all the hot and cold particulars between you two lovebirds." He tilted his head, waiting for her to connect the dots.

As his meaning crystallized, her growing nausea mounted into a stabbing headache. "All of you?" she croaked, her throat tight with the humiliation of discovering these people knew every intimate facet of her relationship with Finn.

"Well, not *all* of us. The Holy Tree Spirit only shares the visions with me," he said, rolling his Celtic r's reverently.

His clarification did nothing to ease her outrage. Having this punk wise to her personal business and all their weaknesses made her blood boil. "Okay, so you *think* you stopped us. What now?"

Yawning like he was suddenly bored, Rory motioned to the fisherman. "Take 'er to the Tree. I'll be along shortly. And Gar, no defilin' the sacrifice like last time. This one's real special."

Gar's weathered features twisted with resentment as he seized Fate by the arm, careful to keep his delicates angled away from her knee. "So long as she *behaves,*" he said, shoving his face at Fate, once again polluting her air with his foul breath.

In a fit of rage, she spit at him—kind of surprised at herself since she'd always been grossed out by the act. But then again, she'd suddenly come to understand the true meaning of spitting mad.

He recoiled, swiping his arm over his eye.

Secure in knowing he wasn't allowed to harm her, she started to smile but his fist came down hard and swift. Pain filled her skull and everything shattered into an explosion of stars.

♠

The left side of Fate's head ached. Memory nagged her for a second as she tried to pin down what was happening. Then she remembered Gar's punch. *Dirtbag.* She tried to touch her sore temple but her wrist was tied, no, both wrists *and* her ankles. They'd roped her to a T-shaped stake in the ground. Her pulse spiked. She hadn't thought any time had passed. But she'd obviously been out long enough for them to carry her outside and tie her up.

Raising her head slightly, she peeked at her surroundings through her hair, first seeing a tall narrow stone carved with glyphs a few yards ahead of her. There was another stone in front of it, smoother than the first with a two-inch round hole bored through the top half. There were three other pairs of standing stones, all set in a half-circle formation around the base of the oak's massive trunk. As she focused on the tree, fear swelled in her throat and her breathing escalated into dry gasps.

Its twisting paths of black bark were seeping blood like ill-healed scabs.

"Ah, look who's awake."

Fate tensed against her bonds as Rory sauntered into view. He wasn't alone. The other villagers circled round, all holding pails and beaming with excitement like they were getting ready to watch a baseball game on a sunny afternoon. Thankfully, Gar wasn't among them.

Standing on tiptoe so he could look her in the eye, Rory hovered inches from her face.

The strong smell of fish on his breath gagged her. Was there anyone on this island who owned a breath mint? Anger burned in her gut. She'd never hated anyone as much as she did these people, especially this adolescent worm for invading her privacy. If she could still shatter bones with a shriek, they'd be nothing more than mushy skin bags. Since she couldn't do that, she settled for spitting in his face too.

"Now, now. Ya don't want another knock upside the head, do ya?" he said, wiping the spittle off his pink, freckled cheek.

She didn't feel nearly as satisfied as she had before. At least she'd gotten Gar's goat. Rory's calm infuriated her.

The boy squinted at the setting sun blazing bright orange across the distant horizon, lighting the ocean with blinding sparks. He walked over to one of the standing stones and peered through the hole, which cast its dark shadow on the stone behind it. "Listen up now. When the sun moves just a little lower, its light'll shine through the hole onto this part right here." He ran his finger over a carved symbol of a circle where one half was made deeper than the other. "When that happens, the earth below yer feet'll start rumblin,' and somethin' both terrible and glorious will come burstin' out of the ground fer ya."

Icy fear crept up Fate's spine, effectively dousing her anger.

Rory saw it. "Now don't fret," he said, confusing her with a sudden tone of compassion in his voice. "You won't suffer. Not as Finn's creator. It's already been decided you'll die quickly."

"What do you mean?" she yelled, her confusion worsening. "What do you want with Finn?"

Rory's blue eyes rounded. "Are you really that daft?"

She waited for him to elaborate but he'd become distracted. He was staring at the standing stones. The sun's sinking light had descended enough to direct its rays through the hole in the stone. Her mouth went dry. The circular beam now touched the very top of the symbol on the stone behind it.

Rory turned to his sister, motioning for her to come forward. With her pail in hand, she walked up to Fate wearing the same unsettling smirk on her face. The notepad hung round her neck by a string. The other children lined up behind her with their pails. Fate's stomach tightened with dread. They looked at her like she was subhuman—something to be poked at. She knew children could be cruel but these creepy kids scared her.

Rory's sister thrust her pail at Fate, filling her vision with a blur of red. She clenched her eyes shut as lukewarm liquid smacked her in the face. Blinking, she looked down to see blood dripping onto her clothes. Unable to keep the blood from seeping through the barrier of her pressed lips, she retched from the bitter taste of iron.

The other children joined in, giggling while they drenched her with the blood in their pails. Shocked and unable to escape the onslaught, Fate endured it with eyes closed and head down. When it was finally over, she lifted her gaze, glaring at them through the sting of blood in her eyes. The adults laughed hard, slapping their knees as if she had pie on her face when she must look as horrifying as bloodied Carrie at the prom.

"You're all *insane!*" she yelled, her whole body shaking with fear and rage.

Rory was next to her, wiping the blood from her eyes—a kind gesture that shrank her anger and made her want to cry. "The blood blackening is a tradition of ours," he explained.

"Rory," she said, trying to keep the desperation out of her voice. "You must know you're making a terrible mistake. I can save you and all the others from having to live like this. You know what I can do. If you just let me go, I *promise,* I can write all your problems away."

He held still and looked at her. "You would do that?"

Hope sparked in her heart. "Yes, of *course.*"

Glancing over his shoulder at the others, who'd moved about fifty feet away, he turned back with a furtive smile. "Why didn't ya just say that before?"

"I-I guess I didn't really think of it 'til now."

"Hmm," he mused as his gaze turned toward the rickety village at the bottom of the barren hillside. "Would you conjure up a fancy new town and make our crops grow?"

"Absolutely."

"And free us from the tyranny we're under?"

"That kind of goes without saying. But yes, you'd no longer be forced to feed innocent people to this evil."

The smile left his eyes. "What makes you think we're bein' forced?"

Her hopes sank into a sea of cold fear. "You're not going to let me go, are you?"

"Sorry," he chuckled, "I couldn't help messin' with ya."

"You *weasel!* I hope you die!" she screamed at his back as he walked over to the other villagers.

Tears blurred her vision. Why had she believed he would let her go? A sob welled in her chest. Where was Finn? He should've woken by now. Why wasn't he swooping in like Superman and saving her already? The fact that he wasn't, meant chances were good he'd gone dark. What a horrible mess. Everything had gone terribly wrong. She didn't even want to think about what might be happening to Sithias and Gerdie.

She glanced nervously at the standing stones. The shadow of the stone with the hole in it now overlaid the stone behind. The last of the sun's rays beamed straight through, casting a perfect circle of light.

Time had run out, and with it came a chilling roar from deep below.

CHAPTER 33

FATE TWISTED HER WRISTS, straining hard against her bindings as the ground quaked beneath her. Biting back the deep burn in her skin, she pulled with all her strength. As her blood seeped under the coarse twine, she wrenched her arms in a panicked frenzy, hoping to make the ropes slippery enough to slide free.

The ground exploded in front of her. Clumps of dirt and rocks blasted into the air. Unable to raise her arms to shield herself from the falling debris, she bent her head, cringing. As the dust settled, thick crusts of earth cracked wider as something huge thrust upwards.

Fate stared in horrified silence.

An enormous monster formed entirely of gnarled roots snaked up out of the earth. Its misshapen head had no eyes or features of any kind except for a gaping mouth of deadly, bloodstained fangs. Arms of twisted roots extended from a dense, tangled torso, which spiraled downward and held fast to the base of the giant oak.

Terror washed over her like a wave, her heart slamming in her ribcage so violently she thought she'd die. Adrenaline flooded her system, doubling her supernatural strength as she fought against the ropes. Her wrists slipped free at last and she started to run. Forgetting her ankles were bound, she tipped over, grabbing at the ropes as she looked up.

The root monster loomed, swaying in place, its head twisting to one side as if to look at her. She struggled with renewed frenzy, her pulse pounding in her ears. A tentacle lashed out and coiled round her waist. She screamed—a violent rending that burned her throat. Its grip tightened, squeezing the breath from her lungs and stifling her cry. A forceful yank broke the ropes, bending her shins the wrong way. She heard the horrible popping sound of her bones breaking, felt the sickening snaps. As crippling pain exploded in her legs, the world tipped upside down and the earth swallowed her whole.

❦

Finn woke with a start, gasping for air as fear stabbed into his heart. "Fate!" he cried, sitting up and clenching his chest.

"Oh thank goodnesss," Sithias said. "You're finally *awake*. Where's Fate? Why isn't she with you?"

Gerdie hunched down next to Finn. "Is she okay? Did she get away?"

"No, they got her too. I don't know where she is exactly, but I know she's in trouble," he said, choking out the words as he stared straight ahead at the craggy, moss-covered walls surrounding them. Desperate to locate her, he frantically pushed his senses out over the island, but the grating ache near his brain stem locked him inside his body. An unbearable feeling of emptiness descended. He needed to find her right now. Jumping to his feet, he staggered from a dizzying bout of nausea. Every part of him hurt, especially his back. If he didn't know better, he'd swear an elephant had danced on it.

"Take care, sssir," Sithias said. "You took a nassssty blow to the back of the head. Gerdie found a huge lump."

Finn waved him off. "It's nothing. I'll survive." He looked around. "Where are we?"

"This is their dungeon, I guess," Gerdie grumbled.

"Can you believe they caught usss in a net when we climbed down the hatch under the inn?" Sithias said. "Had I not been carrying Gerdie on my back, I could've put up a fight."

"Yeah, and we've been stuck in this stink-hole ever since." Gerdie said, wrinkling her nose.

"I wasss working up the courage to make myssself sssmall and essscape," Sithias went on to say. "To come and help you of courssse. But then they threw you in with usss."

"I'll get us out of here," Finn said, glancing up at the layers of nets webbed across the pit opening. The walls were at least thirty feet high and too slick to climb. Not that he needed to worry about that. He flew up to the covering and pressed his face up into the nets, looking through the weave for any guards. The creep who'd touched Fate was the only one in sight.

As soon as Finn laid eyes on him, blinding rage took over. Heaving on the nets until one end ripped from the stakes holding the covering in place, he shot through the narrow gap and crashed into the fisherman, landing him on his back. "Where is she?" Finn yelled.

"Yer too late. The Tree's got 'er," he said, coughing and gasping for air.

"No."

A sneer formed on the man's leathery features. "Don't fret, I gave the she-devil what she deserved and sent 'er off right."

Savage fury exploded at the front of Finn's brain, burning away all reason. Hauling back his arm, he drove his knuckles into the man's nose, wanting to mash his face into the back of his head. But he yanked back on the punch at the last second. Stumbling backward, he stared at the dazed fisherman's bloodied face and broken nose. The sleazeball didn't deserve any mercy. None of these people did, but with Fate's life hanging in the balance, he couldn't afford to go into a mindless rage and risk Mugloth taking over. The bastard had lucked out for the moment, but if anything happened to her, all bets were off. He'd be back to bury his fist in his skull.

♠

The dank smell of soil closed in around Fate. She clawed at the dirt, grabbing frantically at whatever she could to keep from being pulled farther down. Her fingers hooked something solid. For a second she thought she had a firm handhold, but it came loose. In the dimming light, she discovered she was gripping a human skull.

She instinctively let go and the grinning skull tumbled down, chasing after her with its promise of death as she was hauled through the crumbling earth. Dirt and rocks collapsed in. All light vanished as suffocating soil packed in around her.

Close to passing out from the sharp stabbing pain of her broken shins, she gasped for air, certain the smothering earth would kill her before she lost consciousness. But she was suddenly pushed upward into an open space. As she let out a tortured groan and spit dirt from her mouth, the roots slowly uncoiled from her waist, leaving her alone in pitch-black darkness.

Finally able to suck in air, she retched from the stench of blood and decay. In her panic, she groped blindly, recoiling when she touched cold slime. The space was small with only a tiny bit of elbowroom. Lifting her arms, she felt a curved ceiling right above her head and her hands squished into a thick layer of ooze. Putrid ichor dropped on her, trickling down over her face. Convulsing with nausea and a frightened sob, she feverishly wiped it off, remembering the blood she'd seen seeping from the bark of the oak.

On the verge of completely losing it, she willed herself to remember her training and drew in deep, shaky breaths, in spite of the rank air. Slowly, her eyes adjusted to the dark and the faint glow of her rapidly beating heart shed just enough light for her to see the blood-blackened secretions dripping from the walls.

A view she could've done without, but at least now she knew the loose dirt beneath the little indentation she sat on was the only way in or out.

Clenching her teeth against the excruciating ache of her broken bones grinding together, she slowly pulled her legs up out of the dirt and positioned them on either side of the soil. She ran her hands over her swollen shins, grateful no bones had punctured the skin. Eustace would freak out if he knew she was injured and in such dire straits. She'd never broken so much as a pinky before. "Dad," she whimpered as tears flooded her eyes. Thinking of him only spiraled her further into despair.

"No," she said, swallowing back the huge lump in her throat. "You can feel sorry for yourself later. Time to dig your way out of this mess."

Driving both arms into the dirt, she started scooping mounds up behind her. She didn't care how long it took. She'd dig herself out. But after several minutes of laborious digging, she found it harder and harder to get a lungful of air. Then the awful realization hit her. She was suffocating in her own exhalations. Weakened and light-headed, she slumped against the pile of dirt she'd made behind her.

Something cold and wet squirmed under her left palm.

Recognizing the sensation, she screamed and flattened herself against the opposite side of the hollow, the light of her heart flaring brighter as she looked down into the upturned soil. Undiluted panic flooded her nervous system when she saw the slithering multitudes of thinly wrapped tubes of viscous goo.

Worms. They were everywhere, and there was no way out.

Having retrieved his flute from the inn, Finn shot through the air, slowing only when he reached the gigantic oak. He hovered high overhead, scanning the ground for Fate, afraid of what he would find but needing to know if his greatest fear had become a reality. She was nowhere to be seen, only a dreadful hole at the base of the massive trunk, which the villagers approached with slow caution.

A sickening wave of fear welled up inside him as he descended.

The startled villagers scattered when he landed out of nowhere. All but a red-haired boy and girl. She sidled next to the older boy and took his hand as Finn zeroed in on Fate's notepad strung around her neck.

"That's Fate's!" he growled. "Where is she?"

"She's fine. All's well, Finn," the boy said. "Or should I say, *Emrys?*"

The aching knot at the back of his skull throbbed upon hearing his Druidic name. "Who told you that name?"

The boy stepped forward, blocking the half submerged sun blazing on the horizon, plunging his face in shadow and lighting his carroty hair into a flaming halo. "I think ya know. I think you've always known."

In that moment Finn did know, the realization crashed in on him. Every twig, acorn and leaf that had ever come from the Bloodthirsty Oak was a direct conduit for Mugloth to slide through. Which meant when Sabirah broke his Ogham wards with the oak's tainted branch, the land was poisoned, or to be more exact, infected by Mugloth. And because his Druidic name had been carved into Glenna's hut, he'd been laid open to an invasion. His blood suddenly ran cold. He'd assumed none of these people were in communication with Mugloth. He'd thought they were prisoners of the oak. But this lad knew his spirit name. How stupid he'd been!

His throat constricted with grief. Not only had he made a fatal error in coming here, his very presence put Fate, Sithias and Gerdie in direct danger. It's no wonder they'd been outsmarted. This whole time Mugloth had been seeing and hearing *everything* through him. He'd only been allowed to believe he'd mastered some control over his dark influence. When in actuality Mugloth had been toying with him, most likely manipulating every thought and action to make it seem like they originated with him. A sickening mixture of rage and sorrow thrashed in his chest.

He had to destroy the oak.

The moment he set his intention, a roaring blackness surged into his pounding head, fast blotting out his thoughts and memories. Mugloth had opened the floodgates and Finn was drowning in the gloom.

A malignant chuckle penetrated the silence. It seemed to come from nowhere in particular. The rumbling laugh simply filled the cramped space.

Fate shrank back in alarm. Her heart light pulsed a rosy gleam within the dank hollow, illuminating a gnarled root pushing up through the worm-ridden soil. She wanted to pull her knees up to her chest but she already knew her broken limbs couldn't bear the weight. Forced to leave her legs extended straight, she stared at the root swaying upright like a cobra between them.

"Time to sample the offering," said a deep, raspy voice.

Whipping through the air snake-quick, the point of the root struck her. Gasping, she grabbed her lacerated arm, feeling the slickness of fresh blood.

"*Mmmm,* tastes rich—full of fear and so much anger."

Terror stretched her nerves thin as another cruel swipe lashed out, this time cutting her cheek. The violent blow rattled her.

"Delicious. Sadness always sweetens the broth," the voice hissed. "And you have so much to be miserable about. Your true love stands above you, surrendering to his glorious destiny while you slowly die below, soon to have the worms working on your carcass."

Another shudder rocked her body. She had to shove the appalling image from her mind, force herself to focus solely on Finn and trust in his strength to resist. Yet uncertainty tormented her. She didn't want to believe he might've succumbed already, but what if it spoke the truth? He should've come for her by now.

"You named him well…Emrys, the immortal. He will certainly live on forever through us, adding to our strength with his knowledge of the Elder race language," the voice rasped with pleasure.

The name startled her. "How do you know that name?" she whispered.

Another malignant laugh coiled around her. "We know because we're in his blood, shaping his thoughts, calling him home," whispered the cruel presence.

A deeper understanding of what she'd learned from Rory seeped in. The poison had never been some sort of worsening condition in need of a cure. This was a possession. This evil thing had been hiding inside Finn all along. She felt violated, not just for herself but for Finn.

A persistent question pushed aside her revulsion. What or who exactly was speaking? The fable had said Mugloth's union with Grandfather Oak had transformed the tree into a hellish monstrosity. The voice kept saying "we", not I. Was Grandfather Oak part of this "we"? If so, she might have a fighting chance.

"We don't ever speak to the offerings," the voice continued, "but *you* are the exception. As the Shining One's creator, your blood flows with *his* essence. After we drink your blood, your essence will make our call to him irresistible. He will *need* to be one with you, as he has since the moment of his inception."

So Finn was resisting. But if she died, she knew he'd give up. She couldn't let that happen. "I want to speak to Grandfather

Oak," she blurted out.

Her pulse quickened as several more roots slithered up through the dirt. "Grandfather Oak is here. His spirit is part of our greater whole."

"No, I don't believe Grandfather Oak is anywhere near here. If he was, he'd never have allowed centuries of senseless killings to take place," she said, hoping to goad it into letting Grandfather Oak come forward as proof.

"There is nothing senseless about justice being carried out."

Not the response she was looking for. She'd have to push harder. "Thousands, if not millions of innocent people have died because of you!"

"The only innocents in this world are nature's tender creatures. Reckless, greedy humans abandoned the sacred laws. They've destroyed everything in their path, scarring entire continents in their gluttonous quest for more. You don't hear how Earth weeps for her children. But her healing will begin now that Emrys has joined us. With our combined power, we will wage a holy war upon the barbarian horde, and out of it shall come a garden as unspoiled as the original."

A chill streaked up her spine. She was frightened of this grand plan. Frightened for Finn, for her friends, for this world. "I'll admit we humans are flawed, but we're waking up. Where I come from lots of people respect nature, and they fight to protect Earth," she said hurriedly, deciding it might be better to steer the conversation in a more positive direction. Maybe a glimmer of hope would draw Grandfather Oak out. "What of those who honor nature's sacred laws? Would you also put an end to them? I know Grandfather Oak wouldn't. He was too loving and forgiving for that."

Silence. Scary silence.

Her pulse thudded loudly in her ears as her beating heart threw a brighter light on more roots snaking up into view.

"Nature does not suffer even them to live," the voice seethed.

Terror pulsated along her nerve endings. The increasing impatience in the voice only confirmed Grandfather Oak no longer existed. If he did, he would've spoken to her by now. Her last chance was to make Mugloth see the error of his ways. "Not nature. *You.* Or should I say Mugloth? You've been lying to yourself, haven't you? Grandfather Oak isn't with you. He's long dead. I'm sure you didn't mean to, but it's time you faced the fact that you killed his spirit with your hatred and rage. Nothing good has come from—"

"No! You are the liar!" the voice thundered, shaking the tree's very foundation.

The roots thrashed and stabbed into her. Paralyzing pain shot through muscle and nerves as they burrowed beneath her skin. Nothing could save her now. Mugloth had begun to feed.

Mugloth's dark tide crashed over Finn, sucking his awareness deep underground, down into the oak's sprawling roots. He tried to remember what came before this black wave and why it was important to resist and push against the current. But the undertow was strong, pulling him toward the heart of something greater than his own existence. An immense power radiated from there, calling to him to unite with it—to become more.

"Emrys."

The inescapable tug of his spirit name pulled Finn to the beating heart of the oak, where a denser, darker concentration of power resided. There was a seductive purity to the energy—an undiluted expression of purposeful rage unaffected by guilt or shame. He couldn't help but open to it. The emanation offered too much freedom. As he yielded, his awareness expanded, bleeding beyond the borders of the oak and blending with the heartbeat of the earth, the ceaseless thrum of the ocean, the perpetual inhale and exhale of the wind's breath.

And the soft noise of a shallow, dying gasp—a sound that troubled him.

Flashes of his past came and went in the form of blurred pictures as Finn pushed his senses throughout the tree until his dark sight found the source of the sound. The second he saw her face—Fate's face—his memory returned in an instant and his consciousness slammed back into his body. A cry tore from his throat, a savage howl of agony that shuddered through him. Desperation coursed through his veins, firing him into action. He could save her if he hurried.

Something clamped down on him, squeezing his bruised and battered body. That's when he realized he was being lifted off the ground by a tangled mess of writhing roots corded around his torso. Smaller tendrils skewered his skin, slowly drinking his blood. The tricky demon had lured his spirit out of his body, intending to drain him dry while nobody was home. And its two copper-topped minions stood by, looking annoyingly superior.

As light-headed as he was from blood loss, Finn knew what to do without having to think. He uttered the sacred names of the elements in the Elder race language. The roots tightened, trying to cut off his air but all he needed was a whispered gasp to engage the runes embedded in his skin and ignite the internal fire needed to fuel his voice. In the span of a second, the heat erupted in his gut, shooting into his chest and out his throat. His head flung back in the ecstasy of power flowing through him as he roared his command over the elements.

The wind answered his call first, thrashing at the enormous oak with furious gales. A mass of roiling clouds formed into being, smothering the clear dusky sky and plunging the island into absolute night. Thunder cracked as a bolt of lightning dead-eyed the oak on the scar Mugloth had made hundreds of years before. The roots binding Finn flailed spasmodically and let go.

He dropped to the ground, glaring up at the red-haired boy and his sister.

Frightened, they slowly backed away.

"Aye, you should be scared," he snarled, taking pleasure in their fear.

They broke into a run, following the other villagers who were also making a hasty retreat. The evil siblings were lucky he couldn't bring himself to harm children.

A terrible cracking resounded behind him as the colossal tree split down the middle. Darting out from under the two halves crashing to the ground, Finn shot skyward into a sudden downpour of rain.

"You didn't happen to sssee Fate down there while you were busssy bringing about the end of the world, did you?"

Startled, Finn whirled round to see a bird-sized dragonfly, white with amber bug eyes staring at him. "Oh, Sithias." He swallowed hard, not wanting to deliver the dreadful news. "She's underground." He couldn't bring himself to speak aloud that she was close to death.

Sithias worried his thin insect appendages together. "Oh no! We mussst sssave her!" He zigged to one side of Finn, staring down at the exposed blackened cavity of the oak's trunk. Dark rivers of blood washed forth while crimson rivulets gushed along newly opened cracks in the hillside. "Sssir, I think I sssee her!"

Filled with a battling mixture of hope and fear, Finn descended, scanning for her amongst the multitude of bones entrenched in the thick, age-old layers of blood coating the great oak's hollowed trunk. Time stopped for a heartbeat when he saw her lying within the trenches of the ghastly graveyard, so thickly covered in the black sludge and mud he almost didn't see her. His chest tightened, forcing a strangled cry from him as he looked upon the crooked angles of her legs, the countless puncture wounds and her deathly pale face. Seeing her mutilated body and knowing the suffering she'd endured, riddled him with unbearable pain. He hadn't saved her. He died inside knowing she must've thought he'd abandoned her.

A massive tangle of roots suddenly exploded up from the riven tree, bulking together into a monstrous form, its sprawling arms lashing at Finn. Maneuvering out of the way before it could grab hold, he climbed higher into the sky, shocked by this unexpected aberration of nature and furious that it blocked his way to Fate.

Digging in his pocket, he drew out his flute and blew a combination of rune notes to transform it into a wind sword with a blade as long as he was tall. He then launched himself at the root monster, slicing off one of its writhing arms.

Mugloth's insidious voice filled his head. *"She is with us now. Can you not feel her? Join us and you'll be with her forever."*

Even as the rain pelted Finn's face, the invitation disconnected him from all bodily discomfort and immediate concerns, lulling him into a drowsy stupor that enticed him to allow the honeyed darkness to flood over him. If he surrendered, the aching guilt and agony would be washed away and he'd have some little part of Fate with him.

Pain fired through Finn's tenderized legs and torso as Mugloth grabbed hold, the roots coiling fast around him, jolting him out of the hypnotic state. He slashed his wind sword down on its arm, hacking like a madman.

Sithias zipped into view, his dragonfly wings working extra hard against the rain and wind. "Sssir! I retrieved Fate'sss body while you were creating a diversssion. That iss what you were doing, right? Becaussse for a moment there you ssseemed to be the one who wasss dissstracted."

"Is she…?" Finn couldn't say it.

"Oh, that's what I came to tell you!"

Mugloth swatted at Sithias with his other arm—newly grown in short order.

Sithias yelped, zagging out of the way with only inches to spare.

Finn sliced again at Mugloth if only to pull his attention away from Sithias, but he felt polarized, afraid to hope he'd come to deliver good news and terrified he was going to confirm his worst fear.

The buzz of Sithias's wings sounded near Finn's ear. "She'sss alive!"

"Really?" Finn said, jerking his head in his direction.

"Barely, but yesss."

All at once the soreness in Finn's body fled. Strength and lightness returned. "Go take care of her, Sithias. I'm going to finish this."

"Happy to, sssir."

Mugloth roared and lunged at Sithias once again. Squealing, he zoomed out of reach. His grip loosened enough for Finn to lean forward and slash through his clenched fist. The slack roots fell off him as he landed in the slippery, blood-soaked mud. Scrambling to his feet, he looked up at the same moment Mugloth turned his attention back on him.

With his fanged mouth gaping wide enough to swallow him whole, Mugloth dove at Finn. Dodging to one side, he turned and swept his wind sword down, hewing off Mugloth's knotted head in two strokes. Even as the body lurched backwards, more roots grew from the cut ends, reforming the misshapen head with astonishing speed.

That's when Finn knew he was fighting an endless battle. Letting his wind sword die out, he slipped his flute back into his pocket and spoke in the clipped language of the Elder race. He thanked the storm elements for answering his call and released them from his control. Then he invoked his power over

Air. Rune energy crackled and surged up through him, the spell-rich words streaming from his mouth in rippling heat waves.

As Mugloth shrank from the power in the words, he wormed his way back into Finn's mind. *"Emrys, you cannot destroy us. We're in your blood. We'll always be with you."*

The energy inside Finn sputtered. He glared up at the twisted, tangled behemoth swaying in place, its aggression curbed for the moment.

"Unite with us and you'll become as immortal as the Earth, the Sea, the Sun and the Air. Be their champion, as you have for those undeserving, weak mortals."

"If it's a champion you want, you've got it. But it'll be for the humans you've wreaked so much misery upon! You were a Druid! You were supposed to heal and protect, not kill!" he yelled, sensing a sudden shift between them. For the first time in centuries Mugloth was the one feeling fear, and in turn losing more and more control over Finn.

Mugloth raged and lurched at him, a long snarled arm slamming down where he stood.

Evading the blow, Finn shot up toward the night sky. The rain had vanished and the high winds were fast thinning the clouds, revealing glimpses of stars and a bright moon. A calm came over him as he looked down on the island, his gaze resting on the dim figures of Sithias and Gerdie huddled around Fate a safe distance away. His instinct to go to her pressed hard on him, but he had to finish this first.

Sucking in a deep breath, he invoked Air. The rune power burst into action. Heat and red-gold micro-sparks poured from his mouth, altering his voice into the same deafening roar of the giants of old. Distant winds shrieked in answer, disturbing the ocean's surface as they rushed inland. They blasted into Mugloth and circled him, creating a solid wall of churning air. Mugloth's bellow echoed out over the island as he beat against the air-bound prison building around him like an enormous tube.

Then Finn invoked Water, his gaze fixed on the moonlit ocean. In defiance of gravity, a titanic wave surged upward, a terrible roiling black serpent made only of the sea. The sound of so much rushing water was thunderous. As the massive body of water arced over the island, for a tiny fragment of time, the snaking river seemed suspended in the sky. Then it plummeted to earth, smashing into Mugloth like God's fist. It seemed as if the entire ocean poured into the tube of pressurized air to drown Mugloth and his network of malignant roots.

As the deluge hammered the monster deep underground, his hold on Finn's heart and mind worked loose. Mugloth was dying.

Pain unlike anything Finn had ever experienced seared through his entire being as Mugloth's hooks and chains of hatred ripped away from his very soul, tearing through muscle and skin. Such agony should've left his spirit and body shredded, but in the instant of Mugloth's death, Finn felt whole and unshackled. His oppressive prison had crumbled at last.

Strengthened and renewed, he spoke to Air and Water, expressing his gratitude as he set the elemental spirits free. The ocean yielded, collapsing over the island's cove with a resounding splash. At last all was quiet, save for a soft breeze and the crashing of waves along the shores.

Finn hurled through the air and landed next to Fate. Sithias, having changed to human form but with wings, helped Gerdie to her feet and they stepped aside. As Finn knelt down, Fate's broken legs and open wounds tore at him. Her face had been cleaned of most of the grime but her hair and clothes were matted in blood and mud. Gently, he gathered her up in his arms and held her close to his chest. Her skin was frighteningly cold. "It's over, love," he said softly in her ear. "It's just me here.

I'm free—*we're* free. We can be together now."

Her dark lashes fluttered against the delicate purpled hollows of her eyes as her forehead creased with the effort of waking. "Finn?" she whispered, her gaze unfocused as if she couldn't quite see him.

"Aye, m'love, I'm here," he replied, his voice cracking with fear. "We've got to get you inside now. Get you warm and take care of you." He glanced up at Sithias and Gerdie. "Are they all at the inn?" He'd have to deal with the villagers first if they were lying in wait again.

"Ressst assured, the place isss desssserted," Sithias told him.

"Yeah, they all scatted like a bunch of rats jumpin' ship," Gerdie said. "Except they took their boats to do it."

Finn sighed. "Good."

As he started to get up, Fate groaned in pain. "No…wait," she pleaded. "It hurts too much to move. Just hold me."

He desperately wanted to get her inside and start attending to her injuries but he couldn't stand adding to her suffering in any way. "For a minute," he told her.

She nuzzled her face against his chest. "You're back. I can feel you," she murmured, a tiny smile forming on her blue-tinged lips. "Captain of your soul again."

"Aye, master of my fate." He swallowed back the painful lump in his throat as she lifted a trembling finger to his mouth.

"I love you, Finn," she whispered.

Tears filled his eyes. "And I love you," he said, his voice breaking into a sob.

Her eyes closed and her hand dropped.

Finn's heart lurched as he stared at her bloodless face. "Fate? Wake up." He buried his face against her neck, probing with his senses as he chased her dwindling life force. "Don't leave me, love. Not now. Not when we're home free."

"No! Not my missss!" Sithias wailed.

Gerdie took Fate's hand, pressing her little fingers on her wrist. "Stop your panickin', both of you. She's not dead. But she will be if you don't get her inside where I can start tendin' to her cuts and breaks, and get some blood-buildin' tonics in her."

Finn nodded, grateful to have his marching orders. He needed someone to tell him what to do right now. He was too frightened to think straight.

"Oh thank the godsss! Let'sss hurry then, shall we?" Sithias said, crouching to pick up Gerdie. Flapping his wings, he lifted off and flew down the hill with her to the Royal Oak Inn.

Finn started slowly lifting into the air to avoid jostling Fate when the ground suddenly rumbled and a mountainous tangle of roots rose up from the earth. Afraid it was Mugloth returned to life, he increased his speed but not before a gigantic hand of muddy roots grabbed him by the legs. Tightening his grip on Fate to keep from dropping her, she moaned in pain. With her in such a fragile state, his only option was to summon the elements again. Just as he started to speak, a voice he knew too well crackled with power behind him, with a message that penetrated skin and flesh, pounding its meaning all the way to the very marrow of his bones.

As the hand brought him around to face his captor, Finn knew it was the Green Man even before he saw the gleaming eyes staring back at him from within a face of twisted roots and leafy fronds. "No!" Finn protested in the Dark Speech.

The Green Man pierced his mind, telling him the only way out of his debt was to offer the girl in his place.

A weight greater than any Finn had felt before pressed down on him. Handing Fate over to the Green Man was unthinkable, but leaving her now after moving heaven and earth to be together was every bit as inconceivable. Yet there was no disputing the agreement he'd made with the Olde One back when the giant had released Fate in Callum's cursed forest.

He'd always hoped they'd escape the book before the debt was due. He should've known better.

Finn conceded and the giant placed him on the ground. He walked over to Sithias, who'd left Gerdie at the inn and flown back when he'd seen what was happening.

"Take her," Finn said, placing Fate in his arms. The movement didn't jar her awake this time, which worried him greatly.

Sithias stared at the giant with mouth gaping open. "What isss *he* doing here? Do you have to fight him too?"

Utterly exhausted, Finn pitched his head back in defeat and stared at the night sky. "How do you fight something eternal and ever-present? I've been reminded of a promise I'm bound to. When the Green Man took Fate after she summoned him to destroy Callum, I offered myself in her place. After he spared her, he said he'd be back for me when the time came."

"Uh-huh..." Sithias said, not clueing in.

"Well, that time has come."

"B-but, what does thisss mean?"

"Destroying Mugloth wasn't enough. The Green Man wants me to renew the island."

"How?"

"I have to do what Mugloth did."

Sithias stared at him in horror. "No! What about Fate? She *needsss* you."

He grabbed Sithias by the shoulders. "If I don't go, he'll take her. I'm counting on you to take care of her now. Promise me you'll help her get home."

Sithias remained speechless.

"Promise me."

"I-I promissse." Sithias's amber eyes grew round and watery. "But she may not pull through thisss, essspecially if you're not by her ssside. She could die!"

Finn squeezed his shoulders tight. "Don't you *dare* let that happen. And don't let her do anything *bloody* stupid, like invoking the Green Man to undo this. We all know what kind of mess that got us into." He paused, regretting his words. "Don't tell her I said that."

When Sithias didn't answer he gave him a hard stare. "Agreed?"

"Yesss, I'll do my utmossst bessst."

He let go, patting his shoulders. "I had you all wrong. You've been a good friend, Sithias."

Gulping loudly, Sithias nodded with tears running freely.

Finn dropped his gaze to Fate, wanting so badly to be the one to clean her wounds and watch over her recovery. Lifting her hand to his mouth, he kissed the rope burns on her wrist. The ribbon he'd given her was soaked in blood and muck, the ends frayed. It was garbage now. Reaching into his pocket, he pulled out his leather pouch of holy blend and set it on her stomach.

If only he could stay to whisper a wonderful future into her ear while she slept and healed. To be by her side as the rose returned to her cheeks and see the fire in those brown eyes when she awoke. To be able to kiss her warm, eager lips without holding back. To envision a life together and set their feet upon a path of their own choosing, free to love each other every day without fearing some horrible consequence.

If only he could stay.

He looked at Sithias. "Don't let her wait for me. Make her leave. I couldn't take it if she put herself in jeopardy trying to find some way to free me."

"You wouldn't sssay that if you knew how long she'sss waited for you already," Sithias said, the tears dripping off his quivering chin.

"If you have to, tell her I'm okay with this. Tell her this is bigger than us—that we need to sacrifice our own personal happiness for a grander purpose. *Make her move on.*" It killed him to have Fate think he'd accepted this so easily when leaving her felt like his heart was being cut out.

Sithias nodded solemnly as Gerdie ran up to them. "What's...going...on? Is Mugloth...back?" she asked, out of breath from running up the hill. Her eyes grew round with shock as her gaze trailed along the towering height of the Green Man. "What's *that?*"

"Goodbye, Gerdie," Finn said hoarsely, too emotional to explain.

"Finn?" she said, looking confused and afraid.

Shaking his head, he lifted off and flew over to the riven oak. The seawater had cleansed the bones and centuries-old layers of blood from the two hollowed halves of the trunk. He landed, taking his place within the deep cleft of the splayed tree. As the Green Man lifted the huge halves and brought them up around him, the wood cracked and moaned mournfully, as did his spirit. The fear in him unraveled as every ounce of his being rebelled against an existence he could not begin to fathom. His life was slipping away. He would never again feel the sun on his face and breathe the free air, or know the touch of Fate's skin against his.

Finn looked at the stars, glittering like diamonds scattered over black velvet. Feeling so very alone, he reached up to the dazzling sky, his view shrinking as the oak closed and sealed him off from everything he loved.

Completely and irrevocably.

CHAPTER 34

"NO, IT'SSS NOT FRAGEEL, it'sss *fragile.* Asss in *sssmile,"* Sithias said, underlining the word on the chalkboard so hard he broke the stick in half. "Oh now look what you've made me do." He bent to pick up the chalk.

"What does smile have to do it?" Gerdie said, crossing her arms in frustration. "And who needs a fancy word for weak anyway? Just say weak."

Sithias popped up, his back straight and chin tucked in. "A good writer needsss a varied vocabulary to expresss a rich and interesssting ssstory."

"I don't want to be some brainy writer, I only need the basics of readin' and writin'."

"We've been at thisss every day for a month. Now that you do know the basicsss, it'sss time to move onto more advanced lessonsss," he said, frowning at her through his monocle, which was really only for looks. He'd thrown himself into the role of "headmaster"—an idea he'd gotten from some book Fate had conjured for him back in Beldereth. A role that inspired him to shift into an elderly man wearing a white tie, a goofy black gown and a silly square board on his head with a tassel that tickled his nose and made him sneeze.

"It's borin' and it's hurtin' my head."

"Bor*ing*, use your g'sss in your ingsss," he corrected.

"I am quitt*ing* school. This class is dull," she said, saying each word precisely.

"Oh! Nice sssynonym for boring. You get a cookie for that one."

"That's just skippy," Gerdie muttered. Rising from her desk, she walked to the big window to stare at the deep shadows of the forest on the other side of the pier and the hills rising in green swells to where the giant oak stood, its wide canopy sprawled protectively over its saplings—if they could even be called that anymore. Their trunks had thickened to the size of centuries-old oaks. The rapid growth continued to amaze her. She'd never seen a more beautiful forest.

At least one good thing had come from Finn being sealed away.

Ever since that horrible night though, things had been touch and go. Fate's blood loss was so great there were moments when Gerdie thought she might not survive. But she didn't give up on her. She force-fed Fate her magically brewed fennel and seaweed tonics for a solid week before she was conscious enough to drink them herself. At least the broken legs had been easy enough to set while she was unconscious.

Pulling her through her injuries was the easy part. Telling her why Finn wasn't there when she awoke was a whole lot harder. She became hysterical and inconsolable. When nothing would help, Gerdie had added valerian root to the tonics to calm her. The herb ended the crying jags and allowed her to sleep, which she did a lot for another few weeks. But when the resilience of youth kicked in and she could no longer sleep as much, she wouldn't talk, no matter how much Sithias tried to get her to respond. She'd just lie in bed staring up at the ceiling, pale as snow and so very…fragile.

Sithias stepped up next to her, his gaze fixed on the giant oak. "How long do you think she'll be up there today?"

As soon as she was strong enough, Fate spent every day sitting at the base of the tree. Her nights would've been spent there as well if Sithias didn't keep bringing her back to the inn after she fell fast asleep. She'd also become frightfully thin and they'd had to be diligent about making sure she ate.

Gerdie suspected the few bites she did eat were only to appease them. It was beginning to look like Fate might not ever regain her zest for life. She was practically a ghost haunting the halls—floating to keep the weight off her legs—with a lost look in her eyes.

"The weather's getting' warmer every day," Gerdie replied. "She's almost got no reason to come inside."

"Or any reassson to live, it would ssseem," Sithias said with a heavy sigh. "What elssse can we posssibly do to bring her back to life? I'm afraid if we don't, we'll be ssstuck on thisss island forever."

"I've been thinkin' on that. Fate's legs are pretty much mended. She's still pasty, which tells me her blood's not where it should be, but that'll right itself in time, so long as she keeps drinkin' the tonics. What she's got is a soul sickness, and the only cure for that is hope."

"How do you propossse we do *that?* Short of giving her paper and pen ssso she can write Finn out of that tree—which we've told her isss *not* an option—I can't think what that might be." He gave her a sudden look of horror. "Oh dear, you're not thinking you can do it, are you? Jussst because you've usssed the Wordsss of Making to conjure food sssupplies and improvementsss to our living conditionsss doesssn't mean *you* can ussse them to free Finn. I didn't teach you to read and write ssso you could throw usss into deeper trouble with the Green Man or some entirely different problem."

"Relax, I only *look* like a dumb kid," Gerdie said, openly wearing her annoyance.

"Then what are you planning? A potion or sssome sssort of ssspell?"

"Nope, somethin' even better, the old carrot-on-a-stick trick."

Sithias frowned. "That'sss your grand idea? I know I don't have to tell you how much she lovesss being in cocoa heaven, and what a cocoa hell it'ssss been for me baking all thossse chocolate cakesss, piesss, triflesss, trufflesss, browniesss and fudge jussst to get her to take a nibble. And did she touch any of it?"

"Nope."

"Then what makesss you think she'll want a carrot ssstick?"

"Huh. Whaddya know," Gerdie said, smiling as she moved to the door. "I know somethin' you don't for a change."

Sithias handed her the jar of cookies he kept on his desk. "Take thessse in cassse your carrot failsss to entice."

The lilting notes of a flute floated down from the heart of the woods, tugging at Fate with an invitation to follow. She weaved her way through the trees, knee deep in a lake of ferns and bluebells. The scent of lilacs perfumed the air as she ran her fingers over sun-dappled leaves and climbed the gentle incline to the immense, ancient oak on the hill. As she pushed through the dense foliage into the open, where the massive trunk marked the grove's center, the notes shivered over her skin, reverberating throughout her entire being.

He stood by the oak, lost in his music, his eyes closed and fingers tapping the wooden flute. He was as familiar to her as her own face in the mirror, yet every time she reached for his name it slipped from her mind. Heart thief is what she called him, because he kept stealing precious memories from her, drawing them out one by one with his beguiling melodies, leaving her with nothing but shadowy remnants. She tried desperately to hang onto what little was left, but her shiny treasures and sacred wounds escaped like smoke through the cracks of her fingers. She was angry with him for wielding this power of forgetting over her. Even words had been taken from her, making it impossible to voice her complaint.

As he emptied her heart of pain and all her attachments to

the past, peace filled the hole in her chest, making her sleepy. Helpless to resist the tranquil music, she settled down into the moss and laid her head on the roots. The flute's notes mingled with the breeze rustling the leaves, and together the piper and oak tree sang a lyric only the soul could understand, a song of forgiveness, of letting go and moving on. But Fate didn't want to move on. If she could stay asleep and keep dreaming this dream, then maybe she would cease to exist and her quiet end would become a beautiful beginning.

A discordant, wild note sliced through the serene melody, cutting it short with a jarring abruptness.

Waking with a shock, she sat up within the mossy indentation beneath the oak. An unnatural stillness fell over the surrounding forest, a loud silence that saddened her as the afterglow of forgetfulness faded and her wits returned. She'd been dreaming of Finn again. The gnawing ache in her heart returned. She didn't want to believe he might be trying to communicate with her through her dreams, because then she'd have to accept what he wanted, which was to forget him and leave the island. But the dream was persistent. *He* was persistent.

Well, she could be just as stubborn. She'd vowed to stay by his side until her dying day—which might never come if Gerdie was any example of what she was in for, but that didn't matter. She couldn't leave him. Summoning the Green Man to destroy Callum had been her doing. She should be the one locked inside the oak, not Finn. He shouldn't have had to sacrifice himself, not after he'd fought so hard and long to be free of Mugloth. Yet here he was, a prisoner again. All because she'd been careless with her words.

As always, whenever she followed this line of thinking, the temptation to use the Words of Making to go back in time and avoid her original mistake rose beneath her skin like a sudden itchy rash that wouldn't go away.

The wind rushed in, blasting her in the face and shaking the oak's branches with the noisome thrashing of leaves. Acorns rained down on her and a swallow swooped in, pecking the top of her head.

"Ow!" she cried, rubbing her scalp. Glancing around, she wondered if Finn had called the wind and directed the bird to dive-bomb her. She decided to test her theory. "Finn," she croaked, her vocal chords unused to speaking. "I'm going to rewrite this fable and free you." She waited for another violent wind and a swarm of wrens to attack her.

The wind hushed as if to listen but that was all.

She sighed. Was her dream more of a torturous nightmare, in which she imagined they were connected in some way? She wished she knew what it was like for him inside the oak. Was he even conscious anymore? She prayed he was at peace and one with nature like in her dreams. But she couldn't shake the notion he might be suffering the same isolation and fear she'd gone through when Mugloth had dragged her down into the hollow.

There was no description in the *Book of Fables* as to what he was experiencing. Hoping to find a clue, she'd read the passage until it was scorched into her brain: *At long last, a Druidh of great power named Emrys, came to Innith Tine and purged the island of Mugloth's darkness. The Green Man, the oldest of the Olde Ones, rose from the earth and sealed Emrys inside the ancient oak to ensoul the tree and renew the forest. With this new cycle begun, the island became a sacred place for the annual Alban Eiler Druidhean pilgrimage once again.*

Her hand flew to the ribbon around her neck—the one Finn had given her—stroking the silk in an attempt to soothe her misery. Gerdie had done her best to clean it but the fabric remained a mottled gray, the ends so frayed they were practically tassels now. Fate didn't care about that. She had tied the small pouch he'd left behind to the ribbon to keep them both close to her heart. Lifting it to her nose, she breathed in the rich earthy scent of the holy blend inside the soaped leather. If she closed her eyes, she could almost fool herself into believing he was near.

But almost wasn't good enough. Tears burned behind her lids as a monstrous pain clawed its way up from her stomach into her chest, ripping a sob from her throat.

"Fate?"

Opening her eyes with a start, she saw Gerdie peering at her through the vegetation. She wiped her eyes, turning her head away. Why didn't they understand she just wanted to be left alone? Talking only made the sorrow worse.

"I brought chocolate chip cookies," Gerdie said, holding up the jar.

Fate's stomach twisted with nausea at the thought of eating.

Gerdie nestled in amongst the wildflowers and sat down up to her neck in colorful blossoms. "There's somethin' you need to know."

Blinking to hold back the tears, Fate looked up into the oak's sprawling canopy.

"Back home where I come from there's this secret door my family's been hidin' for a long, long time," Gerdie said. "We've kinda been guardin' it to make sure nobody finds where it leads, to this place called the Keep."

This unexpected topic of conversation momentarily pulled Fate's attention away from her pain. Lowering her gaze, she stared past Gerdie, listening with vague interest.

"It's like a big city closed in by a cage of turnin' hoops. And there's all these vaults inside. Thousands of 'em. Each one holds powerful magic." Gerdie fell quiet and waited.

The buzzing of bees droned in the silence as Fate tried to make sense of what she was being told. She looked at the ancient six-year-old, questioning her with a frown.

Gerdie leaned in, her eyes bright now that she had her attention. "Don't you get it? There's gotta be somethin' in the Keep that's powerful enough to put things right with Finn. And I can get you there."

Fate wrestled with her locked mind, wanting to know more, but afraid to allow the slightest grain of hope in. Any more disappointment would kill her. "How?" she asked.

"We get ourselves out of this book and I take you back to my family's bookstore. That's where the door to the Keep is. Brune can get us in. She's got the Key. And you can bet she'll be there when we get back. If she sent you in for the Rod, she'll be waitin' for you to come springin' out of the book with it."

Fate put her hand to her neck protectively, feeling for the Rod hidden behind Finn's ribbon. The guilt she'd pushed down all those months ago rose to the surface, holding her back from explaining the blood and the mystery around how she'd gotten the Rod from O'Deldar.

"Sithias told me about how you got that," Gerdie said, seeing her reaction.

That burned Fate. He promised to keep her secret.

"Don't blame him. I saw it when I was cleanin' you up. I knew what it was. It's got the same markings as the Orb."

Fate relaxed somewhat, relieved she didn't have to worry about Gerdie taking it from her. She'd had every opportunity to do so and hadn't. "You said your family had a bookstore?"

"Yeah," Gerdie said, the beginnings of a smile forming on her face before turning to a frown. "I only hope it's still there. It's been so long."

"Did the building it's in used to be a granary?"

"How'd you know?"

"I think we share the same family bookstore. It's still there but it's closed now, ever since my Gran died."

Gerdie stood up, an anxious look on her face. "Please tell me your Gran's name wasn't Berdie."

Fate frowned in confusion, puzzling over how Gerdie knew Gran's name, and struck by the uncanny way their names rhymed. "She went by Berdie Biddle."

Tears sparkled in Gerdie's eyes. "Berdie married Hank Biddle? But she hated that freckle-faced carrot top after he shoved her in a puddle and ruined her Easter dress."

"How do you know that story? Gran used to tell it a lot."

"Because—" she said, her voice cracking and her little hands wringing together. "Berdie's my twin sister."

Fate was stunned. Gran had never mentioned a twin, or any siblings for that matter. But this explained the immediate kinship she'd felt with Gerdie when they first met, the instinctual need to protect. She smiled, a faint wisp of a smile. "All this time, and we never made the connection."

Gerdie tried to smile, but she still looked upset. "Berdie's really gone?"

Fate nodded. "Seven years now."

Her face crumpled with grief. "That means Mama's gone too."

"I'm so sorry, Gerdie."

"Guess I should've known there'd be no one left if I ever got back home."

It hurt to see Gerdie cry. Countless years of stifled sadness had broken that seemingly dauntless composure of hers. They'd both lost loved ones. In many ways Gerdie had lost so much more. She'd grown up completely alone—robbed of everything, thanks to Brune. It sickened Fate to know she was related to someone who could abandon her defenseless sister and later throw her niece into the same danger. They each had every reason to hate Brune.

Reaching out, Fate drew Gerdie down to sit next to her, cradling the little girl who, as crazy as it sounded, was her great aunt. "You're not alone. You've got family right here," she assured the softly weeping girl.

While Fate held her, she considered what Gerdie had told her about the Keep. Could there really be a way to save Finn? The wheels began to turn as she watched a caterpillar scale the stalk of a bluebell, its weight bending the thin stem back to the ground. The more she thought about what the Keep might hold, the more compelling the idea became.

Sniffing, Gerdie wiped her nose with her sleeve and sat straight, her indomitable spirit back in place.

"Do you really think there's something in the Keep powerful enough to override Finn's debt to the Green Man?" Fate asked.

"I do," Gerdie said, struggling to open the jar of cookies.

Fate grabbed the lid and twisted.

"There's more magic in the Keep than there is in all the world," Gerdie said, biting into a cookie. "Mmm. Sithias did a good job with these."

Fate's stomach gurgled as irrepressible hope flooded through her, drowning out the deadness inside. "How will I get back to Oldwilde though?"

"Oma said the Keep wasn't just for storin' magic. She said some of the vaults were doors to other places and times. There's gotta be one that goes to Oldwilde."

Fate wanted to believe this was the solution to freeing Finn, but worried she might end up on some wild goose chase with no way back.

A black and white warbler landed in a nearby bush, flicking its tail. As its dark eyes met hers, the bird's coloring made her think of O'Deldar with his salt and pepper hair. When they'd first met, he'd given her the same hard stare while impressing upon her that there were other ways besides the *Book of Fables* to cross the divide between worlds. Could he have been referring to the Keep?

"Okay, I'll go," she said. The moment the words were out,

the warbler flew off. She half expected, or hoped the wind would stir and shake some acorns loose in defiance of her decision but the breeze remained unchanged.

Gerdie let out a big sigh and smiled. "Good, but first we're gonna have to shape you up with some color back in your face and meat on those bones." She held out the cookie jar.

"What, you don't think this whole anemic, skin-and-bones thing is working for me?" Fate said, smiling as she took a cookie and nibbled off a piece of chocolate.

Gerdie screwed up her face and shook her head.

"Darn, and here I thought I was looking so fashionably undead."

"I'm going away," Fate said, her throat closing over the words. She leaned her forehead against the rough bark of the oak, squeezing her eyes shut against the tears. "I *promise,* I'll be back for you, Finn. Just don't give up on me. Okay?"

A hush fell over the grove.

She looked up into the massive umbrella of leaves, sensing the change in the air, as if all of nature suddenly held its breath. "Finn?" she whispered.

Not a flutter of leaf, not a chirp of bird or buzz of insect. Only quiet.

Fate listened with beating heart and ears pricked to a voice, silent to the outside world, but loud in her heart. *We are tied together, always.*

Cool, brisk air blew against her lips, like the breeze of a hummingbird's wings. Drawing in a tiny gasp, she put her fingers to her mouth, certain she'd been kissed—a kiss goodbye. She wanted to clutch at Finn's presence, faint as it was, and never let go. But he was already slipping away. As normal sounds of the forest resumed, she felt the acute pain of his absence all over again. Why did love have to hurt so much?

The tightening in her chest worsened with each step she took away from the oak. No matter how far her journey took her, there would always be this raw, open gash in her heart. But she had to focus on the road ahead because pushing forward was the only way back to him. And only then could she put an end to this gnawing pain. Biting back the tears, she willed herself to leap into the air and flew back to the inn.

"Would you stop pacin'? You're makin' me dizzy," Gerdie complained as Sithias slithered past her for the hundredth time. He'd returned to snake form, complete with his old suede hunter's cap. Since they had to return to *The Lonely Sorceress* and give it a happy ending before they could return home, he wanted to make sure Elsina recognized him. "Why are you so nervous about goin' back?"

He stopped and looked at her. "How do I explain why I've been gone ssso very long and why I'm in the company of enemiesss? Elsssina'sss not to be trifled with. She may be unbearably beautiful, but she'sss made of ice, you know. I sssometimesss doubt there'sss a beating heart beneath that sssmooth ivory ssskin. She can be ssso cruel." He heaved a big sigh. "I wonder what she'sss been doing while I've been away. Do you think she misssed me?"

Fate walked in.

Gerdie hopped off the table, relieved to see that her farewell to Finn hadn't shattered her resolve to leave. They'd worked hard to build up her spirits and stamina, and she didn't want to see her lapse back into depression. Plus she was anxious to finally face Brune, especially with Fate there to back her up. "All set to go?" she asked.

Fate whipped aside her hooded cloak, revealing her sword and daggers strapped over her leather armor. "Ready as I'll ever be after weeks of stuffing my face with Sithias's gourmet meals. Could've done without those revolting tonics though. Sorry, Gerdie, but they really stink." She threw Sithias a smile that didn't quite conceal the lingering sadness in her eyes. "But you, my friend, will make someone an excellent wife someday."

"Oh, you really think ssso?" he asked, looking a little too hopeful.

"You're really holdin' up fine?" Gerdie pressed as she scrutinized Fate.

"Yes," she replied.

But Gerdie noted a flicker of doubt in her eyes before she looked away and strode over to the *Book of Fables*, its huge pages open to *The Lonely Sorceress*.

Fate curled her arm and slapped a well-defined bicep. "Odds are good I could beat a four hundred pound gorilla in an arm wrestling match right now. Don't know exactly how long this leftover super-strength will last, but I'm betting on a few more months before I need help opening a jar of mayo."

"That'sss good to know, misss," Sithias said, his tone deliberately careful as he moved in next to her.

Something inside Gerdie went cold as she joined them by the big book and glanced up at the snake, his wings shivering with fear. Or was that eagerness? Then she realized what was bothering her. There'd been a false note in his voice she'd never heard before. Alarmed, she tugged on Fate's sleeve, but too late.

Fate had already uttered the first word of *The Lonely Sorceress*. The inexorable pull into the fable snatched the words off the tip of her tongue as an explosion of letters suddenly swarmed off the page and swept them away.

CHAPTER 35

THE PLUNGE BACK into *The Lonely Sorceress* immersed Fate within Elsina's all-consuming longing to love and be loved. The sorceress's agonizing loss when she discovered Torrin was devoted to another, seared like salt poured into the open, weeping wound that was Fate's heart. Elsina's pain was the same as hers, regardless of circumstance.

Fate's sorrow increased as the story unfolded toward its new tragic end when Torrin flung himself off the cliffs. The sight of his broken body on the rocks—tossed carelessly by the heaving waves—left her even more heartbroken, the despair intensifying when Elsina's wail of grief shuddered the island.

Red flames brought the fable to an abrupt end, turning everything to ash.

Her knees buckling, Fate dropped into cool sand. Another blast of red fiery light hit the *Book of Fables*, the flames glancing off its pages, vanishing in a puff of smoke. Hugging her waist, she choked back a sob.

Gerdie yanked her down flat to the ground. "What's going on?" Fate muttered, suddenly overcome by a wave of nausea from the jump. Disoriented by the darkness of night after leaving a sunny afternoon behind, she wiped her eyes dry of tears and glanced around. They were back in the cove. The only light was that of the moon reflecting over the black ocean.

Sithias flew out in front of them, his wings flapping like crazy. "Mistressss! I've returned—with the magic book!"

Shock cut through some of the fog in Fate's head. Had she

heard him right? "Sithias," she said, keeping her voice low. "What are you *doing?*"

Ignoring her, Sithias continued flapping in place. "I know how the book worksss. We can travel to other worldsss without ever leaving the island. You can do thisss without fear of losssing your powersss!"

Unable to believe her ears, Fate grabbed him by the tail to stop him from whatever it was he thought he was doing. The muscles beneath his scales twisted in her hand, whipping free of her grasp.

Confusion churned amongst the queasiness in her stomach.

"I knew it, he's turned against us," Gerdie whispered, her frizzy hair smoking and singed down the middle.

Further confused by Gerdie's sudden shift in attitude, Fate rose to her feet, her movements sluggish from the nausea and throbbing in her temples. Or was it a nagging sense of betrayal causing the ache in her brain? She turned her fuzzy attention to the sorceress.

"Have you lost your pea-sized brain?" Elsina said, her winged granite lion on one side and Hatho on the other. "You never left. The book closed and then opened. Now get out of the way!" She signaled the soldier hawk. "Lock them up. And send an ox back for the book."

When Sithias flew off and landed next to the sorceress, Fate's skin erupted with a sweating panic. He really was a double-crossing snake! How could she have been so wrong about him?

Shaking, she freed her sword. The hilt slid against her slick palm as she positioned herself in front of Gerdie, her focus on Hatho, who'd drawn his broadsword.

In a blur of motion, he plunged his blade at her. As rusty as she felt wielding a sword after her long convalescence, muscle memory kicked in and she deflected the blow. The clash of blades vibrated up her arm and shoulder, nearly knocking her over. Regaining her footing, she blocked another swift attack, watching for an opening that never came. Hatho's blade flew at her in precise, unrelenting strokes. She repelled each strike, but her reflexes weren't as quick as they should be. She hadn't completely recovered from the transition between fables.

Desperate to gain the upper hand, she pulled a dagger from the strap at her thigh. With her sword hand, she curved her blade over his, driving it downward, then slashed the dagger above his gauntleted forearm, slicing through feather and hitting bone. As he staggered back a step, she expected him to drop his weapon. Instead he advanced, swinging his broadsword round in an arc before redirecting the blade's angle into a vertical swipe that came down hard and fast. The impact of his heavy blade jolted the light rapier from her grasp.

Disarmed and off balance, she stumbled backward as he lunged, shoving her further along. Tripping over Gerdie who was crouched in the sand, she fell over, the air knocking from her lungs. Suddenly he was on top of her, his hand clamped over her throat and lifting her up to his face. Angry golden eyes glinted from behind his silver helmet.

Struggling for her next breath, she pounded on his arm, ramming her knee into his gut. Pain ground into her kneecap as it smashed against his armor. In return, Hatho delivered a roundhouse punch that met her stomach with the force of a speeding cannonball.

He let her drop to the ground. Curling inward and unable to breathe, she glanced past the soldier hawk, locking eyes with Sithias. Why was he allowing this? Surely any moment now he would step in and help. She searched his amber eyes for the smallest signal they were still on the same team. But nothing even close to friendship registered in his gaze.

"Sithias!" she yelled with a fury that burned her throat. "I'll get you for—" A gag in her mouth staunched the threat.

"Hatho," the sorceress said as she climbed onto the back of her scowling lion, "bring me the witch's spell book."

The hawk finished tying Fate's hands behind her back, then searched the satchel slung across her chest. "It's not here, m'la—"

Fate launched her boot straight into his helmet. Hatho stumbled sideways, but promptly regained his balance and cracked his iron fist into the side of her head.

A fleeting fireworks display exploded inside her skull before everything went black.

♠

"Fate," a voice called from some far off place. "Wake up."

Opening her eyes, Fate stared at a blurry face hovering over her. She had to blink several times before Gerdie came into view. "Wha—what happened?" The moment she touched her aching temple, Hatho's fist flashed in her mind. "Oh right, the gorilla hawk."

"That's a good lump you've got there. That oddball hawk's got some powerful arms."

"Thanks for the news flash," she said, barely able to move her sore, stiff body.

"I was beginnin' to think you'd never wake up. You've been out all night."

Groaning from the head-to-toe body ache Hatho and the stone floor had given her, Fate propped herself up, frowning at the moss-stained walls, the flat straw bed she was lying on and the rusted iron door blocking her way to freedom. "Where are we?" she asked, momentarily distracted by bee-winged spiders weaving peculiar honeycomb-patterned webs over the ceiling.

"Elsina's dungeon."

"Huh, what a surprise. Typical dungeon motif with gothic touches of gloomy gray juxtaposed against yet *more* gloomy gray. Unless you count the freaky insects." Her hair blew about as a brisk wind whipped up from behind. She shivered. "Kind of windy for being underground—now that I think of it—a lot brighter than it should be."

"That's cuz we're missin' a whole wall," Gerdie said.

Fate glanced over her shoulder, squinting into the glare of a magnificent sunrise shining into the square opening of their cell. "Okay, that's interesting. I wasn't expecting a first-class ocean view." From what she could see, their cell was nothing more than a ten-foot indentation carved into the cliff rock. Still woozy but encouraged by this discovery, she stood up and started to take a step when her leg hooked in something. "What the—?" Her ankle was bound in a rusty shackle chained to an iron ring driven into the stone floor. "Really? He told them I could fly?" Hurt and anger tangled in her chest. "Ooooh, I swear next time I see Sithias I'm going to tie him in knots and pluck out his wings, one rotten feather at a time. *Turncoat.* How could he do this to us after everything we've been through together?"

Gerdie shook her head, an angry frown marring her impish features. "He's a tricksy snake. He fooled us all. I shoulda known better. I only caught onto him at the last minute right before we left. Somethin' in his voice hit me wrong."

Feeling sick, Fate pressed her hands over her bruised stomach. "No, I should've seen it. I'm sorry, Gerdie, I was too wrapped up in my own stuff."

"Don't go blamin' yourself. Nobody can think straight after losin' someone they love."

"But it was right there in front of me. Remember how all of his plays and stories had the same femme fatale? Which, now that I'm looking back on it, sounded just like Elsina. But that changed after we got to Innith Tine. After I started feeling better, I noticed the poems he read me were different. They were about a raven-haired woman whose breath was like the sweetest blossom, skin like the glow of a sunbeam and voice like the trill of a blue jay. Of course the description changed from day to day, but you know what I mean."

Gerdie tapped her finger on her chin. "I don't think it was a blue jay. They're squawky."

"Whatever," Fate said. "I can't believe I didn't notice. He's been totally in love with Elsina this whole time."

Gerdie looked doubtful. "No way. He was afraid of her."

"I know. But there was that one time he came right out and called her a miracle of womanhood, followed by a whole lot of fancy backpedaling."

"Oh yeah, that's right," Gerdie agreed, her eyes narrowing. "That means when we were makin' plans to come back here, he was just goin' along with all that talk about how you'd use the Words of Makin' to give Elsina her perfect companion and happy endin'."

Dragging her chains to the back of the cell, Fate slumped against the wall, staring out at the ocean. "He doesn't want her to be with anyone but him."

"Sounds like we're never gettin' out of here," Gerdie grumbled.

A loud grating noise startled them both as a small panel at the bottom of the iron door slid open. A tray of food was shoved through. Then the panel slammed shut.

Gerdie carried the tray over to Fate and sat down. Picking up a small cube of cheese by the toothpick stuck in it, she offered it to her.

Too upset to eat, Fate waved it away.

"Suit yourself. Course, I never pass up a meal since there's no tellin' when the next one's comin'." Popping the cheese in her mouth, she whipped aside a pristine white cloth, revealing steaming hot porridge and warm bread underneath. "Hmm, can't say the sorceress doesn't feed her prisoners well." She grabbed a goblet of dark juice. After gulping most of it back, she wrinkled her nose. "Never been too keen on prune juice."

When loud gurgling noises started in her stomach, she eyed the hole in the floor off in one corner. "Uh-oh. Probably shouldn't have done that."

As Gerdie prattled on, a slow burn in Fate's gut flared into red-hot rage, scorching away the sick feeling Sithias's betrayal had left her with. Every cell in her body vibrated with anger.

"You okay? You're chest is lightin' up like a Christmas tree."

"I'm so mad," Fate said through clenched teeth. "I don't think I've ever been this furious in all my life. Well, maybe when they cancelled Danny Phantom, but this is just so much worse. What Sithias did is unforgivable."

"Yeah, if he was here right now, I'd make him drink this prune juice."

Fate eyed the nearly empty goblet. "Give it to me," she said.

"Be my guest," Gerdie said as she handed it over.

Grabbing the linen cloth, Fate picked up the discarded toothpick and dipped it in the juice. When she started spelling on the cloth, Gerdie smiled and nodded. "Ooh, Sithias is in so much trouble."

"He'll get his, but first we need to blow this hole in the wall and keep Torrin from taking a swan dive off the cliffs."

"What if we're already too late?"

"Oh that's positive, Eeyore."

"I think I'm more like Christopher Robin," Gerdie said, crossing her arms in annoyance.

"Fine, Chris, take a seat over there with Pooh and the gang while I get on with this," Fate said, smiling tiredly at her spirited great-aunt. Looking at what she'd written, she murmured the words aloud. The air quivered, drawing something small and metallic into existence. A key, which she caught before it hit the floor.

Gerdie's eyes widened. "Is that the key to the door?"

"Uh, well no," Fate said as she slotted it into the locked

shackle. The manacle sprang open. "I figured we go out this way." She walked over to the end of the cell and stood at the edge of the steep drop. A roiling broth of crashing waves and sea-foam churned on the rocks below.

"I suppose that's probably better since the guards are on the other side of that door."

"My thinking exactly." Fate bent low so Gerdie could climb onto her back. "Ready?"

"About as ready as a cat hangin' over a bath," she remarked nervously as she positioned herself.

Fate launched into the sky. She was barely in the air a few seconds when a horn blared. Adrenaline shot through her limbs as she glanced back at the pockmarked cliff walls, filled with over a hundred cells from which a dozen soldier hawks lifted off and flew straight at them.

Gerdie went stiff, her grip tightening around Fate's neck, pressing pain into her already tender windpipe. She shot straight up, knowing the hawks could never match her rocket-like aerodynamics. But her speed was hampered by Gerdie's extra weight. She couldn't climb fast enough to outrun their reach. A hand clamped onto her ankle. Another yanked Gerdie off her back.

Gerdie's scream rang out as Fate twisted round to grab her arm. *"No!"* she cried out as the girl's frightened face dropped from sight. Her heart lurched outward, her stomach pitching like she was the one plummeting helplessly to the ocean.

She turned around to dive after her, but the soldier hawk held her leg fast and grabbed hold of her arm. Screaming furiously, she struggled to see past the battery of wings and glinting helmets blocking her view. A second hawk gripped her other arm, carrying her forcefully back to the sky cells. She twisted in every direction, hoping to see that Gerdie had been caught before hitting the water.

They threw her into one of the cells. Tumbling over the stone, she smacked into the wall, cracking her head hard. Pain bloomed in her skull, dulling her wits as blood dripped down her face. She was vaguely aware of being lifted upright and a cold pinch of iron cuffs binding her wrists and ankles. "Where's Gerdie?" she muttered.

"The little one?" the soldier hawk nearest her asked.

"Lost," replied the other.

Grief and fury slammed into Fate's chest. She rushed at them, a savage scream tearing from her throat, the shackles clanging as she strained against them. The startled hawks backed away as she shot them a look of pure venom and hellfire. "I'll kill you!" she screamed. "I'll kill you all!"

Uneasy, they kept their eyes trained on her until they reached the edge of the cell and lifted off.

After everything she'd been through, only to lose Finn in the end, then to suffer Sithias's betrayal, and now Gerdie. The pain was too much. Rage she could deal with, but not this desolate agonizing grief threatening to overtake her. Allowing hatred to push aside her anguish, fury poisoned her tortured mind, distorting all reason as she glared out at Gerdie's watery grave. She narrowed her eyes on the glittering ocean, a deceptive beauty filled with a multitude of dangers. Not just the ordinary kind, but supernatural sorts like sea monsters, sirens and behemoths like the legendary Kraken. She couldn't help smiling as she envisioned the Kraken's giant tentacles snaking out of the water, grabbing hawks from the air and lashing out to crush Elsina's palace.

She drew a shallow breath, fueled on by the idea. But how could she make it happen? Her eyes landed on the crimson spatters near her feet. Dipping the tip of her boot in the blood, she spelled out a barely readable but simple command. Without hesitating, she breathed the vengeful words into the air, *"I summon Poseidon's wrath upon this island."*

Just then a soldier hawk landed in the cell. He was carrying Gerdie.

"Gerdie!" she cried, all her rage draining away as relief poured through her. "You're so much less…dead than I thought you were."

Gerdie ran to her, hugging her around the waist. "Thanks to Sithias!"

"What?" Stunned, Fate watched the soldier hawk elongate, a disturbing distortion, before transforming fully into the winged snake.

Smiling, he undulated forward. "It'sss a miracle I came along when I did."

"Oh really, *Judas?*" Fate yelled, her fisted hands wrenching against the shackles.

Sithias shrank away from her. "Misss, why are you ssso angry?"

Gerdie tugged on Fate's shirt. "Don't be mad. He's on our side. He made sure we had that tray of stuff to write with. And he's been busy makin' sure the fable has a happy endin' so we can go home!"

"It'sss true," he jumped in. "Upon my arrival, I sssecreted Torrin out of the palace and brought him to the sssea nymph—"

"You could've let us know!" Tears of frustration spilled down Fate's face.

The snake's amber eyes rounded with remorse. "That'sss why I'm here. I would have come sssooner, but I sssimply couldn't get away until now."

Fate couldn't catch her breath. Her chest heaved with sobs. She didn't know what to do with this overwhelming clash of relief, heartache and lingering distrust.

Gerdie edged close to her, nervously pointing at the horizon. "What's that?"

Gulping back the tears, Fate looked out at the water. "Oh no!" she whispered.

In a matter of minutes, storm clouds had swept in, disturbing the serene skyline. Poseidon had answered her call. The ocean had changed shape with gigantic waves swirling and crashing into one mountainous swell. The water rose with frightening speed, swallowing the horizon, surging ever higher into the restless, angry sky.

Sithias pulled his panicked gaze from the unnatural tempest, his eyes landing on the telltale words at her feet. "Possseidon? You sssummoned the sssupreme ruler of the sssea?"

"Yes, but I wasn't expecting *that!*" she said, staring dumbfounded at the colossal wave barreling toward them.

A bone-chilling shriek emanated from the towering wall of water. Huge shadowy forms with crawling tentacles lurked within the seething wave. Sithias backed away from the terrifying sight until he banged against the wall. "Oh dear, leviathonsss are in the water! I don't want to die this way," he squeaked.

Fate frantically smeared out one word, then started spelling out a new one in its place. She still had one letter to go when she discovered the blood had dried. "I can't finish!"

Sithias dipped his head down to the dried splotches, making spitting sounds. He lifted his head in alarm. "I thought I could wet it, but I'm ssscared spitlesss!"

The sound of thundering water, along with the alien roar of sea monsters, was almost deafening.

Gerdie pulled a rock from her pocket and scratched it over the stone, leaving a faint white line. "Picked this up from below!" she yelled over the din. "Tell me what ya need!"

Icy winds blasted in. Sea spray spewed into the hole, saturating the air with the smell of brine. Fate inhaled absolute fear as water splattered all over her sentence. She pointed with her toe the last letter she needed. As soon as Gerdie chalked in a 'd,' Fate screamed the altered sentence, *"I forbid Posiedon's wrath upon this island!"*

But it was too late. The wave crashed in, flooding the cell, a crushing force that plowed in, ramming them against the back wall. Held stationary by her shackles, Fate felt Sithias anchor himself by coiling around her waist, but Gerdie was floating unsecured.

The weight of the water pressing in was already lessening, an alternate current pulling Gerdie with it to the edge of the cell, where a window into Posiedon's world had opened. The sight was hair-raising. The turbulent water teamed with a swarm of monstrous squid, fiery eels, jet-black serpents, giant sharks and a horde of other nameless creatures. Then a great head and lipless maw of fangs blotted out the nest of sea beasts, its gullet a dark and terrifying cavern.

Fate screamed into the water. Through the air bubbles, she saw Sithias's tail lash out and grab Gerdie by the ankle. The massive jaws snapped shut inches from her head. She was safe for the moment, but the real threat was the urgent burning in Fate's lungs. They were all going to drown and she was to blame.

With her lungs screaming for air, Fate released what little was left, knowing her next gasp would bring certain death. But the pressurized weightlessness of water suddenly gave way to gravity, dropping her to the floor as her lungs filled with precious air. The ocean spilled out of the cell as rapidly as it had poured in. Gerdie sprawled on the floor like a wet rag, sputtering water and clutching her rock. Uncoiling from Fate's waist, Sithias released his grip on Gerdie as well. As he shook out his drenched wings, he looked at Fate, his mouth a grim line.

She flushed with guilt. "I'm so sorry. I really screwed up this time. I can't believe I almost got us all killed."

"No, I'm the one who'sss sssorry." He sighed heavily. "My performance wasss entirely too convincing. You truly believed I'd turned againssst you. Thisss gift of mine isss too powerful. I may have to give up acting."

His humility-laced arrogance nudged a smile out of her. How could she remain angry? They'd both made mistakes. "It's true, you had us going," Fate agreed.

"You're not the only onesss I've pulled into my grand illusion," he said, going on to describe what he'd done to keep Torrin from killing himself. "The sssea nymph fell in love with him jussst asss she did in the original fable. She wanted to become a mortal like him, but I told her they needed to leave the island and never come back."

"But the sea nymph gave her glamour to me," Fate reminded him. "He must've been pretty grossed out by her fishiness."

Sithias waved his tail dismissively. "Pffff, glamoursss are a ssshell a dozen under the sssea. She wasss agleam with golden hair and ssstormy eyesss. Torrin was ssso completely captivated, he let her turn him into a merman, and off they went into the deep blue. He wasss quite happy, believe me."

As much as she wanted to believe he'd worked everything out, Fate couldn't hide her skepticism. "But Elsina must've been devastated when her true love slipped away like that."

A sly smile crept onto his face. "She doesssn't know. I made myssself to look like Torrin. She thinksss *I'm* him."

Fate exchanged a knowing glance with Gerdie. "So it's true! You're in love with your boss!"

Momentarily speechless, Sithias opened and closed his mouth. "She isss not my bosss. She'sss my sssweet mistresss. She may ssseem cold on the sssurface, but I know how much she yearnsss for that one true companion who truly knowsss and understandsss her."

"I would've thought that was Hatho's thing. Isn't that why she made him with those big strong arms? So he could hold her?" Fate tried to keep a straight face, but she was shaking with laughter.

Sithias frowned. "Hatho'sss more the faithful dog. He'sss quite content to ssstand guard and merely be in her presssence. I, on the other hand, want much more. And what of it?"

Wet and cold, Gerdie shivered. "I think it's real sweet."

"It has been sssweet. We were up all night—the very reassson I wasssn't able to come here. It wasss a dream-come-true. But I'll admit, I'm bog-eyed from keeping up the pretenssse." He glanced anxiously at the now tranquil ocean. "I've no doubt been gone much too long. She'll be worried after thisss near disssaster, and I'm sure the hawksss will return any moment." He slithered to the edge of the cell then turned back. "Oh dear, I nearly forgot. The *Book of Fablesss* hasss locked itssself up. There'sss no opening it. Not for lack of trying on Elsina'sss part."

Fate looked at Gerdie. "What do you make of that?"

Hugging her little body, Gerdie appeared equally baffled. "Maybe the only way it'll pop open and get us out of here is if you write a happy end for this last fable."

"I was afraid you'd say that. But first things first." She shook her arms, rattling the chains of her manacles. "We need some dry clothes and another key for these shackles."

Gerdie smiled and lifted her rock. "No problem."

Fate turned to Sithias. "Can you help me write the end? I don't want to mess up again."

"Not to worry, I have a plan, misss," he said, though he looked embarrassed. "But you mussst promissse not to laugh…again."

CHAPTER 36

FATE DIDN'T LAUGH. She was touched by what Sithias had proposed and was more than willing to do the best she could for him. He deserved to be part of the happy ending to *The Lonely Sorceress* and she wanted to show him how much she appreciated his friendship.

After he left, Gerdie conjured clothing and some straw and blankets to hide beneath so Hatho and his soldiers wouldn't find her when they checked in on their prisoner. Then they waited for nightfall before unlocking Fate's irons.

"Sithias taught you well," Fate said, impressed by Gerdie's newly developed abilities. "You're spelling's really good."

Smiling proudly, Gerdie sat down across from her cross-legged. "Yeah, I'm lookin' forward to readin' a whole lot of books when we get back home."

Fate nodded, not wanting to tell her that all the books back at Fables had turned to dust. It seemed a lifetime since that brief visit back to the family bookstore. So much had happened since then and she had a hard time recalling who she'd been before she entered the *Book of Fables*. If all went well, she'd be going home. But she doubted she would ever fit back into her old life. Finn had left an aching hole in her chest, plus she'd seen and done unthinkable things. Yet as changed as she was, there was still something at her core that remained unchanged and that enduring part yearned to see her father. She needed to go home, make sure all was well with Eustace, spend a little time driving Oz crazy with the laser pointer and tell her oldest BFF about her unbelievable experience. Jessie 'll be blown away.

But her stay would not be long. She had a promise to keep.

Picking up Gerdie's rock, she scratched out a description of a pen and paper. The time had come to bring an end to this long, arduous journey and create a new beginning, not just for Sithias, but also for her and Gerdie. A strange sense of peace came over her as she began to write by the light of the moon. The words came effortlessly. They seemed to flow into her from somewhere else. She trusted them, they felt right.

Done at last, she looked up from the page. "Do you remember how the story began?"

Gerdie bobbed her head.

"I decided to start with Sithias finding Torrin with the sea nymph, rather than one of Elsina's owls, as it's told in the fable," she explained. "That way, it'll line up with what's already happened." Her gaze drifted to the smooth, glossy water, so calm now after Poseidon's storm. She couldn't help wondering why she'd never been able to tap into this feeling of certainty before. If she had, she would've saved everyone so much trouble. Especially Finn. Her insides withered with sadness and remorse as she thought about him entombed within the oak.

"You sure?" Gerdie asked, her brown eyes round with concern. "My brain's kinda twistin' up around it already."

Swallowing back the heartache, Fate forced a smile. "I may be unfamiliar with this feeling, but yes, I'm sure." Smoothing out the paper, she cleared her throat and began reading: *"Sithias discovered Torrin with the sea nymph. He chose not to tell Elsina that the sea nymph had turned the willing Torrin into a merman and that the two lovers had left. Sithias could not bear to break Elsina's heart with the truth, for the snake loved the sorceress more than anything. Using a powerful glamour, he transformed himself into Torrin and returned to the palace.*

"Elsina's happiness grew in leaps and bounds, for Torrin seemed

changed. He returned her love with the same fervor as her own, and for a time all was well. But Sithias began to grow disheartened, for he was living a lie, and his mistress loved Torrin, not him. His only hope was to become real, to be made into the flesh-and-bone-man he knew he was capable of being.

To do this, he called upon Fate, who had the power to make her written words become real by reading them aloud. He asked her to grant him his deepest wish, which was to shed the skin of the amber-eyed, winged snake and become the man he knew he was deep down inside. Fate spoke his wish into the air, and also endowed him with the power of the Words of Making and the ability to shape-shift. When Elsina saw who Sithias truly was, the sorceress recognized him as the true love and life-long companion she had always yearned for. And so, Elsina and Sithias lived happily ever after."

Breathing a sigh of satisfaction, Fate folded up the note and tucked it behind her belt. "So what do you think? Pretty romantic, huh?"

Gerdie nodded with an uneasy smile.

"What? You don't think it'll work?"

"No, I'm sure it will—for Elsina and Sithias—but what about us? I mean…there's no mention of us goin' home."

"Don't worry about that. What goes good for Sithias goes good for us."

"If you say so."

But after more than an hour ticked by, a thread of doubt worked loose and Fate began to worry. What made her think she could suddenly rewrite a fable without it backfiring like before? What horrible price would one of them have to pay this time? "Maybe I should swing over to the palace and see what's going on," she said, trying to sound like she'd already planned a flyby as her next step.

Gerdie's lips pressed together dubiously. "Do you really think that's smart?"

"What choice do I—"

The sound of the heavy deadbolt sliding to unlock the rusty door of their cell had them both scrambling back into prisoner mode. Gerdie barely had time to lock Fate back into her shackles and dive under the blankets before the door swung open to reveal Hatho and two of his soldier hawks standing outside.

After removing the irons, Hatho's two soldiers gripped her by each arm and launched into the air. As they carried her toward the palace, her thoughts raced with questions—fear and hope vying for dominance. Was she being taken to her doom or was she being freed?

They rose over the cliffs, flying over an elegant courtyard. Curiosity got the best of her when she spied a variety of odd creatures with disturbingly human features strolling the moonlit grounds. Sithias hadn't exaggerated when he'd said Elsina went wing-happy designing her peculiar collection of citizens. If the animals didn't already fly naturally, they were equipped with wings of either bird or insect so they could.

As they left the distracting sights behind and climbed high toward one of the towers, she wondered again what she was about to face. Her pulse raced as they landed on a huge balcony lined with billowing curtains.

Signaling his soldiers to watch her, Hatho disappeared behind the filmy fabric.

Craning her neck to see through the drapes as they moved in the breeze, she caught a glimpse of ornate carpets, satin pillows, bowls of fruit and a bored, sleepy-looking stork in satin pajamas waving a large palm frond. A shadow darkened the translucent material, blocking her view entirely.

Hatho stuck his head out and signaled for her to enter.

The sweet, spicy fragrance of exotic oils wafted in the air as she passed through the silken layers. Two figures stood a fair distance away toward the end of the balcony, one of which was

Elsina. Her long ebony hair hung to her bare ankles and she was dressed in a red satin robe hanging loosely around her shoulders. But it was the man at her side who had Fate's attention.

Her hopes crashed. Somehow she'd screwed up again.

This guy was much taller than Sithias had ever been in human form, and much more muscular in a lean, athletic way. A large pair of tawny, white-flecked feathery wings flanked his strong arms and he was dressed in tan leather breeches, but little else. All she could see of his turned face was a Roman nose and square jaw. His hair was braided into one long rope down his back and the color was the same as his wings—golden brown with streaks of white. Whoever this statuesque specimen was, he definitely wasn't her good friend, or even Torrin. But one thing was clear. They were deeply in love.

Seeing the blissful couple further magnified the eternal ache of missing Finn and leaving him behind. They might as well have been posing for the cover of a romance novel and she resented them for it.

Smiling up at her lover like a contented cat, Elsina whispered something in his ear. As the man reluctantly tore himself away, the sorceress let her head roll toward Fate. The second their eyes met, Elsina's expression turned glacial.

Gulping, Fate glanced away from her frosty stare. With the moon at his back, all she could see of the man was the dark cut of his athletic physique as he strolled across the length of the vast balcony toward her. When his features came into full view, she recognized a familiar grin spreading over his handsome face and the twinkling amber eyes she'd come to know so well.

"Sithias," she said, hugely relieved. "It *is* you. But you look so—"

"Handsssome? Dare I sssay sssexy, even?" he said without meaning to be flirtatious.

"Yeah," Fate admitted, heat flushing her cheeks. But she

already missed the gangly, awkward Sithias she'd grown so fond of when he wasn't in snake form.

"I know, I can hardly believe it myssself. Sssomething magical jussst happened a little more than an hour ago. I was ssstill pretending to be Torrin, but I couldn't bear to keep up the lie any longer, ssso I took off the glamour to reveal myssself to her." He paused, letting the words hang in the air as the memory of it overwhelmed him.

"And?" she urged, anxious to hear the rest.

"Well, when I removed the glamour, thisss gorgeousss body appeared. Not the sssnake, not the ssskinny fool who kept tripping over hisss own feet, but *thisss.*" He held out his arms and made a proud twirl, which looked pretty silly in his chiseled form.

Glad to see the Sithias she knew and loved, Fate smiled. "This settles it. You're way too marvelous to be seen with me anymore."

"Never!"

"I take it you and Elsina are happy?"

"*Ecssstatic*. Though she wasss a bit…furiousss at firssst—an underssstatement at bessst. But only for a moment." His eyes grew wide with remembered fear. "And what an eternally *long* and terrifying moment it wasss." He shook his head to release the memory. "Isss thisss your doing?"

She took out the story she'd written and handed it to him. "Yup, and if all goes as intended, you're now a shape-shifting sorcerer with the power of the Words of Making."

His eyes widened in fright. "The Wordsss of Making? I don't know if that'sss sssuch a good idea."

"I trust you'll use them more wisely than I did."

"I don't know," he said, still looking uncertain. "Is it even possssible to grant me that power?"

She shrugged. "I'm not sure. You'll have to test it out later.

I don't see why it wouldn't though. I gave Finn the ability to fly." Her chest tightened. Just saying his name hurt.

He sighed. "Whatever did I do to dessserve sssuch icing on the cake?"

"Well, I figured if I didn't make you Elsina's equal, she'd trample all over you."

"Oh, she wouldn't do that. But thank you, misss," he said, his voice husky with emotion.

"Sithias, my pet, I'm waiting," Elsina cooed, her voice raised so she could be heard from the other end of the balcony. The impatience in her tone was obvious to all but Sithias.

"I'm sssaying goodbye now, my love," he called back.

Fate elbowed him. "See what I mean?"

His eyes had glazed over as he stared at the sorceress and she could tell he wasn't listening.

"We should hurry," he said, suddenly coming out of it and herding her hastily through a set of French doors into a sumptuous bedchamber dressed in gold brocade with woven tapestries hanging from the walls displaying embraced lovers. The room glowed with candlelight and the heady scent of burning incense hung in the air. Sudden stabs of envy made Fate slow down and stop. The room screamed love and passion—another painful reminder of what she'd lost.

He leaned forward with concern. "What isss it? You look posssitively green around the gillsss."

"I'm fine," she snapped. Catching the wounded look in his eyes, she felt instantly bad. "Sorry, I—"

"No need to explain. I know how much you're hurting."

"In all kinds of horrible ways." She tried to smile. "Is there a reason for this torture?"

"Elsina'sss been keeping the *Book of Fablesss* in here."

"Oh," she said, now looking past the room's romantic trappings. The giant book was off to one side leaning against the wall. Her heart raced with a chaotic beat as she walked over to it and tugged at the cover. The book remained firmly closed. She was completely baffled. Elsina was happy and in love, no longer the lonely sorceress. So why wasn't it opening? Out of habit, she turned to ask Gerdie if there could be some other reason before remembering she'd been left in the cell. "You need to go get Gerdie. She hid from Hatho and his goons when they came to get me."

"Oh, quite right," Sithias said, rushing out of the room and closing the doors behind him.

While waiting for him to return, her gaze rested on the *Book of Fables*. The forces within the book had thrown so many hidden and unforeseeable dangers in her path. Now it refused entry. Not surprising really. The only predictable thing about the book was that it was unpredictable.

She could easily curse the day she'd laid eyes on it, but not if that meant giving up a single moment with Sithias, Gerdie and most of all, Finn. Their adventures together, even the most horrific, had taught her so much about herself. She could've done without having her weaknesses and greatest failings made known, but she'd also discovered strengths she never could've imagined. Strengths that would help her blaze a fiery trail back to Finn.

Sithias burst through the door with Gerdie. "I've got sssome explaining to do," he whispered worriedly. "They're all wondering how she sssurvived that fall."

"You'll figure out something to tell them," Fate said before turning to Gerdie. "The book's still locked."

Gerdie shrugged, then glanced at Elsina who was pacing and looking unhappy. "Maybe the lovers are gonna become enemies."

Sithias stomped his foot. "Hey! Thisss isss true love."

"I'm sure it is," Fate assured him. "But if we really do have our happy ending, how come it's not opening?"

He ran over to a small desk and withdrew a roll of parchment from the drawer. "Here," he said, placing the paper next to the quill and inkwell on the tabletop. "Tell it to open with your Wordsss of Making."

"Could it be that simple?" Fate asked.

"We can only hope," he said, his eyes darting nervously to Elsina.

Fate leaned over the desk and penned a short passage.

"Good," he said, beads of sweat gleaming on his forehead.

His growing nervousness made her uneasy. "This isn't some kind of trick to get me to open the book, is it? Not by you, but by *her.*"

"No worriesss there, misss. Before I asssked for your releassse, I warned her if we go roaming through the book we'd have to bring about sssome horrible endingsss now that it'sss filled with happy onesss—thanksss to our hard work. My mistresss may be...prickly at timesss, but she'sss a romantic at heart and lovesss a good ending—which I am quite confident she now hasss. In fact, that'sss the very reassson she'sss willing to allow you to leave. As you well know, there's not enough room on thisss island for two willful and powerful women."

Surprised to be put in the same highly regarded category as Elsina, Fate blushed. "I see."

His eyes grew sad and misty. "Well, here we are." He sighed, his shoulders slumping. "Oh dear, I truly detessst goodbyesss."

Swallowing back the painful lump forming in her throat, she smiled sadly. "Me too." The thought of losing Sithias in addition to Finn, was more than she could bear. She lurched forward, wrapping her arms around his neck.

Giving her a squeeze, he held her for a brief moment. When he let go, his eyes brimmed with tears.

She choked back a sob. "I'll miss you, Sithias."

"And I you, misss."

Elsina positioned herself so Fate could see her past his shoulder. Possessiveness twisted her flawless features. Wiping at the tears, Fate averted her gaze and lowered her voice. "You'd better get back to your girlfriend. We'll take it from here."

Gulping with fear, he glanced back at the sorceress. "Yesss, I'd bessst do jussst that."

"Don't forget how amazing you are," she reminded him. "You've got it all now. Especially if you have the powers I gave you."

He beamed with humble pride as Gerdie stepped up, her small hand extended to shake his. "Bye, Sithias."

Taking her hand, he kneeled down and smiled. "Goodbye, Gerdie. It'sss been…interesssting," he said with a wink.

"Sure has," she said as he made a hasty retreat back to Elsina, her arms crossed and a cold shoulder pointed at him.

As Hatho stepped forward to close the doors, Fate waved at the hawk. "So long, Big Bird. It's been like a party around here, only without the fun." The doors shut without a word, leaving them alone in the bedchamber.

Gerdie slipped her hand in Fate's. "You ready to face Brune?"

Smoldering resentment flared hot in her gut as she touched the Rod of Aeternitis resting beneath Finn's ribbon. Fuming, she nodded, glaring into space. "The first thing I'm going to do is dangle the Rod in front of Brunhilda's warty nose and make the witch think she'll get it back *if* she takes me into the Keep and helps me find something powerful enough to free Finn, and locate a gateway to Oldwilde. But I'll *never* let her have it. I'm going to make her feel what it's like to have someone else have all the control and hold back what she most desires."

"Are you done?" Gerdie said, blinking up at her, seemingly unimpressed by her tirade.

"Well, that's just for starters."

Gerdie shook her head, her cloud of singed curls waving softly. "You can't go chargin' in all hot-headed. Remember, Brune spelled you. More than likely, she still has you under her spell. Could be all she's gotta do is snap her fingers to get you to hand the Rod over."

Fate's anger flatlined.

"No need to pull a face."

"What do we do?"

"You let me handle Brune. I've been plannin' for this day ever since I knew I was goin' home."

"Are you going to let me in on this grand plan?"

"Nope. The less you know up front the better," Gerdie said, smiling sweetly and giving her hand a squeeze.

"Okay," Fate replied, feeling a little deflated. "I had this whole ra-ra speech prepared, but I guess we can just get to the leaving instead."

"Go ahead. I'd like to hear it."

"No, the moment's kind of passed."

Gerdie gave her a worried look. "You're not losin' your guts are ya?"

"No, I've got guts. I'm all kinds of gutsy," Fate said, straightening her shoulders to hide her growing nervousness for what lay ahead. She was about to confront the person responsible for basically chucking her into shark-infested waters without a single care. It didn't sit well with her that this evil great-aunt might still have power over her. Fate had thought the days of being a victim were well behind her.

Burning up with frustration, she clenched her fist around the parchment. She was done being knocked around on the winds like a kite without a tether. Not only had she survived running this gauntlet of hell, she'd come out the other end a warrior capable of kicking some serious ass. "Let's do this."

Unwrinkling the parchment, she held it out in front of her, reading, *"I have turned all eight fables into their mirror opposites. The Book of Fables can no longer hold me. The lock must open and return Gerdie and I to where we came from."*

A loud metallic click sounded within the lock and the *Book of Fables* swung wide open. A huge shadow stretched across the room, engulfing them in darkness. Holding onto Gerdie, Fate hurtled through the black toward a pinprick of light growing larger by the second. Glimpsing the dim interior of the bookstore, she felt torn from Finn all over again. There was no way to know if she was leaving him behind forever. But the time for second-guessing had passed. She had to believe the path leading away would somehow take her back to Finn.

EPILOGUE

"THE FOREST OF INNITH TINE IS RESTORED… your debt is fulfilled… you are free to walk the Earth once more,"* a voice rumbled from deep below the colossal oak.

At the core of the tree's massive trunk, where all was dark and peaceful, the promise of freedom unearthed hope and expectancy. A face materialized like a half-remembered dream, kindling sparks of human emotions, forgotten and put aside. Cinnamon-brown eyes gazed back with a look of longing, igniting those sparks into flames of desire that scorched away the Earthmind, revealing a former existence.

The groan of cracking timber resounded as living wood peeled away from the body interred within the trunk. Hindered blood-flow burst into compressed veins, tissue and muscle. Limbs quivered with prickling pain. As the narrow slit curled back, light pierced the snug darkness and air blasted through the opening. Sheltered eyes watered and skin shivered with revived feeling. Stiff joints struggled to move, pushing with tremendous effort from the quiet warmth out into the harsh elements. Sunlight burned and sounds cut deep.

A tidal wave of memories slammed in with the crushing weight of the world. Ferocious currents of anger, fear and guilt bashed him about, forcing him to relive the sins of his past. When at last the punishing undertow ceased, he floated weightless to the surface, caressed by a stream of blissful recollections —of Fate. The mere thought of her sent a surge of strength throughout his body.

Rising to his feet, Finn gazed out over the sweeping forest of oaks and smiled with satisfaction at the island's renewed majesty. Breathing in the fresh sea air, he could clearly see he was no longer needed here. Free to move on, every part of him hungered to reunite with Fate, to hold her close and kiss her without a single thread of fear. But where was she? He couldn't feel her on the island.

Closing his eyes, he probed farther out, skimming across azure oceans, over snowy mountain peaks, golden deserts and lush forests, questing for her spirit's dazzling red-gold flame.

It seemed as if he stood there for an eternity, searching every corner of the world, his heart growing heavier with every passing moment. Then he felt it—stretching endlessly in all directions—a barrier of sentient fire hissing with powerful magic meant to destroy whatever ventured too close.

Fate was on the other side.

Finn's eyes flashed open and his jaw tightened as he stared at the distant horizon. "Not to worry, love," he said under his breath. "We'll find each other, come hell or high water. After all, it's what we've grown used to."

READ THE FIRST CHAPTER OF

Book 2 of Her Dark Destiny

FATE'S KEEP

T. RAE MITCHELL

I

BACK TO THE BEGINNING

FATE FLOYD TUMBLED THROUGH space toward a world in which she no longer belonged. A dull, ordinary place, where most everyone craved make-believe and magic, because without it, reality was too dreary to face. She used to be one of those addicted daydreamers.

Not anymore.

She'd since found out magic was real, and there was nothing pink and sparkly about it. Magic was scary and far deadlier than she could've ever imagined.

Yet she would've stayed in that dangerous realm, risking her life, over and over, if she thought it would help Finn. She closed her eyes against the sudden tears and sharp pang in her chest. Leaving him behind inside the *Book of Fables* had left a hole where her heart used to be.

The second she opened her eyes, the hardwood floor of the bookstore filled her vision and slammed into her shoulder. Pain drilled down her arm as she rolled with the momentum of the fall and slid to a stop. She was almost grateful for the pain, because all thoughts of Finn vanished…at least for a moment.

Rising on an elbow, she searched the dim interior for Gerdie. They'd been holding hands only seconds ago. Instead, her gaze landed on the *Book of Fables*. The ten-foot-tall book, which had just spit her out like some giant who didn't care for how she tasted.

She could hardly believe she was back. The massive tome was closed and leaning against the brick wall of the deserted bookstore where she'd originally found it, in what seemed like eons ago. She'd been so clueless then, thinking the book was just a big sign that once hung on the outside of Fables Bookstore. Nothing could have been further from the truth. Giant chroniclers had created the *Book of Fables* to preserve a record of ancient magic within its yellowed pages in the form of eight horribly unfortunate fairy tales, each of which she'd had the great displeasure of experiencing up close and personal.

Fate started to stand, when a blow from behind flattened her to the floor, knocking the air from her lungs.

"Sorry," Gerdie muttered from where she'd landed on Fate's back. "But thanks for the soft landin' all the same."

"Glad I could be of service," Fate groaned, though relieved to have her small companion back.

Gerdie jumped off. She blew a frizzy, fawn-colored strand of hair out of her brown eyes. A serious expression hardened her elfin features as she took in her surroundings.

As Fate sucked in a lungful of air, a horrendous stench caught in her throat. Gagging, she covered her nose while searching for the offending odor. She was surprised to find her grandmother's old bookstore exactly as she'd left it. Dark, decrepit and lit with a feeble fire burning in a metal wastebasket.

She'd been gone such a long time, yet she was certain this was the same fire Finn had lit the night they first met. She could almost see him kneeling there, the flames lighting the dark gold of his hair, the sweet curve of his mouth and smiling, leaf-green eyes. Tears welled up again as she reached out to the flickering light. Was it possible she'd somehow gone back in time to when he was there?

She was about to call his name when the next inhale assaulted her nose, pushing her to face the awful truth. She'd been forced to leave Finn behind in the last fable and no amount of wishing for some time-twisting miracle was going to change the dismal reality that he'd traded his own freedom to save her from being imprisoned inside a giant oak.

The cloying, sickly smell was thick now. Bile burned at the back of Fate's throat as she peered at her shadowy surroundings. The hair on the back of her neck rose. Someone was sitting in one of the wing-backed chairs of the reading corner. The person sat still. Unnaturally so. Fate's skin crawled as she stared at the figure. The moment she registered what she was looking at, she scrabbled back on all fours until she banged into the giant book. "Is that what I think it is?"

Gerdie hadn't moved. "Yup. Looks like a pruned-up carcass to me." Stepping closer to the seated corpse, she poked its arm. "I take that back. It's still juicy."

Fate jumped to her feet. "What are you doing? Hasn't anyone told you not to play with dead things?"

"I'm no stranger to dealin' with the dead. Pretty much comes with the territory, when you've been livin' near an evil old hag who's eatin' babies for breakfast, lunch and supper."

There wasn't much Fate could say to that. Gerdie had managed to stay out of Old Mother Grim's clutches all by herself, for what may have been centuries before they'd met. It was still easy to forget Gerdie wasn't a child. The six-year-old had been suspended in time the moment her black-hearted sister, Brune, had abandoned her inside the *Book of Fables*.

Brune was responsible for throwing Fate into the cursed book as well. Worse yet, she and Brune were related. Fate's grandmother, Gerdie and Brune were all sisters. Fate was happy to have Gerdie as her great-aunt, but she hated sharing Brune's bad blood.

Covering her nose with her sleeve, Gerdie leaned closer to the dead body, staring at the necklace hanging around the shriveled gray neck. "Just like I thought," she muttered. "It's Brune."

"Really? How can you be sure?"

"She's wearin' the Orb of Aeternitis."

Unwilling to move any closer, Fate strained to see through the gloom to get a better look at the Orb. The whole reason Brune had forced Fate into the *Book of Fables* had been to find and retrieve the Orb's counterpart, the Rod of Aeternitis. From what little she understood, combining the two powerful pieces grants the owner godlike powers. With that kind of power she could free Finn with a mere thought and save him from an eternity of suffering.

Fate reached for the slim gold bar resting against her breastbone. The chain holding the pendant was cold, but the Rod was warm and vibrating, calling out to the Orb. She took an uneasy step forward. She'd paid a terrible price to get the Rod and her hands would be stained with blood forever because of it

Gerdie glanced back at Fate. "How lucky are we? And here I thought I'd have to duke it out with Brune to get the Orb."

"Yeah, dandy. How about I leave you to the grave robbing?" Fate had seen her fill of rotting corpses one too many times inside the *Book of Fables*.

Gerdie tugged on the Orb, tipping Brune's corpse forward. She shoved it back and gave the necklace a harder tug. Fate shuddered as the head lolled to one side with a bone-cracking sound and dangled at a disturbing angle. Undaunted by the grisly interaction, Gerdie gave the necklace another solid yank to break the chain, when a bony hand shot out and grabbed the girl's wrist.

Gerdie and Fate both screamed.

Brune pulled Gerdie close to her mummified face. They were practically nose to nose. "You really think it'll be that easy to take what's mine?" Brune's voice was a wet rattle. The smell had to be atrocious, because Gerdie convulsed with nausea.

Gerdie wrestled free and ran over to Fate. "She's alive!"

"It's not a she," Fate argued. "That's what you call a zombie. And FYI, they eat brains."

Fate reached instinctively for one of the daggers she was used to having strapped on her thigh. There was nothing there. "Damn, I forgot to get my gear back," she grumbled. She'd been relieved of her sword, dagger and crossbow when an army of soldier hawks had captured her and Gerdie. They'd been allowed to leave in the end, so why hadn't she asked for her weapons back?

Stupid.

Brune remained seated while she swung the Orb on its long chain in wide circles. Golden tracers began to build into a solid band of light with every swing.

Gerdie dug her hand in the pocket of her dress, pulled out a little ball of dark red wax and aimed her clenched fist at Brune. "*Avra Kedavra*, Brune!"

"Whoa, whoa, whoa," Fate interjected, worriedly. "That sounds an awful lot like the Killing Curse. But just so you know, that's fiction. Fantastic fiction, but fiction nonetheless."

Gerdie frowned at her. "Don't know what you're goin' on about, but you need to stop interruptin' and make yourself useful." She shoved a cloth bag full of dried, ground herbs into Fate's hand. "Pour this all the way around her. And do it fast!"

Holding her breath, Fate raced over with the pouch, hastily sprinkling the herbs.

"I cast this circle and bind you, Brune!" Gerdie commanded, though her voice quavered. "*Avra Kedavra. Avra Kedavra. Avra Kedavra.*"

Fate finished laying down the circle and ran back to Gerdie, encouraged by the dying gasps and croaks coming from Brune. Fate undid the clasp of her own necklace and swung the Rod in plain sight. She'd been looking forward to this moment for a long time. "I've got the Rod, Brune. But guess what?

I'm keeping it! How do you like them apples? Look who's in control now."

Brune's body shuddered as she continued to swing the Orb round and round, its light now sweeping out in concentric circles, rippling further and further out, expanding toward Fate and Gerdie. Fate's blood ran cold with the realization that Brune was shaking with fits of laughter. And they weren't dying gasps. They were raspy cackles.

Before Fate could ask Gerdie why the counter spell wasn't working, her mouth filled with a coppery taste. The air turned hot, stinging her skin, scorching her lungs. An explosion of molten sparks penetrated deep inside, searing tissue and cells, pulling her muscles so tight she couldn't move.

Fate knew this fiery pain. She'd experienced it before. The constricting pain, combined with the stench of Brune's rotting flesh, had been her last memories before waking inside the *Book of Fables*.

"Bring me the Rod," Brune croaked.

An invisible force seized Fate. Spasms of pain shot through her muscles, forcing her limbs into action. Tears blurred her vision as her body marched of its own accord across the room. Fate fought and resisted from within, but no amount of will power could stop her legs from carrying her forward with the Rod held out to Brune like a gift. All that was missing was a silver platter.

This concludes the
first chapter preview of

Fate's Keep

Read more by T. Rae Mitchell for FREE!

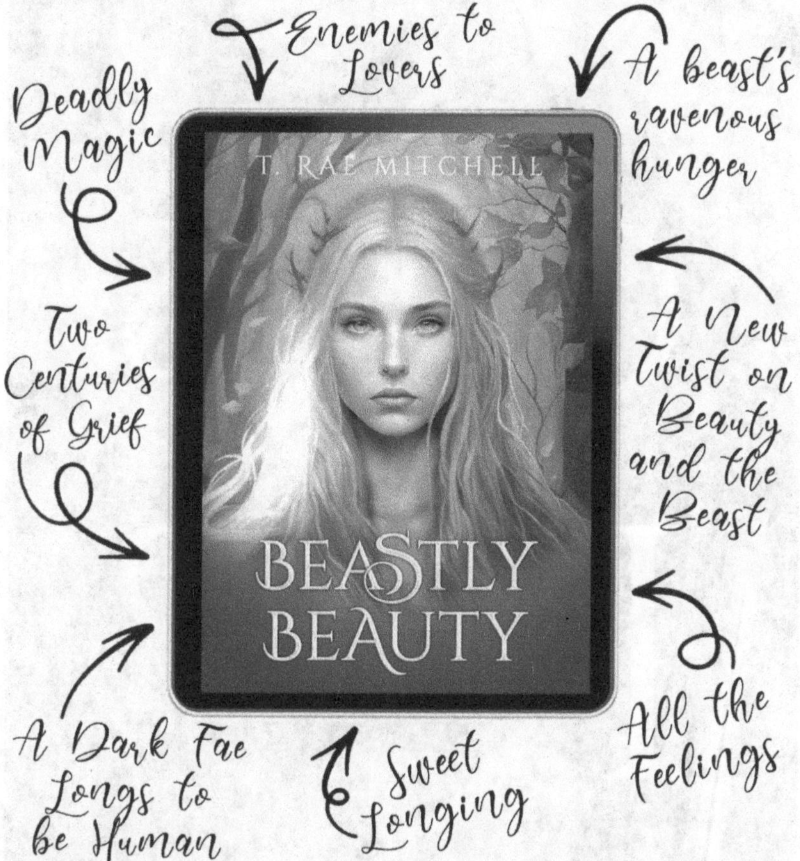

Visit www.traemitchell.com/signup

Turn the page to read the Bonus Prequel
CHAOS IN THE KEEP

Hidden in the deepest of space, the darkest of magic is caged within a place called the Keep. When the Keep Guardian makes a mistake that could unleash chaos through-out the universe, she's forced to find her successor, who just happens to be Fate Floyd.

CHAOS IN THE KEEP

T. RAE MITCHELL

Every great mistake has a halfway moment,
a split second when it can be recalled
and perhaps remedied.

~ Pearl S. Buck ~

SUCH A SMALL MISTAKE

THE LIGHT WAS FADING FAST. Start of sunset was when she always left, and she was well past that. The rules were clear: *Never* remain inside the Keep during twilight when gateways unlock.

Nevertheless, Brune landed in front of a massive stone arch, smashed on one side. She flicked off the ignition, silencing the whirring wings of her aeronaut pack. Kneeling down to read the Old Norse runes surrounding the empty indentation beneath the archway, a quick glance told her the immense and immovable hammer of Thor had sat there for untold ages. There could be only one explanation for its disappearance. Another scavenger.

Anger burned hot in her chest. A weapon that used to level mountains had become spare parts for a walking scrapheap. "What a waste," she fumed.

Generally, scavengers were easily dealt with. They were really nothing more than hairballs coughed up by the Keep whenever there was too much magic congesting the pipes. Scavs were more pests than anything else. Voracious eaters of whatever element they first came in contact with. The last one had been a small, porcupine-shaped creature made of crystal, seemingly harmless until it laser-beamed her in the ankle. Stomping it under her boot and disintegrating it with her pistol had taken care of that. Though judging from the damage this new scavenger had already caused, dining on Thor's hammer had given it a scary amount of strength.

Uneasiness squirmed in the pit of her stomach as she looked up at the dwindling light. Tangerine hues bled across the blue expanse of the Keep's artificial atmosphere. The revolving hoops of the titanic armillary sphere sweeping round and round high overhead, grazed the firmament with crackling golden tracers. The only sign of the force field protecting life and precious cargo against the exposure of deep space. The cargo being countless vaults, each of which held something far too powerful and dangerous for ordinary realms. The very reason the enormous storehouse had been chucked to the ass-end of the universe. But to Brune, the Keep was more of an enclosed city, like a snow globe wrapped around a tiny jewel of a metropolis.

Where the sky had deepened to indigo, she could just make out the sickly green and clotted red of the Hades Nebula and the smoldering, molten surface of the planet, Titus, looming large against the glittering backdrop of distant stars. She had forty minutes before total night descended, but only fifteen before twilight.

She lowered her gaze, briefly registering a pearlescent cathedral and copper pyramid rising into view beside where she stood under the broken arch. Miles of architectural wonders stretched out on all sides—new from one day to the next—the landscape always in constant motion. An ancient, magically infused technology powered the complex system of underground cogs and wheels with clockwork precision. Each unique structure slid into view, while others returned into the Keep's mysterious depths in completion of a century long cycle. It still boggled her mind as to why this design of perfect orderliness would have a flaw that could bring about its own destruction.

Tension knotted her shoulders as she teetered on the edge of indecision. Her instincts urged her to get out, but her devotion to the Keep made her stay. A scavenger, possibly more dangerous than any she'd encountered before, was loose. She couldn't just allow it free rein for the next hour to devour other priceless instruments of magic *and* grow even more powerful. Not to mention, if it damaged even a single gateway during the gloaming, all hell would break loose.

Her job as Guardian was to prevent that from happening at all costs.

"Damn the rules," she said, sliding back the compass ring on the navigation watch strapped to her left wrist. She set the timer for twelve minutes, allowing three minutes to get to the breaching door of the sanctuary. As the bronze ring snicked back over the clock face, the ticking began, loud and urgent. The marks measuring the seconds lit up a bright red path that was already building fast.

Tugging her goggles down over her eyes, the amber tint of crystal lenses turned her world a dark gold. She dialed back the controls, bracing for the nausea-inducing sensation of her retinas adjusting to high frequency particle emissions. As the initial queasiness subsided, feathery streaks of blue vapor revealed the scavenger's telltale path.

Brune sprinted after the vaporous tracks past a gilded chapel. The elaborate Byzantine-style structure sank steadily into the subsurface, a jade mausoleum advancing in its place. With everything in perpetual motion, she feared the scavenger's tracks might've shifted too much from where they originated. She jumped onto a moving walkway, maintaining the same rapid pace. As it snaked to the right and rounded a sprawling panel of silver filigree, the vaporous trail thickened. She was close.

Skidding to a stop, she scanned for any movement out of sync with the rhythmic motion of her surroundings. The clock ticked. The red path lengthened. Only nine minutes left.

She continued on, forcing herself to slow down, to move cautiously along the winding walkway. A crepuscular blue glimmer emanated from behind a massive glass clock tower. Easing down behind the low wall bordering the walkway, she fixed her gaze on the tower's base, refocusing the lenses of her goggles. Visibility sharpened, cutting through the structure's multilayered glass cogs and wheels until she saw it on the other side.

"Gotcha," she muttered, flipping another set of lenses down over her goggles. The magnified view tightened in on a hulking shape of twisted metal shrouded in a dense blue haze. Slowly, she gripped the handle of her disintegrator pistol, pulling it from the holster.

The walkway circled the other side of the clock tower, moving her into the scavenger's corrosive cloud. The stench of crude magic always burned her nostrils and made her eyes water. But the result was further intensified when used to animate metal, especially iron, which this one was seeking out and consuming.

The seconds ticked incessantly, pushing her nerves to the edge. Six minutes left.

Realizing her jaw ached from locking her teeth, she unclenched and sucked in a shaky breath. Fear sat on her shoulder like a vulture, ready to swoop in and pick her clean of courage.

Pushing off the goggles, she brought her target into the cross hairs of the pistol's scope. The air was growing more caustic the closer she got, making it hard to see. Wiping her eyes, she screwed up her face. "Lousy scavs."

She saw its misshapen head jerk up and around. Adrenaline shot up her spine. This one had excellent hearing. It's eyes flamed ice blue and fixed on her. Then it lunged, its blade-like claws grappling the tower and breaking glass. Shards rained down over the bronze steps encircling the structure. Wincing from the damage it wreaked, she kept her pistol aimed.

"Come on…a little closer."

As if in answer, the scavenger leaped from the tower and shot toward her.

"No…no, too close." She reared back in a panic, pulling the trigger too soon.

The pistol kicked hard in her hand, emitting a gaseous red cloud. Had she held her aim, the gas would've engulfed the creature. Most of it missed, hitting only its legs. The particles went to work fast, oxidizing metal limbs into crumbling rust. An angry shriek resounded throughout the Keep as the creature spun out of control. Before hitting the ground, the twisted metal in its back reshaped into razor-sharp wings. The scavenger righted its fall with surprising agility, swept up and circled overhead, its gleaming eyes fastened on her.

With shaking, sweating hands, she removed the pistol's purged canister. Feeling for a new charge, she pulled it from her belt. The ticking counted down, drawing her gaze to the watch face. Two minutes left. Perspiration dripped in her eyes as she fumbled with the cartridge.

The scavenger plunged. It was on her just as she loaded the next charge.

The hot slice of its claw drove into her shoulder, sending her hurtling through the air, the pain excruciating. Fighting to stay conscious, she lifted the pistol with her good arm and pulled the trigger. The shot reverberated through her, ringing in her ears. Red gas filled her vision as a cloud of rust choked her lungs, a sure sign she'd hit the mark.

Then she heard the scavenger's shriek and realized she'd failed.

She crashed to the ground, the air slamming from her lungs. Pain exploded throughout her body. Her head swam as impending darkness pressed in.

The timer rang, a clamorous sound in her muddled mind. She had three minutes to get out. Dull panic badgered her to get up. She tried to move but her body wouldn't respond, the connection to her brain severed as she sank inexorably into a depthless black.

•

Searing jolts burned up her left arm. Brune woke gasping and slapping at her wrist where the prongs from the watch dug into skin, shocking her with short bursts of electricity. Pressing the button, she shut down the alarm's built-in safety mechanism—designed to initiate if the timer wasn't turned off after the first ring of the alarm. Why had she set it?

Disoriented, she squinted at the watch, trying to remember past the last minute. Her vision was blurred, her head thick. Struggling to sit up, she cried out from a knifing pain in her shoulder. She unbuckled the aeronaut pack, putting her hand over the open, throbbing wound. Blood gushed between her fingers.

Nauseating fear welled up inside her. What had happened? Eerie, unfamiliar sounds echoed all around her, sending cold shivers up the back of her neck. She gulped, realizing she sat in darkness beneath a pale-lit sky. Twilight was upon her. She grabbed for her pistol, only to find the holster empty.

Then it all came back to her. She had shot the scavenger and missed.

Clicking on her light ring, she pointed her fist, shining its radiant beam over the floor. Her pistol was nowhere to be seen.

Her first thought was that the scavenger had devoured it. But if that were the case, she would've found the wooden grip and its empty cartridge with traces of deducting fluid left inside. No, this scavenger somehow had the foresight to take the pistol before it flew off to restore itself—a worrisome notion in and of itself, but something else bothered her more.

Why had it left her alive?

Brune rose to her feet with difficulty. A deep, bone-weary fatigue nearly overwhelmed her again. She'd never experienced such weakness before. This was just a stab wound. She'd been through worse than this before.

A dreadful fear reared its ugly head, a demon she'd thought she'd conquered long ago. Her mind shrank from it.

"Focus," she said, brushing the fulvous dust from her clothes.

She checked her punctured shoulder. Pus and far too much blood had soaked into her tank top and canvas corset. She was almost relieved by the sight. Blood loss would account for the fuzzy thinking and severe drag. Pulling her leather skirt aside, she tore a strip of cloth from her petticoat and bound it round her shoulder.

That done, she briefly considered pursuing the scavenger, more out of habit than anything else. But her rapidly failing energy decided the matter. She needed to get through the breaching door and patch herself up before she could come back to finish the job.

She turned her attention to inspecting the aeronaut pack. One of the wire dragonfly-shaped wings was bent, but the netting was still intact and the fuel pump and storage cells glowed green with ample energy. She straightened the wing and turned on the ignition. Satisfied it would hold, she cut the motor long enough to gingerly slip the pack onto her back. Searing pain brought stars to her eyes as soon as the strap pressed down on the wound, but she had to keep it on. Walking was out of the question.

She was just about to lift off when her slowed senses registered the sound of rushing water behind her. An archway flanked by gilded Atlantean seahorses had opened to reveal an inner chamber with a pool fed by waterfalls. Now she knew why the scavenger had left her lying where it had dropped her. Water, even in the form of mist, destroyed all iron animated by crude magic.

A shadow moved across the wet tiles of the interior, a human shadow, but the footsteps sounded more like hooves. As the shadow neared the entrance, a magnificent set of horns preceded the bent head of a gazelle, followed by quivering wings of aquamarine. The graceful creature had round liquid eyes promising pure gentleness, yet nothing could be further from the truth. Brune froze when she recognized the creature. A peryton with a human shadow craved one thing only: the taste of human flesh.

Dizzy with terror, she stepped backwards, hoping it hadn't seen her. Then its eyes met hers. Revving the throttle of her aeronaut pack, she launched skyward. After covering a fair distance, she glanced back. The peryton was nowhere in sight. Relief flooded through her. She faced forward and cried out in shock.

The creature had flown with silent swiftness over her head, now charging straight at her. She shot up but not fast enough. Its horns ripped through the flare of her leather skirt, ramming into her shins with bone-shattering pain. She tumbled through the air not knowing up from down, only hearing the beating of its wings. Panic hammered in her heart. She didn't stand a chance if she stayed airborne. In the terrible blur, she spotted a nearby turret. Righting herself, she sped towards it and landed.

The peryton dove from a great height, its soft muzzle gaping with fangs. Shuddering, she unsheathed her sword, probably a useless gesture but it made her feel better. The sword's blade glanced off its back like a butter knife against rock. She swerved to one side to avoid being impaled by its horns. Her weak legs buckling, she hit the wall as hooves clattered over the stone behind her.

Her unreliable legs forced her to take flight again, but not soon enough. A horn caught in her skirt, flipping her directly onto its back. She was stuck, flat on her belly with her legs straddling its muscular neck. Never had she felt so helpless as she struggled to free herself.

A terrifying roar rumbled from below. The peryton gave a violent buck, or so she thought. Something had seized it out from under her. She hovered in place, confused by the sight of huge, flapping bat wings, a serpent coiled around the peryton's body and a lion's jaws crushing its neck. It took several seconds to realize this new beast was one creature, not two.

"Oh God, a Chimera!"

As the lion half of the Chimera gorged on the peryton, the serpent part abandoned the bloody feast, locking eyes with her.

"Note to self," she muttered, "less thinking aloud. And no more skirts."

Jetting in the opposite direction, Brune searched for the breaching door, but her wondrous city was lit with a confusing gleam of open gateways, some shooting out ensorcelled flames, others oozing with glowing plasma or sparking clouds of faery light. More disturbing than any of these were the thick shadow forms made of glinting stardust, which blotted out large sections of the Keep.

At last she saw the breaching door about a mile away. As she flew toward it, a movement from below caused her to drop her speed slightly. A small band of deformed humanoids crept close to the walls. One had the head of a dog and another was more like an upright eel, while most of the others were grotesque distortions of humans, slithering and crawling within the deep shadows.

Revulsion and terror pooled alongside increasing exhaustion. She sped up, hoping the Fomorians hadn't seen her. The last thing she needed was to draw the attention of an ancient race of chaos-makers.

She was about a half-mile from the hatch when she heard the Chimera's roar behind her. She glanced back, only to see the lion's flaming maw less than a hundred yards away. Cranking the motor to full throttle, she weaved between two spires, almost crashing into a bell tower. The beast gave chase, both leaping and flying from one structure to the next, the more fragile ones collapsing under its great weight.

Brune didn't have to look back to know it was gaining on her. She sensed its closeness by the raised hairs on the back of her neck. The escape hatch was only moments away, but she wouldn't get there before she was either incinerated or clawed out of the air. She struggled to think, her instincts clouded by desperation. Years of close calls shouted at her to take cover. So she dove into the shadowy depths, dipping under a wrought-iron bridge before skimming through a series of narrow passageways.

Behind her, the behemoth's angry roar and the shrieking crush of the bridge echoed throughout the expanse. She stayed close to ground level, hoping it would pursue her on foot at a more hindered pace. Looking back, she caught a glimpse of leathery wings fighting the restraint of narrow confines. The head and body were cloaked in darkness except for the glistening scales of the serpent's head and those awful, staring eyes.

Forcing her gaze straight ahead, she ducked into the courtyard of a fortress to buy more time. She passed through the gate, shooting straight up but heard smashing stone as the

Chimera burst through the cramped passage only seconds later. She raced to open the hatch, bashing into the wall as she punched the button. The sliding sound of iron against iron as the door opened like the dilating iris of a camera lens was music to her ears.

"Come on!" she screamed, her heart pounding in her throat.

Growling flames and scorching heat surged at her back as she shot through the opening and tumbled across the floor. As the iris spiraled shut behind her, the Chimera crashed against the solid barrier with a resounding roar that shook the sanctuary's walls.

Choking back the acidic tang of adrenalin flooding her system, Brune lay there like a limp rag. Her body begged to lose consciousness, but rest was the furthest thing from her mind. After seventy-five years of keeping order in the universe, she couldn't believe such a small mistake could very well unleash an eternity of chaos throughout the cosmos.

ONE GAMBLETUNITY

"THIS IS A SOUR QUANDARYMENT you've dropped me into, Brune. What am I to do now that you're defunctional?" said an irritated Farouk.

Cringing at the grating sound of his amplified voice blaring through the transmodulator, she narrowed her eyes at him. He stared back, his whiskered snout poking through the bars of his cage. He had the coloring and features of a fox, large devil-pointed ears, a body resembling a monkey and eyes that glowed with an inner fire suggestive of great mischief.

"Turn that down," she grumbled, "you're hurting my ears." She'd always found his quasi-East Indian accent and outlandish word amalgams amusing, endearing even, but not when he was chastising her at an unbearable pitch. She turned away, unable to face his accusing gaze.

"Where's the rescue kit?" she said as she eased the battered aeronaut pack from her throbbing shoulder and peeled off her fur-lined pilot's cap and goggles. Welcoming the cool air hitting her sweat-drenched hair, she rose on trembling legs and leaned heavily against a large table full of ancient tomes piled around glass vials of bubbling liquid connected by copper tubes dripping into a complex arrangement of brass funnels and reservoirs.

Farouk pulled on a gear, his ears drooping sullenly. Long mechanical crablike legs extended from the bottom, lifting his cage. His arms moved the levers with practiced precision as he steered his noisy transport across the wide sanctuary to a circular wall of bookcases. He ratcheted up the height, pulled a box from the top shelf and blew the dust off. Swinging back around, he placed it on the table and unlatched the lid. Several tiered drawers sprang up, offering their belongings in an orderly fashion.

He reached for a bottle of luminescent gold liquid. "You should have undone your doggenacity. You know well enough that tomorrow comes perpetuously," he said, finally dialing down the volume when she covered her ears and glared at him again.

Dropping her hands she heaved a sigh. He was right, but she wasn't going to admit it out loud. She'd never hear the end of it. Untying her makeshift bandage, she peeled the bloody cloth away from the already putrid wound. Before she could defend her actions, he poured the bottle's contents over the festering flesh, holding his nose as the seeping puncture fizzed and smoked. Pain shot up her arm; she bit down on the back of her fist to keep from crying out, watching as the flesh turned a healthy pink.

Relief set in as the stinging eased. "I would've come back in and waited, but *this* scav likes the taste of iron."

Farouk's eyes widened with alarm.

"That's right, the Keep could come to a grinding halt if it gets into the underpinnings and starts eating away at the gears—"

"Or perforgrates the breaching door," he said, his expression foreboding. "You do know what would happen if the Keep's seal is breaktured?"

"Of course I do." Guilt gnawed at her. "Stop looking at me like that. It's my mistake, and I'll fix it as soon as I get my strength back. There's no way I can go back in the way I'm feeling right now."

"But the scavenger will be doublfied soon, and I know I do not need to mention the mixcellaneous creatures you've already unleashed."

The thought of going back in there in such a worn-out state terrified her. "Listen, if I hadn't been forced to run for my *life*, I would've gotten the scav."

"You were indubitously slower than usual." Farouk's sharp ears flicked toward her like fingers pointing the blame. "There are logicalities for why no human should be present in the Keep during the gloaming—"

"I know," she snapped.

"But you did not heed why humans are such a fascenticement. Mortals have always been the playthings of the old forces, and quite often the *food*."

"Having nearly been the blue-plate special of the day… I think I got that."

"You don't comprestand. You exposed yourself to all levels of magic—crude, raw, dark, refined, wild. It's more than the human body can abssimilate at any given moment."

She stopped breathing a second. Was that why she felt so weak and brittle? "And you're only telling me this now?" she yelled.

He shrugged. "I thought the first rule was enough motivcentive." He gave her a sideways glance filled with distaste. "You are destructalized, Brune. I am seeing it already."

"What are you talking about?"

Farouk's steady gaze burned into her. "The years you've been holding back are surfmerging—and swiftly."

An icy dread crawled over Brune's skin. She rushed over to the mirror ball sitting atop a pile of books. Leaning in, she stared at her convex reflection in horror. Her full lips looked like shriveled rose petals. Fine lines had carved themselves into her smooth skin, while puffy folds crowded her hazel eyes. Her fresh nineteen-year-old face was gone, replaced by a stranger in her forties.

She pushed away from her reflection, unwilling to watch the

inevitable arrival of the ninety-four-year-old crone she'd cleverly evaded for the last seven-and-a-half decades. How was this possible? The Orb of Aeternitis should've protected her. Panicked, she checked to see if the small gold orb was still on the chain around her neck. It was still there.

"The Orb pickled you well these last seventy-five years," Farouk said, picking up on her thoughts, "but it isn't enough to insulguard you against an ill-mixed cocktail of monumantically potent magic."

"Oh, God," she muttered, holding up a lock of long blonde hair swiftly turning to coarse threads of gray.

"You'll get no help from that lofty compartment," Farouk said. "This is no time for hystericalness. You must face this messbacle and find your successor. You need help to restructify the Keep."

As weak as she was, Brune resisted. She would not be replaced. "I can do it myself. All I need is the Rod to reverse this."

He paused, nodding. "Yes, the Rod would completify the Orb. You would be omnivasive. But how will you get it? The same way you pilfaged the Orb?"

A terrible heaviness pressed down on her as she staggered to a chair and sat down. She'd always intended to go back to Oldwilde for the Rod. But the Keep had held too much fascination for her. The artifacts in the vaults were only part of its allure. The sanctuary had a library full of ancient texts, scrolls, tablets and books of magic. She could live a thousand years and not even scratch the surface of knowledge contained within the Keep or its library.

But there were other reasons she hadn't returned to Oldwilde. That place was full of ghosts. She couldn't face them. It was enough they haunted her from within.

"Brune. There is no time to proquire the Rod. Leave now and summon your successor this very night."

Startled from her thoughts, she nearly fell off her chair. As she caught herself, she noticed the ring of keys attached to her belt. The Key to the Keep was three sizes larger than the other keys, and still growing. If she left now, the Key would never fit the Lock, which opened the gateway between here and Earth. She looked at him. "Did you *know* this would happen?"

His ears twitched with exasperation. "The Key knows when the Keep needs a new Guardian."

Brune rushed at the cage, pushing against the bars, almost knocking it over. "This is all your fault! I never would've stayed during the gloaming if I'd known this would happen!" Her chest constricted with fear. "Why didn't you warn me?"

His slanted eyes turned to gleaming slits. "I never thought I needed to. In all the time I've been condemnified to this prison, I have never known a Guardian who dared as much as you to get and keep her position." He shrugged. "Guardians come and go, but none of them ever lasted as long as you. I was cheering for you, waiting to see how far you would get. Disfortunately, your overconfidence was very much your own undoing."

She quaked with fear. "I won't leave. This is my *home*—it's where I belong."

"Then I'm sure you'll be quite pleased to host a salutorious greeting for the nastilence that will soon pour through that breaching door. And be sure to serve some flavoriscious donuts, only save the creamy white ones for me. What were they called again? Cumulus One-More-Than-Eight?"

"Cloud Nines," Brune mumbled as she slid to the floor in defeat.

"Ah yes, pure heaven," Farouk said, licking one side of his snout. "Oh, stop brooding. You won't be shut out for long. You'll gain admitrance with the new Guardian. After all, you must eduprime your replacement."

"Yeah, someone too soft and green to handle *this* mess."

"And whose fault is that? You should have summoned and trained someone long ago."

His voice droned on in the background. She was reliving the domino of mistakes she'd made over and over, wishing she could go back and undo each one. As the bitter reality set in, she made a decision, one that iced into her heart. She would do whatever it took to reclaim her youth and rightful place within the Keep. She was the only one who could protect it.

Using the Key—now the length of a cane—she struggled to her feet and hobbled over to the spell book section of the library. After finding the volume she sought, she tucked it under her arm and turned to leave.

"You cannot take that with you."

"Listen, you overgrown rodent, you know I need the summoning spell." She hadn't called him that since their first year together, but she was furious with him.

Looking wounded, Farouk's ears fell as he buried his nose against his shoulder. "What happens if you expirate out there? We cannot risk a book of magic falling into unignorant hands."

Knowing he was right, she put the book on the table with a weary sigh.

Directing his cage to a tall curio cabinet, he pulled out a jar with a gnarled root tied to its lid. "I prepurated the honey pot with calamus root." He set it down. "Don't forget to add a teaspoon of your own blood to connectify to those who answer the call."

"You saw this coming, didn't you?"

Farouk placed a small pouch on top of the jar. "It is my job to previsionate your every need." He nudged his snout toward the pouch. "I included John the Conqueror root—ground to a fine powder for better discatterment."

Its sweet, earthy scent rose up around her. "I see you've brought out all the heavy hitters."

"It is not enough to compel those who are summoned. You must governate them until one commits to becoming the next Guardian."

"I have the Orb for that."

"It may not be enough. You have one gambletunity. You cannot afford to misbotch this too."

"*All right*. But do you really think there's anyone left to answer the summons after all these years? They could be dead for all we know. It's generational. Surely I've outlived them all."

Farouk gave her a sidelong look that told her he knew better. "You may wish it otherelse, but rest assured, your successor lives. There will always be a Guardian as long as the Keep exists."

Frowning, Brune returned to the spell book, nearly tearing its fragile sheets as she flipped angrily through them. When she found the spell she needed, she grabbed a quill and dipped it in ink.

"No scribing. You must rememborize the spell."

She threw the quill at him, making the spry creature dart to one side of his cage. "My brain's turning to mush as we speak! I may not be able to remember the spell in the next five minutes, let alone an hour or more!"

Farouk's furry face wrinkled with irritation when he saw ink spots on his immaculate coat. "Fine, you made your point."

She copied the spell down. "I'll be sure to eat it after I'm done," she muttered.

His gaze slid to the floor as she shuffled over to a round iron door, its edges trimmed in bronze and etched with symbols. Without a word of goodbye to her only companion of seventy-five years, she pulled the lever. As the iris spiraled open, anguish filled Brune's heart. She desperately wished she was only going through the portal on a donut run for Farouk. Other than his occasional yen for junk food, there had never been any other reason to return to Earth. No one waited for her on the other side.

She stared at the circular tunnel. The inner rings activated, each rotating in opposite directions, the spin generating a flux path. Its strong gravitational pull tugged at her as the tunnel filled with waves of neon-blue light. The moment she stepped through the threshold, she hurtled through space and time. As hot bolts of electricity bombarded her, an unexpected and incredible pain ripped through her body, like the melting of skin and G-forces imploding her bones.

The jump was over in a fraction of a second. She stood panting in the dark, reeling from the shocking assault. She groped at her face expecting to touch skinless mush. Feeling dry, papery skin was almost as upsetting. She should've known her old, broken-down body wouldn't withstand a ride like that without feeling every bump. She was lucky she even survived.

Still shaking, she felt around in the blackness for the doorknob. The door's hinges creaked as she stepped into a musty-smelling storage room of the bookstore. She was back on Earth, the last place in the universe she ever wanted to be. Sadness crashed in as she trailed her mottled hand over the faded letters spelling Janitor on the ordinary door concealing the portal. She reached for the Lock attached above the doorknob. It was gone. A surge of fear went through her before she remembered. Just as the Key had returned to its original size when she became incapable of guarding the Keep, the Lock had been drawn back to its place of origin, where it would remain securely hidden until the new Guardian claimed it.

She hated the thought of someone else taking her place. Every part of her being resisted handing over that much responsibility to an underling. But she had to accept the cold hard facts. A new Guardian was her only hope, no matter how green the recruit might be.

SOFT AS A MARSHMALLOW

BRUNE HID IN THE SHADOWS behind one of the tall bookcases, anxious for her successor to arrive. She had no idea who would show up, but she prayed for a battle-hardened marine fit for the grueling gauntlet ahead.

She got a drenched powder puff instead.

"Well, there goes my odds," she croaked, her hopes deflating like a punctured life raft.

At least the waiting was over.

Her feeble condition and shriveling brain had slowed her down in every conceivable way. Just preparing for the summoning spell had been an exhausting task. Performing it had been even harder. Being so dull-witted, she'd had to repeat the conjuration steps multiple times. But dealing with the ravages of old age was a cakewalk compared to the nightmare following her tumble down a flight of stairs.

The crush of her skull and the nauseating crack of her neck when she landed at the bottom in a grotesque heap of twisted limbs should've killed her. But she'd survived. Her right arm had popped out of the socket, wrapped around her head, while one leg bent forward at the knee and the other hung loose from her pelvic bone. Using her one good arm, Brune had forced each body part back into its proper position, trying her best to disregard the disturbing sounds of grinding bone and snapping tendons.

It took her addled mind a few minutes to realize she should've been in unbearable pain. That's when the hideous truth hit her.

She was undead.

The Orb of Aeternitis, having given her eternal youth as she continued to wear it round her neck, now animated her lifeless limbs with its powerful and unpredictable magic.

Having dispatched her share of undead within the Keep, her revulsion toward becoming one of them was so great she wanted to end it all right there and then. It would be simple, just remove the Orb and the lights would go out. She came close to doing it several times, but there was still a greedy spark of life in her refusing to let go.

Her gruesome condition changed everything. She needed a new game plan. The Rod of Aeternitis was now her only option. Once she merged the Rod with the Orb, she would have unlimited power—the ability to create or destroy with a mere thought. *All* her problems would vanish like they had never happened.

But she had to work fast. Being magically alive hadn't stopped her from rotting at an alarming rate.

At least the summons had worked. There was just one small hitch: the mysterious young man who'd appeared out of nowhere after she'd cast the jumbled spell. This wasn't the first time the Orb had conjured something unexpected when combined with incantations. But based on past experience, an accidental manifestation was never good. Another reason she needed the Rod. Using the Orb alone was like trying to use a nail without a hammer. She would've done a reversal spell if she could remember it. Not that there had been any time to do so. The girl had walked into the bookstore too soon after his appearance—mistaking Brune for a cat of all things.

The sound of voices pulled Brune's attention back to the present. The girl had discovered the boy and the *Book of Fables*. That was good. She had her inside the ring of John the Conqueror powder she'd sprinkled around its base. Now all she had to do was keep her there with the Orb.

Brune tried to listen to what they were saying, but the flies buzzing around her head drowned out their voices. Cursing her failing hearing, she peered through an old set of opera glasses in time to see the girl shiver and be given the young man's jacket.

"Just as I thought, soft as a marshmallow," she muttered in disgust.

When they started heading straight for her, she jerked backwards, causing her neck to further dislodge from her spine. With her head pitched at a grotesque angle, she reached for the Orb. It was imperative she keep them in the circle to activate the governing spell. As she swung the pendant from its long chain, she watched the two youths stop in their tracks. She almost fell over with relief.

"Time to get on with this," she said, her voice a dry rasp as she focused her intent.

They turned and marched back to the giant book.

The Orb's swing increased of its own accord, its pale glimmer thickening into a band of glowing light. She shambled through the maze of bookcases and stopped behind the spellbound couple. Her gaze dropped to their clasped hands. She considered separating them but decided it would be more bother than she had time for.

The Orb's spiraling coil of light descended to the floor, splashed over the wooden floorboards in a haze of liquid gold and pooled around the girl's feet. As the light curled up her legs, Brune funneled her burning desire for the Rod into the Orb.

Suddenly a torrent of emotions surged out of her. All her desperation, fear, determination and primal instinct for survival poured into the girl. The current was strong, frightening, as if her very soul was abandoning her.

Brune grabbed the Orb, halting its swing. As the golden

light thinned to twinkling specks, the connection between them faded.

Wondering what had just happened, she staggered to a nearby chair. Her body was so stiff with rigor mortis she had to tilt into it. Her hips cracked like dry twigs as her weight hit the back of the chair, snapping her into a sitting position.

She fixed her blurred vision on the ancient *Book of Fables*. Seeing it open distracted her from a troubling thought that had been whispering within the fog of her infirm mind. She hadn't seen those ensorcelled pages since her eighteenth birthday—the day she'd opened the giant book and plunged into its wondrous tales. But they hadn't stayed wondrous, had they? Sinister forces had orchestrated the unpredictable rules within the book, and in the end, each fable had turned more hideous than anything she could've ever imagined.

She tore her gaze from the towering tome too late. The dam had broken. A flood of regret slammed into her. Stomping her foot in frustration, she heard it crunch under the force. "Useless bones," she grumbled.

The girl glanced over her shoulder, looking straight at Brune.

"Turn around," Brune commanded.

The teenager kept staring.

Brune could tell the girl was still in the trance. But somehow she'd managed to awaken within the spell, much like becoming aware of being in a dream while asleep. The ability to do such an extraordinary thing spoke of a strong and stubborn will. Maybe there was a backbone inside that marshmallow after all.

Struggling from her seat, Brune shuffled across the floor, her loose leg dragging. She drew within inches of the girl's face, scrutinizing her through the clouding film coating her eyes. She was pretty, long wet auburn curls framed fine-boned features and wide trusting eyes, the irises a bright swirl of golden brown with sparks of red.

Brune touched the girl's pale cheek. When she saw her dry, dead fingers against the smooth, alabaster skin, she jerked her hand away. The sting of envy pricked her, poisoning her thoughts. She wanted to gouge holes in that creamy skin. She recoiled from the vicious impulse. Good looks had never been her concern. The boundless energy, strength and stamina of youth were what mattered to her. But it was maddening to stand next to this fresh-faced beauty while she decayed at record speed.

Enough of the pity party, Brune told herself. Time to get back to business. Especially since the girl had awakened within the trance. "I am Brune Inkwell," she said, revolted by the awful rattle in her cankered throat as she spoke. "I'm sending you on a very important mission, for which failure is not an option. You will die before you give up. Do you understand?"

The girl nodded yes to the question.

"It doesn't matter how long you take to accomplish this task, because time passes differently in the *Book of Fables* than it does here. I'll experience a few minutes from the time you leave to when you return, whereas you might experience months, or even years. So there's no need to hurry and make unnecessary mistakes."

Brune paused a moment, watching to see if the girl was registering the information.

Her expression remained devoid of emotion, perfect and empty as a porcelain doll except for her eyes, which followed Brune's every move.

"Tell me what it is you're supposed to bring back," Brune asked, testing the spell's influence.

"The Rod of Aeternitis."

"And who has the Rod?"

"O'Deldar."

Brune's confidence increased. She knew the spell would hold fast until the Rod was in the girl's possession. A wavering sense of guilt rose to the surface. The odds were good she was sending the girl to her death. "What's your name?" She figured she should at least know the name of the person whose life she was risking.

"Fate."

"You'll be needing this." Brune removed her aide mémoire, a family heirloom she always wore on her waistband, and clasped it onto Fate's skirt. She hated parting with it, but she knew she needed to arm the girl with all the help she could get. Without the little writing tablet, she never would've survived her own journey through the fables. "You'll know what this is for when you read the warning at the beginning of the book. Do that as soon as you enter the first fable."

A fly skittered over Brune's eyeball. She batted it off, almost losing her balance. An image of maggots squirming inside her rotting corpse swiftly banished any lingering sympathies. "Time to read those fables you're so curious about."

Fate's gaze turned to the open book and the first fable's elegant title penned at the top.

As Brune limped out of the way, she eyed the boy with uncertainty. "Don't know about this one, but hang onto him if he proves useful." She stood outside the circle, her crooked shoulders hunched tight in expectation. "And Godspeed," she whispered.

Fate murmured under her breath, "*The Lonely Sorceress.*"

And that was all it took to propel Brune's desperate plan into motion. She watched through fogged eyes as the giant *Book of Fables* lurched forward and slammed shut over the young couple.

An unnerving thud of finality echoed through the bookstore. Brune hobbled back over to the chair, sat down and set her watch to track the passing time. There was nothing to do now but hope the powder puff had enough grit to stay alive and return with the Rod before she turned to a pile of dust and bones.

This concludes the bonus prequel

Chaos In The Keep

Acknowledgements

First and foremost, thanks to the love of my life, Tony, for believing in me. Without your encouragement, guidance and unwavering support, this book would not have been written. Thank you for working side by side with me in the trenches to bring this book to publication, designing the gorgeous cover and helping me to create the beautiful book trailer. And to my amazing son, Tyler, for your quiet confidence in me to write a story you enjoyed enough to read twice—an unexpected phenomenon that spoke louder than any words of praise ever could.

Thanks to my mom, Corry, for planting the first seeds of magic in my heart with our walks in the woods to find fairy rings and my dad, Larry, for knowing I had it in me to do this. Also to the rest of my wonderful family and all my good friends for your unfailing enthusiasm, even when I had to answer "no" to that seemingly eternal question, "Did you finish your book yet?"

A big thank you to my editor, Rhonda Helms, for steering key story elements in the right direction and guiding character development to a much richer level. Huge thanks to Bernie Tilley for walking the last mile with me to catch copy editing issues as well as the added bonus of your invaluable insights. And also to Nora Schroeder for giving me great pointers on my book jacket copy. Special thanks to my beta readers, especially those I tortured with the early drafts: Thora Gleason, Vicki Rautenberger, Madelon Stent-Fischer, Nadine Tegart-Kanaugh, Raquel Larson and Bonnie McKee. And a big smiley thanks to all my well-traveled friends from IWWG/CWC for your combined wealth of knowledge and ready support.

Last but not least, thank you, dear reader, for choosing this book. I hope Fate took you on a great adventure.

Acknowledgements

First and foremost thanks to the love of my life, Tony, for believing in me. Without your encouragement, guidance and unwavering support, this book would not have been written. Thank you for working side by side with me in the trenches to bring this book to publication, designing the gorgeous cover and helping me to create the beautiful book trailer. And to my amazing son, Tyler, for your quiet confidence in me to write a story you enjoyed enough to read twice—an unexpected phenomenon that spoke louder than any words of praise ever could.

Thanks to my mom, Gerry, for planting the first seeds of magic in my heart with our walks in the woods to find fairy rings and my dad, Larry, for knowing I had it in me to do this. Also to the rest of my wonderful family and all my good friends for your unfailing enthusiasm, even when I had to answer "no" to that seemingly eternal question, "Did you finish your book yet?"

A big thank you to my editor, Rhonda Helms, for steering key story elements in the right direction and guiding character development to a much richer level. Huge thanks to Denise Tilley, for walking the last mile with me to catch copy editing issues, as well as the added bonus of your invaluable insights. And also to Nora Snowden for giving me great pointers on my book jacket copy. Special thanks to my beta readers, especially those I tortured with the early drafts: Thora Gislason, Vickie Hadersberger, Madelon Scott-Eichen, Nadine Tegart-Reaugh, Raquel Larson and Bonnie McRae. And a big smiley nod to all my stellar writer friends from RWA-GVC for your combined wealth of knowledge and ready support.

Last but not least, thank you, dear reader, for choosing this book. I hope Fate took you on a great adventure.

Bestselling author T. Rae Mitchell is an incurable fantasy junkie who spent much of her youth dreaming up worlds and bringing characters to life. While most kids outgrow such things, T. Rae didn't and sometimes took playing make-believe a bit far. Like the time a wizard hid a bottle of dragon beans in the back yard and left her son convinced he could grow his own dragons. Needless to say, the beans failed to produce and disappointments were had. That's when T. Rae decided to funnel her crazy imagination into writing young and new adult fantasy.

Sign-up for T. Rae Mitchell's
Exclusive VIP List
for upcoming notifications:
www.traemitchell.com/sign-up

You can also find T. Rae Mitchell on...

Instagram: www.instagram.com/t.raemitchell

Facebook: www.facebook.com/mitchelltrae

Bookbub: www.bookbub.com/authors/t-rae-mitchell

Goodreads: www.goodreads.com/author/show/6926344.T_Rae_Mitchell

Twitter: www.twitter.com/TRaeMitchell

Pinterest: www.pinterest.com/TRaeMitchell

www.ingramcontent.com/pod-product-compliance
Lightning Source LLC
Chambersburg PA
CBHW010446310726
48979CB00018B/2827/J

9781999024192